THE ENGINEER

Parts Two and Three

T P NASH

Troubador Publishing Ltd
Unit E2 Airfield Business Park,
Harrison Road, Market Harborough,
Leicestershire. LE16 7UL
Tel: 0116 2792299
Email: books@troubador.co.uk
Web: www.troubador.co.uk

ISBN 978 1805142 614

British Library Cataloguing in Publication Data.
A catalogue record for this book is available from the British Library.

Printed and bound in Great Britain by 4edge Limited
Typeset in 11pt Minion Pro by Troubador Publishing Ltd, Leicester, UK

For Roger

ONE

There was a man he hadn't seen before, a stranger who walked these narrow streets as though he owned them, but nobody spoke to him. Indeed, everybody turned aside, stood in doorways or engaged in sudden conversations, all to observe the stranger over their shoulders, between the backs of friends, through windows or dark glasses. But this was a man who carried weight with a threat that was as hard to weigh as the anger of a scorned woman. And there were many who had suffered under that torment.

Bernd sighed and recollected that he was retired. He gazed at the sky, an enduring blue, at the house across the street, curtains closed as always, and wondered for the hundredth time what went on behind those curtains and whether they were spying on him and out of habit looked up the street beyond the stranger. A narrow street, the rendered houses closing in, small shuttered windows, red tiled roofs. What did he want with a stranger? Really, this man could be no part of his life, unless... unless the Conglomerate was still pursuing him.

He put his cup down and looked at his cafetiere with regret; he had become accustomed to an easier life and rarely thought of his early days, the Hitler Youth, the Stasi, and his own business. They were part of another life, one long past, and he looked forward now no further than the next week and the next visit of his girlfriend, though that description failed the true nature of their relationship. He sighed, checked his underarm holster and stepped into the street. It was cool, still early before the blast of the southern sun. He walked up to the main street and descended on the shady side, rubber soled shoes silent, the old blue worker's jacket unbuttoned. A few nodded to him as he entered the bar and settled on a stool near the door; he had been a neighbour for long enough to be recognised and to not be suspicious in a small town where suspicion grew like ivy. There had been a few problems in the early days, difficulty in getting served at the shop and bar; mutters behind his back, children drawn hastily indoors when he passed. But that had all passed, particularly after one incident.

It was nothing really, he thought, but it had opened doors and people had started regarding him as one of them.

There were three of them, or was it four? He couldn't remember now, and closed his ears when yet another villager recounted the tale, the history of it, embellished each year. It might have been a stag party or a group celebrating some football victory. They were young and wealthy, throwing money around at the bar, shouting, throwing up in the street; but that was nothing. Albert and his cronies could deal with that. But when they started accosting the girls of the village, Albert's daughter in particular, there was a groundswell of indignation; growls of anger and threats uttered but not carried out. For the young men, the three, or was it four, produced knives, laughing, and one, leaning over the bar, slit the front of Albert's daughter's dress from

2

top to bottom. She screamed, clutched her dress around her bosom and fled.

Berndt was sitting at the far end of the bar; he had missed the earlier violence, the anger and threats, sitting quietly in a corner, perusing the local paper; what a rag! He thought. The scream alerted him; he rose quietly, checked his pockets. No weapon except for his gun and that was over the top. He could grab a bottle but not yet; it would draw attention and that he didn't want. Not just yet.

He dropped down behind the bar taking his belt off as he went, listening to the crowd and the strangers and crawled along. Looking up he could see the man who had slit the dress leaning back against the bar, still laughing. When Berndt was behind him, he rose in a silent smooth movement and dropped his belt around the man's neck, pulling it back tightly but not too tightly; yet. The man twisted, swinging his knife around but Berndt increased the pressure until the man gasped and was still. There was no sound, apart from two children passing the door, chattering.

'Drop your knives.' He had spoken quietly, no sign of anger or excitement. Two men stared at him and lunged forward together. Twisting the belt tighter, he grabbed a brandy bottle from the counter, half full, and held it over the throttled man's head.

'Do you want him to die?' They paused, looked at each other; who was this man who had dared to challenge them? No villager for sure.

One spoke. 'You wouldn't dare! Let him go. Now!'

Berndt said nothing. He was waiting. The oldest lesson in the book; let them come to you and then pick your moment.

3

The two men circled, approaching him from either side, knives held high. The bar remained between them and Berndt swung the bottle against his captive's head with a satisfying clunk that rendered him unconscious and sliding to the floor, vaulted onto the bar and threw the bottle into the face of one of the men, who swung back, half stunned; Berndt kicked the knife out of his hand. Really, he thought, this is not my type of fight. Give me a gun and 1000 metres but I have no choice, do I? The other man approached him fast, swinging the knife at his legs; timing the swing and hopping over his arm, Berndt kicked his neck, a precise calculated blow that rendered the man semi-conscious, gasping on all fours. There was a silence.

The villagers had remained aghast, amazed at the speed of the attack on the men that had taken no more than a minute. They came to life as though waking and grabbed the three men, shouting for rope. There was a fourth; he held his hands high and rushed for the door. A solid wall of villagers stood across his path, arms folded, grim looks. He hesitated, dropped his arms and began to cry.

'Don't kill me; I didn't do anything!'

Berndt had dropped down to the floor. 'Tie him up with the rest; you don't want him fetching reinforcements.'

At which the villagers dragged him to the others, tied them all up, wrists and ankles, and Albert made a telephone call to the gendarme in the next town.

'Please, could you come; terrorists in my bar… no, they have been captured… well, it's a long story… but yes, they are tied up here, and… how did we defeat them? Well, it was like this… no, I'm sure you don't, but… well, when are you coming?… Not till tomorrow? But what are we to do

4

with them?... I don't see why we should feed them; maybe pour a bucket of water over them... yes, all right... yes, yes, I hear you... no, we won't lynch them, though after what they did to my daughter... why yes... but it is true, they assaulted her... right here in the bar... she is seventeen, my very own daughter... what are you saying?... So you will be here soon... a bientot!' Albert gave a huge shrug. 'They said they are coming, but you know what the gendarme are like. Now, Gilbert, a drink, hein? But where is he? Did anyone see him leave? We all owe him, that's for sure. Did you see him kick that bastard in the neck? My God, that was some move. Where do you think he learnt that? He is a mystery man, is he not?'

There was a buzz of conversation, the tale growing in the warmth like dough until 'Gilbert' had defeated a dozen men armed with guns with only a bottle of brandy. The Mayor had to warn them from taking revenge in the old-fashioned way.

Berndt had been suddenly aware of the attention that he was drawing upon himself. He smiled an apology for the loss of the brandy and slipped out of the door. Back to his home, where he prepared a simple meal and sat in the dark contemplating his future; he didn't wish to stand out from the crowd. It was bad news.

But after that, he was welcomed everywhere, found small parcels of food and bottles left at his door and was not allowed to pay for a drink at the bar for a whole month. Until another village feast day came along to take the attention away from him.

As he settled onto a stool at the bar, Albert poured him a cognac, left the bottle close, and said with a shrug, 'Nobody knows him; who does he think he is, walking our streets like that? I should warn Marie, tell her to keep the school door closed. Why, he might be one of those!'

Berndt grunted, knocked back his drink and slipped into the street. It was not difficult, rather like following the path of errant cow; he followed the gestures, the looks and shrugs as he walked down the hill on the cobbles. Until he saw the stranger ahead, hesitating as if he was searching for something, looking for someone.

Berndt took a small alley to his left, jigged right and passed quickly through a cowshed and a yard, another right and emerged abruptly in front of the stranger, close in case he should be thinking of drawing a gun. The stranger was taken aback, and stepped back, his hands up and a scared face. Berndt noted the city suit, the black shoes which wouldn't last a day on their cobbled streets, the gauche tie, and the face above, not young but soft, untried.

'Could you... I wonder... I'm looking for—'

'Of course you are,' said Berndt, taking him firmly by the arm and pushing him against the wall. 'Would you mind?' And without waiting for an answer, he frisked him, including ankles. He was clean. The man looked bemused.

'Please, I can explain. I'm looking for a family, but I don't have the name; I believe she has remarried. But why do you treat me like a criminal? I protest, take me to the police.'

'There's no police here and you are not known. It makes people unhappy, not secure.'

'Well, is there a post office? They might be able to help.'

'Come with me,' said Berndt. The man resisted, struggling. Then he looked into Berndt's eyes and followed meekly beside him. Up the street they went; a few smiled

6

at Berndt, laughed behind their backs. A small boy threw a stone and hid when Berndt looked round with a frown.

The bar fell silent as they walked in; it looked like a scene in a Western as the locals backed away from the bar and Berndt led in the stranger. One man stepped forward, the Mayor. He was a butcher, the bloodied apron giving him an unfortunate badge of office.

'Messieurs, I am sorry if I have caused any distress. I am looking for a family, but I believe the woman may have remarried.'

'And what is your business, Monsieur?'

'I am a lawyer. I represent a man who has unfortunately died and I seek his niece who I believe lives in this village. She was born Sophie Dumoulin.'

The room erupted; there was laughter, much shuffling and a buzz of conversation.

'Ah, Monsieur, I believe that we can help you. Yes indeed. She is married to Chauvet, a good man you'll see. He farms around here, a small way. Let me take you to their home. But first, a little drink, hein?'

Berndt nodded to Albert and left the bar.

Well, you never knew. He often wondered how long it would take the Conglomerate to find him; it didn't help when he exposed his innate skills and people talked. It wouldn't do him much good if the villagers spoke of a hero in their midst who defeated three men in a couple of minutes, who could disable a man with a kick and take any stranger in hand. He had escaped from Paris with a little difficulty but taken a zig-zag route through France to this small village on a hill where he had adopted another of his identities, all backed up with identity cards and passports. It had taken a while but he was settled now and learning happiness. His girlfriend, Francine, visited once a month, staying a few days only; it was enough to assure him of his humanity, that he was not altogether a lost soul, enough to satisfy his needs and hers. He had to trust her and assume that her father, now a retired policeman, did not know of his place of residence or try to ascertain where she travelled to once a month. In fact, she would travel to the nearby town by train where there was a University, carry out some research and spend the rest of the time with Berndt; he had brought her to his village on the hill only twice, as much to protect her. He didn't want her to be harmed by the Conglomerate if they should find him. And it was likely that one day, maybe years in the future but one day, he would be found.

But he could not know how long it might last, how long he could settle into a quiet domestic life enjoying the simpler things in life, a life so different from his past life and yet so satisfying. He did not miss his sophisticated weapons, his armoured car, the rich lifestyle. But the thought of surrendering to them, of being executed, never crossed his mind.

Years passed; never again did he feel the need to take matters into his hands and restrain a violent man. He took part in harvests, trod grapes for the local vintage, helped with birthing calves, and even took a role as part-time barkeeper to give Albert some free time. It was wonderful and he felt a change in himself, a change towards trusting life. But he could never quite cast off the automatic surveillance of those around him and of the street. It was second nature and on occasion he would scoff at himself for not relaxing and leaving it all in the past. And he would have if it were not for the Conglomerate.

It was Albert who warned him.

A man had been asking after any new arrivals in the village. Albert had assured him that there were no new arrivals. 'Who would want to live here?' he said with a shrug. 'What is there here for a man or woman except a hard poor life?'

'This man would be able to look after himself, if you see what I mean.'

'Mais non, we are all able to look after ourselves, we are country folk.'

'No man of speed and strength, who probably lives alone?'

A young man jumped up from his stool. 'Mais Albert, there is—'

Albert looked at him, a strong commanding look that pinned the young man to the spot.

'You were saying?' The stranger turned to the young man, offered him a drink, smiled and produced a sheaf of notes.

'Well, there was... a man... ' he stuttered.

'Enough now,' commanded Albert. 'You should be off home; you've had enough.' And when the young man protested, Albert gave him another look and the young man slunk out of the door. After a few moments, the stranger followed. Albert turned to one of his regulars. 'Georges, would you be so kind? Tell Gilbert that there is a stranger looking for him. He is an unsavoury character; I wouldn't share a bottle of wine with him or tell him the time of the day.'

Berndt was sitting at his table when Georges arrived. At once, he felt a sinking in his heart. Georges passed on the message, and left. Shortly afterwards, there was a knocking. Berndt heard Tante Marie, his landlady, at the door.

'Who do you want?'

'I understand that you have a man living upstairs. Could I see him, please?'

'Who are you?'

'That's not important.'

'It may not be to you but it is to me. I don't know you. How do you think I feel at letting a stranger into my house?'

'Madame, please, get out of my way!'

'Quoi? You think to threaten me? Me, who has seen the dirty Boche tramp over our country, who has seen English immigrants buying up our houses, who has... Get out of my door.'

'But Madame—'

'I said, get out of my door. If you wish to meet someone, do it like everyone else; go to the bar. Au revoir.' The door slammed.

Berndt went downstairs, his arms raised in apology.

'Madame, I fear that there is trouble that I bring you. No, I do not know this man, but there is trouble in the air; I smell it. You have been good to me; thank you for your hospitality.'

'Mais non, Gilbert, you must not think of giving in to these salauds; they are dirt under our feet. You must stay.'

'Tante Marie, I am not sure that I can.'

'Ah, what nonsense! You have paid me for the rest of the year; you must stay for the rest of the year. I will hear no more of it and I shall not be threatened by these salauds.

We shall tell the Mayor and Albert to see them on their way at once.'

Berndt retreated up the stairs; he feared for Tante Marie.

At three o'clock in the morning, four shapes materialised out of the darkness on two sides of the house, moving smoothly, silently. They were dressed in black with black balaclavas, combat boots; all four carried sub-machine guns. They stood around the house wondering how to get in.

Berndt watched them. Dressed also in black, he was armed and carried a small rucksack. On the table was a note to his landlady.

'Chere Tante, I fear for your safety; these are bad men. They are after me, not you, and I shall leave you for a while. I may be back, I may not. Please, do have all my food and drink; there is a full bottle of Armagnac in the cupboard; it is yours. Thank you for your hospitality. Gilbert.'

The men were gathered outside the door; they appeared to be talking quietly. Berndt had feared this day ever since he had moved in and had chosen an apartement with the same facilities as his Paris apartement. He slipped out of the rear window onto the roof and tiptoed around to the side. The four men were almost below him, at the door. He coughed quietly, retreated from the corner and dropped down to the foot of the roof, lying flat and screwing the silencer onto his gun. One of the men came round the corner, peering along the alley. Berndt waited. He came further and when he was just below, Berndt leant out and shot him in the back of the neck, his hand no more than half a metre above the man, a brief 'phut'. The man dropped like a stone, face to the ground.

There was a pause, a silence broken only by a shuffling

of footsteps around the corner. A voice called out quietly, urgently. 'Carlos, Carlos, where are you? I can't see you.' Another man came into the alley but stopped when he saw the body, calling out, 'Hey, here, Carlos is down. Where is the bastard? Where are you all?'

There was a crash as the street door was broken in; he heard Tante Marie cry out, a door slammed and thundering on the stairs. Berndt walked up the roof and pressed himself against the wall by the window.

There was a muttering indoors; Tante Marie was silent. A gun appeared through the window; there was a curse. 'Gottdammit! Wo ist the bastard?' 'Get out there and look.' 'Me? What sort of an idiot do you think I am?' 'Get out there and wipe him out, now!'

A face emerged briefly; Berndt froze in the darkness. A foot slowly extended over the cill to touch down on the tiles, followed by an arm and a head. Berndt waited until the man looked towards him and shot him between the eyes; the man collapsed onto the tiles as Berndt retreated across the roof and dropped down to the alley. Damn, he thought, this isn't my type of work; give me a rifle and a bit of distance. Not much chance of that now.

He walked up to the corner of the alley and peered round the corner; there was one man standing looking into the house. He coughed and stood back from the corner. But at that moment, he heard a noise of someone walking across the roof tiles above his head. He ran as fast as he could deeper into the shade of the alley and ducked into a doorway. A cat took off, howling in disgust.

The two men were talking. 'Where is he, the bastard? Come on, Berndt, give yourself up, we might not have to kill you.' A gunshot whined down the alley, a chip of brick flying near Berndt's ear. Too close, he thought, too close. He looked across the alley, only two and a half metres wide at this point; his night vision was improving and he could see another doorway into a barn. There was a latch.

He jumped into the alley. A bullet whined past his ear as he reached the doorway reveal, pressing himself against the door as he lifted the latch; more bullets whistled past him, plucking at his rucksack. He stepped into the barn and closed the door behind him. There was a warm smell of cattle and the restless stirring of beasts. The floor squelched beneath his feet. He looked up and hoisted himself up onto the roofbeams, sliding back to a hay loft. He could just make out the doorway.

The door was opened, two figures dark in the night peering in. Idiots, Berndt thought; where did they get their training? I could pick them off now, but if I miss one he could get me. Berndt waited.

'He's run, the bastard. You follow him through, I'll get around the back.' And one disappeared, leaving a man feeling his way slowly along the wall inside. He lit his lighter, peering around. The cattle stirred and moved towards him and the open door. Berndt watched as they surrounded him and pressed him against the wall, watched him drop to the ground, crying out for help as they made for the open door. Berndt felt no compassion; he found an end of rope on the loft, dropped down to the ground, pushing the cattle aside and looped the rope around the man's neck and hauled him up on a pulley clear of the cattle. The legs shook for a while and were still.

Berndt waited.

There was a rustling of straw, then a voice, urgent in the dark. 'Milos, did you get him? Where are you? I went all the way round the back, but I didn't see him; he must be in here. Did you get him?' Berndt saw him bump into the hanging body, gasp with surprise, swore, crouched down and started to run for the door; the cattle would not move aside and he was panicking, pressing against a cow's backside. Berndt lined up his shot and when the man was just inside the door, fired. The bullet entered the man's back on the left side, passed through his heart, exited and lodged in the doorframe. As he fell, the beasts trampled him into the mire.

Four men accounted for; were there more?

The door was clear, the cattle wandering down the alley towards the streets. Berndt slipped between them, concealed by their warm comforting bulk as they walked slowly up the alley and he left them to turn into the house, his gun ready. There was a muffled howl of rage and a door being kicked.

He opened the kitchen door, alert for any interruption and looked through the hinge gap; the room was empty. In the kitchen, the noise was greater and he opened the pantry door to be faced by an enraged Tante Marie, her mouth taped. He quietened her with a raised finger and pulled the tape off in one jerk; tears came to her mouth as she filled her lungs to scream and he placed one hand over her mouth, whispering, 'Hush.' Leaving her in the pantry with the door closed, he checked the house, silently, downstairs and upstairs, moving from room to room without a sound, ascending the stairs avoiding the steps that he knew creaked until he was sure that the house was empty. Looking out of the rear window, there was the body of the man he had shot. He locked the window.

He went downstairs and assured Tante Marie that her house was free of the salauds and that he must be away for a while; she would be safer, he would deal with the menace. She wept, implored him to stay, but he said he must deal with the bastards. She wished him luck, said that she would pray for him.

At the door, he could see nobody near and dropped down between the last of the cattle to emerge onto the main street, still hiding between their warm sides. The cattle had chosen the easier option, turning left downhill towards the bar rather than uphill away from the centre. It was still early, about four, but there were one or two men around, alerted by the sound of the cattle, who, unsure of their surroundings and lack of enclosure, set up a melancholy lowing.

Down the street, Berndt could see a car, a four-wheel drive Mercedes station wagon standing in the centre of the road. A figure sat behind the wheel. It was unlikely to be a friend or a random visitor. It was no doubt stationary because of the cattle or because it was waiting for an elimination squad to finish their work.

Berndt slipped between cattle to the right side of the road, keeping a beast between him and the car. When he was past the car, he doubled back and listened. The driver was swearing softly. 'Where the hell are you? What's taking you so long? What do you expect me to do? Run or finish the job for you?'

Berndt stood up against the door, reached through the open window, and grabbed the man's neck. He waved a gun towards Berndt, who started to twist his neck. Further and further until there was a click and a slight crunch and the man drooped in the seat. Berndt opened the door, pulled him onto the road, propped him up against a building and climbed into the driving seat.

The car felt warm. The cattle had finished walking past and he started the engine and drove slowly out of the town. Where should he go now? The Conglomerate might respect his skills but they would not stomach the loss of a whole elimination squad. It wouldn't be long before the car was reported as stolen, and the hunt would be on for him.

TWO

Four a.m. Driving away from the village.

It felt wrong to be running again. And running, not from the police, but the Conglomerate. He had no fears of being discovered by the police. It had been Interpol who sought him rather than the French police, except for Francine's father and he was now retired after that unfortunate encounter in the railyard. He regretted that he never could come to terms with felling Francine's father. It had been unavoidable. And he valued Francine, now more than ever.

He drove quietly, choosing minor roads and small towns, avoiding cities and police attention. Mist hung low, swathes between the banks; it was not dark but a dim pre-dawn and an intense blue sky. Once he found himself at a dead end, the road petering out in a farmyard. It was early for visitors and the farmer appeared with a shotgun and two hunting dogs. He didn't wait to talk it out but reversed at speed, back out of sight, the dogs leaping at the doors. At other times, he found he was driving a ridge road, above the valley mists, fully exposed to helicopters or surveillance should there be any at this hour. Buzzards soared above him and there was a view of distant hill ranges stretching in the distance into the rising sun; early morning cloud still hung in the valleys and the air was crisp, clean. It reminded him of the Bavarian hills of his youth. He drove off the hills into the valleys, gradually working to the east.

It was instinctive; the need to find another remote rural area where he hoped he could be accepted to the level that they would warn him, protect him as the last village had. And he had to stay in France because France was where Francine lived. Did the Conglomerate know of Francine? He believed that it was unlikely for they would have found him faster and possibly eliminated her; at least, they would have taken her, held her hostage against his capture; what would he have done? Submit and face the inevitable, or run again? No, he could never leave Francine to their ministrations; it was unthinkable.

There it was again; his whole working life had been based on his independence and ability to move at will. And now he felt tethered like a goat unable to butt and fight a predator. Is this what it felt like to be a married man? It was not a future that appealed to him but he could not lose Francine.

What was she to him?

Ah, a simple question and no simple answer. She was a source of physical satisfaction and he believed that it worked both ways; she was good company, intelligent and not too demanding, apparently happy with the frequency of their meetings, happy to continue her work and happy not to be a housewife. And essentially, Berndt had to recognise it, she provided a feeling of security that had been missing in his life almost from the time that the family left Augsburg.

He had never thought it necessary; he must be getting old, he thought, and maybe that was it. Getting old and seeking a nest to allow his bones to rest, a harbour against the world and company as he aged. What was the alternative? He had never considered it but now he supposed that he would have worked on until eliminated, either by another man's gun or, if taken, by his own; the last thing that he could allow was to stand in a court, exposed to cringing lawyers and gloating policemen.

He smiled at the thought of being taken. How many years had he worked in Europe with no sign of being detected? Yes, there had been François but nothing since his retirement; it had been no more than an idea, a suspicion that François had been unable to prove. The railyard incident had been unfortunate but no proof of his former life.

The sun rose in his eyes as he crested another hill to drop down into another valley. He estimated that he could keep the car for another eight hours and then dispose of it. That would be a problem, would draw the Conglomerate closer to him and he could think of no way to dispose of the car unless it could be sunk beneath water or buried in a pit. Neither were easy solutions. He had not considered it and it would be a problem; how could he travel without it?

He turned north on a main road into a more populated area; it was dangerous, inviting detection by the police or... someone.

On the outskirts of a town was a supermarket, advertising 24 hour service. He drove into the car park and left the car in a slot about halfway back where it should be surrounded by shoppers. In the supermarket, he sat in the café, coffee and a croissant, and planned.

He ordered more food; better to stoke up while he could. He gorged, chewed, and sat back bloated and ready for sleep.

The car. It was too close.

He dragged himself around the supermarket: food, high energy and easily carried; clothes, a working man's overalls, quilted jacket, padded knees, an anonymous dull green; and maps. And he went back to the car, changed and drove to the local railway station.

It was busy, the early rush-hour buzz of blue collar workers in a hurry. The policeman at the door yawned as Berndt hurried past among the other passengers. He stood in a crowd, bought a local ticket from a machine and pushed into a crowded carriage. Standing, a quick reconnaissance around him: a few suits, many blousons bleu headed for manual work somewhere, some secretaries, the younger ones eyeing up the men, the older ones yawning and dozing. There were four soldiers, young and looking a little nervous, perhaps on a first posting. And there were two nuns. Always nuns. One was young and pretty, a vivacious smile; the soldiers were trying hard not to eye her up and failing. Eventually, the older nun had a few words in her ear, stern and brief; the younger cast her eyes downwards.

'Always a crush! Mon Dieu, you would think that we could get our money's worth, a seat. Mais non! Look at us.'

Berndt turned. A small man, a creased face like oak bark, and the fingers, a heavy smoker. The hands were rough, the clothes poor and worn. Berndt grunted.

'I haven't seen you on this train before; apart from the soldiers and the nuns, I know everyone else, the same old, same old!'

'They send me on an errand, moi, an errand boy. Huh!'

'Eh bien, it could be worse weather for an outing. My boss, he never sends me for anything, just tells me to mix

20

more mortar. Always more mortar!'

'Where do you work?' said Berndt.

'Here and there. Mostly there and I am expected to get there on time. Zut alors, late already. Ah, this is my stop; bonne journée!'

Berndt blew the stale fumes of cigarette smoke out of his lungs and took an empty seat. A ticket collector came along. Berndt held up his ticket without raising his eyes.

'Monsieur, you have missed your stop; you should have descended at the last station. Where are you going?'

'Ah, pardon; I was not thinking. My wife, she is not well, I slept poorly last night. Pardons! What do I owe you for the terminus?'

'You understand it is an offence to travel on the train without the appropriate ticket; there should be a fine!'

Berndt wondered how long this would go on; what was the point in thinking that he could kill this objectionable official, snap his neck in a second? Ah, for his armoured Audi. That was the way to travel. He grunted, bent himself into a humble hunch and said how sorry he was, it was a mistake, his wife was so ill and the child cried and he was very sorry, he hadn't meant to and his boss was telling him to be at the town as soon as possible.

The ticket inspector hummed, drew himself up and said, 'Monsieur, it is early in the day. This time... this time, I will excuse your attempt to travel without the appropriate ticket, and you may pay ten euros to me now!'

Berndt passed up a crumpled note, the inspector laboriously wrote out a ticket and passed up the carriage.

'Salaud! Who does he think he is?'

'Pardon?' Berndt looked at his neighbour with surprise.

'These petty officials; they think they can rule our lives; which gutter does he come from, I wonder.' It was the older nun, her eyes flashing, spit on her lip. She looked straight ahead as though addressing the whole carriage. There was a mutter of agreement, a murmur of conversation broke out and a few men grinned and exclaimed in agreement.

After a few more stops, the train passed through the suburbs of a town and pulled up. The carriage emptied, Berndt walking with the crowd. On the concourse, he ambled into a café and sat drinking coffee while he looked at his maps.

'Monsieur. Monsieur!'

He looked up. Oh God, a beggar. And not French, he was sure.

'Monsieur, can you spare the price of a coffee? And perhaps something to eat? I have been travelling…'

She was ageless, a bent bundle of ragged clothing carrying a shopping bag full of clothes.

'Where do you come from?' said Berndt.

'I'm looking for my daughter, but I don't know where she is. Perhaps Paris, but I can't get there. No money.'

It struck Berndt that here was someone who was worse off than himself, someone existing on a faint hope and little else. And for a moment he felt troubled, unable to feel sufficient compassion for her, used to considering himself alone. And Francine, of course. Come, Berndt, look at yourself; are you not seeking your own haven?

'Where have you come from?'

'Are you police? An official?'

'Mais non, I am a worker, that's all. Not one of those salauds.'

'I come from the East.'

'But where?'

'It's been a long way, I was lost many times; please Monsieur, do you have the cost of a meal?'

Berndt wondered if it was all a fraud; but then she looked starving. The face was drawn, dirty, eyes sparking out of deep hollows, straggled hair beneath a head scarf.

'Come with me.' He took her to the counter, bought her a large meal and carried it back to his table. She looked at his maps.

'Are you travelling too, monsieur?'

Albania? Hungary? No, further East. Bulgaria, Rumania, perhaps, or Georgia. She has escaped from the Soviets, as I did. Her daughter? A fiction? But... a thought struck him, and he smiled to himself.

'Madam, it was Rumania, was it not? And you are an illegal immigrant, I guess. But do you really have a daughter?'

The woman collapsed in tears, rocking to and fro, her food ignored; a few people looked round, summing up the two of them. Berndt spoke softly.

'Madam, you have nothing to fear from me. We can help each other. Would you do that?'

She sniffed, wiping her nose on her sleeve. 'Help you, Monsieur? Some hope of that!'

'Ah, but I think it might be possible. Do you really want to get to Paris?'

'Yes, my daughter—'

'She is real?'

The woman sat up with a jerk, a scowl of outrage. 'What do you take me for? Of course she is real; she got out before me, some student trip; managed to escape the escort. They threatened to put me in prison so I fled.'

'How?' Berndt was interested; it had been easy for him, with the papers he held. But a poor woman?

'A train. Nightime. I hid under the seat; they were too lazy to check and there was no dog. Or I would have been done for; a prison for life, I should think.'

'Finish your food and we'll get you some clothes. That will help in Paris, won't it? And then we'll travel.'

'Travel?' she said. She looked at Berndt, a grave look of suspicion, but dug into her food, mopping up the plate with bread and sitting back with a grunt of pleasure. 'That's the best food I have had since leaving home.'

'Home?'

'Brasov. Three weeks ago. My God, I'm tired.' She dropped her head on the table, and in a moment was snoring. Berndt looked at her; would it work? It was worth a try. He let her sleep for ten minutes then woke her; the café staff were starting to pay attention.

'Let's find a clothing store. Oh, by the way, say you are my cousin and then if anyone demands your papers ... What do I call you?'

'Brit.'

As they left the station, there was a man standing on one side, smoking, pretending to read a paper and looking around, all the time. He had a narrow face, like a weasel, a greasy cap pulled low over his eyes; he was wearing an anorak and jeans, and slick lounge shoes. They looked out of place to Berndt who hunched his shoulders, bent his head and held onto the woman's arm, an old couple on the way home. Sure, the woman looked a bit dishevelled but perhaps she had been working in the fields. The man shook his head in the direction of the car park. Berndt scanned the parked cars casually; a Mercedes, German plates, third row, a man behind the steering wheel. He recognised the type, certainly not a chauffeur.

They hobbled off down the street until they found a cheap supermarket. Inside, the staff looked at the woman with distaste but looked away when Berndt returned their look. It didn't take long; she found sensible warm clothes, a suit and coat, underclothes, blouses and a hat, and changed in the cubicle. Berndt located a shoulder bag for the spare clothes and the worn rags were left in the cubicle. They returned to the station; the man was still beside the door and now he examined Berndt more closely.

Inside, Berndt directed the woman to the Ladies Toilets, suggesting that she have a wash, no hurry, he would meet her in the café. He went into the Gents and waited.

A few minutes later, the man came in; he glanced at Berndt, went to the basins watching Berndt the whole time in the mirror, and when Berndt was standing at the urinals, came at him fast, a knife held low. Ah, Berndt thought, where do they train these idiots? He swivelled, noted the look of alarm in the man's face, and propelled him into the urinal, the knife clattering into the trough, and gave him a sharp chop in the neck. The man collapsed; the urinal flushed. Berndt was washing his hands at the sink when a man came in; it was not the man in the car.

He shrugged towards the man in the urinal. 'Huh! Some drunkard, I suppose. I'll call the station staff.' And walked out.

In the café, he had to wait a while, drinking coffee, until the woman appeared.

'We go now. We're late' he said. Taking the woman by the elbow, he hurried out towards the platforms. When they reached the ticket office, she dug in her heels.

'Hey, where are you taking me now? What do you take me for? I've heard about the slave trade. And it's not for me.'

'You want to go to Paris? I shall pay for your ticket, but first I need you to come to Lyons with me. I can explain on the train.'

At the office, he asked for two singles to Lyons, and a single onward to Paris; this he gave to Brit, who looked much cleaner and happier. As they left the ticket office, he saw the driver of the Mercedes standing in the concourse, looking around. They went to the platform and boarded the train. A few minutes later, the driver was on the platform, examining the passengers in the train; Brit stared at him.

'Who does he think he is, looking at me like that?'

Berndt was busy doing up his shoelace. He hated the fleeing; how much better it had been to eliminate the opposition, like the thug in the Gents. But he could not draw attention to them now; it was only a matter of time before they caught up with him again.

The train pulled out, a slow stopping train that ran across country, a zig-zag route that took a whole day. Berndt wondered what awaited him in Lyons.

THREE

It was raining. The train pulled through the suburbs, dull afternoon light, dull colours, dull wet walls and roofs. Berndt looked at Brit, wondering what she made of this change in her circumstances and wished that his circumstances could change. She seemed content, gazing out of the window with interest; she had spoken a few times during the day of her past, a quiet life, a husband who had worked for a state logging company and was away for days at a time, a hard drinker. She had left him. She had worked in a library and brought up their daughter. Their home, a flat in a modern block, small and uncomfortable, looked out onto a road, and more blocks; she remembered her grandparents' home in the country, always warm and welcoming. A humble farming life where nobody went without; there was no opportunity of making a bit of spare money in a city flat. She didn't speak of her parents, or the War.

Berndt rested, taking his pulse and breathing down so that he slept, a little at a time, preparing for Lyons. It was inevitable; they would be waiting at the station, would have tracked his departure and had time to telephone ahead. He wondered how large the organisation was, whether he had met the leaders in Munich or lieutenants only. He wondered how large their army was and what it consisted of; what proportion of mindless hard men to those who used their brains. He assumed that the force in the village had consisted largely of hard men, expendable if necessary, and possibly one lieutenant. So far, he had eliminated six men if the man in the urinal had succumbed to the blow. How many men were they prepared to sacrifice before he was defeated? It couldn't be good business for them and he had left them alone. Until now.

And now, perhaps, was the time to stop running. What sort of a life was it, being a fugitive? Francine must wait while he takes the fight to the enemy.

When they arrived at Lyon, there was no immediate sign of trouble; he scanned the platforms and concourse but all seemed quiet, the evening rush not yet started. Brit turned to him, her eyes full, and hugged him; she was a different person from the tramp who had accosted him. Now she stood tall, a bag in hand, thanking him and looking for the train to Paris. He helped her on her way but did not dawdle in the station, leaving for the street. On the way out, he paused to examine a street map, discovering that to all effects he was on an island, and islands allowed limited escape routes. Still, he turned north across a square into a shopping street, where he slipped into a budget clothing store.

Half an hour later, he came out wearing a suit, shirt and tie, beret, and carrying a briefcase into which he had stuffed his working clothes. His shoes were still workers' boots, but he hoped they didn't stand out. Now he was a travelling salesman, free to cross France without notice. Except for those who took the trouble to observe him. He walked up the narrow street, scanning casually as he went, changing

28

course, doubling back, dropping into shops to emerge again in a few minutes. He was sure that he was not followed and went into a café to drink coffee and eat.

He hadn't been at his table long before he became aware of a girl at his elbow. Of course, he had seen her enter but taken no further notice of her.

'Pardon, monsieur.'

He turned; she was about eleven years old, quite small, simply dressed. A quiet face, he thought. Not one to show emotions.

'I have a note for you,' she said, and laid a folded piece of paper on the table.

'Who gave it to you…'

She was gone, winding through the tables, slipping out of the door into the street, out of sight almost immediately.

Berndt sighed; so they were employing child labour. And he had been spotted arriving and followed through the streets. In all his working life, he had never known the use of children for tracking. Though, come to think of it, it made a lot of sense particularly in a city where they knew every corner. And then he recalled his time in Hitler Youth and how they were trained to hide in the narrowest of crevices, crawling through the ruined buildings to follow the enemy, laying traps and mines. He was good at it, rewarded with a tap on his shoulder by the Führer himself.

The note: brief and to the point. "Call this number; we shall expect your call within 30 minutes." He guessed it was a local number.

There was a phone in the corner. He dialled and waited. A voice.

'Oui? Who goes there?' A gruff man's voice.

Berndt was silent; was this a joke? He replaced the receiver, staring at the 'phone. Lifted it, dialled again.

'Oui? Qui va la?'

Berndt snorted. 'You wanted to talk?'

'Oui. Moment, s'il vous plait.' There was a buzzing, the line went dead, and then a loud German voice spoke slowly.

'Berndt. It is a while since we met at the railway station; I'm sorry you felt it necessary to eliminate our man.'

Berndt made no comment; he remembered the occasion vividly and still felt some anguish that he had been taken so easily.

'And now, a further five, or is it six men? This is not good business. I am a businessman and I thought we had an arrangement; we give you work, and reward you well. What happened?'

Berndt cleared his throat. 'I'll be no man's servant.'

'Proud words and I sympathise with your principles. But my dear man, are we not all servants in one way or another? To the state, to a woman, a family, a tradition?'

'You punished me, interfered with my method of contract.'

'Why, you were taking for ever, for ever I say, to carry out your contract. What sort of an employer, or any person who is paying for work, is prepared to wait upon the wiles of a contractor? Why, if I employ a builder, if he delays, dawdles, goes elsewhere instead of my contract, I cancel our contract and seek remuneration.'

Berndt could imagine what that might consist of; his own experiences made him wise to the methods of this man.

'I wasn't working for you,' he said.

'Aah, there is the rub, as the English say. You had no idea for whom you were working; it was not important to you. You had no qualms about eliminating a nice man or a pretty woman, or even a child.'

Berndt remembered the Italian student who he left on a hillside.

'So, my Berndt, how are we to move forward? Am I to lose still more men trying to bring you down? It is not good business; they are too expensive and not as expendable as you might think.'

Berndt was silent.

'What do you want, really, my friend? What will satisfy you? It would be such a waste to fritter your skills on eliminating my soldiers. There are greater uses for those skills.'

Berndt shrugged. 'Those days are past.'

'Is that so? Really? No... no, I don't think so, not at all, not by the standards of the last few days.'

Berndt was silent.

'I have a proposal. A simple proposal. Why don't you carry out one more contract for me, not an easy one I confess but that would bore you; one contract, and I will release you of any obligation and you can retire.'

'One contract only?' Berndt doubted him and could see a long line of 'final' contracts. 'My money is running out. Call me back if you wish to discuss it further.' He put the phone down, and stood in deep thought. Was this really the way out? The phone rang.

'Qui va la?'

'Don't waste my time,' snapped Berndt.

Silence, a pause. The smooth German voice.

'Ah, my friend. Have you considered my offer?'

'It stinks. But I accept your terms; if you break your word, it will cost you more soldiers. And, as a sign of your word, place one hundred thousand English pounds in the same account as usual and a further one hundred and fifty thousand to be held by the bankers towards the completion of the contract.'

'The details of the contract will be delivered to your table there in one hour. But understand one thing; when I say retire, I mean retire. You will do no more work, no more little eliminations, for any persons or organisation; is that understood? Have a good meal, you can afford it.' There was a merry laugh, and the line went dead.

Forty-five minutes later, the girl was beside his table once more. She left a thick brown envelope, smiled and slipped away. Berndt weighed the envelope in his hand; not light. What could be so heavy about a simple instruction? He slit the end, drew out a sheaf of papers, maps, timetables, directions, and noted that there were to be two murders. Not one. He had never been contracted to carry out two; it increased the complications enormously, the dangers, the escape route. He rang the number again.

'Allo?' A different voice, a woman's, not young.

'Put me onto him. Now.'

'Allo? Qui va la?'

'Where's the German? Get him.'

'Pardon, monsieur, you must have the wrong number.' Click, the line went dead.

Berndt found a small hotel out of the centre, and opened up the papers. It appeared that the research had been carried out; some person had been meticulous in his observations, noting weather, timings, dress, the number of persons involved, any security, the distance from a police post and including photographs. The contract was for the owner and his son of a general contracting firm based in Lyon. It required that they were eliminated in or directly outside their offices and the notes made clear that they never arrived together. Merde, it was two contracts, not one. Berndt considered his alternatives.

He could run and deal with the hard men as they came; a tiring restless existence and one from necessity without Francine. He could hang around until he was contacted again and have the opportunity of discussing the case. Or he could contact his armourer, his car builder, and his banks, and plan the contract.

The next morning, he took a taxi out to the offices; a black glass block set gleaming in a builder's yard, worn-out storage sheds, rusting machinery, concrete mixers, trucks, bricks, cement bags, blocks and timber. Across the road stood a primary school and a church. There was a happy squealing of children at play, a single teacher glued to a letter. He walked past twice and was not noticed. In one hour, nobody came or went from the offices, though the odd truck entered and left the yard.

He didn't like the setup. There was nowhere to site a sniper gun at a distance and he didn't fancy a drive-by shooting; the days of gangster shoot-ups was long gone as cars were too easily tracked by helicopter.

He went back and purchased more detailed maps of the area and a local paper. In a café, he looked at the maps and read the paper.

On page five, there was a whole page article about the owner of the building firm. He had lost his grand-daughter to cancer at the age of five and started a local charity for children suffering from all forms of cancer, injecting a large sum of money into the charity and building a respite home for them in the hills, fully staffed. He was due to retire, having built up the business from a two-man firm started by his father, and the article welcomed his son, the son who had lost the daughter, as the new proprietor. The son supported the local football team to the tune of several thousand euros and installed the Christmas tree outside the Mayor's office every year.

FOUR

It rained, and Berndt sat in cafés, his hotel room and elsewhere, trying to come to a plan for the contract. He was sure that the Conglomerate would not strike him; after all, was he not working for them? He was also sure that they would not like a delay; there might be a re-occurrence of the Station incident. And while he did not feel that he had to bow to their preferences, he did not wish to draw more trouble down onto himself. He was lightly armed, the Glock that he had taken off the driver in the car, with ammunition clips but no rifle or scope. He pondered his future and kept out of the rain.

Eventually, he went out and bought a good raincoat, a hat and a good pair of shoes; he could not go around looking like a soaked salesman. The coat bought him a measure of respect in the restaurants that he visited; they no longer found that they were fully booked or placed him at the rear near the kitchen door. He lived well and built his personal resources, strength and will.

After a week, he rang the builders' yard and made an appointment. Arriving in a taxi, he walked slowly to the door, stepping carefully around the puddles and builders' mess to preserve the immaculate shine on his shoes. In the reception, the girl stopped chewing, came from behind the desk and asked his business. Before long, he was ushered upstairs into the boardroom, a large well-lit room looking out to the rear of the plot, a park of timber sheds, joinery shops, and implements. There was a long table, by the windows, and the other side of the room, the boss's desk and a number of comfortable chairs to which he was directed. He was served with coffee, offered gateaux and alcohol that he refused.

'Monsieur, welcome to our offices. How can I help you?' The man was in his sixties, a comfortable build, double chin, and a sharp eye that took in the details of Berndt's cheap working suit and expensive shoes.

'I represent a gentleman who has heard of your charitable work and wishes to join in helping the unfortunate children of Lyon. I understand that you have donated and constructed a rest home and subsidise its maintenance.' Berndt spoke slowly, in no rush to establish his credentials.

'That is true. But, excuse me monsieur, a simple donation would not come to our offices; the charity has its own offices in the city. A visit…'

'Oui, je comprends. But my gentleman wishes to go a little further.'

'Moment, may I call my son? He will be taking over from me shortly, and you may prefer to do business with him.' He buzzed his phone and asked his secretary to send his son in.

'May I introduce my son? And your name, monsieur?'

'Jacob Lign. But I cannot give you my patron's name; a matter of discretion, you understand.'

The son looked at Berndt's suit and curled his lip in suspicion. He stood leaning back against the board table, hands in pockets, looking down on Berndt. About thirty-five, he was lean and slightly raffish, a sharp suit, shoes that would never be worn on a builders' site. Against the light, Berndt had difficulty seeing his expression but his manner and the way he held himself told Berndt all he needed to know.

'Alors, you wonder at my clothes. I must tell you that my patron is very strict about these things; he does not wish his employees to appear too well paid; it is a measure of his humility and charity. Money must not be spent on frivolous appendages; I apologise for my shoes and coat, but the weather came upon me.'

The older man laughed, frowned at his son and pointed to a chair.

'Didier, take notes if you please. Now M. Lign, what do you have in mind?'

'Well, my patron believes that you have done great works for the poor children and wonders, with your opinion of course, whether a building in the city, a day shelter for sick and recuperating children, would be useful.'

'Well, we would have to address the board of the charity but I believe that they would be grateful for the suggestion; at present, they only have small offices and a single room for the children. How were you suggesting that this centre might come about?'

'To be constructed by yourselves, funded by my patron on a regular basis.'

'That would be a good scheme; we would ensure that construction costs would be kept under control so your patron would not feel that his contribution is wasted.'

'I have looked at your reputation and buildings in the

city; I assume that you would have little difficulty with zoning and construction laws.'

'Indeed, that is so. Have you a site in mind?'

'I do not know this city well; I hoped that you might suggest somewhere suitable, bearing in mind the location of the homes of the sick.'

'We would be delighted to suggest suitable sites and buildings.'

Berndt coughed, eased himself in the chair and looked from the older man to the younger. 'There is one source of concern.' He produced the newspaper article.

The older man looked troubled, glanced at his son and sipped coffee. 'If you are concerned at the change of the proprietor, I must assure you that my son has my fullest confidence. He has ten years experience in this firm and worked for a national firm before then after college.'

Berndt smiled, raised a hand. 'I am sure that you would not leave such a business in hands other than those who would carry on such a tradition. No, there is another matter.'

There was a pause; both builders looked concerned, speaking silently to each other, shoulders shrugged.

'There is nothing that should concern you, monsieur,' the older man said stiffly. 'Please, tell us of your concerns.'

'There have been whispers of a take-over, a German company.'

There was a long pause; the older man was having difficulty re-arranging his face and the younger gazed at the floor.

'Am I mistaken?' said Berndt.

A pause.

'I am surprised that you have heard anything of this matter; can I enquire how you came upon it?'

'Unfortunately I can't tell you. My patron passed it on to me to check the soundness of your business.'

The older man sighed. 'It was two years ago. We tendered for a big job in Bavaria but to carry it out we would have had to refinance; you know how it is. We made arrangements for the financing but never needed to draw upon the funds as we withdrew from the project. It was too big for us, too complicated; we came to the conclusion that we would not have completed the work to the satisfaction of the project.'

'And this funding would have involved a take-over?'

'That was not our understanding; it would be most regrettable if the finance company assumed that we were handing our company into their hands.'

Berndt sat back, sipped coffee, and looked at both men. 'You can appreciate that my patron wishes to be quite clear on this matter.'

'Naturally, we would be happy to reassure him in any way.'

Berndt smiled, a smile that did not reach his eyes.

'Then why is there a contract out for both of you?'

There was a long silence. The younger man reacted violently, flinging his hands in the air, staring. The older pondered, looking down, and then said, 'What sort of contract, monsieur?'

'Oh papa! There is only one sort of contract in this case.' Turning to Berndt, he said, 'How do you know of this contract? How are we to believe you? Surely, there must be a mistake!'

'No mistake.'

'But,' the older man broke in. 'What have we done? Why are we the targets?'

'I cannot tell you; I do not know.' Berndt was cool, detached.

'You haven't told us,' said the younger. 'How do you know?'

'Because I was contracted to carry it out.'

The younger man stared and moved towards the door. The older just looked down and mopped his brow.

'I should be grateful if you would sit near your father,' said Berndt to the younger, who stared, hovered near the door and then sat next to his father.

'When are you going to do it then?' he said.

Berndt smiled and didn't reply.

'Perhaps,' said the older. 'Perhaps, as he has not already killed us, there is some negotiation that we can pursue.'

Berndt smiled and nodded.

At that moment, there was a sharp crack and the younger man cried out, clapping his hand to his left shoulder.

'Down. Now!' Berndt was sharp, and they obeyed, the older man groaning as he lowered himself to the floor. Berndt stepped to the long table and upended it as more shots came through the window, embedding in the polished mahogany. A few moments and a small canister came through the opening and exploded with considerable force, deafening the three men; the table held the blast while the ceiling showered plaster and the walls shook.

So, he thought, the Conglomerate (he did not doubt that it was their operatives outside) was trying to eliminate him with the builders. How very neat, except of course, it was not neat at all. Just messy thuggish bungling.

Signing to the builders to stay put, he opened the door quietly and peered down to the hall. The receptionist was nowhere to be seen; in her place lounged a man, medium height, close cropped hair, army kit, with a semi-automatic leaning against the desk next to him. Berndt considered how confident the attackers had been on success. On the landing, he sighed quietly; still the man ignored him. He tut-tutted and as the man wheeled round, his hand reaching for his gun, shot him between the eyes. The man fell back against the desk, staring sightlessly at the ceiling. Taking the stairs three at a time, he recovered the semi-automatic, checked the clip, found a spare clip and turned to the rear of the building. Through a door he found the receptionist and two secretaries, all shaking with fear, tears and wide eyes as Berndt appeared with a gun. One pointed to a door to the rear and put her finger to her lips. He indicated to them to be quiet and opened the door quietly.

In front of him was a man, back to him, calling out into the yard; he was having difficulty in hearing a voice outside. Berndt went back through the door, slamming it behind him; in a moment, the man came through the door.

'I told you, keep quiet and—'

Berndt stepped from behind the door, and gave him a single sharp chop to the neck. The man collapsed as though poleaxed.

'Tie him up, tight. Where are all the yard staff? Why haven't you called the police?'

'He said we would all be killed if the police came. There are only two men in the yard, old Pierre who sweeps up and Henri in the joinery shop.'

'Don't call the police just yet; I have something to do first. Is there a window looking out to the yard?'

He was directed to a small office; he slipped into the room, crawled to the window and stood at one side peering out into the yard. Behind the offices was a clear space about fifty metres wide; a killing ground. Beyond that, there were a series of alleys running to the back of the site, between stacks of bricks, blocks, timbers, and sheds. Prominent in the centre was a larger construction; Berndt guessed it was the joinery shop. At first floor level was a window looking towards the offices; Berndt focused on it, and after a few minutes saw a man moving inside and then the barrel of a gun. He wondered how large the team was and how skilled; he didn't think that the Conglomerate would have sent dull soldiers to be eliminated by him again.

Oh well, there wasn't any choice; he would have to face them.

He went back into the offices and out of the front door, turning to the right down the access drive to the yard. It was wide, a parking space on one side with a Mercedes and a Toyota Impreza among other small cars. Guess who drives the Impreza, he thought. He slipped across the roadway and made his way down the line of cars. At the rear of the building was a security fence and gate, standing open; a man lounged there, semi-automatic hanging in his hands; he seemed absorbed in trying to hear words from the joinery shop.

Berndt crouched down about ten metres from the gate and remembered the old Stasi training. Surprise was more powerful than all the guns in the world. He coughed. The man swung round, staring. And turned back.

Berndt coughed again.

The man came towards him, down the roadway looking between the cars. It was so easy, thought Berndt. He followed his feet and came up behind him, slipping an old piece of rope round his neck and throttling him, dragging him back between cars to the fence where he was concealed. He checked there was no life and walked towards the yard. How to cross the killing ground? Going back to the front yard, he picked up a sheet of steel cladding and walked openly up the roadway and across the killing ground; he heard a shout but no shots. The gunmen would be wondering why the man on the gate had disappeared, but hadn't yet left their nest. Berndt found it easy to walk down the alley, cross over to the joinery shop and come up behind it; there were large doors on the side, one slid back to allow a man to enter. Berndt flattened himself against the building and peered into the shop; there was nobody in sight. He slipped around the door, keeping his back to the wall inside and moved to the rear, checking between the machines, the bench saws, planers, sanders and drill stands.

At the back of the building was a rough staircase leading to the loft; one way upstairs but if it creaked he would be dead. Of course, he could always set fire to the building but Henri would perish and it would seem a little excessive. His training should overcome such an obstacle. He looked round. The machines stood silent, neat rows, bins of waste, stacks of timber, some partially finished windows. It was a timber-framed building, sawn timbers, constructed simply. The floor overhead... yes, the floor overhead was boarding with 19mm gaps, no doubt for ventilation. He crept to the front; two pairs of feet moved about restlessly.

'Where is he? The idiot, he's meant to be by the gate. Can't see him. Why don't you go and find him? 'spect he's dawdling with the secretaries inside. Haw haw!'

'I ain't going, why me, it's always – OK, OK, I'm on the way.'

Loud stamping footsteps across the floor, down the stairs, out the door. Berndt pursued him silently, across the floor, out of the door into the yard. The man was tramping towards the gate, shouting. Berndt slipped across an alley, dropped a brick, and retreated behind a stack. The man stopped.

'What you doing? Having a piss? Come on, you meant to be on the gate!'

There was a pause, and he shouted again, 'I ain't standing here all day!' And then, 'Where the… are you?' And walked across the killing ground, down the nearest alley. Berndt waited, tossed a brick to the rear and followed it cautiously. He chose a short piece of 75 x 75mm sawn hardwood, weighed it up in his hands and waited. In no time, the man appeared at the end of the stack; he had a moment to register Berndt before the timber hit him with full force in the face. He staggered, stood and advanced; Berndt was astonished; what sort of an ox was this? He swung the timber again and the man went down, still moving, blood pouring from his head. Berndt finished him with a sharp stab to the neck. One man to go, he reckoned. He looked up; old Pierre was standing looking at him in amazement. Berndt didn't stop.

Back into the shop, he walked to the front. The man was calling out, 'Who's there? Where are you all? Stop pissing about, and get back here!'

Berndt stood beneath him, located him by the shouting, and fired upwards through the floor. A body crashed down on the floor above, shouting for help. Berndt took the stairs three at a time; the man rolled towards him, struggling to raise his gun. Berndt shot him in the head. Henri was tied up at one side; he released him; Henri burst into a wail of gratitude, of shock and release.

At that moment, he could hear police sirens.

FIVE

Berndt froze; how far off were the police? What would they think of a man who eliminated a gang of gangsters, a tough group of professional killers? It might not go down well. And then there might be questions and records perused and who knows where it would end up. Probably in prison. Great.

'Henri, tell me now. How do I get out of here?'

Henri stared, wiped his hand across his face. Stared, and coughed.

'Why, down the stairs, through the yard, out the front… Oh!' A light dawned, he smiled, wiped the smile off his face, shrugged. 'I don't know.'

'What is at the back of the yard?'

'A high fence, steel.'

'Fetch me a ladder.'

'But, mon ami, there is a deep ditch the other side.'

Berndt thought, and sent him for a scaffold pole.

The fence was about three metres high, barbed poles, galvanised steel. Berndt put the ladder up, and started climbing. Stopped.

'Henri, thank you, I don't want to put you in trouble. Please, can you see to Pierre? He saw me eliminating a man and I don't want the police to catch me. They don't like others doing their dirty work.'

'Non, zut, you rescued me, go in peace, may the power be with you!'

They shook hands and Berndt climbed to the top of the fence. Putting the pole over the fence, he stood on the horizontals between the barbs, and pole-vaulted the ditch to the opposite bank. Thrusting the pole back through the fence, he waved; Henri had already removed the ladder.

Beyond the ditch was a grass embankment, not high. Beyond the grass was a road, light traffic travelling at speed; nobody paid a moment's notice. Beyond the road, more grass and then the River Rhone. Berndt strode over the road to the riverbank, looking up – and downstream. It would take some luck, he thought. How long before the police spy him from the yard? It was not dark, and although cloudy, visibility was good.

There were a number of boats, small and large, tied up along the bank. Most had awnings covering them. He chose a larger vessel, perhaps ten metres long, and slipped under the awning. There was a teak lined cockpit, a wheel and binnacle, engine throttle and ignition and the entrance to a deckhouse; it was a smart motor yacht, designed for long trips, perhaps even along the coast.

Berndt lay down, and reflected that it had been a busy day and that he had failed in one of his objectives, to remove the builders, father and son, from Lyon and place them in a secure location for a while. How long? No idea. He felt hungry and thirsty. It would have to wait; that was nothing new. After all, he had breakfasted well that morning. He wondered whether he had caused Francine concern, being out of touch; it was days since he had spoken to her and then was unable to give her a location or an idea where and when they might meet. The boat rocked slightly on the current as vessels passed and Berndt fell asleep.

It was dark. Voices, laughter, the smell of Gauloises, a hiccup and a belch.

'Ah, Gaston, you are dégoutant! Here let me carry the food.'

The awning was pulled back and three persons froze, looking down into the cockpit. Berndt lounged on the floor, apparently at ease, the gun concealed in his lap.

'My apologies,' he said. 'I was tired and this boat was very comfortable.'

'Who are you?' The woman was strident, without fear, dressed in a smart tight skirt and silk blouse with a shawl round her neck. 'Get out of our boat!'

'Ah, you see, that would be the obvious thing to do but I wonder if you could do me a little favour?'

'Mon Dieu!' The man was also smartly dressed, blazer and slacks, smoking, a look of horror. Berndt smelt the fear that he gave off. The other man was older and came forward. He showed no fear and took in the situation without alarm.

'You are running from the police? Well, how can we help?'

'Could you take me down as far as the station? I shall be happy to leave you there but I would be obliged if you told no-one of my presence here.'

'If you think—'

'Be quiet, Isabelle! I think we can accommodate this man. If he wished to cause us harm, I think he would have by now. And it is easy to take him that short distance downstream.'

Berndt recognised an old army man, the type hardened by sun and experiences. He wondered where he had served, with what kind of unit.

'Thank you, I am sorry to cause you trouble.'

The awning was rolled up and Berndt ushered into the deckhouse and offered a drink. He wondered why they were so hospitable, why they didn't just wish to throw him off the boat. It seemed to come down to the older man who cared for him and appeared to see something the younger two did not; he had left them to cast off and get underway. He sat with Berndt looking at him with interest.

'Well,' he said. 'I don't know where you have come from and I don't want to know. But I imagine that you have no wish to use that gun on us.' He smiled.

Berndt looked him over; the man was lean but had a hard look that he recognised. 'You have fought in a secret unit in the army?'

'It shows, does it? I guess you have served in something similar. I like to think that army man will always help army man, whichever side you are.'

'Can you tell me? How can a man disappear in this part of the world?'

'You are running from the police?'

'Let us say police or other forces.'

'If you are a deserter, I'm not sure that I can help.'

'No deserter. A long time since I was in the army. But there are others who wish to eliminate me.'

'You must have made them unhappy.'

'It happens.'

'Do they know you are here?'

'Yes.'

'Can I help? It is some time since I have had some action but a little exercise would be good.'

'I would not wish to bring them down on your family or your friends.'

'They are like that?'

'They are.'

'And—'

'And what do I plan to do? They have a commander and I don't know where he is located. I have only seen his soldiers and his spies.'

'Spies?'

'If you are one of them, I have not told you anything that they do not know.'

'I cannot prove that I am not your enemy. That is for you to believe. But, in truth, I have not used a weapon in five or ten years and I live a life of unadulterated luxury and idleness.'

Berndt looked at the man and didn't believe him. 'Where are you heading?'

'Avignon. It will take us two or three days.'

'Can you take a passenger?'

The older man looked at him thoughtfully, then nodded. 'Let me ask the others; it's their boat.' And disappeared into the darkness of the cockpit.

There was a loud altercation, swearing and shouting gradually dying away. Berndt thought he heard a sob. After a quarter of an hour the man reappeared.

'Well, that was not so easy. You see, the woman is my niece and the man is her fiancé; they were looking forward to a romantic holiday. But let me introduce myself; I am Marcel, my niece is Isabelle and her fiancé Gaston. We are limited in accommodation but you are welcome to sleep in the cockpit; you found it quite comfortable, hein?'

A strange time followed. The younger couple avoided Berndt as though he was not there, looking through him, never addressing him, making sure that they were never alone with him. They gave him hours at the helm and his meals were passed to him in the cockpit and they kept to the deckhouse or sprawled on the foredeck. But they caused him no harm.

Marcel, on the other hand, was intrigued with Berndt's situation and offered help again. Berndt had never had an accomplice and was suspicious of any attempt to help him, fearing that he was becoming vulnerable. But Marcel talked of his own days in his unit, of eliminating spies and others from Eastern Bloc countries, of serving for a while in the desert and facing fighters on camels. He remembered months in Vietnam and was harshly critical of the French forces there. Berndt revealed a little of his Stasi days, of his training and exercises; he did not talk of Hitler Youth. By degrees, he spoke a little of the Conglomerate, how they pursued him across France, how many soldiers they used; he did not reveal his former life as a hitman though Marcel possibly guessed that his occupation had not been lawful. And Berndt did not tell of the number of Conglomerate soldiers he had killed. Eventually, he revealed that there was a job that he had left unsolved in Lyon and perhaps Marcel could help him.

'I was visiting a builders' yard; you might know of them. They have done much charity work and—'

'I know who you mean. The son is about to take over from the father; I saw it in the paper.'

'There is a contract out to kill them.'

'Mon Dieu! Why?'

'I understand that they got into a mess, some business deal. Not intended, I don't think they have caused any debt or difficulty but some party is choosing to believe that the builders cheated them.'

'And what could I do?'

'It's not so simple and you may be put into a situation of danger.'

'Huh, about time. I have been going mad sitting around playing the retired man. What do you want?'

'Remove the builders.'

'Remove? Take out? Eliminate?'

'Non, non. I meant take them somewhere safe for a while.'

'How long?'

'I don't know. If I only knew where the commander of the Conglomerate was or how to hit him where it hurts… But if they are removed to a safe house, there is a chance they will survive.'

Marcel thought for a while, head bent. Then laughed.

'Bien sur. I know where to take them; it is not so difficult. And you, what will you do?'

'What I always do.'

Marcel did not ask and they talked of other things, armament in particular. Each enquired of the other whether they were armed and compared gun types, ammunition, and availability. It seemed that Marcel was a crack shot, had shot for the Army and had a number of weapons; he was not interested in semi-automatics – so vulgar, so messy – but liked the kind of sniper rifle that Berndt had used in his working life. Hand guns were not a problem, as long as they were at hand.

The land rose on both sides, vineyards and small fields, many towns that beckoned with fresh bread, cafés and groceries. Gaston and Isabelle would disappear, arm in arm, only to reappear later, apparently sated. Occasionally, large freight barges would come upriver bound for the docks at Lyon, a friendly wave, perhaps a toot on the horn. Sometimes they saw another cruiser, not often.

It was on the second day; they had just passed Les Roches de Condrieu. Berndt was taking his trick at the wheel, swinging round the large bends in the Rhone as Marcel stretched out on the side deck. He hated sun-bathing, he said, such a waste of time and not good for you, but what else can I do… Gaston and Isabelle were sun-bathing on the foredeck, flat out under the hot sun. They became aware of a high humming behind them, like a hornet or a swarm of bees.

Marcel sat up, shading his eyes. They could see a white bow wave, like a proud man's moustache, approaching them rapidly. Berndt and Marcel faced forward and Marcel said, 'I think it better if you concealed yourself.'

Berndt dived into the deckhouse and down the companionway to the saloon. He had been below before. A large comfortable saloon took up the centre of the yacht, with two small cabins in the quarters to the rear and a short corridor forward with a bathroom, a small bedroom, and a large suite in the bows. Berndt slipped into the bathroom.

The launch throttled down and circled the yacht before coming alongside. Gaston and Isabelle sat up; Marcel signalled to them to stay where they were. There were three men, all wearing dark blue army blouses and trousers and kepis, and belts with holsters. No badges, no unit insignia.

The driver called, 'Cut your engine. We are coming aboard.'

'Why? What warrant do you have?' said Marcel.

'We don't need one; we are looking for a dangerous terrorist and he may be concealed on your yacht.'

'That's not possible—'

'Stand aside.'

Two of the men came aboard and the launch stood off maintaining a position off the stern. Marcel looked at the men; they were swarthy, one had not shaved and was wearing brown shoes. One of them told the other to search below while he kept watch on the captain.

Berndt heard the man stumbling down the steps and helping himself to a croissant from the table. It seemed he looked into the quarter cabins, slamming the doors, and then came forward. Berndt could see enough through the louvred door and when the man came near, he slammed the door back into his face, chopping down onto his gun hand; the gun skittered forward on the floor. The man punched Berndt through the door, louvres splintering, and caught him on his side. Slamming the door away from him, he faced Berndt in the corridor. It was only about 60 centimetres wide and no more than two and half metres long. Berndt found himself in a small space facing a large man who paid no heed to the blows falling on him but was causing Berndt harm on his body and his arms.

It was a long time since he had engaged in this sort of exercise though the Stasi had trained him well in physical combat. But the man he faced was a brute, insensible to pain, even apparently enjoying himself, a low gurgle of pleasure.

Berndt fought for a while and then, as though defeated, retreated suddenly into the little cabin, ducking to one side; the man laughed and ducked down to retrieve his gun. Berndt jumped on his arm, punched him in the ear and grabbed his head, twisting it violently sideways and back until there was a small crunch and the body subsided to the floor. Berndt stood over him, breathing heavily, rubbing his arms, and picked up the gun, checking the magazine.

In the cockpit, the engine was still idling. The other man could hear nothing of the action below but was becoming concerned. He opened the door to the deckhouse, leaning forward to call to his mate. Marcel moved quickly; he tipped the man down the companionway stairs and shot him as he attempted to stand at the foot. Berndt emerged from the corridor, smiled, and dragged the first man out of the corridor.

Behind the yacht, they heard the launch accelerate and come near. Marcel strolled into the cockpit, hands in pockets.

'Where are my men?'

'Oh, I think they are searching all the cabins and the engine room and the bilges. I guess it takes a time, hein?'

The captain on the launch looked unhappy and picked up a semi-automatic. At that moment, Marcel saw a large freighter barge coming towards them; they had drifted onto the wrong side of the river; there was a loud hoot from the barge. Marcel threw the yacht into gear, full power, and ducked around the barge's bow, running between the bank and the barge. The launch was left in mid-stream on the other side of the barge. The skipper of the barge looked down at Marcel, shouting and cursing, something about fancy yachts that were no better than... and should stay in fancy... yacht stations where they could... themselves. Gaston and Isabelle looked up in horror and huddled together. Berndt had come up into the deckhouse, watching Marcel.

As the yacht emerged from the stern of the barge, the launch came roaring up from the other side, the captain raising his semi-automatic. Marcel had waited for him, and fired. His shot hit the man in the shoulder and he dropped the weapon, swearing loudly, and turned the launch towards the yacht. Before he could raise his gun, Marcel fired again, hitting him in the head.

The launch collided with the yacht, running alongside, the captain slumped over his wheel. Berndt leapt from the yacht onto the launch, cut the throttle and passed the painter to Marcel. He heaved the man clear of the wheel, dragging him under the launch's awning, and climbed back onto the yacht.

'Three dead bodies; they seem to have a death wish. Could be an embarrassment.' Marcel had enjoyed himself and poured them both a brandy. 'Mind you, the launch could be a problem.'

Berndt sighed; his ribs hurt and his arms were bruised; where was the quiet retirement? 'I suggest we sink the bodies at night and leave the launch on the bank. OK?'

'Sure, sure. I wonder who they were? Did you see those

brown shoes? Army or police unit? I don't think so.'

'Probably East European, Georgian or Serbia. We used to practise our skills against them; they were never missed.'

'And they were the Conglomerate you spoke of? Nasty brutes. How many more of them?'

Berndt shrugged.

Gaston and Isabelle had come back to the cockpit; Isabelle was crying and shivering and both looked shocked. Marcel pressed them to sit down and drink some brandy.

'There are three dead bodies to dispose of tonight.'

Isabelle gave a shriek and collapsed against Gaston, who stared ahead.

'It's time I left you,' said Berndt.

'Not quite yet, I hope,' said Marcel. 'I was just beginning to enjoy myself.'

Isabelle shrieked. 'Oh Uncle, how could you!'

A little later, they tied up for the night and sank the bodies when it was dark, weighted with old mud anchors; the launch they had set adrift. Isabelle suggested that Berndt use it to escape but he had no wish to escape. Gaston and Isabelle had retreated to their cabin in the bows, having wished Berndt a good journey and hoping that they would never meet him again. Berndt and Marcel sat in the cockpit, drinking.

'I will visit the builders in Lyon. Might there be trouble there? I do hope so,' said Marcel.

'I'll come with you,' said Berndt.

'I'd enjoy that but we need more arms. I must get my rifle and some ammunition. Do you have anything?'

Berndt shrugged and showed him the two guns and

the semi-automatic he had retrieved. At that moment, a car appeared on the bank above them, headlights shining out over the river. A loud voice, a German accent.

'Bitte. Pardon. If you please. Have you seen a black launch with three men? I believe they were here.'

SIX

'Achtung! Excuse me! Do you hear me?'

Berndt spoke quietly to Marcel. 'Keep him talking.' He crawled along the hidden side of the deckhouse. The car was on the bank, well above the river level. The headlights shown out above the moored boat. Otherwise, the night was filled with a soft blackness, the outlines of trees and people just discernible. In the distance there was the sound of a small car being driven at speed, a night bird calling and the perpetual murmur of cicadas. The moon was just rising.

Berndt dropped off the boat and crawled up the bank. It was covered with a short spiky bush and his progress was slow. He peered over the top.

The car was about ten metres short of the edge of the bank. On either side of its beam stood a soldier, army wear, semi-automatics hanging casually; Berndt was no more than five metres from the nearest. And then he saw the man who was speaking, standing at the edge of the bank talking down to Marcel, well lit by the headlights; a slight man, well dressed with a long raincoat and a homburg hat.

'Do you hear me now? You must have seen the launch, black with three men, dark clothes, a fast boat.'

'Yeah, yeah. I expect so. There were many boats on the

river today; you should have seen. There was this woman driving—'

'Nein, nein. No woman. A fast launch, three men.'

'Maybe, maybe. I don't know. We are on holiday, you know, just cruising slowly. We stopped at the last town, very pretty; have you seen it?'

'You are sure, then? No launch?'

'I didn't say that; I don't know. Why? Do you want it? Can I let you know if I see it?'

'Ach, you waste my time. Komm, let's leave this French idiot!'

The two soldiers immediately got into the car, ushering the man into the rear. Berndt had considered a move against them but he would have needed a rifle and a little distance; otherwise he would have been shot down before he could lay hands on the gentleman in the long raincoat, who must have been one of the Conglomerate, possibly the one who spoke to him in Munich Station.

But he was frustrated at not acting; as the car turned, he put a bullet into a rear tyre and slid back into concealment on the bank. The car continued a little way down the road and stopped. He could just see one of the men get out of the driving seat and walk around the car. He was swearing. He shouted at the other man to join him and help change the wheel. The gentleman did not appear. Berndt watched for a while and then crept forward in the darkness keeping a low profile. Behind the road bank he stopped, scarcely one metre from the men who were still swearing, trying to work out how to operate the jack. The road was quiet, a dark country lane.

He stood. 'Want some help?'

They wheeled round in confusion, fumbling for side arms. Berndt shot them both in the head; it was a little too dark to aim for the eyes. They collapsed over the spare wheel without a sound. Almost immediately, a window was lowered and a gun barrel poked out; Berndt could see the whites of his eyes.

A voice spoke out of the car. 'Who is it? What do you want?' A pompous voice with a vein of fear. Berndt did not reply.

'Do I know you?' A long pause. 'Is it… is it Berndt?'

Berndt had anticipated this dilemma for some time; what would he do when he caught up with one of the Conglomerate? How many of them were there? Where were they? Were they all German? What would happen if he eliminated one of them? It was tempting. He waited.

'Do we meet at last?'

Berndt waited.

'Well, what do you want? Shoot me now?' Silence. 'But no. I think there is more sense to talking, don't you?'

Berndt was gruff. 'What about?'

'About why you kill my men, perhaps.'

'And why your men try to kill me.'

'I apologise; they are not very… what shall we say… intelligent! You take too long to carry out your commissions; I ask them simply to prompt you. They have a rather crude sense of "prompting". I don't understand; we pay you very well. And yet you—'

'Enough.'

'Enough? What do you mean?'

'I have had enough of your gorillas. Enough.'

'Gorillas?' He laughed. 'I like that.'

'So when will it stop?'

'Stop? The gorillas?'

'Stop. The commissions.'

'Aah, you can never stop. Did you not realise? We own you, we do.'

'Who are we?'

'It is not important to you. You only have to do what you do, and you do it very well.'

'Who are we?'

'There is always a quiet word to Interpol. Or the French police. They could make your life a little warm. No, you are better working for us.'

'I resign.'

'Surely, it is a joke; why would you want to give it all up? The luxurious lifestyle, the cars, the food, the houses? Why? I really don't understand.'

'No, you don't.'

'What can we do to entice you, to draw you back into the fold? Money? No problem. Privacy? No problem. Weapons? Ach, you can have what you want. We can raid the war chests of any country we choose: Russia, America, France, Britain... why would you want to give up? Please, help me.'

'You wouldn't understand.' And Berndt shot him through the opening at the top of the window, taking the top of his head off.

What would happen now? How long did he have before another director of the Conglomerate caught him? He sighed into the warm soft darkness, and strolled back to Marcel.

On the boat, the other two were raising hell, complaining, shouting, cursing, weeping. Marcel was standing in the cockpit, his arms raised, attempting to bring peace. The sight of Berndt renewed the anger; Isabelle came at him clawing at his face, Gaston behind her. Berndt held her arms and spoke to Marcel.

'I should leave you. I apologise, I did not wish to cause trouble.'

Marcel nodded towards the bank, a question.

'All taken care of, but we should move on,' said Berndt.

Marcel nodded and started the engine. Isabelle slumped down on the seat, weeping. Gaston tried not to look useless, patting her shoulder.

They motored slowly through the night; there was just sufficient light and the river was wide enough to proceed. The next morning, they arrived in Valence and tied up, Gaston and Isabelle disappearing into the town, washing their hands of the two men.

'So,' said Marcel. 'Do you have a plan?'

Berndt shrugged.

'These builders,' said Marcel. 'They are important?'

'Why should they die?' Berndt surprised himself; he had never had such a thought in his life. Berlin 1945? A question of do or die. The Stasi? Accept orders, learn an efficient way of elimination. And since then? Commissions to eliminate individuals. But never, in all that time, any consideration of saving lives. It was true; one didn't seek to involve innocent people in carrying out his commissions but that was a pragmatic decision, to reduce the amount of notice and attention from the authorities.

He looked at Marcel, who had killed the driver of the launch. He appeared to be completely unfazed by his experience, even lusting for more action. And yet ... another man, always a complication. What did he know of this man except that he had similar experiences, similar armed service? He might turn him over to a 'friendly' policeman, or be slow to cover him when it mattered. Was Marcel really prepared to put himself at risk and not reveal their actions to some friend in Lyon?

Another man, always a liability. Because what could he know of how Berndt operated, how could he know to recognise the Conglomerate's operatives? Perhaps it would be best to leave him to deal with the builders alone; he had said that he could, had seemed confident.

And how would he feel if there was a problem, that Marcel had been killed while involved with a problem that he regarded as his own?

Berndt knocked back his coffee. 'I'll deal with the builders; thank you for your help but I shouldn't involve you in my business.'

Marcel shrugged, thought for a moment, and then laughed loudly. 'I get it. You think I might be a liability, of no use, possibly another man to be rescued.' He laughed coldly, chucking his dregs overboard. 'Come my friend, you show me a glimpse, no more, of a life of action and want to cut me out. No, no way. I'm in.'

When the others returned, much later, Marcel and Berndt left the boat to go to the railway station. Isabelle had been unhappy.

'You said you would manage the yacht; skipper us down to the Mediterranean. What shall we do now? Oh Marcel, what a disappointment!'

Marcel looked at Gaston, who shuffled to and fro, and

said, 'You have your man. You will be fine, just fine!'

He had to explain the workings of the yacht to Gaston twice, emphasise the importance of watching fuel reserves, warned him against navigating at night, and clapped him on the back. 'Away you go! Isabelle will crew for you.'

Isabelle gave him a look of hate, spat out, 'Marcel, you'll regret this!' And turned her back on him.

Away from the yacht, Marcel laughed. 'God, how good it is to get away. Yes, I know, she is my niece, but... '

It was not long before they had returned to Lyon where they parted, Berndt to his hotel and Marcel to his home. He had pressed Berndt to stay with him but Berndt said that he wished to carry out a little surveillance, to ascertain whether the Conglomerate was still on the streets. They would meet the next day; Marcel would pick him up at eleven.

Berndt dropped into the café. The proprietor served him and then picked up the phone. Berndt saw it, made no comment. He sat in peace for about half an hour and the little girl was standing suddenly at his table.

'You are to come with me.'

Berndt smiled. 'No, it doesn't work like that. You tell your bosses. They can come to me, or...'

The girl vanished. Berndt left the café and stood over the road in a doorway. He felt his gun in his shoulder holster and kept his head down, watching the pedestrian movement, up and down the street, shopping, eating, groups of girls in arms together, laughing at anything. There was no traffic; deliveries only he read on the signs.

After a while, a big giant of a man walked down the street and straight into the café. There was a loud altercation and he emerged, the proprietor behind him.

'I tell you; he left, after the girl… No, I don't know where he went. What do you think I am? I have a café to run!' He turned and went back into the building, but only after the big man had grasped his collar, shaken him like a rat and told him to telephone if there was any sign of the salaud. The big man scanned the street; Berndt was a tourist, gazing into a shop window, exchanging comments with another tourist, watching the reflection of the thug. A few minutes and he was bored, stomping off up the street.

Berndt was about to leave when a Mercedes came up the street, nosing between the pedestrians, free use of the horn, and stopped at the café. Two men got out. Berndt recognised the type; over developed shoulder muscles, thick necks, crew cuts, black suits cut too small, glowering stares at anyone who dared to meet their eyes. And intelligence not much advanced from an ape, Berndt reckoned.

One man opened the back door of the car and stood staring around as though expecting a challenge. At that moment, a policeman appeared, swinging his baton casually. 'It is not permitted to drive in this street. Remove your vehicle immediately.'

The thug snorted, looking down at the policeman and did not attempt to say anything.

'At once, if you please, or I will be obliged to take your details.'

The thug ignored him as though he was deaf. A man emerged from the back seat and spoke to the policeman. 'Officer, officer, I apologise for my man's behaviour. He did not know that driving in this street was not permitted; I instructed him to bring me here. It is all my fault.'

'Well, monsieur, please remove your car.'

'Of course, of course. But may I have a few moments in this café? Only a few moments.'

The policeman looked at him, at the two thugs who loomed over him, and said, 'Be quick! I shall return in a few minutes and expect you gone.' He wandered away.

Berndt watched with interest; the man was slim, dressed smartly, a dark suit, a homburg hat, frameless glasses, shiny black shoes, black briefcase. He looked like a bank manager, or a lawyer; accustomed to using reason and being obeyed. He spoke to the two men; they did not seem happy with their instructions but scanned the street and then drove off, free use of horn. The gentleman looked up and down the street for a few minutes and went into the café where he dislodged a tourist couple sitting at a window table and sat there, looking out with great patience. The proprietor brought him coffee that he ignored. After a little while, he took some papers from his briefcase and pretended to read while looking out at the street under a lowered head.

Berndt sighed. Well, he had invited it, only he did not know the back door to the café; perhaps there wasn't one. He walked down the street a little way looking for the car and the thugs. No sign. Walked back past the window; there was no reaction. The man did not recognise him. That was a surprise. He slipped into the café and sat opposite the gentleman.

'Ah,' the man said. 'You must be Berndt.'

Berndt waited. He was good at waiting.

'You seem to have difficulty in understanding our needs. A surprise! You are not a stupid man.'

Berndt waited.

'I am told that you have killed my colleague when he was not threatening you in any way. Perhaps he said the wrong thing.'

Berndt waited.

'And now you summon me as though I might be able to provide answers. Me! What do you want?'

'To be left alone.'

'Ah, if only life was that simple. Now, I have brought you a contract; it is quite clear, a simple contract that provides you with benefits, even a pension.' He beamed over his glasses as though that had been his particular contribution, and passed it over. Berndt did not even look at it, but tore it in two, and poured coffee over it.

'That is what it is worth.'

'Couldn't you even look at it? I think it would tempt you. We know that you don't find the work difficult but even enjoyable, and only about thirty days a year. I can't think of such a generous remuneration for that amount of time; why, your daily rate must be—'

'Enough. Leave me alone.'

'Surely, you don't mean it—'

Berndt rose and went out of the door. The two men were approaching from one side and saw him; they paused in front of the window, saw the urgent signs from the gentleman and came in pursuit.

It was not a difficult situation. He remembered his Stasi training well and had kept fit even if he had not had much practice. Then he recalled the encounters that he had had in the last few days. He had generally avoided any such confrontation in his own working life, preferring to eliminate at a sensible distance and clear of crowds. But this street! So many people, all with time to wander and notice and comment.

The men had separated, one on either side of the street, barging through the shoppers. They were planning a pincer action, one on either side to prevent escape. They would time their action when there was a gap in the crowds and close in, perhaps making the excuse that their 'friend' was unwell.

It didn't go to plan. Berndt allowed one man, the closest, to approach him while the further was encumbered with crowds, particularly a group of children playing tag. He was just about to carry out a simple martial arts move that would leave the man face down on the road with a suspect broken neck, when a girl came up to him, flung her arms round his neck and said, 'Ah chérie! Where have you been? I've been so lonely and you left me; you left me!' She was looking now at the hard man, who hesitated in shock, backing away a little. Berndt was nonplussed; what does one do now? Who was she? He had been keen on eliminating these two guerrillas, somehow. But he could not risk an open scene and he embraced the girl, and walked away arm in arm.

Behind him, the men came together, muttered, and went back to the café.

SEVEN

Berndt looked at the girl; she was in her twenties, he guessed, as tall as him and quite strong; that was evident by the way she had embraced him and taken him under her arm. He was unused to girls, particularly ones who embraced him in the street. But who was she?

She had rescued him from the soldiers but she might be another Conglomerate soldier, a clever ruse to bring him in. My God, they would try anything! He was about to extract himself, with force if necessary, when she spoke.

'Berndt, please do not worry. I am taking you somewhere safe.'

'Who are you?'

'Moi? I am Juliette. Pleased to make your acquaintance!'

'And you are working for the Conglomerate and when—'

'Ah, cherie, what is this "Conglomerate"? I have never heard of such a thing.'

She turned suddenly into an alley and all Berndt's instincts rose up and told him to react. He swivelled quickly towards her, twisting the arm that had held him behind her back and pulling her in front of him as he backed against a wall, scanning the alley and the street for the 'soldiers'. They would have followed.

'Aagh! You hurt me; I don't understand and I came to rescue you.'

'I don't need rescue. Who are you?'

There was a shout. A man came up the alley. Marcel.

'Well, Berndt, so you have met my daughter. She's quite capable, wouldn't you say?'

Berndt looked from one to the other as he released the girl, who stood looking at him, rubbing her arm. He couldn't see any similarity.

'Oof, Papa, you did not warn me that he is a guerrilla!'

Marcel laughed. 'I thought you might have a spot of trouble,' he said to Berndt. 'I was watching and sent Juliette to intervene. Successfully by the looks of it.'

Berndt grunted. 'There was not a problem.'

'Such gratitude!' said Juliette, turning her back on him.

'My dear, you do not understand. Berndt and I come from a place where we have to rely on ourselves. I'm sure that he would have extricated himself safely but in view of the crowded street… well, I thought it best to intervene.'

Berndt was not happy with the idea of someone intervening on his behalf and wondered if he would want anyone ever to intervene on his behalf. Well, Francine, maybe; if she ever found herself in such a situation. Marcel obviously feels that we are a gang; I would not want to make an enemy of him and perhaps we can work together for a while. A short while, and then…

One of the soldiers appeared at the end of the alley and stepped towards them. He took in Marcel, the girl and Berndt, and hesitated. Berndt was about to act when Juliette gave him a look and stepped forward.

'Can I help you?'

The man grunted, made as if to turn away. Juliette made a short skip and kicked him in the groin; as his head came down, she brought her knee up smartly under his chin and he collapsed onto the road.

'All yours,' she said.

Berndt stared. He had not known female operatives in the Stasi, except those used to lure targets, but they were not expected to practise strong arm tactics except in defence. Where had Juliette come from? He was about to dispatch the man when Marcel held him back.

'It's not worth it. It only makes trouble for us; if there are any questions, Juliette will say that he made inappropriate advances and she had to react to protect herself.'

Berndt was beginning to feel more and more compromised; he had not worked with another person since his Stasi days; even then, it had been a rare occasion. He kept quiet, and followed the others back to Marcel's car, a Ferrari saloon. Juliette squirmed into the front seat leaving Berndt the back. Marcel accelerated rapidly out of the city centre.

Marcel's house sat on a hill to the east of Lyon. It was a little like a blockhouse, yet there were generous windows on the corners. The steep pitched roof, zinc covered, had wide eaves and at the centre of the ridge was a small tower, windows all round. Berndt was surprised that there was not a flagpole to top it all.

'Papa's fort. He loves cowboy and Indian films,' said Juliette.

'Well, you never know. Where we are situated…' Marcel shrugged.

'You haven't told him about your machine guns,' said Juliette.

'Hush, dear. Well, Berndt, you might as well know. There are remote controlled machine guns situated in the eaves; I control them from the tower. The technology has been around for a long time; the Americans had it in the Second World War, in a bomber.'

Berndt wondered if they would ever be used, apart from shooting the odd deer. They went inside; he was struck immediately by the unusual layout. There were no through passages or two rooms together; always a dog-leg between doors.

Marcel saw him looking, grinned and commented, 'It prevents a through shot. Much harder for someone attacking if they get in.'

'Just paranoia,' said Juliette, giving her father a hug. Marcel shrugged. Juliette disappeared and Marcel brought together some food.

'Perhaps your hotel is compromised,' he said.

Berndt was silent; he could look after his own hotel.

'Now, the builders. I have done a little research; the depot is still working but the office is closed down. They say for an annual holiday but I don't believe it.'

'He may be at his house.'

'Just my thoughts. We'll go and take a look, yeah?'

'I wonder; could I make a phone call?'

'Mais bien sur. It is through there.'

Berndt found a comfortable study, a superb view over the city and a telephone on the desk. He dialled; there was a long wait.

'Allo?'

'Francine, it's me.'

'Bernard, where have you been? I have been... yes, I have been worried. It has been so long; what is the problem?'

All of his past that he had not revealed to her came flooding to the front and he struggled to think of an explanation that would not have her hang up immediately.

'Francine, it is difficult to tell you all on the phone. But it is related to my work.'

'But Bernard, you were a mining engineer, were you not? What can be the problem?'

'Some of my clients have unfriendly acquaintances, who have decided that they have been cheated. It is not true, of course, but I have had to make myself disappear.'

'Oh cherie, that is awful! You must go to the police, at once.'

'Ah Francine! I did speak with them but they said it was a civil matter and they couldn't intervene unless I was threatened physically, actually hurt.'

'Cherie, how can I help? I could speak with my father.'

'My love, I will stay clear of them and speak to you soon. Please, don't bother your father; how is he?'

'So-so. But Bernard, I miss you. Call me soon; can I come to you? Where are you?'

'Lyon at present but I won't stay here. May go to Switzerland.'

'Switzerland? I could come to you there.'

'Well, I will let you know. Au revoir, my Francine.'

'Au revoir, my Bernard. I love you. A bientot!'

Berndt sat staring out of the window. Now was the time to take the battle to the Conglomerate, but how? He wasn't afraid of the soldiers; he had killed so many already. But where were the officers?

Outside, Marcel made for the Ferrari.

'Marcel, it is not a very discreet car. Do you have another?'

Marcel looked surprised. 'Does it matter?'

'It may.'

They took Juliette's Clio and drove down into the city. Marcel took a route around the centre towards a suburban district, large houses set in large plots.

'It's just along here,' he said, slowing up.

'Keep your speed up. Drive past.'

The house was a traditional three storey house, trees and grass in front, garages on one side. In the gated drive was a police car. A little way down the road, they parked, checked their weapons and walked back.

The police car was a little way only within the gates and they could see the single officer, fast asleep. A little way along the path a tree overhung the fence and they swung up into the branches, dropping down in the garden. They checked that nobody had seen their entry. There was peace. They ran to the house and around to the back.

A large conservatory extended into the garden and inside they could see the older builder, reading the paper. The doors were open and a small dog came out, barking.

The builder looked up and immediately leapt up to go back into the house but Berndt reached the doors and pointed his gun at him. The builder froze until he recognised Berndt.

'How did you get in? The policeman—'

'No matter. Probably better not to call him.'

'But he is there for my protection. You were right; there is a contract out for my life. All that shooting; you saved our lives, I am grateful but if you are not the killer, there must be another out there.'

Marcel stepped forward. 'You're right. We saw them earlier; they are in the city and it won't be very difficult for them to find you. As I did.'

'Mon Dieu, what do I do? How long will this go on?'

'I have come to take you to somewhere safer than this house. Your wife—'

'She died last year.'

'I'm sorry,' said Marcel. 'I had not heard.'

'But the police; they are here for my protection.'

'And we walked in.'

'Walked—'

'Well, almost.'

'Can I gather some things? And what about my son?'

'Where is he?'

'He has gone into hiding with his family. I don't know where they are; will they be all right?'

'I can't say. Quickly, please. We can go now or as soon as you are ready. Berndt, how do we get out?'

Berndt went back around the side of the house. The policeman was standing beside his car, stretching, scratching his behind, yawning. Berndt gave a low whistle, and ducked back behind the corner; in a moment, the policeman was in front of him, staring at the gun that Berndt levelled at his stomach.

'There will be no trouble here,' said Berndt.

'What do you mean? You hold a gun on a police officer, you have broken into a protected zone, and—'

'Silence. We are taking your man to a safer place. No, you may not know where it is. I mean you no harm but you must stay here.'

'Who are you? How do I know it will be safer?'

'Talk to the builder.'

'What will my sergeant say when he sees me and the man has gone?'

'Shall we tie you up?'

He took the officer around to the conservatory where the builder confirmed that Berndt was not there to kill him and they tied him into a chair, not too tightly.

On the way back to Marcel's house, a Mercedes came the other way, driving fast, swinging around the corners. Berndt ducked down, pulling the builder with him.

'They haven't wasted any time,' he said. 'Don't drive fast, look like you're going shopping.'

Marcel chuckled.

The builder was shaken. 'Mon Dieu, it was them? Already? Have you saved my life a second time? What do you want?' He shrank back into the seat, staring at Berndt.

'Let's get you somewhere safe, eh?' said Marcel.

'They may have somebody inside the police. Do you think they saw your registration plates?' said Berndt.

'Not a chance,' said Marcel. Berndt was not so sure; they had been near the builder's house, and there was little traffic on the road. He wondered whether they would treat the policeman with respect.

At Marcel's house, Juliette took the builder under her wing, finding him a room, making him comfortable, answering his questions as best as she could. He wanted to telephone the firm and was discouraged from doing it. She chatted to him, assured him that he couldn't be in a safer place. A fort, she said.

Marcel had disappeared. Berndt sat down, wondering when he could escape; he had had enough of joint operations and wanted to disappear in his own way. When Marcel came into the room, he stood and wished him farewell.

'But Berndt, this is a poor time of day to leave. And in any case I thought we, the two of us, were going to demolish this Conglomerate. Stay a night, do. We can talk about it. And if you still want a lift, I'll take you in the morning.'

Berndt felt tired, and it was late afternoon. He said he would stay, and they relaxed. That evening they talked about what was possible and what was not possible without coming to any conclusions. The conversation relapsed into their memories of working practices, bad and good.

'After Vietnam,' said Marcel. 'I was commissioned in a unit to tackle the Stasi, particularly when they were operating in France. Mon Dieu, but you had some careless operatives!'

'Vietnam? I guess that was not a good place to be.'

'The Americans are welcome to it. I gather you people are still operating in France?'

'Are they? Not my people. As I told you, I got out. Years ago.'

'What did you say you did for a job?'

'Mining engineer. All over the world, except America. Never got jobs to go there. Guess they have their own.'

'I have too little to do. Ever since I retired. Really good to have a bit of action!'

Berndt grunted and they went off to bed.

Berndt was dreaming. He was on a boat and Francine was lying next to him, kicking him, and he was laughing… He woke with a start, instinctively rolling out of bed, gun in hand, naked. The room was not quite dark and he could make out another person in the bed. He stripped back the duvet as the light came on.

'But cherie, I have never had that effect on another man before.'

Juliette was lying on her back, totally naked, gazing at him. Berndt took in a compact slim body, flat stomach and small breasts, and a big grin. Then he realised that he was naked and pulled bedclothes in front of him.

'Do you always sleep with a gun? So does Papa. But I've never tried to climb into his bed so I don't know how fast he would react. I would give you full marks but I was in bed with you while you were still dreaming. Wow! You were moving about! Was she very active?'

'Are you leaving now?'

'That's not very friendly. Is that the way to treat your beautiful hostess?'

Berndt was lost. He had little knowledge of women; his experience had come from rare unemotional couplings, mostly at Stasi college, until he met Francine who had taken it on herself to teach him about close relationships and bring him out.

'There is someone else,' he said.

'Ah! But she is not here and I am, no strings. We could have a good time; it looks as if you need it,' she said gazing at him.

Embarrassed, he started to pull on clothes.

'All right, all right. I get the message. What a pity! A tout a l'heure!' And she was gone, flouncing out and slamming the door. Berndt thought of Marcel and determined that he would leave the next morning. Early. He went back to bed and drifted off without difficulty after wondering what it would have been like, Juliette and him.

It was early, the light just creeping over the land. A loud alarm was ringing throughout the house. Berndt was up, dressed in minutes. On the stairs, he met Marcel.

'It's the perimeter alarms; I set them last night. We are under attack, and it's not deer.'

EIGHT

They ran up to the tower lookout. Around the house was a break of light brush low to the ground, about one hundred and fifty metres wide; beyond, the forest was dark and dense, except on the west side where the slope fell away steeply to the city. Coming out of the woods on three sides were men dressed in dark army wear carrying semi-automatics. At the edge of the trees on the drive they could see vehicles and a cluster of men. A deer sprang up from the hillside and darted away, zigzagging down the slope.

'So,' said Marcel. 'Your Conglomerate, they mean business. I assume it is them? You don't have any other enemies?'

'It's them. Unless you have enemies.'

Marcel laughed. 'If only. Let's give them a taste of their own medicine.'

'Marcel, I'm sorry. I have brought you much trouble. I should leave now and you can tell them you don't have me.'

'And how would you leave, mon vieux? No, let us have fun!'

The 'soldiers' had advanced into clear sight and stopped. The black Mercedes came up the drive, a man waving a white handkerchief out of the window. It stopped about fifty metres away. There was a pause. A man stepped out of the passenger seat, a dark suit, homburg hat, deferential air.

'Excuse me, can you hear me?' He was shouting, shook his head, spoke into the car and was passed a loudhailer.

'I regret inconveniencing you. I assure you my soldiers mean no harm. But I believe you are housing a dangerous criminal, guilty of many murders, and I should be grateful if you could hand him over.'

There was no answer from the house. Marcel gave Berndt a hard look.

'A dangerous criminal, eh? And I have never enquired what work you did since retiring from the Stasi. I thought you were on the side of the angels, rescuing the builders. Is this true?'

'Mining engineer. That's all.'

'Ah yes. Of course. Silly of me, I forgot. But not quite "all", I suspect. Well, we'll see. Let's deal with these salauds.' He bent to a microphone. 'Allo, allo. We have no criminal here. You are trespassing on my property; please remove yourself and your men immediately.'

The man in the suit shrugged, raising his hands. 'But Monsieur, he has been seen coming here. Do you refuse to hand him over?'

'It is no business of yours what I choose to do. Depart, now!'

'Quelle dommage! I very much regret that we shall have to come and get him. Please put yourselves in the open so you are not damaged in the process.' He got back into the car.

'Now for some fun,' said Marcel. 'You operate these controls, the guns pointing up the hill there.' On an intercom, he said, 'Juliette, cherie, lock-down, now.'

Juliette emerged from the staircase. 'Hey, which guns are mine?'

Marcel sent her down to a room above the entrance.

The Mercedes accelerated hard at the front door.

'Armour plated, damn it!' muttered Marcel.

The car crashed through the doors and came to a stop in the lobby. There was the sound of shots fired and the car suddenly reappeared, reversing down the drive.

Marcel smiled. 'It's an old medieval trick. Juliette gave them raking fire from above. There may be a body or two down there. Anyway, no problem.'

The 'soldiers' were advancing slowly down the slope towards the house.

'Shall we tickle them?' said Marcel, opening fire on his side. A couple of men went down, another limped to the rear and the rest halted before retreating. Berndt repeated the fire, felling three men who were dragged back by their comrades as they fell back. Silence fell.

A siege began, the 'soldiers' occasionally advancing a little, only to be deterred from further advance by fire from the house. Marcel left Berndt to handle the incursions, saying he was going to check the front door status and their guest the builder. Time passed and Berndt wondered how things might progress. He had little experience of sieges and little patience for them. In the Stasi, sieges had been handed over to special elements of the army; Stasi operatives were trained for more immediate action. Juliette brought him some food and they chatted.

'Such a pity, last night. I would have enjoyed it, you know. And there would have been no recriminations.'

'Do you not have boyfriends?'

'From time to time. But you know, they are all so boring, or fearful. Just boys really.'

'Where did you learn martial arts?'

'Here and there.' She had looked away, gazing at the 'soldiers' still standing on the hillside, looking bored. A sharp rain had begun to fall and some had retreated under the trees.

There was a new sound; Berndt recognised it immediately. Two black helicopters came up the valley, approaching the house from the west, circling the house at a low level before setting down either side of the drive between the house and the Mercedes. Armed soldiers, black uniform, masked balaclavas, semi-machine guns, streamed out of the helicopters and took up a defensive position around the drive to the house. Almost immediately, there was an exchange of fire between soldiers and the Conglomerate.

Berndt looked out and felt a great sadness. This was the real army but how had they come to be there? Was he to become a captive? It would not be long before difficult questions from Interpol arose and he would be done for, and he had promised himself that he would never appear in a courtroom.

Marcel came upstairs, alone. 'Eh bien, mon vieux, I am sorry but it was standard procedure.'

'Standard procedure?'

'You must have had it in the Stasi. Any member of the force, retired or active, is entitled to full protection from the State. I had to make a phone call. But you have nothing to fear from the army? We have both been acting the privateers. You need not be alarmed; I shall not introduce you.'

Berndt looked at him and said nothing; what could he say? Except that he was disappointed in the man, had thought that Marcel enjoyed a bit of action and would not need to involve the authorities. He felt trapped; there might be questions. Why didn't he leave last night, or even before then? He could not remember a situation when he had been led by the nose into capture and he was determined that it should not happen now. He scanned the hillside; the 'soldiers' had melted away, the Mercedes had gone and the army soldiers were relaxing, looking at the 'fort' and smoking. A commander was coming in the ruins of the front door and Marcel went down to greet him.

'Is there any other way out of here?' Berndt asked Juliette.

She had turned her back on him, looking out over the valley. The sun had reappeared, a watery smear towards the west. The city below them glistened, wet roofs and glass. A crow glided low over the house and away over the city. A train drew into the station and lighters moved on the river. She turned to him, looking up into his face, smiled suddenly, grabbed his sleeve and said, 'Come with me.'

Berndt could see no alternative; after all, perhaps he could take her hostage to bargain his way out. But she was running ahead of him, down through the house, two staircases, a short corridor, down again into a cellar, opening a hatch into a dark space, the far wall and pulling on an iron door, entering a low tunnel that ran into darkness. Berndt tried to talk to her but she hushed him to silence and pulled him into the tunnel, crawling through darkness for some distance. He was wondering whether he was bound for some dungeon when there was a slight glimmer of light ahead.

She heaved at a counterweight on the side of the tunnel and a hatch opened. Daylight streamed in; ahead, the hill fell away, the city before them.

Emerging into the daylight, she said, 'It's our emergency escape. Go straight down the hill; they can't see you if you are quick. Good luck. Look me up when you have time.'

And she was gone before Berndt could say anything, the hatch falling, a square of grass and bush, unidentifiable from the ground around.

It was a miserable afternoon, occasional rain, a keen wind from the north. The weather had broken and people were hurrying to seek shelter, too busy to notice a man who emerged from the hill above the city, who walked with purpose without a care for the rain, who was indistinguishable from any other worker returning home at the end of the afternoon.

The city had become too dangerous. He could tackle a few men, some of their dumb 'soldiers', but the display at the 'fort' had been impressive. How many men could the Conglomerate call upon? He went straight to the station, had a quick meal in the café and looked up trains, all the time maintaining observation. There were a few men who appeared to have time heavy on their hands, pretending to read newspapers, check train times or drink coffee, but nobody troubled him. Perhaps, he thought, they realised that when the numbers were small, Berndt always got the better of them. They would be passing on the sightings, perhaps even the train that he chose.

He followed old procedures, woven indelibly into his training. He took a local train north, fifty kilometres. Then a fast train south, passing through Lyon, towards the Mediterranean. A night's break in a small hotel, the room at the rear, a car park behind, easy escape. A small train over the mountains into Italy.

Ah, Italy. He remembered his work there, the man who supplied his arms and ammunition, the car builder, his beloved Audis. All in the past; what was he now? He thought of Francine in Paris, and wished he could be back there in his flat in Le Marais. Another night in a small hotel, another tourist travelling alone. No questions.

An Italian train, north, to Geneva. He liked Geneva, a clean city wedded to money and authority; indeed, he had funds in banks there. The Stasi had sent him there a few times, chasing Russian plutocrats who had large funds that had appeared from nowhere; when he asked why the Stasi were doing the work, he was told that the KGB was above such work, the Stasi could do their dirty work for them.

He walked up the hill and booked into the Hostel.

One night was enough; noisy, full of nosy students and poor escape provision. He moved to the other side of the Rhone, towards the district La Colline, a quiet residential area, and found a small family hotel. And after visiting his banks, became a tourist, an unusual role for him, wandering the streets and the lake front, the Jet d'Eau, the grand buildings, museums, cafés and views. All the time looking for signs of the Conglomerate, heavy East European thugs trying to hide among the smart shoppers, and dark suited gentlemen emerging from black Mercedes; but there were plenty of those, all bankers he assumed. Bankers didn't wear homburgs, it seemed. There was no sign of the 'soldiers', the East European thugs.

Four days later, Francine arrived at the station; he had implored her to fly but she had arrived by train, from Lyon.

'Flying; it's so boring, you know. On the train I can talk to people, enjoy the countryside, read, take time. And the train from Paris to Lyon is very fast, you know. Grande Vitesse.'

He took her up the hill and ensconced her in another small hotel, not far from his hotel. She was shocked.

'Alors, Bernard, what is this? I come all this way to see you and I can't even stay in your hotel.'

Berndt explained that it was safer, if the 'bad guys' should pursue him; he couldn't bear the thought of her being captured or injured by them. She didn't reply, didn't comment but unpacked and waited for him to suggest the next move.

A restaurant, not cheap. He wanted to spoil her, an apology for the hotel. She was quiet, keeping to herself her thoughts and moods. But when they had eaten, she put down her coffee cup, rested her elbows on the table and fixed him with a direct stare. Berndt could see the storm coming and mentally ducked; what was it now?

'So, Bernard, cherie,' the last spat out. 'I know so little of your life and you know so much of mine. It's your turn. Where do you start?'

'I was, well, am a mining engineer. I have worked here and there, and—'

'I meant start; that is no start.'

Berndt was silent; what could he tell her? That he had murdered people for a living? That he had at least three different identities? That he knew how to kill a man or a woman a hundred different ways, some which looked like natural death? That he had worked for the Stasi, the hated East German organisation? That his real name was Berndt?

'Well,' he said. 'I was born in Augsburg and moved to Berlin just before the War.'

'So you are German.'

'Naturalised French, but I retain my accent.'

'And then?'

'I was only a small boy when the War started. My elder brother disappeared fighting on the Eastern Front. I was a Hitler Youth.'

'A Nazi?!' She spat the word out, looking down at the table.

'No. Not a Nazi. Us boys, we had no choice; my parents were dead, bombed. My sister disappeared when the Russians invaded. Hitler tapped me on the head, told me to die for the Reich, saying that to a ten year old boy. But we were fed.'

'Ah, I'm sorry. It was not easy in an occupied Paris; I imagine it was not easy in a bombed out Berlin.'

Berndt sipped his wine and looked out of the window; he had taken a table where his back was to the wall and he had a view out of the front window, the entrance and the kitchen door.

'After the War must have been difficult. No parents, no home, no big brother or sister. What did you do?'

'Whatever it took.'

'Anything?'

'I didn't murder; some did, for a pair of boots or a loaf of bread.'

'Mon Dieu!'

'I survived.'

'But things changed? Yes?'

'At first I was in a gang of boys. Lived in ruins. Ate rat. Found clothes in wardrobes in bombed out houses; weren't allowed to but they couldn't stop us.'

'How long did that go on?'

'I don't remember; a long time for a small boy.'

'And then?'

'They used soldiers' barracks for hostels for us. And there was some food. Horrible. The big boys stole off the little ones; one learnt to fight, protect what was one's own.'

'So, you were a street fighter.' She smiled.

Berndt grinned. 'Yes, until I joined the police.'

'A policeman!'

'Not for long. I went into the army.'

'Why?'

'The police force was too constricting, boring. Following rules. The army gave more... more training, travelling, experiences.'

'Have you ever killed anyone?'

Berndt swallowed; he had no idea of the number of his victims; perhaps a hundred, perhaps more. He looked grim. 'Francine, I was in the army!'

'Well? Have you?'

'One or two.'

'Why? You were in no wars, were you?'

'United Nations forces.'

'Ah. Of course.'

A long pause.

'I didn't know the East German army contributed to United Nations forces.'

'Oh yes.'

'Why a mining engineer?'

'I learnt things in the Army. Engineering. Mining.'

'But you were in the East.'

'I got out.'

'How? Honestly, Bernard, it's like extracting teeth.'

'I hid in a train to Greece. Out of Rumania. It was easy.'

Francine gave him a hard stare.

'Oh, I joined a firm in Italy. Mining engineers. Trained with them, then set up by myself.'

Francine pushed back from the table, crossed her legs, and gave him another straight stare.

'Where do we go from here?'

'What do you mean?'

'Bernard, I have come all this way to spend time with you. As we did in your French village. And now you place me in another hotel; have you finished with me?'

Berndt was horrified; is that what she really thought? Where had he gone wrong? He was so glad to be with her and assumed she felt the same.

'It's not enough, Bernard. I don't know you anymore. My father; he warned me against you. Said there was something he could not place. I never heard how he was wounded; was it you?'

'But, Francine... I was so glad you could come—'

'Do you love me?'

Berndt stared. Love? He had never thought in those terms; he knew he wanted to be with her, but was this love? He couldn't remember 'love'; he supposed his mother loved him but that was not the same at all. He had never felt this way before, but he couldn't label it.

'I don't know what—'

'Don't know? Don't know?' She spat out the words. 'Mon Dieu and I had thought that we were together, somehow, forever. I was happy to see you every month and hoped that it would be more often. Preferably every day. And night. But you don't know.'

Berndt stared at the table; he had no tools for dealing with this personal assault, no experience of negotiating his way out of it. He couldn't get any words out. How could he explain the danger they were in? He had told her already, hadn't he? But he couldn't tell her why the Conglomerate were pursuing him and what they wanted... And now she wants to talk of being with him all the time and he wanted it but how...

'Have you nothing to say to me?'

He could not look at her, panting slightly, lost in a vacuum. She pushed back her chair, summoned the waiter for her coat. 'Please see me back to my hotel.' And started for the door. Berndt thrust money at the waiter and followed.

The next morning came slowly; Berndt had spent the first part of the night persuading himself that it did not matter, he could manage well without her, hadn't he for years and years, and the second part on the street outside her hotel. He felt raw, his armour crushed like an eggshell. He still could not understand what had happened the night before; he had accompanied her up the road in silence and she had turned in to her hotel with a 'goodbye', rather than a 'goodnight'. And not a glance back at him.

His procedures were in ruins, his surveillance down, his body slack and exhausted. He couldn't think straight, couldn't see a way forward. He slumped against a wall the other side of the road.

At eight o'clock, she emerged, a suitcase in tow, striding swiftly down the road. He walked down with her but the other side of the street, not knowing how to break through to her, what to say, how to keep her.

She crossed a junction without slowing; he was held up by a car turning slowly in front of him, and fell behind. Just beyond the junction, a black Mercedes, the same car that had held him up, slowed beside her. Two men, heavily muscled, wearing black, emerged from the car. One picked up the suitcase, the other persuaded her into the car without a pause, the car scarcely stopping before it accelerated gently and went off down the street.

NINE

Berndt stared.

He could not comprehend it. Why? When had they connected her to me? How? And slowly, as slow as his dull state would allow him, he looked back at the past twenty-four hours.

She had arrived by train. From Lyon. Damn. Lyon, where they would have been watching the station, looking at anyone travelling; disregarding routes to the west – hadn't I just come from there? – and possibly those travelling to Paris and certainly commuters, but looking at those travelling directly to another city, Geneva or elsewhere. I begin to suspect they have seen me here, and I have not seen them. The manpower; it must be immense, all those eyes watching, reporting. And how many false leads? And who has seen me here? I have seen no thugs on the street, certainly not here, but is it children again? Or students? In any case, I must have been seen and reported. And now they are here.

His head buzzed and he leaned back against the wall; a housewife passing by gave him a sharp look, some muttered comment about alcohol consumption, layabouts, ne'er-do-wells... He grunted, straightened up and gave her his cold stare that sent her scurrying down the street in fear for her life. And then he went in search of the Conglomerate.

It was a different Berndt that walked the streets of Geneva. No sightseer wandering the attractive ways, eyes swivelling all directions, but a man in pursuit of some object, walking fast, in all weathers, always with purpose, stopping rarely, occasionally dropping into the less expensive cafés and waiting to see if a contact was forthcoming. But there was no contact and no sign of the thugs who had emerged from the Mercedes. He felt depressed, an unusual mood for him, more used to the absorption in tackling a task, the satisfaction of working. And Francine meant more to him than he had realised; the sight of her being abducted into the car came back to him again and again, the worst nightmare. He would give himself up to release her, he was sure. If he could find the Conglomerate.

He stalked the streets, grim and unyielding; his stare made a clear way between the crowds, who flinched under the icy glare. Still no sign of the thugs.

Until the third day. He was becoming exhausted, walking for sixteen hours a day, always fast with purpose. And sleeping like a dead man in his hotel to rise and repeat the surveillance of the day before.

But early on the third day, around seven in the morning, he saw a man who seemed too brutish for the civilised streets of Geneva: the familiar East European visage, odd clothes and shoes, a man walking with purpose. Berndt watched him drop into a small supermarket, buy milk and bread, tinned food, bacon, butter, beer, enough for a platoon. And followed him back to a flat near the station.

A mixed neighbourhood, offices, light industry and private residences, not smart. The flat: first floor over a shop, two entrances, front and back to a staircase hall, no balcony, two further storeys above. A security door but no warden. And no surveillance camera. He walked down a side alley, earning a gruff query from a neighbour that he ignored, and saw that there was a rear entrance giving onto a fire escape. Drop-down ladder; no chance of an assault there.

He crossed over the street, stood in the shade and looked up at the windows; occasionally, a man appeared, shaving, eating, scratching himself. The men did not spend any time looking out of the window; strange, considering that they knew that Berndt was in the city. Was Francine a prisoner here? He doubted it, suspected that this was a barracks for the 'soldiers', a place for them to rest, eat, and relax before being summoned.

Where were the officers, the directors?

He guessed that if he was to assault the flat that he would set alarm bells that would drive Francine and her captors further away. Better to observe; he found a quiet corner and settled to wait.

It was not a long wait. An hour later, the front door opened and three men came out. A moment later, the Mercedes drew up and the men hustled a woman out of the entrance into the Mercedes. Francine. He would recognise her anywhere. He cursed his assumptions, his delay in assaulting a nest of thugs. It wouldn't have been difficult; a slight risk that they would have hurt Francine while he was entering but he would have been fast and unexpected. A bad mistake; he was getting careless. He reminded himself: don't make assumptions, use the advantage of surprise, and always be the first aggressor.

He stared after the car; it was driving slowly away. He shouted, waved his arms. Come and get me, you bastards.

Traffic screeched to a halt around him, shouts and horns; he stared around him, gave them the benefit of his cold assassin's stare and ran off down the pavement. The Mercedes remained in sight for a while, held by traffic and lights, and then swung off to the left towards the Lake. He stopped a taxi by standing in the road in front of it. The driver blinked in incomprehension; passengers in Geneva did not behave like that; they were polite, stood at the kerb, signalled and waited until the driver was ready for them. He gave swift instructions, clear and to the point: don't lose sight of that Mercedes. The driver started to speak into his radio; Berndt leant over, switched it off, warned the driver to concentrate on his driving and no stopping at lights. When the driver objected in the strongest tones, Berndt stared at him, the same icy stare that brought silence and obedience. He checked his gun, the magazine, the spare; the driver looked and blenched, an audible swallow. He looked fixedly ahead, his eyes glued to the road.

Good progress for a while; two lights crossed as they changed. The Mercedes continued at a gentle speed alongside the Lake, past the Jet d'Eau, onto the Quai Gustave-Ador, and turned into the yacht Club. Berndt paid off the taxi driver, hoping that his generous tip and warning would deter him from reporting Berndt as a danger to the civilised society of Geneva.

The yacht Club was a smart affair, limited parking for a range of large Mercedes, Rolls, Audis and other large saloons. A uniformed doorman looked over the cars and bowed as the Mercedes drew up in front of him; a tip pressed into his hands, no sign of disapproval as the three thugs escorted

Francine into the club. The driver remained behind the wheel, parking on a double yellow line not far from the door.

Berndt passed by the Club, following the quay. On his left, pontoons with day sailing boats and the odd motor cruiser. At the end of the pontoons a row of launches, several quite large. One, a varnished mahogany Riva, was occupied, its engine rumbling quietly, two uniformed sailors sitting at ease in the cockpit.

Berndt withdrew quietly and concealed himself behind a post. The launch might be waiting for Francine, or Conglomerate generals, or even the thugs. If he took the launch, what would he achieve?

The launch left the quay, a low burble of exhaust; large inboard engines. It would be a fast boat. It turned the end of the pontoon into the harbour. Berndt saw it come alongside a pontoon adjacent to the Club; a moment later, the three thugs appeared from a side door with Francine. Now she was struggling, kicking the men near her; her hands were bound and she had a gag. She shook her head, kicked out and twisted against the men. There were no passers-by, no pedestrians near.

Berndt shouted and sprinted down the quay towards them, his gun drawn. A couple walking towards him screamed and dived for cover. He was aware of the distance he had to run, the launch already untied and ready to depart, Francine struggling.

Two thugs simply picked up Francine, chest and legs, and carried her to the boat, ignoring her struggles, her kicking; a shoe fell off and was left. The third man went into a squat and drew his gun, firing rapidly at Berndt; he felt a bullet skim his shoulder, another hit his leg, and he fell, still shooting. He saw his bullets hitting home and the man drag himself off the quay onto the pontoon. The others pulled him into the launch and took off at speed, a fast swing out into the Lake to disappear in a sheet of spray.

Berndt rolled over; his leg hurt. The couple who had been walking stood over him, concern written on their gentle faces; words, offers, a handkerchief offered. Berndt looked away, sat up; the launch was a distant cloud, fading into the dull morning. He stood and hobbled down the quay; the couple stared after him. In the distance he could hear a cacophony of police sirens.

Ignoring the doorman, he crossed the car park. The driver of the Mercedes was reading a paper, the window open, his cap laid beside him on the seat. Approaching from the rear of the car, he came alongside the driver's door and pressed his gun against the driver's neck.

'Unlock the rear doors. Don't move.' Berndt slipped into the car. 'Put your cap on, sit up. Drive. Out of here. Back to the flat. Slowly, don't draw attention. Go.' He ripped open his trousers; the bullet had embedded itself in his thigh muscle but had not hit the artery. There was some blood.

As the car came to the road, a couple of police cars, sirens screeching, swung round the corner, tyres screaming as they charged towards the Club. The Mercedes turned right onto the Quai, settling into the traffic, almost silent.

'What is your name?' Bernd said.

There was no answer.

'It would be better for you if you answered me. Now, what is your name?'

A pause. Then 'Tomas.'

'Well, Tomas, we are going to drive out of the city. If you want to cause trouble with me, you will have an uncomfortable death. Do I make myself clear?'

Silence.

'Do I make myself clear?'

'Yes.'

They continued for a while through the centre, and Berndt indicated the road out of the city, past endless dreary housing, offices, and industry. They stopped at lights, were held up in queues of trucks, and still pursued the same road. Eventually, the buildings fell away and they were driving along a major route. The clouds had cleared a little, and patches of sunshine dried the road. The land rose on either side with farms and woods; a gentle rural scene.

Approaching a small turn, Berndt told him to turn right off the road and pull up. The driver began to look terrified and at the same time, Berndt could see that he was readying himself to retaliate. Berndt gave him an icy look and told him to relax and climbed into the front seat.

'Now,' said Berndt. 'Where are the bosses?'

Silence.

'I repeat, where are the bosses?'

Silence.

'Which bit of you shall I shoot first, Tomas? Can you answer that question?'

'I don't know.'

'Try a little harder. A little effort usually provides answers.'

'I only drive the car, where I'm told.'

'And where do you drive the car to? Some house in the hills?'

'No, never in the hills.'

'There. A little progress. A townhouse, then?'

Silence.

Berndt slammed his gun down on the driver's fingers as they gripped the wheel. There was a scream, hastily muffled, as the man turned towards Berndt, raising his arms. Berndt pushed his gun under the man's chin; the driver froze. Berndt frisked him, removed a gun from a shoulder holster, and a knife from a waist sheath.

'Where is this townhouse?'

'There isn't a townhouse. They…'

'The yacht club; what has that to do with it?'

'Bugger you, they'll kill me! Go on then, do it!'

'Not so easy. How painful do you want it?' Berndt punched the man's thigh, as hard as he could. The man rolled his head, clenched his teeth.

'Where were we? Ah, the yacht club.'

'They… they have a yacht. It moves about, where they want. I just take them to the club.'

'There. That wasn't too difficult, and now, Tomas, I shall let you live. Get out.'

The driver scrambled out of the car and started to run up the road. Berndt slid into the driver's seat, watching him. When he had run a little way, the driver stooped, pulled a knife from an ankle sheath and threw it at Berndt; it was too far. The knife clattered onto the road. Berndt pulled his gun and fired low; the bullet hit the road at the man's feet, the ricochet stinging his legs. He ran faster, away from the car. Berndt recovered the knife, closed the door, and drove back onto the main road, heading away from Geneva.

A few kilometres down the road, he came into a small

town and stopped outside a pharmacy. The girl behind the counter stared at a gaunt man limping in with a rent in his trousers, stained with blood. She stepped back and called the pharmacist.

Berndt explained that he had had an accident and was supplied with antiseptics and ointments, bandages and advice. The pharmacist asked how he had been injured but received no answer and was deterred from further queries by a look. Berndt took his purchases, drove to a car park and parked at the rear. There, he cleaned the knife with antiseptic and dug into his thigh to remove the slug; it was about 30 millimetres deep. The pain was relative; he had been inured to pain early in the Stasi, taught how most of it was imagination and that it could be managed, except in the most dire cases when unconsciousness would relieve the injured from any action. Treating the wound, he bound it up and took a painkiller to bring him back to operational level.

As he was digging the slug out, a small boy had appeared beside the window, staring, his mouth open. Berndt gave him a single look; the boy stepped away, threw up, and ran away, screaming in tears.

Berndt sighed, wished he could rest for a while. He started the car and drove down the street, parking outside an outfitters'. Limping in, there was another girl who retreated at the sight, calling the manager. Before long, Berndt had equipped himself with new clothes, a different colour than before, bundling up the old clothes and disposing of them in a rubbish bin. The new clothes were smart casual, suitable for day or night wear; and practical. The jacket concealed his shoulder holster very well. He would be welcomed in any restaurant or club.

He was beginning to feel hungry and exhausted. He found a road café and ate, plenty of protein and carbohydrate, left and found a small hotel, where he slept for eighteen hours, waking in the early hours and checking out before breakfast. He doubted that the police would be pursuing him; there was no body, and any witness would tell of the kidnapping and the man who had been shooting and escaped in the boat. Of the man who had been hit and walked away, there would be no record.

But he still had to find Francine, and it had become more difficult. A yacht on the Lake Geneva, somewhere. A yacht with an unknown number of guards and bosses. And Francine.

TEN

It was a problem, and one that was hard to solve. He wasn't used to problems that were hard to solve; his working life had always, or almost always, been simple: a simple elimination. But now he was faced with his own safety and more importantly Francine's deliverance and safety. What she would think of him after that, he refused to consider. It would not be a surprise if she threw up her hands in disgust and returned to Paris and her sterile academic life. But he couldn't leave her. He had never been responsible for another person in his whole life, since his older sister disappeared in Berlin as the Russians invaded. And then he was only a ten year old boy.

And there was the matter of the Conglomerate: where they were, what they consisted of, how important they might be in polite society, and how to remove their threat from his back. Permanently.

He realised that he now deplored killing for the sake of it; that had been in the past. If the Conglomerate chose to put thugs in his path, he would only kill if there were no choice. Otherwise, like the driver, he would release them into the wild like so many animals to survive as best they may. It was unlikely that the Conglomerate would look kindly on a 'soldier' who had failed.

He drove back to Geneva; he had no choice; the riddle would only be solved there, on the lake and around it. The Mercedes was a nice car; he had always had big Audis, but he enjoyed the luxury and quiet of the car. It was with regret that he left it on a side street not far from the thugs' flat; he took the keys with him, and disabled the electrics. Why make it easy for them?

At his hotel, he paid off the bill, told them that he was moving on to Italy, and booked into another hotel about two kilometres away, still in a residential area. His wound was troubling him, some pain and a blood-soaked dressing. He wished that he could rest for a few days but felt driven to continue his struggle.

Back to the streets. He wondered if Francine would be returned to the flat; it was unlikely and he didn't waste time watching it. Instead, he concentrated on the yacht Club, at a distance, looking out for the Riva launch. There was no sign of it.

It was a quiet morning in the centre of the city, shoppers and working people going about their business, a weak sun shining on them all like a blessing to the privileged. He was walking through the streets at much the same pace as everyone else, not standing out in his city clothes, when abruptly a young girl in front of him wheeled round and faced him. She was wearing school clothes, dark skirt and a jacket with an emblem. He came to a stop, staring down at her; before he could react, she slashed at his arm with a knife, yelling some words. He stepped back and sideways; she pursued him. Around them, a circle of shoppers formed in no time, staring, mutters of 'men who could not leave little girls alone' and 'honestly, that sort of man ought to be locked up'. He glared at the girl who was not in the least bit terrified; his attempts to escape the circle were hindered by the shoppers themselves, intent on seeing him arrested.

There was a whistle and the shoppers turned to look for authority. The girl vanished. As Berndt was about to escape, a woman came up to him.

'Shocking, just shocking. I do apologise, on behalf of the residents of Geneva. I can see you are a visitor. It is so embarrassing the way the young behave these days.'

'It's nothing. Excuse me, I must be on my way.'

'But you are bleeding! No, no, we must help you. I work with the Tourist Office. Please, let me accompany you to a private clinic I know nearby; you will be treated without delay.'

Berndt was now bleeding from his arm and his leg and knew that any treatment was preferable to having to continue on his way. His jacket was torn and he could not settle back into the role of an unseen observer. The woman seemed genuine; middle aged, hair cut short, little make-up, a dark business suit, some sort of little badge in the lapel, a silk scarf at the neck. Good shoes. And obviously Swiss.

He allowed himself to be taken in hand and followed her back up the street, into a small square, and into what appeared to be a discreet office. There was a plate beside the door, some organisation, and there were blinds in the windows. He paused on the threshold; she had gone ahead and was holding the door.

'It won't take long, and you must let us remunerate you for your damaged clothing. It is shocking, quite shocking the way the young behave these days.'

'What was she saying?' said Berndt.

'I don't know. Some nonsense. They get so worked up these days. I blame it on their education; we would never have been allowed such views.'

Berndt followed her into a room, obviously some sort of clinic but hard to identify its speciality. There was a surface with equipment including a steriliser and a couch for patients partially concealed behind a curtain.

'Would you make yourself comfortable? If you could remove some clothes it would help.'

She went out of the room, closing the door. Berndt took his jacket off, and replaced it when he realised that his shoulder holster was revealed. He pulled the torn sleeve up.

Outside the door, he could hear talking; picking up a glass from the surface, he stood close to the door listening through it.

'Yes, I have him here… No, I'm sure it's him. He doesn't suspect; why would he have come here if he did?… How long?… Well, I'll try. He is bleeding, it can take a time… Don't be long. Bye.'

Berndt heard her footsteps in the hall; he stood behind the door. Idiot, idiot, he said to himself. She wasn't East European, and he was deceived. Idiot. Now, to get out of here.

She came in, unsuspecting. Berndt had only to step behind her, put an arm round her neck, and tell her quietly to behave. She froze, then a moment later, kicked back hard at Berndt's shins. It hurt. He twisted her arm behind her until he heard a slight chink, and she gasped and cried out with pain.

'You were not behaving. Now, we are going to walk out of here. Go.'

She resisted briefly, but a kick to her ankles prompted her to move. Out of the office, along to the door.

'Open it.' As she did so, he twisted around her, looking into the little square. Nobody. Two exits, the one that they had walked in, and one opposite, neither suitable for cars. He pushed her ahead of him, walking close to the walls around the square to the other exit, a short alley leading to a shopping street. As they walked down the alley, a Mercedes drew up on the shopping street, and two thugs got out; Berndt recognised them from the flat.

They started up the alley towards him. He stood in the centre, the woman in front of him.

'Don't shoot, don't shoot,' she cried. 'He'll kill me. Help!'

The men stopped; they had no idea how to solve this problem, looking at each other; perhaps they were waiting for assistance from the other side of the square. Berndt had considered that option, and decided that the only way out was to push forward. He moved slowly forward towards the men. In turn, they retreated towards the street, looking confused. He drew his gun and prepared for action.

One of the men saw him drawing his gun and fired. The bullet entered the shoulder of the woman, lodging on a bone. She fainted; Berndt found himself holding her up like a shield; not a position to be held for long.

He called out, 'Help, here, please. A woman has fainted. Help, call an ambulance!'

A few people came into the alley from the street, full of concern; they sent a man to call for an ambulance, and asked if Berndt knew her, and why she had fainted. Berndt indicated the two men, suggesting that they had assaulted her; they were nowhere to be seen. The Mercedes had vanished. He laid her carefully on the ground; the entry hole for the bullet was scarcely visible, though the ambulance men would find it. A bevy of women huddled around the woman on the ground; one covered her with her coat, another wiped her face with a tissue. Berndt slipped away. He was in pain, bleeding from arm and leg.

He purchased bandages and antiseptics from a pharmacy, and took a taxi to his hotel, where he stayed for three days, by which time he was able to walk without a limp and his arm was healing well.

Onto the streets again, back to the yacht Club.

ELEVEN

He strode the streets of Geneva again. Was he the target of some pot shooter? He doubted it but it didn't feel comfortable. Not a situation that was within his experience. But he knew that they wanted him, a valuable commodity to serve in some grubby crime. What a laugh; crime had been his speciality, of a particular and almost clinical nature. Hadn't he been practising it for the last thirty years? At least his targets had been remote from him, except in a few rare occurrences. And few had been innocent of any wrong doing but had been in the way, a necessary elimination. He had always ensured a clean stroke; well, almost always. And in a remote location of his choice, away from other people, away from immediate interception, simply carrying out a job that needed doing and it might as well have been him.

A remote location, except for the Munich job, dammit, and that had led to the present situation. And now he was reduced to working in the raw, like a Stasi apprentice, dealing with thugs without his weaponry, without his adoptive procedures and tradecraft. It was depressing and he would be far away if it were not for Francine.

Oh Francine! How was she? Had they confined her to a dungeon, tied up as he had been at Munich? Had they tortured her in any way, physical or mental? Was she in pain? He could not bear to think of it, gritted his teeth. A small boy, crossing in front of him, burst into tears when he saw his face and fled to his mother's side.

Downtown, a spread of luxury shops, large displays, expensive goods. He cruised the windows, scanning the reflections, occasionally wondering at the dresses themselves, wondering if Francine would like them. He would bring her here, when it was all over, give her a free choice. His suspicions now fell upon all, including children and bourgeois mothers, all potential risks but he could see not one person who paid him the slightest notice. Until he came into a square and was aware that he was approaching the apex of a triangle composed of the paths of three policemen, all casually wandering from different directions, looking around but bent on the same spot, a place beside a fountain where he could be easily confined.

Perhaps they wanted to question him, suspected him of being a threat to their civilised society, a rather tough looking man walking alone at some speed. He didn't want to be questioned; it might include an embarrassing body search, either on the spot or in the police station. And he was carrying, of course; a gun and a knife, suitably sheathed and concealed under his clothing but easily available.

He turned suddenly, a clean right angle with no change to his pace; it took him out of the triangle and between the two police most widely spaced. They had progressed too far towards their target and faltered at his change of direction as though awaiting instructions. And then pursued him but without speed as though they couldn't be bothered to expend much energy on him. He entered an alley, shops on either side; the police were about twenty metres behind him, the two who had faltered, the third coming on fast behind them. No whistle or call. No distant siren.

Ahead he saw a department store and slipped through the door concealed by a gaggle of housewives, all exclaiming at the prices, the dresses, their husbands. He glanced to the right as he entered to see the police searching the alley. Inside the store he made for the main entrance and came out on a main street turning towards the lake.

The police; what had he to fear from them? Were they in touch with Interpol, with the remote possibility of an investigation into a series of unsolved murders around Europe? Most unlikely. More likely that he appeared to be a stranger, an unwanted stranger walking the town a little too often; they would want to know who he was, where he came from, how long he was staying. He did not want another group pursuing him, endangering his plans for eliminating the bosses of the Conglomerate and freeing Francine.

But he could not believe himself as he walked into the central police station. He had had nothing to do with the police of many nations, in spite of their pursuit of him. Indeed, he recalled a simple exercise in this very city, the removal of an irritating union official, who mired the city's reputation with threatened strikes and libellous claims against the city fathers. He doubted that they would ever find him, under the calm waters of the lake. And he wondered where the contract had come from. The bankers? Or the city fathers themselves? Or an interested party, political or social? It was of no interest to him; it was simply another elimination and not a difficult one.

He recalled following the man from a bar where he had been drinking with his cronies, befriending him,

112

congratulating him on his prowess, bidding him a goodnight and shooting him from a little distance when he was sure that there was nobody around. The disposal of the body was a hassle; the man was gross and it took all his energy to load him into a mobile waste bin that was then rolled into the lake at night.

He asked for the Chief Inspector, giving one of his identities, a French one. Before long, he was invited into an office and had coffee and gateau pressed upon him.

'Monsieur, what can I do for you?'

'Inspector, you must excuse me if I come directly to the point. I suspect that three of your good officers were pursuing me this morning.'

'Ah monsieur, I am sorry if there is any inconvenience. Would you excuse me while I investigate the matter?' The Inspector left the room; Berndt felt his gun warm against his body; the knife was in an ankle sheath. He hoped it would not be necessary to fight his way out of the station; perhaps it had been foolhardy to address this problem so precipitately.

The Inspector returned in a short while. 'Well, monsieur, it is a delicate matter and I am sorry that you have been troubled. You see, you have been observed by a number of officers in the streets; they have remarked on the frequency of their sightings of you, all written up in their notebooks of course.'

'I'm sorry to have caused concern. Is there a problem? I am on holiday and enjoy your streets.'

'Of course, monsieur. May I ask what occupation you have?'

'I am retired. I have never been here before and I was enjoying your city. It is an old city, isn't it?'

'And your work; what was it?'

'Mining engineer. I like to identify the types of stone used in the buildings, both old and new. It is interesting the volume of granite used, a hard stone to work, though available locally. And then limestone is more commonly used for municipal buildings. You only have to look at—'

'Well monsieur, I must apologise if there has been any interference to your enjoyment. I hope you understand that our officers are diligent in their observations and always on the lookout for signs of terrorism or any other assault on our city businesses. And therefore a visitor like yourself who is observed day after day must come under suspicion. How long are you planning to stay?'

'I don't know; there seems to be a large number of different quarries involved. Perhaps I should make myself known to your officers.'

'That won't be necessary. Your image has been posted to all stations, purely for security reasons you understand. I shall inform them that you are interested in the fabric of the buildings. Good day.'

Berndt left the station not entirely convinced that the Inspector had believed him. But what could he do, but look for the thugs and the Riva motorboat?

Leaving the city centre, he turned towards the lake and the Yacht Club, where the Conglomerate had been. It was a sunny day and a number of day yachts were setting out upon the lake in a light wind. Crews chatted across the water to each other; brightly coloured clothes, caps and loafers. It was a world of which he knew nothing, the social side, the technicalities of racing, the parts of a boat. He had spent enough time in the water, both at Stasi college and since then, but never learnt how to sail properly; he remembered a frustrating experience off Cassis, drifting away from the coast.

He stood on the end of a pontoon, watching the dinghies depart like so many ducklings taking to water. How could he take to the water here, without raising suspicion? He had seen fleets of small boats out in the evening, apparently following a meaningless course around some buoys. Was there a sailing school where he might enrol and borrow a boat?

The pontoon shifted under his feet; there was a man standing at the far end, blocking the way back to the quay. There it was again; the bull's head, close cropped, a short neck set upon a torso with over developed muscles, squat legs set well apart. And a blank stare that suggested a lack of deep thought. He had seen the type before: those who rose to the rank of a sergeant in the East German army but never above. Berndt hoped that he was not about to ruin his own reputation with the city police.

The options looked bleak. He could tackle this animal, but it would take time and draw attention to himself, whether he succeeded or not. He could dive into the water and escape; he hated the idea. He could wait for the man to come to him, and then what? He stared out over the water, an attitude of deep calm while keeping an eye on his adversary out of the corner of his eye. Could he distract him somehow?

A day yacht pulled into the pontoon by him, a young couple, obviously experienced sailors; tying up, dropping sails, tidying the yacht all without instructions or debate.

They looked friendly; he stepped over to the boat and spoke down to the crew.

'I say, I am looking to purchase one of these but I need a sail to get to know them. You know, like a test drive. It's very impertinent, but could you give me a sail?' Berndt was sweating lightly. What a lot of words. He was not used to putting himself out and talking much to strangers, and certainly not used to asking strangers for help.

The young couple looked at each other, exchanged a few words, and the young woman spoke, 'We were just going in for lunch. Could you come back later?'

'I'm tied up later.'

'Why don't you come up to the Club with us and we'll see whether anyone else is free.'

The woman and her male companion sprang onto the pontoon; young, fit, and wealthy. And friendly.

'Where do you come from?' the young man asked.

'Oh, I've just come over from the Bordeaux region.'

'Sea sailing?'

Berndt thought of the Cassis experience, and shrugged. 'Not very keen on that. I like your lake.'

As they walked down the pontoon towards the quay, the thug had started walking towards them. He stared at Berndt, a look of hatred and frustration. Berndt smiled at him, chatting with the young people. It was too much for the thug.

'Allo!' he shouted. 'A word. You're wanted!' He laid a hand on Berndt's arm. Berndt looked down at it, a pause, and looked the man full in the face, who quailed and withdrew his hand.

'No, but you're wanted. Come with me,' he said to Berndt.

'Got the wrong man. Sorry!' Berndt turned to the others. 'Do you know this man?'

'No,' said the young man. 'Never seen him before.'

'Should we call the police?' said the young woman. 'He looks like trouble.'

The thug stepped back, a look of concern. And fell backwards into the water; there was a floundering and splashing. He couldn't swim, that was obvious. Then he stood up; the water was shallow. The young man stepped forward, offered him a hand up but he ignored it with a sneer and hauled himself up with speed. For a moment, he stood looking at them, Berndt in particular, and then climbed the steps to the quay and strode off towards the Clubhouse. It was unlikely that he would be admitted; his suit was dripping, water and weed, and his legs were covered in a soft black mud.

'Well, I don't know. What a character!' said the young man.

Berndt smiled and walked on with the others, up the steps onto the quay and along to the Yacht Club.

He adopted a novel form of mobility; a bicycle. It allowed him a freedom that he had not considered before; cyclists broke all the traffic laws, rode the wrong way up one-way streets, down footpaths, and across traffic lights on the red. And he had equipped himself with a camera, carried prominently on his chest, with a powerful telescopic lens. The perfect tourist. Nobody troubled him and he was free of pedestrians; even a thug would have difficulty arresting his progress.

He rode up the Quay de Cologny, on the footpath beside the Lake, looking out over the water for the Yacht. He wasn't sure what type of yacht it might be; cursed himself for not getting more out of Tomas. But he thought it unlikely that it was a sailing yacht. There had been a number of smart motor cruisers tied up at the Yacht Club and he imagined that the Conglomerate yacht was one of those. And a sailing yacht, in spite of having an auxiliary motor, would require more handling and be more prominent than they might wish. It must be a motor yacht.

But it might be a great distance from Geneva. Nevertheless, he was enjoying the ride; it was warm and there were a number of other cyclists, all who waved and greeted him as though he was one of them, one of a select number who chose to be above the common pedestrian. The pedestrians chose to keep out of the way, except for the odd one, often a German, who insisted on his rights and walked in the middle of the path, irritated to uttering loud curses at the loud ringing of bicycle bells around him.

Berndt stopped on a promontory to eat a roll that he had brought with him; a salami roll prepared as he waited by a concerned woman who pressed on him serviettes, a drink and a bag to carry it all. He had never considered himself the type who attracted the concerns of women; what was it about these Geneva residents?

There was no sign of any motor yacht; a few sailing yachts were coming up the lake in the light wind but all were too small to have a prisoner on board. He began to despair of finding the yacht and decided to turn round at Anieres, just coming into sight. In any case, the light was fading and he had no lights to see his way back.

In front of the small town, he dismounted and sat on a bench looking out over the water. A couple of teenage girls descended on him, hooting with laughter, hovering around him; he gave them a look and they retreated silently, breaking into embarrassed giggles some distance away. He began to feel hungry and wondered whether there was a restaurant nearby; he looked back at the town, scanning the streets. And turned back to look at the water.

The light had fallen, a soft evening light that made the water appear lighter than the land. A motor yacht came slowly into the bay and dropped anchor, without fuss or noise; only the chatter of the anchor chain. It swung to the breeze, sideways on to the shore. It was an old-fashioned design, about twenty-five metres long, with a fully glazed deckhouse and a small bridge at the front. The stern was clear, easy chairs and tables. A row of portholes, mostly lit, ran the length of the yacht.

Berndt looked at it idly with no expectations of success; he was feeling hungry and tired, ready to return to Geneva or find a meal in the town. The lights came on in the deckhouse and there appeared to be a number of people, presumably seated at a table; others moved around them. At the stern end, one person seemed to be sitting alone, the others grouped towards the other end. An odd arrangement, unless this was the owner, an old man given his place at the top of the table. Berndt smiled and raised his camera to get a better look.

His breath froze and his heart missed a beat; he became unaware of anything around him. A pulse pounded in his ears.

Where was the skilled operative, always cool in a crisis, always ready for the unexpected? For seated at the end of the table on the yacht was Francine.

He watched as she raised a glass, sipping. He watched as she appeared to be in conversation with one or two of the men at the other end. He watched as she appeared to laugh, her arms outstretched. Turning his lens, he scanned the rest of the group; there were four men seated and two men behind them, pouring wine, holding dishes. He recognised Tomas, the driver, and the man who had fallen off the pontoon. So neither had been sacked in spite of failing in their tasks, failing to bring him in. The four men all looked like prosperous businessmen in their fifties; they wore suits and ties, but there was nothing to distinguish one from another at this distance. He could see how one turned to the man at the very end, who seemed to be leading the conversation. He took a closer look at him and clicked the shutter. Was Francine simply taking part in their talk or being interrogated?

And then he took a shot of her. He couldn't leave, couldn't stop staring at her, wondering how she was managing, whether she was siding with the Conglomerate now, the Stockholm syndrome.

Eventually, a car drew up behind him and a noisy gaggle of people emerged, walking onto the grass around him, pointing and exclaiming at the evening, the yacht, the stars, and each other. He dropped his head and slipped away, disappearing into the dark on his bicycle.

TWELVE

Early dusk. The light settled on the water that shone briefly like mercury under an early moon. The shores were dark, pierced by spots of light except over Geneva where a glow lit the sky. The evening still lay on the lake, the wind dropped to a light breath. Berndt dropped his anchor and lay on his back gazing up at the stars, putting off the moment of action.

He had not taken a sail in the day yacht, nor encountered the thugs from the Conglomerate. A few days had been spent preparing for this evening; a small dingy, hired by the week, wet suits, fireworks and other materials. He had felt an unusual excitement to be planning an operation, something that he had not done for many years. But he had had neither the resources of former years, nor the budget. The operation was only in place to release Francine, at some stage; beyond that he had no plans except a general wish to disappear to another country and to survive with or without Francine.

Because it was a question that he could not answer; he had no idea whether Francine would be pleased to see him. Perhaps she had been content to entertain the bosses of the Conglomerate and would not welcome an unruly awakening in the form of Berndt bursting in upon them. No, it was inconceivable that she should wish to remain on the yacht and even if she was ambivalent about spending time with him, he was committed to her release, committed through guilt that she had been taken, committed to at least asking her what she wanted. It was hard, this being with someone. He could take over, determine what should happen, what the outcome should be, but not be floating about on the lake with a harebrained plan in his head, not knowing if she wanted to be rescued. He gasped with frustration, and steeled his will; the plan would proceed. He ate an energy bar, sipped water, and waited.

Inshore from him was the yacht, lying still in the water, a warm light glowing from the windows. He trained his telescope and could see a number of men sitting in the saloon, but of Francine there was no sign. A couple of men, the thugs probably, circled around them; on the deck, he could see nobody. At first. Then the glow of a cigarette on the aft deck.

He waited.

About an hour later, Francine appeared in the saloon; the men stood, and waited until she was sitting. Something was offered, food or drink. They sat around the table, apparently enjoying a good conversation; he saw Francine throw back her head in laughter, and gritted his teeth. But it made no difference.

As dusk settled into darkness, he slipped into the water; in his wetsuit, it felt warm and he swam slowly towards the yacht. He was approaching from offshore; he would be hard to see against the distant lights of the far shore. The water had turned black as the moon rose and only the odd bird alighting on the surface raised a splash that could be seen. It was a long time since he had carried out a waterborne operation; his Stasi training had involved underwater swimming in freezing water, and since then he had carried out an elimination underwater in the Mediterranean. His waterproof bag knocked against his legs and he adjusted it; there was no hurry. The cigarette glowed on board the yacht, the saloon rang with laughter and conversation, and Berndt quietly approached out of the dark. Twenty metres away, he submerged and swam underwater; he found that he could look up and see the hull of the yacht against the night sky.

At the stern there was a diving platform projecting about a metre; he surfaced without a splash on the offshore side and listened. No change; the man on the aft deck stood up, moved; Berndt could hear him walking around. And then he was gone. But where?

Berndt eased himself onto the platform and peered onto the deck. There was a stack of emergency rafts in the centre and two big ventilators. The man appeared from the foredeck, an aimless wandering, sucking on a fresh cigarette. He was humming to himself; Berndt saw him glancing into the saloon as he passed and curl his lip, obviously frustrated at being left outside. He slumped onto the rafts, lying back with a grunt, sucking on his cigarette.

Berndt moved. Two steps onto the aft deck, three steps to the side of the rafts, a cord around the man's neck as Berndt crouched down out of sight of the saloon. He pulled; there was a gasping, the man started to kick his legs, drumming them on the deck. The saloon door opened.

'Come in, Berndt. You were expected. You can leave him, he will survive, useless man.' A man stood by the door, dark suit, right hand in his pocket, glass in the left. 'What will you have to drink?' Berndt stood. 'No, don't leave. I might have to shoot you. Come on in. There's someone you must meet.'

He led the way into the saloon; Berndt followed; his gun was in his bag, the bag on his shoulder. He stood by the door as one of the thugs took his bag and gently pushed him to a seat by Francine.

The saloon was a grand space, mahogany framed with large windows, mouldings around the columns, a white ceiling with a central painting of a goddess disporting herself in breaking waves. At the far end the doors opened to a bridge where the wheel could be seen, mahogany brass bound. Behind him were two doors at the corners leading out to the aft deck. Between the doors at the fore end was a staircase descending to the cabins below, the companionway. The floor was scrubbed teak boarding, covered with a stretched canvas. All was in beautiful condition, lit by wall brackets on the columns between the windows. A mahogany table stretched down the middle, large enough to seat twenty. But there were only four men at the far end.

'I believe you know each other.' The man was looking very pleased with himself. The other three gentlemen sat in silence at the other end of the table watching. A glass was placed before Berndt and wine poured; he considered taking out the thug who poured but could see no advantage at the present. It might earn him a bullet.

'Now, my dear. Do you have anything to say to this man?'

Francine turned her head, surveyed Berndt without change of expression and said, 'No. Do I know him?'

'Come, my dear. You were seen together. This is no time for sowing false seeds.'

'Yes, but do I know him?' said Francine. 'The man I knew before has no resemblance to this man.' She looked Berndt up and down; he sat in his wetsuit, the hood and boots, looking like a creature from a science fiction movie.

'There is no similarity to the man I knew. The man I knew was gentle, capable, an artist with his hands, but not this man. Who is he?'

Her words were like daggers in Berndt's body; why had he thought to come here to release her? The man looked nonplussed. 'I don't understand. I thought this was your lover. Shall we throw him to the fishes?' He laughed.

Berndt turned to Francine; she was still gazing at him, as though he was an exhibit in a museum. He looked at her, recalling her laughter, her joy in love-making, her argumentative approach to a new idea, her care for him. He looked down, burnt by her disregard, and said softly, 'Do you want to leave?'

She laughed, saying, 'Do you hear what he is saying? Should I leave with a sea creature?' And laughed again. And beneath the table she moved her foot over his and pressed.

Berndt felt a spark alight in him, like a fire brought back to life; he hadn't realised that he had been so depressed at the thought of her detachment, her leaving him on the street as she had done. But there would have to be a conversation, an exchange of news followed by an open disclosure of his life; and he had no way of knowing where that might lead. He was afraid that the current situation was about to reveal more than he had already revealed to her, of his occupation as a hitman, a contract killer. It was a mountain of a problem that he had thought to avoid forever. His conversation with her in the restaurant had been as far as he had hoped to go, ever, and since his days of killing were over, there should have been no need for disclosure, for a frank description of what he had been. It took him back to the first days after the War, when it was every man for himself, though he was but a boy. He had killed nobody then, but had been schooled in the hardest school of survival. Which had been followed by the police and the Stasi, where he had killed as a matter of duty. But how would the work he pursued after the Stasi be seen, when he had convinced himself without much thought or introspection that he was doing a job that needed doing, that somebody else would do if he did not? Often removing enemies of the state, of society. There were exceptions, but he did not see any purpose in dwelling on those. They were the unfortunate side issues of his occupation.

Francine rose. 'I'm tired. Do you mind if I retire? I don't wish to see more of this... this thing.' She walked to the companionway; the men rose, bowed and wished her goodnight as she descended below and sat again around the far end of the table with one of the thugs standing behind Berndt. He realised that the situation was not desperate. He could take the man out, duck beneath the table from bullets, lift it as a shield, retreat out of the door and dive into the water. He might even be able to retrieve his bag. But it would negate the whole reason for being there, and he had resolved that somehow he would take any chance of releasing Francine. He sipped the wine; it was good.

The men left all the talking to the one who had greeted him.

'So. We are seated around a table at last. All of us. I realise that you know none of us by name; that is not important. You know who we are, and we have no problem in contacting you. I'm sorry that some of our men have little sense of delicacy; it is their calling. They are soldiers, not employed to think but to act and, if necessary, take pain.'

The man behind Berndt shifted and gave a low growl. A little like a wild animal on a leash.

'How are you?'

Berndt sat up, sipped more wine, and asked for more. The man gave a gesture, and the thug behind him filled his glass. So civilised, thought Berndt, so far from the Stasi regime. But there is always a price.

'We have always regarded you as valuable; you must realise that. Otherwise, you would have been... But no more of that.'

Berndt wondered how easy it would have been for them to eliminate him; a shot in the street, possibly, not easy to be sure of success, but still possible. Otherwise, he had managed to succeed over the thugs, their soldiers, who lacked much in the way of brains, though they tried to make up for it with brawn. But brawn rarely wins the day, he thought. And remembered Marie in the street, taking the two soldiers in hand. Berndt stayed silent.

'Now, we have a job for you, we have had it for a while, because we wish to pay you the compliment of saying that only you could carry it out. There, I've said it. We know that you are that good, the best that can be found, can be bought.'

Berndt said nothing.

'We have been slow to realise that money does not tempt you anymore. For years you worked for us, though you did not realise it, but then you seemed to disappear, to withdraw from our workforce. That's not acceptable; one does not withdraw from a workforce without giving notice. You will understand why we were offended. And perhaps rather overplayed our hand, like the team that came to find you in the French village. They had mistaken their instructions, though I don't think that any of them survived, did they?'

Berndt stared at him. He remembered the time with clarity, the old woman who was his landlady, the flat roof behind his room, the cattle shed and the explosion of cows into the street. And the bodies left behind. It was not a good time; he had enjoyed his seclusion in the village, the friends and those who valued his stay.

'Mind you,' the man continued in an even tone, almost a supplication as though everything he said had the force of reason behind it. 'Any soldier who fails is expendable, wouldn't you say? The driver who took you out of the city; what a waste. It would have been the same in the Stasi, wouldn't it?'

Berndt remembered those who had failed in their first operation in Munich, when they had failed to take out the dissident in spite of his efforts. A few had been seen again, downrated to guards and simple soldiers; others had disappeared and he had assumed that they had gone to the Army. Why waste all that training?

'So, will you do a job for us?'

Berndt looked at him; how old was he, and where had he come from? He resembled a faceless senior manager; one would have difficulty in picking him out of a line-up. Average height, a smart business-man's suit, black shoes, well polished, a black waistcoat, white shirt with a dark tie, no insignia or decoration, hair going white but neatly cut, not too short and brushed back, no glasses, teeth perfect, bland expression with a very slight bronzing of the skin. He looked so assured of his position. Berndt looked at the others; they were like clones, all similarly dressed, varying only in the colour of their ties. They looked like bankers to him and perhaps they were, some discreet merchant bank ensuring that their investments grew well, that nobody interfered with their business. He wondered how far their operations stretched, whether their influence had expanded into all of Europe, Britain and Scandinavia. He wondered whether they had opened operations in North America and in the Far East. And following investments would come political influence, to ensure that the 'right' parties ruled and protected their business. He could not imagine a country refusing them, except perhaps Cuba and some South American states.

'Why would you want me?' he said.

'Come, come. I have already told you. You are the best.'

'But I have been retired for a few years.'

'We don't think that you will have lost the skills. Indeed, you have already proved to us that your skills are as they were before.'

Berndt was silent again.

'We thought that you could qualify for retirement if you completed this job for us. There is no problem with money; you could name your sum. We could organise a generous pension.'

Ah, there it was; they must be bankers.

'Of course, we need to take out a little insurance. I think you can understand that.'

'I don't do insurance.'

'But you will this time.'

'What insurance did you have in mind?' Berndt suspected what they would say, with a sinking heart. 'And what proof can I have that your word is good, that this is the last job, that there is a generous pension? That I will be allowed to live without interference wherever I choose?'

'Proof. A difficult word. I suppose you will not accept my word?'

Berndt smiled, a thin smile that did not reach his eyes.

'Very well,' said the man. 'We shall deposit a suitable sum in any bank you care to name; you may check it when you are released from here to carry out your task. As to not interfering with you, I think that you will have taken yourself off so far away to escape security forces that you will be of no interest to us, though we wish you well in your retirement.'

Berndt feared the worst; the need to flee so far. What could be the job? 'Name the insurance.'

'I am sure that you have guessed it. We shall keep Francine here to entertain us until you have completed your task. And then we shall release her into your arms.' He gave a little laugh, as though that was something that might never happen.

Berndt wondered how Francine would feel when she learnt that he might become a hitman. She might well have no interest in him, a deep loathing for his type, a wish to return to her university life in Paris without such a burden. 'It will only work if you tell her nothing of my past or my task. I do not wish to tell her of my occupation. If you tell her, I shall be obliged to make your future operations very difficult.'

'A threat, hein? Well, well. We shall see how you get on.'

'What is the operation?'

'We wish you to assassinate the President of France.'

THIRTEEN

Berndt stared at them, the four bankers sitting at the far end of the table. He was silent.

One of the bankers became excited, started waving his hands about, as though reasoning. 'You see, it is a matter of national policy, and—'

The boss waved at him impatiently, a sharp downward stroke; the excited one silenced immediately. There was silence. A clock ticked; Berndt could see a handsome wall clock the other end, over the expanse of the mahogany table. He gazed at the bankers, said nothing.

The boss stirred. 'It's all right. We don't give Berndt any reason or explanations for his work, we never have done. And now he will go about his task as always before, efficiently, quietly, and without creating a disturbance, which is why we employ him. He is the best.'

There was a silence. A man, one of the thugs, poured Berndt more wine, and stood back. Berndt sipped; it was good wine, expensive wine. The bankers would not drink anything less, would they? They lived in a charmed world where anything they wished for was available, women, food, wine, houses, money, governments and assassinations. He wondered how often they were frustrated in their ambitions, whether they ever settled for second best.

Their suits were immaculate, their shoes the best, shirts and ties all impeccable. And if there was one fault it was that they were all similar, clones of the perfect professional businessman.

Berndt sipped his wine; it was really very good. He thought about escape; how many thugs were there on board? How many behind him? He reckoned just two; they would not be a problem. Were the bankers armed? Unlikely. His wetsuit was beginning to feel uncomfortable; he was over-heating. He tugged the hood back, pulled down the zip at the front. And spoke.

'How much disturbance would be caused by the death of the President?'

'That is not your concern.'

Berndt was silent. After a while, the boss spoke again. 'We imagine that the death would be made to look like an accident, or suicide. We would be ready to deal with the fall-out. There would be no witch hunt.'

'Do you have any particular requirements?'

'Just death made to look like a heart attack, or an accident. Of some sort.'

Berndt was silent.

'It is true,' said the boss, 'that the assassination of the President might be deemed to be above and beyond any of your former assignations. However, it is your last task, after all. We have promised you a pension and the release of your friend. Though I must say, we have greatly enjoyed her time with us.'

Berndt was silent; he was calculating how the task might be met, or how he might evade it and the bankers and release Francine. It was complicated.

'We understand that you will have some research to carry out and the need to compile a list of armament. We are inviting you to stay the night on board and we shall meet tomorrow when you can inform us of your needs. You may ask for anything in reason; we shall attempt to satisfy your demands.'

The bankers rose and descended the stairs, single file; a hand on Berndt's shoulder indicated that he should remain. After a short while, he was beckoned to rise and follow a soldier, another behind him. They did not speak. Berndt knew how easy it would be to take them out but that would leave Francine in the hands of the bankers and negate his whole purpose in coming aboard. He followed the man down the stairs, through a large saloon into a corridor, and was taken forrard to a small cabin where they ushered him inside.

The walls were timber panelling, varnished, the ceiling white painted boards, and the floor rose up towards the outside, the curve of the bows. Clean clothes were laid out on the bunk; a sailor's smock and trousers. And there was food, cold refreshment and water. A small porthole looked out onto the dark water; he could make out the twinkling lights of the town nearby and a few moored boats, all dark. He stripped out of the wetsuit, towelled himself down, donned the new clothes, stretched out on the bunk and closed his eyes; then remembered the food that he consumed fast without pleasure before lying on the bunk again, putting himself to sleep, an old habit learned in the Stasi days, the ability to take rest whenever and wherever one could.

He woke early and fast; there were sounds of scratching on the panelled wall adjacent to his head. Mice on board?

Unlikely. He tapped lightly on the panelling. Silence for a few minutes. Tapping followed from the other side, Morse code, SOS; the Ss were repeated, a long hissing message. He tapped back an affirmative. Silence. He smiled to himself; Francine was communicating. Who else could it be? He bent to his task of assembling an arsenal of weapons and explosives. He did not stint himself; indeed, he knew that he could not carry all that he listed. It would give him more latitude.

The sun was high before his cabin was unlocked and he was ushered through the saloon, up the stairs and into the upper saloon to sit where he had before, breakfast laid before him, a pad of paper and pens. There was nobody else there apart from the two 'soldiers' who waited upon him.

He wrote out his long list, clearly, giving exact specifications to the rifles, sights, handguns, explosives, detonators, remote firing devices and rockets. When he was done, he pushed it away and completed his breakfast. A 'soldier' took the list and disappeared below.

Berndt looked out on the lake. It was a beautiful morning, the sun dazzling off the water; a small fleet of dinghies was setting out from the marina, and a tourist boat went past towards the north. He could make out the little dinghy that he had used last night rocking in its wake. A gull flew over, a long way from home.

The boss emerged and sat at the other end of the table. He smiled at Berndt.

'I must say, those clothes suit you. Better than a wetsuit, wouldn't you say?'

Berndt was silent. The boss looked as immaculate as

ever, not a hair out of place; Berndt wondered if one of the 'soldiers ' was a valet.

'Your list; interesting, but all these explosives? And the rockets?'

Berndt was silent. Well, did he want the job done, or not?

'Well, if you need them ... I suppose so. These things will be available at the flat in two days; you can collect them there.'

'There is one thing more,' said Berndt. He wrote on a pad and passed it to a 'soldier', who took it to the boss.

'A car? An Audi 6? French plates? Two years old? That should not be a problem. Perhaps you would like to keep it afterwards; I shouldn't imagine that it will be of any use to us, spoilt goods, you know.' He laughed, a thin sound, brief without humour.

Berndt was silent.

'Well, I hope you enjoyed your stay with us. I shouldn't imagine that we shall meet again. Your banking details remain the same, I assume? Your pension details will be sent to them. And we shall release Francine in due course. Goodbye.'

He rose and without looking back descended the stairs out of sight.

Berndt stood up and stretched; the thugs stepped back, looking at each other. Berndt asked for his wetsuit but they ignored his words as though they did not understand and ushered him onto the rear deck. Tied up was the Riva launch, engine rumbling, crew of two. Berndt stepped down into the launch; it promptly took off with a flourish of spray, a wide turn towards Geneva. Berndt beckoned towards his dinghy and was ignored.

Two days. No fear of walking the streets, but much work to do before he picked up the car and armament. He booked into a comfortable hotel and treated himself to long sleeps and good meals, building up a reservoir of energy. And in the day, he walked and sat in coffee shops, planning.

He established his general intentions, where and when, and allowed for contingencies. He allocated his resources, guns of various types and explosives. He considered time of day, weather patterns to avoid excessive cross-wind deflection, weight of bullet and strength of charge, size of rifle when broken down, and clothing to pass in any conditions including a long wait in inhospitable conditions. He used the local library to examine maps and research into use of explosives, telling the librarian that he was writing a novel. He researched the President's pastimes, his interests outside of his office, and discovered that he liked shooting and fishing. And throughout he built in contingency plans, the possibility of being discovered at any stage, the chance that ammunition might be dud, the effect of a non show of the target, escape plans, evasion plans. He planned for the best and allowed for the worst.

Two days later, he was at the flat. There were two of the thugs there but they made space for him as though he was now one of them; they offered him coffee, food, and their own opinions on his task, and on their bosses. At first he did not trust them, assumed that it was a test but they assured him that their working conditions were not good; they were slaves, they said, and they looked forward to returning to their own countries in East Europe. They showed him the armaments.

Berndt made a close examination of everything. He broke down the rifles and handguns, checked the firing pins and action, the ammunition, the weight of everything, the state of the plastic explosive, and the age of the rockets. The firing mechanisms and the detonators looked sound, but he rejected the rockets and some of the explosive; too old, unstable. He told the thugs he would return in two days; they gave him the keys to the Audi and wished him well. A bit bizarre he felt, having killed so many of their colleagues. Perhaps they were not so close to each other; it was probably a good strategy to employ 'soldiers' from different countries, to avoid fellow sympathies and to encourage competition and efficiency.

The car was standing outside in the private alley. Before using the key, he examined it closely all over, including underneath; he knew the model well, its crevices and construction. Eventually, he popped the hood and looked around the engine compartment, noting the state of the engine and fluid levels. The boot was clean, a spare tyre in good condition, nothing below the carpet except for a tool kit. Internally, he noticed a loose door panel in the rear, and pulled out all the door and roof linings and found, at last, what he was looking for in the rear doors and the roof; he ripped out the cameras, listening devices and aerials, crushed them underfoot, and took the remains to the thugs upstairs. They were embarrassed, swore that they had only carried out instructions and flinched when Berndt asked which of them he should crush like the electronics.

He left them, bearing the guns and telling them to stay in the flat for two hours; otherwise, he would be obliged to eliminate them and had the means to do so. They assured him that they would do so, let him know that they would do everything that he wanted and offered help with his task. He left them and drove off towards the south of the city.

Before long, he was aware of a tail, a dark Mercedes, keeping two cars behind. He dawdled at traffic lights, causing a barrage of horns and crossing the junctions at the last possible moment; the tail jumped the lights to keep contact.

He accelerated suddenly, turned into a side street, parked in a loading bay, and waited. Emerging half an hour later, he found the Mercedes waiting for him. He parked and ran towards it; it reversed at speed, staying in visible contact. There were two men in it, dark clothing, dark glasses. He returned to the Audi and drove gently towards the main road out of the city; at the city limits, he accelerated again. The Audi leapt into action, far outspeeding the Mercedes; he enjoyed the roar of the engine, remembering his own Audi, lost in the past. He turned in to a country lane and onto a farm track up to the top of the hill, wide open fields on either side. At the top of the hill was a copse, close branches, bending to the breeze. He buried the car in it, covered it with branches and watched the track. There was a gentle breeze; otherwise a deep silence.

A low roar; the Mercedes came slowly up the track; a lower car, it did not like the rutted way, the high central grassy ridge, loose gravel. Berndt waited until it had passed the copse, took the rifle out of the boot of the Audi and placed a bullet in each of the Mercedes, rear tyres. Reversing the Audi onto the track, he drove off; in the mirror he could see the men standing either side of the car, staring after him.

Turning into a deserted farmyard, he parked behind a barn and started his examination of the car again; there had to be something. The boot and engine compartments were clean, the interior, the hardest to search, also clean though he pulled the seats out, lifted the carpets, and looked within the dash. Underneath, he started at the front, looking at the suspension components, the drive transmission, the brake cables, fuel line, tank and exhaust. He found it above the fuel tank, very hard to see until he had inserted a branch to probe. A transmitter, quite small; he estimated its range at no more than ten or twenty miles, but that was enough.

He began to feel annoyed.

He had been entrusted to carry out a task, and the Conglomerate were keeping tabs on him, watching his progress. He did not work like that, he never had worked like that. He was offended.

Putting the transmitter onto the front seat, he drove back into town. They may not be able to follow, or there may be another car, he thought. The resources of the Conglomerate were unlikely to be limited to one Mercedes and they had probably spread a wide net to cover him. He saw his work extended, to keeping clear of them as he pursued his last task. Driving out of the city on a main road south, he stopped at a road café. Walking round the trucks he found an Italian team, a tractor and trailer ensemble carrying French cars. He placed the transmitter in the exhaust pipe of a Renault. The Conglomerate would probably notice the discrepancy quite soon, but it gave him a breathing space. And he still had to pick up the replacement explosives.

He drove out of town to the east, found a small town with a local hotel, and rested. During the day, he drove up into the hills and fired his guns, adjusting the telescopic sights and finding that his aim, in spite of a lapse in practice, had not deteriorated.

FOURTEEN

He rested on his oars as the dusk deepened, the warm day still lingering in the velvet darkness. He was not in a hurry. He was here again, at the hour that the lake turned black and when all movement seemed to have ceased, apart from the occasional car lights hurrying along the shore and the light murmuring of the water against his dinghy. Far away, a duck exploded into loud calls, silenced almost immediately.

He had picked up the explosives, all made to his satisfaction. There had been no mention of the radio locator; indeed, the 'soldier' who met him at the flat had been full of goodwill as before, offering to help him in his task. Berndt was surprised, even a little wary. He put it down to competition between the 'soldiers' as he refused the offer.

And then the yacht had disappeared, and he had taken to his bicycle and rode up the coast, past Anieres towards Chens-sur-Léman. And there she had lain, anchored as before about five hundred metres off the shore. An inspection with the binoculars had shown him the bankers and Francine sitting in the deck saloon, apparently engaged in some meal. She looked totally at ease. Had she not touched his foot, tapped a message through the bulkhead? She was revealing hidden qualities that he had never suspected; he had thought her as straight as a ruler. He wondered at the conversation;

was she a turncoat, giving him up to these suave gentlemen, telling them that he was not to be trusted, a duplicitous sort of person, one didn't know where one was with him, he had seemed so straight, and now... these 'gentlemen' could no doubt offer her a luxurious life, at any cost? Or was she playing some deep game, with a target of her own, saying that perhaps she could help them, but at a cost, and naturally they would have to let her go, and then...

With the bitter taste of frustration, he had swung his bicycle round and returned to his small town outside Geneva.

Sitting in the growing darkness, he changed into his wetsuit, a new one, and ate a little energy food, washed down with water. Filled his waterproof bag; it was heavy but it would be much less weight underwater and help to keep him submerged. He did not question what he was attempting to do, what his target was for tonight. He did not stop to wonder whether he would survive; that was in the hands of fate and his skills. But he knew he was playing a game where the odds were weighted against him, a situation that was foreign to him, and he was not even in full working trim. Life had been too good for that. But what was the point of it all if he could not make war against his enemies? And rescue Francine? He adjusted his mask and snorkel and slipped into the water. It was surprisingly warm.

Approaching the yacht, he could see no sign of the thugs on deck. He submerged as he approached, holding his breath to prevent bubbles giving him away, and cruised up to the yacht. Relaxing for a few minutes against the side, he submerged and went first aft and then forward, placing his charges beneath the hull and setting the timers for about one hour. They clamped onto the varnished hull adjacent to the keel; the detonators and timers were already connected. They would not be disturbed unless the yacht was to take off at full speed; that was most unlikely. And he doubted that the thugs carried out a regular underwater hull check. They did not seem to be around anyway. He swam to the stern and climbed onto the diving platform, breathing deeply.

The thug smoking a cigarette concealed in his palm, hunkered down behind the life-rafts, was out of sight of the bosses; he had had enough of being ordered around for a while. They could whistle if they wanted him. And right before him, removing his mask and headpiece, was number one fugitive; what luck. Should earn a bonus. He delivered a sharp blow to the back of the head. Berndt reeled, almost fell into the water until he was grabbed by the shoulders and dragged back onto the deck. Two thugs picked him up and manhandled him into the saloon, his feet dragging; he was only vaguely aware of what was around him.

For a while he sat in blissful silence. It was warm and he began to float away, to lose consciousness. Slumped in his seat, he struggled to keep awake; eventually, a man began to speak to him, loudly and slowly, clear words hammered down the table; what was he saying?

'What... have you heard... delay again... Munich... hit him too hard?'

One of the thugs behind him protested. 'He's dangerous, sir.'

Berndt was hearing a little better, his senses were returning; his head ached abominably. He tensed the muscles in his legs and arms; they were slow, a delayed reaction; his heart was running hard, working to bring his brain into action. He would not be able to move fast for a while. So he remained slumped and listened.

'Well, Francine, your boyfriend has not been a good boy; we taught him a lesson some little time ago, to carry out his tasks without delay. He does not seem to have taken it seriously. I appreciate that he has been *hors de combat*, as you might say, but that is no excuse in our business. And he knows that. Haven't we been generous, supplied everything he asked for, offered him retirement and a large pension? What more could we do?'

Berndt felt himself becoming too comfortable and fading; it was tempting to drift away, to sleep and relax and forget the pain in his head. He drew on all his strength to keep conscious, driving his fingernails into his palms, inflicting as much pain as he could to keep awake. Francine had made no reply and he felt her closeness, smelt her perfume and was reassured by her presence.

'Perhaps we have not punished him enough, to ensure that he has learnt his lesson. What do you suggest, Francine? Francine?' He looked concerned. Francine was silent. 'Ah now, Francine, you are not going to disappoint us, are you?'

'I am not sure what you mean by punishment. And I am unaware of the task you set him. He is a retired geologist and I cannot think how you gentlemen could find him useful,' said Francine.

'Punishment? An incentive to perform well. The task? Something that he can do well. Can you suggest some simple punishment?'

Francine looked at Berndt, wrinkled her nose and said, 'But perform what well? Why don't you just ask him?'

'Ask him? Well, that is original, my dear, but I believe we need a little more incentive. Marc, how is he? Is he responding?'

One of the thugs bent over Berndt, looking into his eyes; Berndt kept his eyes half closed and made a low moan.

'I don't think he is with us yet,' said the thug called Marc.

'Well, perhaps we should—'

There was a loud crump from the stern. The explosive punched upwards, forming a large hole in the hull boarding, shattering the stern propeller shaft and the gearbox, dislocating the engine bearings, and knocking out the generator. The deck boarding was loosened but held, though the hold-down bolts for the liferafts popped. The engine slipped sideways and jammed in the hole, half in the boat, half out. The lights failed and there was a rushing of water as the engine room flooded, cracking the weakened bulkhead to the kitchen galley. The cook left the kitchen at a run, appearing up the companionway in a panic, leaving the gas cooker baking a soufflé.

The bankers had sat as though frozen, possibly enjoying an experience beyond their comprehension; the appearance of the cook brought them to their senses and they rose, turning this way and that. Meanwhile, the crew, with the 'soldiers', had taken to the life-rafts that had been released from the rear deck, and were afloat a little way off.

The yacht settled by the stern, water washing into the lower saloon. The forward charge exploded, another crump that blasted upwards into the anchor compartment, shattering the bulkheads to the front cabins, including the one that Berndt had been held in. The spare anchor and chain dropped to the lake floor; lightened of the load, the bows rose for a few minutes, but water was now pouring along the corridor to the lower saloon, meeting the flood from the kitchen. An odd medley of flotsam swirled on the joined waters: books, flowers, shoes, a half-eaten pizza, a chef's hat, papers, clothes.

The engine fuel, released by the shattering of the fuel line, had poured into the kitchen and was ignited by the gas cooker, several minutes after the first explosion and shortly before it was flooded. There was a massive explosion, the fuel tank disintegrating with the port side of the hull. The upper works of the deck saloon caught fire, a bright glare in the darkness.

At the first explosion, Berndt had felt himself abruptly dragged backwards, his chair falling beneath him. One or two pairs of hands, he could not be sure, pulled him over the side and into the water where he sank before his wetsuit brought him to the surface; as he rolled in confusion, coughing, a strong pair of hands took him under the arms and he was pulled away from the yacht, the person beneath him swimming strongly. He had no idea who it could be but he was being rescued; he understood that and lay still.

The swim seemed to take hours; he drifted out of consciousness and back again. Odd memories filled his mind: walking in Paris, swimming underwater in the Mediterranean, sailing toy boats with his sister in Berlin, riding a horse, sleeping in a train, laughing. He laughed aloud, coughing.

'You think it's funny, do you? Perhaps you should do your own swimming.'

That voice; he knew it well and yet could not connect it with anything. He lay quiet, allowing his senses to heal. His head hurt and he had difficulty in making his brain work, but otherwise his body was developing feeling. Way back from where he had come, the yacht was a brilliant pyre on the water, remaining level and sinking slowly.

The swimmer stood suddenly and Berndt rolled over, kneeling in the shallows, his arms around his rescuer's legs to hold onto something solid. Not so solid, he thought. The legs moved.

'Let me go, Bernard. Enough, you can stand by yourself.'

Mein Gott, it's Francine; Francine who pulled me out of the yacht, Francine who towed me here. Mein Gott. Francine.

He stood. It was dark and he could make out little of her face. 'Francine,' he said.

'I don't know whether to leave you here or come with you,' she said.

They stood still in the water near the shore that appeared to be deserted. Away on the lake the burning hulk was now settling fast, only the roof above water; a police launch, with a white moustache of wash, was scything through the water. The klaxon and spotlight cut through the dark.

'Come with me. It's not far,' said Berndt.

They walked up the shore and along the path, an incongruous pair, Francine in a soaked evening dress that clung to her, attempting to walk with her usual grace, and Berndt in a wetsuit staggering forward, a dribble of water on the path behind them. They met no one, except a young couple who moved away from them as though they were dangerous escapees from a home.

Before long, they came to Berndt's car. He had parked it nearby on the off chance that he would escape, though he had wondered if he would ever see it again. The sight of it provoked an unusual sense of relief; he couldn't resist a smile. Francine said nothing, but took her seat, pulling her wet dress around her. There was a strong smell of wet fabric, mixed with something vegetable.

It was not a long drive to the little hotel in the hills; there was not one word spoken. At the hotel, they retired to his room where she disappeared into the bathroom, borrowing some clothes. Still silent later, they went out to a local auberge and sat opposite each other at a small table. Berndt was hungry but did not feel that he could eat. Francine ordered a salad and played with it for a while. She sipped her wine. There had still been no conversation except for the briefest words.

She sat back, pushing her plate away. 'And now, I think you should tell me what task the gentlemen wanted you to do.' She did not look at him but addressed the table in front of her.

Berndt sat in silence; what could he say? That he was a hitman? That he had had a career of killing people? That he was meant to be killing the President of France? That he loved her and could not conceive of a life without her now? And that was a shock in itself because he had never told her he loved her, never considered it, never believed that it was something that he did. That it was possible. To fall in love. There had been no place in his life for love, since the death of his parents and the disappearance of his sister, and that was a different sort of love. He had felt himself removed from 'love', something that happened to other people, something that would be a burden to him. At Stasi College it had happened to other students; he had seen how they went off the rails, lost that keen edge of performance that was required of them. And disappeared to some mundane job.

And now he felt the burden himself, like an anchor around his neck dragging him down to a place where, to his surprise, he wanted to be, a place of commitment to somebody else, a vulnerability that he accepted. Could he yet win Francine, persuade her that he was a different man, worlds removed from his past life? But how?

He sipped his wine, choked, wiped his mouth with a napkin. 'I'm not sure that you want to know; indeed, it might put you at risk.'

Francine looked up sharply, was about to protest.

'No let me speak,' he went on. 'I told you something of my earlier life, my life in the Stasi. It was not nice, not civilised, but I felt that it was necessary, serving the state. We all have to serve in some way. After I came to the West, I continued to serve in the same way, with the skills that I had learnt. But it was a hideous life and I was ready to give it up. And then I met you. And now I want nothing or nobody but you.'

Francine was silent. Berndt waited; he could not tear himself away from observing every slight change of expression on her face, hoping beyond hope.

At last she stirred and spoke. 'You deliberately misled me. A mining engineer! Huh. Do you want to tell me the details of the "hideous" life you lived? And how far have you removed yourself from it? The gentlemen, presumably, had a "hideous" task for you. And now, you are right; I don't want to know what it was. But I am angry with you, and full of remorse. Who are you? What am I getting myself into?'

'I… I'm sorry, deeply sorry, did not wish to hurt you, of all people—'

She burst into tears, a deep choking crying that shook her, her hands up to her face, bent over in her chair. Berndt felt shocked, glanced around; such a public display was dangerous; it was noticed and remembered by people. The waiters approached at first and then withdrew as they met his look.

And then a great pity arose in him and he went round to her, kneeling on the floor and hugged her. At first, she half turned away from him, then allowed him to hold her close as she continued to weep, now silently, tears dropping onto her napkin, until she ceased and turned to him, swollen eyes, a wet mouth, nose running, and gazed into his eyes. And kissed him: on his forehead, his eyes, his nose, his lips. He felt her tears running down his cheeks, mixing with his own that came suddenly and surprised him. After a while, she stood, pushing back her chair, and he stood beside her, still looking into her face, still trying to read her mood, her thoughts.

They left the auberge, walking back to the hotel hand in hand, a first for Berndt. And went to bed, both falling asleep after a brief hug.

Breakfast the next day. Berndt was down first, choosing a table towards the rear against a wall from habit, a good view of all doors. Francine appeared, looked at Berndt and chose a table in the window and waited. He joined her; a quick survey of the car park and gardens outside; bushes that could conceal a hidden gun, the car park within close range, the sunlight full on them providing an easy target for anyone outside. He worked to control his nerves that buzzed at such folly.

Francine was smiling. 'I am not sure that I want to know more of your past. It is illogical, I know; I have always believed in the truth; it is the only way to study for a Doctorate, by the earnest pursuit of research, the presentation of facts that are verifiable. But you are not a Doctorate, my love, and I must learn to trust my instincts that we can make a life together, somehow. We are not out of the woods yet, are we?'

Berndt was silent; he felt he was just holding onto a great weight and if he moved or talked, it would slip out of his grip and all would be lost.

'You have to tell me,' she said, 'how bad, on a scale of ten, was the task that you were set, and whether we are in danger now.'

'Ten. That is the truth. And yes, we are in danger. We should move, right now, away from this window and preferably to another country.' He paused. 'And I love you; you are more important to me than anything else.'

They breakfasted at a table at the rear, Francine happy to follow him and sit back to the room so that he could maintain surveillance, and left the hotel shortly afterwards. They packed the Audi with Berndt's things; he had clothes, a handgun and a rifle, ammunition and some paperwork but little else. Francine was fetching in a man's shirt, oversized jeans, loafers, and a sweater; she had no clothes or sanitary things, no money or bankcard, no passport.

As they drove away, Berndt glanced in the mirror. A black Mercedes was following them, gaining on them.

FIFTEEN

They drove out of the village; there was a peaceful silence between them; a pleasant morning, the sun breaking through early cloud, warming them. It felt like a blessing after the night of explosions and immersion. Berndt thought of where they might go: a holiday in Italy, perhaps, or Switzerland.

A black Mercedes had appeared behind them. Berndt glanced at Francine.

He accelerated; he knew his car well. It had been his favourite Audi model, though his old one had received some specialist attention and was capable of surprising bursts of speed, in spite of the armour-plating. But this car was straight from the dealers: a sound vehicle in good condition, new tyres, but no spectacular performance. In fact, the only thing that this car really had in common with his own car was the colour.

The Mercedes kept pace with him, around fifty metres behind, round bends, across junctions, up and down hills. It appeared to be playing a patient game.

'What do they want?' said Francine. She sounded anxious. The explosions on the yacht did not seem to have worried her, Berndt noticed, but she was jumpy, looking over her shoulder, flicking her nails. Perhaps she had thought that trouble was all over. Berndt did not reply; he was calculating the process of confronting the occupants, of bringing it to a conclusion so that he could escape with Francine. He had no doubt that he would succeed, but it was a question of how to do it. And how to protect Francine.

He turned into a lane, single track to prevent the Mercedes coming alongside, and was forced to drive slower, negotiating blind bends and many side roads without priority. At some junctions he skimmed the front of other cars; a chorus of loud horns: no way to drive in quiet civilised Swiss countryside.

They rounded a bend and came face to face with a tractor. The driver, a greasy cap pulled low over his eyes, unshaven, stained overalls, stared at them and slowed but continued to come on, his rusty tractor chugging. What were they meant to do? Leap into the hedge? Berndt slowed.

As they crept forward and the distance to collision became less and less, Berndt was aware of the Mercedes closing behind them. A gap in the hedge on the right appeared and Berndt swerved into it onto a farm track, rough concrete, running across a wide field. He accelerated to sixty miles per hour, breaking hard as it suddenly deteriorated into a rutted earth track climbing a hill, a high grassy ridge running up the middle, overgrown hedges on both sides. The Mercedes had fallen back, perhaps sensing that Berndt was trapped.

Berndt put the Audi to the track, a low gear, engine roaring as they charged up the hill, the wheels sometimes spinning, the car bouncing as the grass ridge rubbed the underside of the car, a weird roaring sound. The Mercedes fell further behind. At the top of the hill, there was a copse, mature oak trees and beeches, a quiet retreat where the trees grew close. Berndt turned in and stopped the car behind a tree.

There was silence, broken by a gentle breeze. A gust raised leaves, a soporific sound. They stood by the car, looking at each other, listening for pursuit. Before long, they could hear the Mercedes, whining and grunting slowly up the hill. He told Francine to hide and took out his weapons; she looked at the guns, with more interest than surprise. The Mercedes was approaching; it had less ground clearance than the Audi. They must have been clipping the central ridge. He looked round, saw Francine back behind a tree, indicated that she should keep quiet, and placed himself behind a tree near the front. He set up his rifle in the crook of a branch and checked the ammunition in both rifle and handgun.

The Mercedes turned into the copse and stopped at the entrance. Two men in dark army fatigues got out; one was holding a handgun, a Glock, the other an Uzi sub-machine gun. They stared around themselves, apparently without fear. Berndt knew he could pick them off, but hesitated. The men spotted the Audi and laughed; the Uzi man made a comment about how it would not be difficult, and then they could have a good meal. The other laughed.

Berndt waited.

The 'soldiers' moved apart and started to move deeper in to the trees; Berndt considered picking them off one by one before they could reach Francine. He aimed a shot at the car, the bullet ricocheting off into the trees. The men immediately returned, standing either side of the car. Berndt again considered shooting them down, considered that if he did not they would shoot him. But he could not.

The back door opened and the head banker got out; he looked as immaculate as usual, unperturbed by the situation.

'Berndt,' he called. 'We need to talk. Can you hear me?'

Berndt was silent.

'I say, can you hear me?'

'I hear you,' said Berndt.

'I was distressed that you hurt us last night. I assume it was you; though I suppose it might have been some enemies of our organisation. No, no, I do not believe that; it must have been you. An imaginative bit of work. Which is exactly why we admire you so. But I really do not understand. You have a profession that we wish to purchase, and yet you keep delaying your work. And now you spend time attacking us. But why?'

Berndt was silent.

'Perhaps I am being naïve. There is Francine; perhaps we should not have captured her. It was a crude move, I admit, intended to persuade you. We should have known better. And we have paid the price; sadly, two of my colleagues were drowned last night and the yacht was lost. It is easily replaced, but my colleagues are not so easily replaced. Could we not talk? You are still a valuable commodity to us.'

There was a scuffle; one of the men, the one with a handgun, had run into the trees and dragged Francine out, holding a gun to her head.

'We seem to be back to square one,' said the banker with a sigh.

Berndt cursed himself for his folly in having Francine near him and stepped out of his shelter, holding a gun on the man holding Francine. He formed the peak of a triangle, himself facing the two 'soldiers', some two metres apart and the banker, between them but a little further away. How fast could he shoot both men? A fast tap-tap, wheeling from one to the other, needing to be accurate to five centimetres. He was not a small firearms man, though he used to win prizes.

'Let her go. Now,' he said.

'This is unfortunate,' said the banker. He didn't sound at all concerned.

'Let her go,' Berndt repeated.

The man holding Francine looked at the banker, at Berndt, and shook his head. Slightly. Frowning as though he was trying to work something out, the situation or his own position in it.

'Are you sure that I cannot persuade you, Berndt? You must realise that if we cannot use your skills, we cannot allow anyone else to use them. It is a rather... er, final way of putting things, but I can see no other way forward.'

Berndt looked up at the sky; blue with a few puffy clouds. The gentle breeze fanned his head. Not a bad day to die, he thought. I'm no killer, anymore. Where is this thing going? Should have picked them off at the start. Francine will survive; once they have killed me, there will be no need for them to keep her. She will be able to return to her academic life, well away from guns and hitmen and thugs. Won't she?

There was a sudden movement. The man holding Francine dropped her arm, wheeled, and shot the other 'soldier' through the head, a single shot that echoed over the hills. The Uzi clattered to the ground as the man crumpled after it. Birds rose from the trees with loud exclamations, flying off in all directions. The banker's face went through a series of expressions, firstly almost amusement as though at a vulgar joke, then wonder, the eyes wide, and then fear. His hands raised against his chest like a shield, one above the other.

The shot changed the equation; two against one became one against one, and it was possible that the one was not the enemy. Berndt smiled to himself at the change in balance, the change in fortune. It did not happen often; he used to allow for contingencies, to allow for the worst possible outcome. But that was in the past.

He fired. His bullet hit the banker in the stomach, below the hands; the banker collapsed onto his knees clutching his stomach, murmuring, gasping, 'What a waste... why... Oh God...'

The remaining 'soldier' went over to him, looked down with no change of expression, and fired a single shot into the top of the head. Francine retreated from him, standing a little way from both men, and looked with wonder and a little horror from one dead body to another, at the remaining 'soldier', at Berndt. He saw the triangle altered, a new integer to the left, and wondered whether Francine was allied with him or whether too much had been experienced that would split her apart from him. A cloud of fear blew over him, leaving him depressed and slow.

She muttered, 'Is it... can it be... surely ...' She started to shake.

Berndt reached her in a few quick strides and folded her in his arms, turning her away from the scene, away from the other man. The 'soldier' looked at them, shrugged, and said, You owe me.' Turned and stepped into the Mercedes, reversing out of the entrance and rolling down the hill, quite slowly. The sound of his engine died away and there was silence again, broken only by the wind in the leaves and birds returning to roost.

It was fortunate that Berndt was not far from the workshops of the men who had provided the means of his business, guns, vehicles, paperwork, and all the other items of his trade. It did mean crossing a border to reach them, but a night-time crossing on a small mountain road proved no problem; the barrier was not even down, and nobody manned the outpost.

His suppliers greeted him with a degree of caution; they had not heard from him for some years and had assumed that he had been eliminated. But his money opened doors and the will to please. The car was replaced, another Audi but with a more powerful engine, the weapons were changed for the type that he had always used, and a passport was produced in a very short time for Francine. She had to accept a new name, and a new nationality; she became Frances, an English woman with a French mother and English father, brought up in Bath.

She was not happy about the change of name. They stood outside the forger's workshop. 'Do you expect me to lose my life, my work and family?'

Berndt gazed across the valley. 'I'm sorry. I can offer you a good life, but if you return to your old life, I can be no part of it.'

'And why not? How long did I travel down to your French village to see you while continuing my research?'

'I fear for you. The Conglomerate know you now, and would torture you to reveal my whereabouts. I do not fear for myself; what will be will be. But it would destroy me if the Conglomerate hurt a hair of your head.'

'Oh Berndt, what has happened to us?' She turned away from him, looking across the valley as tears ran down her face.

'If you wish to return to Paris, you must go, but I don't know how safe you will be. I love you.' The words, only recently a part of his vocabulary, still sounded alien, full of a promise that he did not know whether he could fulfil. And yet he feared that she would leave him now and he would be unable to stop her, for her own good; after all, the Conglomerate might well leave her alone when they see that he was gone from her life. But they might not.

They left Italy, travelling north on minor roads, sometimes only fifty kilometres a day, spending time in remote inns, close to each other. But something crept between them, a choking cloud that prevented them from talking to each other clearly, and with it a sense of estrangement. Francine became more independent, sometimes going for long walks on her own; Berndt grieved the loss of his lover, the grief overflowing into their time together so that Francine tended to withdraw, or chide him for failing her. They still continued to meet in bed every night from physical need, though it was becoming more mechanical.

Approaching the Channel, Francine called upon Berndt to stop.

'Eh bien, mon cheri, this is as far as I can go.'

Berndt stared. 'Won't you come to England with me?'

'You ask too much of me. I love you, but you destroy me.'

'I would destroy myself rather than you should be hurt.'

'But those are just words. Aren't they?' There were no tears now.

'Where will you go?' he said.

'Home. Where else?'

'And your life?'

'It will be as it always was. Friends, research, a little teaching if they have not forgotten me, my parents at the weekend.'

'Would you come to England? For a holiday?'

'Who can say?' she said with a shrug. 'Time must pass.'

'Take great care of yourself. For your sake and mine.'

They spent a final night together, and Francine caught the train for Paris. As she climbed aboard, she gave him a long look from the steps, an examination as though she wondered what sort of man she had met, with no smile or tears, then turned and disappeared. Berndt, shaken, went to the station bar and drank brandy until he staggered into the station hotel and slept like a dead man for twelve hours. The next day, after a breakfast of strong coffee and croissant, he drove to Calais and caught a ferry for England. Arriving at Dover, he turned west, avoiding the high roads, and made his way to Bristol.

PART 3

ONE

'Ere, get out of ma way! Gawd, struth, you don' arf get some dozy bastards!'

Berndt stepped off the pavement, to be rewarded with a loud hoot as a bus came down on him. He stepped back onto the pavement and watched the back of the man wheeling a sack trolley recede; a filthy donkey jacket, cap pulled down over the eyes, boilersuit over hard shoes. The English! Would he ever get used to them?

Bath had been a civilised town, full of polite people who would never require you to vacate the pavement; the only minor hassles came from American tourists, particularly the younger ones who seemed to expect everything to get out of their way. He had expected that Bristol, just down the road, would be cut of the same cloth, but it was very different. A working industrial town, tobacco and a trading port in a minor way; and quite rough in many parts, in spite of its great historical background, railway and port. Perhaps that was one of his problems; he was not working. He was a retired man with a foreign background in a strange town full of working people, many of whom seemed to have strong views, from the type of beer you drank to the colour of your skin to the accent in your voice. He sensed that things were changing, but slowly. There were strikes and demonstrations, in this town as in others; and the Queen was having her Jubilee Year, whatever that meant.

Still, he was not going anywhere, and he did not want to visit Paris and bring danger to Francine. He had written to her a few times but received no reply. It was harder than he had expected; he had come to assume that she would be with him. They would be a couple like other people, accepted and welcomed into that level of society where life seemed straight forward; you found a house, decorated it, filled it with your things, and sat back doing life, whatever it might be. And now he was alone, in a rented house on the south side of the city, using it as a place to sleep and eat, but little else. He was not domesticated; even in his French village, meals had mostly come to him, rather than the whole buying, cooking, serving, washing thing. He was in danger of falling through the mesh of the place, unknown and unnoticed, unplaced and easily forgotten. He spent the days walking the streets, learning the town.

His area was not rough; small terrace houses in neat streets, all aligned north and south. Or so it seemed. Corner shops and pubs. His own house was newer than some, with a hall entrance, bigger windows, a different front door, a bathroom upstairs, small garden at the rear. The main problem was security; he had not yet identified an escape route, as he had in all his other homes: the Paris flat, the Bath flat, the village flat. His garden was jammed between others, with high fences, hedges, ponds and drying lines; he feared that he would find himself trapped between buildings, but he still held out hope that somewhere there was an alley, or a garage roof.

The next Sunday, he went to the local Church; he had read in a local paper that it was an essential way to join your local neighbourhood, to be recognised and to have friends. Friends! He wondered how to make friends here; most 'friends' in the past had been doubtful colleagues a long time in the past, or those who served him, his suppliers and armourers. He did not know the role of a friend; would one be a trouble, nosing into his private life, his past and problems? But it might be good disguise, if nothing else, to be recognised on the street, as he was in the French village, to nod to acquaintances, to have a passing knowledge of the way the neighbourhood worked.

Church was a novel experience; he was welcomed as if he was a long acquaintance, not judged in any way, not criticised when he had no idea what to do. For he had never been to a Church before, except once or twice in other countries to accumulate knowledge of a target's lifestyle. Of course, he was asked questions: where did he live, how long had he lived there, did he work, did he have family, was he really a refugee from another country (ha-ha!).

He was ready for all of the questions; he had done his homework, prepared his contingencies. Yes, he had been out of the country for a long time, working as a mining engineer. But he was British; his father had been a fugitive from Nazi Germany and married an Englishwoman. No sadly, they had both passed on. No, not Bristol; he was born and brought up in Walsall. No, not a very nice place, but his father had to accept a menial job when he came to England; in Germany, he had been a university professor. His mother had been a housewife, except in the War when of course she had worked; well, they all had to, didn't they? But he was only a boy in the War; he remembered the bombing, the barrage balloons, the anti-aircraft guns… Do you know, my father insisted that I learn German, and German was spoken in the house as much as English… my mother learnt it too. I suppose it might be unpopular still, I'm sorry. But it is very good to have a second language, isn't it?

He learnt to have conversations, learnt not to limit his words, to say the obvious things without revealing his thoughts, his background; it was a new experience that left him sweating. And he was accepted, somewhat to his surprise. A few invitations to join the men at the pub introduced him to the local drinking holes; it took a while to become used to the beer. Nobody had invited him to their homes, but it didn't seem to matter; he joined in decorating the church and Church Hall for festive occasions, and even offered to lend a hand with small maintenance jobs.

It began to feel like living in the French village and he began to drop his guard, to not always walk on the safe side of the street, to not always sit in the safe seat at a café or pub. Surveillance was very hard to drop and there were some occasions when his reactions had shocked those around him. On one occasion, he had been sitting in the pew waiting for the Service to begin when a hand had been put on his shoulder; he had risen and in one swift movement swivelled, grabbed the hand, twisted the arm behind the back and was just putting his other arm around the neck of the person, to be greeted by the very surprised face of the Vicar. In some confusion he had stepped back, too embarrassed to apologise, wanting to escape and be elsewhere. But the Vicar laid his hand on his arm, calmed him and said that if he ever wanted to talk, just talk, he was very welcome. There were others nearby who were not so easily mollified and gave him suspicious looks; it took a while for them to feel easy in his presence. After the Service, he apologised to those around him, told them that he had had a bad experience working in South-West Africa. The Vicar shook his hand, repeated his invitation. Anytime, old chap, anytime. He looked at the Church noticeboard, and saw the word 'Cantab' after the Vicar's name; what did it mean? He did not like to ask.

And so life continued, walking, a little socialising, visits to pubs and cafés, museums and the harbour, an area of deep fascination. Known as the Floating Harbour, it was quite large and there were ferries that crossed it; he used them regularly. He looked out for the small trading vessels that still came up river, at the yachts, some large and beautiful, and the repair yards, always busy with a boat on the slip. He came to know the main streets, the railway station and the university, the tobacco factory and the Brunel locks that gave access to the river. And then he became restless, unable to find an occupation that would keep him occupied. He was no great reader or writer; the newspapers were enough. Photography was interesting, but only for a purpose. Volunteering in a charity shop was impossible; not only could he not stay in the same place for more than an hour but he would be thrown into contact with too many people. He thought of becoming a one man litter machine; dismissed it almost immediately. He would draw attention to himself. He did do a little maintenance work at the Church, by himself.

One Sunday, he accepted the Vicar's invitation to drink sherry before lunch. He didn't like sherry and he did not eat lunch but he assumed it was a social convention and accepted.

The Vicar was an elderly man, well into his seventies. A lean man, a shock of unmanageable white hair, gaunt in his face with hairs growing from his nostrils and ears, he was tall and tended to stoop. He wore old corduroy trousers, stained with drops and crumbs, and a worn tweed jacket, leather patches at the elbows. But his look was always benign and he appeared to find his parishioners interesting, their problems not above solving. Berndtt found the house, a large corner detached building, overgrown with ivy, and knocked on the door. The garden was overgrown, and there was no car to be seen. He was ushered into the study; it appeared that the Vicar lived there, surrounded by books and photographs.

Berndtt studied them as the Vicar sought dry biscuits for the sherry; he lived alone. There were scenes of rowing eights, with the name of a Cambridge college beneath; the Vicar had been Stroke. Berndtt did not know what that meant. There were group pictures, all in blazers and boaters, before some College building, words chalked on the walls. They looked old, long before the War. There were also pictures of some hot foreign country, Vicar surrounded by native people. And there was one picture of many Vicars standing in a chapel or church. The books, apart from the single row of religious volumes, were a catholic mix ranging from geomorphology to philosophy, literature to art. Not all the books were in English; French and German was also represented.

'Ah, you are examining my photographs.' The Vicar had come into the room quietly and watched Berndtt. There was a sharp enquiring look, quite different from his usual parish demeanour.

'What does Cantab mean?'

'Cambridge University. I was up in the '20s. Long time ago but they were precious years. Weren't your twenties precious?'

Berndtt thought of the Stasi college; had it been a special time in his life? He did not think so. He remembered the Hitler Youth clearly, but it was a muddled memory, one in which he was meant to feel guilty but could not.

'And then,' said the Vicar, 'I was sent to Africa, Kenya. That was a good time, although the Mau Mau had not been forgotten.'

'I have never been to Africa,' said Berndtt, immediately remembering that he had told friends in the Church that he had had a bad time in South-West Africa. 'Well, only once for a short time.'

'Where did you go?'

'Namibia. Mines.'

'Sounds interesting. I can't imagine what it would be like working underground in a hot country.'

'I am retired now. It's all a long time ago.' Berndtt hated being confined and had always worked above ground, preferably in open country.

'How do you spend your time now?'

'I thought retirement would be ideal. But it's not. I have been used to an active life.'

'I've seen you working on the Church. You have a practical bent; it is not as common as you might think.'

Berndtt was silent.

'Where was most of your work; the mining work, I assume?'

'Europe. All over.'

'And where did you live?'

'Here and there.'

'And now you have come to settle, after a lifetime of moving around?'

'Maybe.'

'I sense that your life has not been easy, possibly involving violence. You appear to be a loner, well capable of looking after yourself; if you have left a lover behind... I'm sorry; if you wish to talk about it, it would only be between us, you know.'

'No. Just mining, but it is not a gentle industry.'

'The only time I was not a parish priest was in the War. I had a quiet War, but it was not what I wanted. How was your War? You must have been a boy.'

'Yes.'

'I'm sorry, I do not mean to pry, but these things are important in our lives, mould us in ways that we don't always recognise. I wanted to be at the Front; I had been in a quiet rural parish and I wanted a life of action, to serve the fighting man. But they put me in a training camp where the recruits did not need counselling, or Last Rites, or any blessing. Apart from a few.'

'I was orphaned in the War; my parents were killed in bombing.'

'Where was this?'

'Berlin.'

'I wonder; were you forced to become a member of Hitler Youth?'

Berndtt was silent; his memories flooded over him like a cold shower, suffocating and enervating at the same time.

'Here I am, an inquisitive old man. You must excuse me.'

'You are right, of course. It was one way to survive, and I wasn't old enough to survive the other way.'

'No ... no. It must have been an awful experience. I am so glad that you rose above it to become a mining engineer; it must have been quite a struggle.'

Berndtt thought of his brief time in the police followed by the Stasi College. It had not been easy, it was true. He smiled.

'I wonder; you must excuse me if I am impertinent, but do you want more work, some other form of work that would be very different from what you have described? It seems to me that you are frustrated, still very fit, and not suited to static life. This town could be too small for you. Am I right?'

Berndtt did not say anything; what did the Vicar want?

'You must think about it, but I may be able to direct you in an interesting direction.'

'I don't think I would be suited to become a Vicar; I don't even know what a Church is.'

The Vicar burst into laughter, rocking to and fro; he stopped.

'I do apologise, please, I am sorry. I do not mean to mock you. I had not thought you suitable or even desiring a life in the Church. Though... no, do not let us pursue it. No, I had something altogether different in mind.'

'What is it?'

'What is it? I can't tell you, I am only exploring it. Just an idea, but if you would like to look outside your current life, I may be able to introduce you to some people who have an interesting business. But it would be improper of me to describe it now. I just thought that you might be rather good at it.'

Berndtt shrugged; he couldn't think of any other occupation than what he had left behind and he did not wish to return to the life of killing, and running.

'No matter,' said the Vicar. 'Now, tell me of your parents.'

And Berndtt told him what he had told the others, of Walsall, his father's menial occupation, his patient mother, no siblings, a tough school where he had survived, before an apprenticeship. And they talked of other things, the harbour and the town, people in the parish and the city, the Vicar promising to introduce him to various people, men and women.

It was three o'clock before he left; the Vicar thanked him for coming, for brightening his day. And said that he might get back to him about that job. Perhaps. He couldn't say.

The pub was noisy, a large neighbourhood place full of families enjoying their free Sunday. Berndtt knew a few and was pressed to join them. He sat on the end of their table, content to be silent and listen to the chatter around him. Children ran here and there and parents ignored them, happy to catch up with their friends. A few old boys sat apart, watching the scene. There was continuous traffic to the bar, brimming mugs and glasses, shouts of warning as a heavily laden man or woman returned to the table. They offered Berndtt a drink, and accepting, he took his turn in buying a round; the women thought it very unfair; there was only one of him and eight of them. Berndtt did not know what to say; he had no experience of these busy women, so different from those that he had met before, all so keen to be heard and laugh and joke with the men. It made him feel lonely.

A young man slid onto the bench opposite him. 'Anybody's seat?'

Berndtt looked at him. He was not quite like the men at the table; he was of similar age, late twenties he guessed, but neater, more contained. He had seen the type at College. There was the feeling of a tightly wound spring that might unwind explosively at any point. He wore clothes much like those around and his manner was similar, as though he was working to fit into the background.

The young man put his hands on the table and played with his mug. 'Busy today.'

Berndtt was sure that he had never seen him in the pub before and had the feeling that it was his first time. But he did not challenge him.

'Nice day. Thought I'd drop in for a pint.'

Berndtt nodded.

'Is this your local? I haven't seen you around.'

'I haven't lived here long.'

'Great city, isn't it? I know it's a bit rough, but it's going to change. Don't you think?'

'Rough? Is it?' Berndtt expressed surprise. Who was this young man?

'Well, there are areas I wouldn't go. Still, quiet enough in the centre where I work.'

'An office job?'

'Yeah. My name is Mike.' And he held out his hand across the table. Berndtt shook it solemnly. These English! All this handshaking.

'What do you do?' Mike was being casual, but it was an effort.

'Not much. Early retirement you could say.'

'Lucky you! I wish I could retire early.'

'What would you do?' said Berndtt.

'Write, I think. You know, novels and perhaps a serious history book.'

'What about?'

'Oh, I dunno. Quite interested in what happened to Europe after the War. Too young to be in it, of course, and my father had a cushy job in an office. But look at what happened to Europe, what with the Iron Curtain and all.'

'What happened?'

'Aren't you from the Continent?'

'I've been working all over.'

'Really? What as? A reporter?'

'No. Mining engineer.'

At that point, one of the women on his table called down, 'Hey Bernard, want another pint?'

The conversation continued, in dribs and drabs. Mike started an argument with one of the fathers; they didn't seem to care for him. Berndtt watched. After a little over an hour, Mike stood. 'Well Bernard, good to meet you. See you around.' Gave a cheery wave and went out of the door. The fathers at the table looked after him and made dry comments; they had not liked him.

'Mike' appeared a couple of times more, always as though he was waiting for something, always slipping onto a seat opposite or adjacent to Berndtt. Berndtt suspected that something was happening, but felt no danger; after all, if they suspected him, they would have picked him up without delay. Mike seemed interested in Berndtt's views on Europe, NATO, and world politics. Berndtt heard no more of novels or Mike's writing, and was limited to talking about the subjects that Mike pursued. He was waiting; he suspected that it was a version of the honeytrap. But that involved the entrapment of a foreign agent and he was certainly not an agent.

One day, Mike seemed more restless than ever; he drank half a pint, left the mug on the table, fiddled with it, chatted a bit of nonsense, and said, 'I say, there's someone I would like you to meet.'

'Why would I want to meet someone?'

'He said he would be interested to meet you.'

'What does he know of me?'

'Oh, he's a friend of the Vicar. That's what he told me.'

Was this the Vicar's introduction, the work that he might find 'interesting'? Or was it a trap?

'Well,' said Mike. 'You don't have to meet him, but he is very keen to meet you.'

'Why doesn't he come in here?'

Mike paused; he had not envisaged this question, and looked around as though the answer was hanging in the air. Then he said, 'He's in a car outside. He can't park, he's waiting there.'

Berndtt considered walking away, but recognised that it might mean running again. And suddenly he felt weary of the games, of the subterfuge and pretence; he had no Francine, he had no job or meaningful pursuit and he turned towards the door. After he had finished his drink, while Mike stood up, sat down, fidgeted with his glass, his clothes, talked little.

Outside, there was a large black car drawn up in a parking bay, a Ford. Mike opened a back door for Berndtt and closed it on him, a particular click. He went round the car and sat in the driver's seat. Next to Berndtt was a man, tall, a straight back, toothbrush moustache, short grey hair, a grizzled complexion; Berndtt recognised the type at once. An army man. He was wearing a British warm and leather gloves, brown. The only things missing were a swagger stick and cap.

'Ah, there you are. Do I call you Bernard or Berndtt?'

Berndtt tried his door. It was locked.

TWO

The army man gave a brief laugh, more of a snort. 'Well, you sound like a German, so I used your German name. What did your father call you?'

Berndtt was silent; he was wondering what was going on.

'Excuse me; bad manners, what? Captain Smith, at your service.' He offered a hand, the glove stripped off. Berndtt looked at it. A large hand, he took it; soft, as he suspected. This man had not been much in the field. The grip was firm, unnecessarily firm, as though he was to be impressed. He said nothing.

'Corporal, drive on.'

'Where to, Sir?' said Corporal 'Mike'.

'Just drive. Back here in sixty minutes.' And to Berndtt, 'That should do it, what?'

The car pulled away smoothly; one of Berndtt's neighbours stopped and stared as they drove off. Berndtt wondered what would be said in the pub; it didn't matter much, but it wouldn't help his integration into local society. He gazed out of the window; there was light cloud, little wind. A flat uninteresting day.

'You might be wondering why I've chosen to meet you in this fashion. I do not intend to kidnap you, no, not in the least.' Another snort. 'But I thought you might choose to leave us before you had heard me out.'

Berndtt looked out of the window; they were coming onto the A4, about to pass under the Clifton Suspension Bridge. He peered up; there were cyclists passing over.

'Young Mike here tells me that you have an interesting past. Can you tell me about it?'

Berndtt swivelled in his seat; the Captain had a bluff confident look. Berndtt considered wiping it off his face, a quick movement that would leave the Captain unconscious that 'Mike' would be in no position to prevent.

'You have locked me into your car, removed me on false premises from my friends and are now driving me away from where I live. I am still waiting to hear what you want from me.'

'I say, old boy, I'm frightfully sorry. There was no intention to upset you; on the contrary. It's just that I wanted to have a rather confidential chat with you. Not the sort of thing to spout about in front of people, what?'

'Then talk.' Berndtt sat back, his arms folded. He was getting bored with this idiot.

'The Vicar is a friend of mine. He told me that you might consider some work that takes you away from your rather quiet life of retirement and uses your undoubted skills. Whatever they are; he seemed to have a better idea than I do.'

Berndtt waited.

'It's not very easy to describe the work; let us say that it involves a reasonable degree of activity outside normal legal restraints, but working on the side of the angels.'

Berndtt looked at him. The Captain was frowning, his hands were gripped and he looked out of the window, avoiding meeting Berndtt's eyes. What was it? The mention of angels, or his inability to describe the work that made him embarrassed?

'You see,' he continued, 'I represent an organisation that works for the Crown under a rather special and not very public profile.'

Now we get to it, thought Berndtt; Army intelligence or something. Could be an interesting way to spend my time and, if the Conglomerate were ever to catch up with me, a good defence.

'Of course, you would be told all about it by someone else; if you are interested to know more, I could put you in touch. Otherwise, you are of course free at this very moment.'

Berndtt looked out; they were speeding down the A4.

'Take me back, please.'

The Captain instructed 'Mike' to turn round. Berndtt said nothing on the return trip. As they neared his area, he asked the car to stop. 'Mike' ran around the car and opened his door, avoiding his eyes. He looked embarrassed to have been involved.

Berndtt stepped out and leant back into the car.

'Tell Mike to meet me in the usual pub in one week's time exactly. I'll give him my reply.'

'Just one thing,' said the Captain. 'Before you go any further, you would have to sign the Official Secrets Act.'

Berndtt walked away.

The following week did nothing to convince Berndtt that he should stay in the parish, mending the church, drinking at the pub, and sitting alone at home. He tried travelling into

Wales, visiting the cities and walking the valleys. He tried spending all day in the pub but just felt uncomfortable. He joined a gym and spent some hours on the treadmill, working up a sweat; he felt virtuous and bored. It did help his fitness, but at too great a cost. He joined in every activity of his neighbours that he could, including picking litter, and felt that it was all a waste of his abilities. He considered talking to the Vicar; he was beginning to suspect that the Vicar had been sparing in describing his own career. Perhaps he had been involved in Army Intelligence or some similar organisation; it did not seem unlikely. What had he seen in him, he wondered?

The neighbours were an interesting lot on the whole, though rather young, babies and small children in attendance. They had almost all attended university and worked in a variety of places, schools, banks, lawyers' offices, the University, and shops. There was one, Fergus, who had read languages at Warwick and taught at the University. He had talked to Berndtt about Germany, asked him about his own career, where he had learnt the mining business. He was a happy man, not worried about the world situation, hoping for German Reunification; he was sure that it would come in ten years or so; the world was waiting for it, and so were the Germans. What would the Russians do? Probably approve it.

The following week he sat in the pub; the crowd of neighbours was subdued. One had been diagnosed with breast cancer and the women were conferring with each other in whispers, while their husbands sat nursing a single pint and being unable to think of anything to say after consoling the unfortunate husband. Berndtt did not know them well enough to join them and found that the whole business was entirely outside his experience. He had no idea how fatal the diagnosis could be.

The door opened and a subdued Mike entered. He looked across at Berndtt and silently signalled, indicating an empty table. Berndtt did not move. Mike went to the bar and returned to the empty table, drinking alone. After a while, Berndtt joined him.

'Well, Corporal, have you brought your Captain today?'

Mike gave him a grudging look, ducking away from Berndtt's eyes.

'What regiment are you?'

'Er… Signals, actually.'

'And I guess that your name is not Mike.'

'Er… no.'

'In that case, I'll call you Corporal.'

Mike gulped beer and sat watching Berndtt.

'Your Captain,' said Berndtt, 'did not give me much detail about the work.'

'Er… no.'

'Well, it is difficult for me to reach a decision. Perhaps you should tell him that. He's outside, isn't he?'

'No… well, he's not far away.'

'Well, I suggest you fetch him so we can have a frank discussion.'

Mike looked mortified; he had obviously been sent to obtain a quick reply and now he was acting as a runner between the two men. His Captain would not be happy; he was not used to receiving orders. Particularly through a Corporal.

'Could you… come outside?'

Berndtt gave a cold stare. It worked and Mike shied away as though he was scorched. He got up and disappeared outside. There was a lengthy pause; Berndtt considered rejoining his friends. Eventually, there was a shuffle at the door. Mike was standing to attention holding it open.

A pause.

Then the Captain entered, ramrod stiff back, his coat firmly buttoned, face frozen. He stopped inside the door, barked something at his Corporal, and strode over to Berndtt. He remained standing. Berndtt ignored him. The Captain was nonplussed as though he had just discovered that he had walked into the wrong place. With a loud harrumph, he sat down. A barmaid came up to him and asked him, Was there anything I can get you, dearie? He ignored her completely, looking at Berndtt.

'I thought I made myself clear last week. And now you send my Corporal running around like a headless chicken requiring my attention. Perhaps,' he said in a chill voice, 'you could tell me what was not clear.'

Berndtt looked at him, gazed away as though bored and said in a lifeless tone, 'Perhaps you would tell me what you were talking about.'

'I thought I made myself perfectly clear.'

'Something about activity outside normal legal parameters. Doesn't say much.'

The Captain coughed, looked in turn furious, knowing, and then perplexed.

'Can't say more than that. Official Secrets and all that.'

For the first time, Berndtt started to wonder whether the Captain had any idea what he was recruiting for. The Captain took a small pad and a propelling pencil out of his jacket inner pocket, sat very upright, harrumphed once more, gave Berndtt a piercing look and wrote two words on a clean sheet, tore it out and pushed it across the table, avoiding beer spills, turning it to face Berndtt with another purposeful harrumph. Berndtt read the words, SECRET AGENT, in large capitals, and stared at the Captain, who looked embarrassed as though he had been caught canoodling with a barmaid. The Captain immediately withdrew the piece of paper and screwed it up into a tight little ball that he put into his inner pocket with the pad and pencil. Berndtt laughed.

The effect on the Captain was unexpected; at first he looked shocked, then he gave an unearthly grin. Berndtt could imagine that grin being delivered to some poor subaltern before punishment was issued.

The Captain rose, turned on his heels as though on parade and strode to the door; halfway there, he stopped, raised a gloved hand to his forehead and turned. Berndtt had remained, facing away from the door. The Captain walked, rather than marched, back to Berndtt and, bending stiffly forward from the waist, spoke quietly into his ear.

'Any idea, eh? Got an inkling of an idea whether you are interested?'

Berndtt swivelled in his seat, looked up at the Captain, and said, 'Take it to the next stage. Let me know.' And turned back to his drink. The Captain stood upright, turned as before and marched to the door, already held open by 'Mike' who scuttled after him.

This activity had not gone unnoticed in the pub. There were some amused comments directed at him from his neighbours, a few quips about how they always knew he was an army deserter, and laughter in which he did not join. Fergus gave him a meaningful look. But he returned to their table, withstood the teasing silently and bought the next round.

A week later he found himself driving to an army base in Wiltshire; he had received his directions from 'Mike' at home. There had been a ring on the door at nine in the evening. Berndtt did not like evening callers; they tended to be trouble. 'Mike' had handed him a sealed envelope, plain white but stiff, A4 size, and retreated without saying anything. Berndtt heard him drive away.

In the envelope there was a letter, a pass and an official form, something to do with the Official Secrets Act. The letter ran as follows:

> Dear Mr. Lipmann,
> Further to your exploratory discussions with Captain Smith, please report to the Signals Base at Lt. Wandike at 3pm on Monday 3 September.

There had been nothing else: no date, no name, no heading. But it did refer to Captain Smith, who probably did not give his actual name, and to 'discussions'; Berndtt could recall no discussions, only the ludicrous little note pushed across the table and hastily withdrawn. It would not change things; he had decided what to do after Mike's first approach. But he wanted to test the waters, to see what calibre of official they, whoever 'they' were, used to recruit. On the whole, he decided that the Vicar had done the recruiting.

It did not appear to be a large base; there were a number of two storey brick buildings, built in the usual Ministry of Defence style, a larger number of Nissen huts dating from the last War, and a large field, no doubt for helicopter landings. The roads were paved, concrete kerbs, mown grass between, mature trees. There were a number of Army vehicles, vans, some with odd aerials sticking out of the top, Land Rovers, even one tracked personnel carrier and private cars. Passing through the gates and a high fence, he was scrutinised at the guardhouse, checked against a list and told to wait in a parking area close by. The armed sentry looked at him with suspicion and warned him against getting out of his car. He sat there for half an hour and was just about to remonstrate with the man when an officer appeared, bearing a clipboard; the clipboard evidently had a photograph on it as he compared it with Berndtt. Berndtt gave him an icy look and he retreated, leaving Berndtt for a further fifteen minutes. He was wondering whether to simply drive away when the officer returned.

'This way. Bring your bag. Lock your car.'

Berndtt followed him to a general parking area where there was a closed three ton van parked among the other Army vehicles. The officer opened the rear door, said Get in, closed the door on him, and left. Berndtt was sitting in the dark, a bench seat running down one side. Far from being alarmed, he began to find amusement in his situation. Nobody had welcomed him, nobody had introduced themselves and there was no sign of Captain 'Smith' or the Corporal. He was good at waiting; he sat still for an hour, listening to movements outside. Eventually, the door was opened again, and Corporal 'Mike' climbed in.

'There's about an hour's drive; I hope you won't be too uncomfortable. Do you have your bag? Good. Well, cheerio!' He hopped out, closed the door, and walked away. Shortly after Berndtt heard a driver climbing into the cab and the journey started.

Berndtt had observed the wind direction while driving over; it had been a beautiful afternoon, white puffy clouds speeding across the sky, a strong south-westerly breeze. He felt the van leaving the base, the Bedford engine accelerating; he found that he could tell the direction they were going by listening to the wind when they stopped at junctions. Even on straight roads he could feel the van leaning from the wind. The driver had no concern for a passenger in the back; he drove as though the van was empty, swinging around the bends, braking late at the junctions, and accelerating hard when he could.

Before long, they ran onto a major road running east; Berndtt could hear the traffic overtaking, and lorries in the slow lane. Estimating their speed at 50 mph, he timed the journey and came to the conclusion that they travelled fifty miles before turning off at a junction. They drove north, slower, probably 40 mph, for half an hour, a road with many bends, and turned off left onto a loose gravel surface. The wind was ahead of them. They stopped, the engine running; there was a pause, some conversation. Then the van drove on at a slow speed, turned abruptly and stopped.

On the basis that a soldier should take his rest when he can, Berndtt had stretched out on the floor, jammed against a bench, his head on his bag, and relaxed. The officer who opened the door was surprised to see his new recruit apparently completely at ease; he coughed, resisted the temptation to bark an order, and held the door while Berndtt leisurely stood up and recovered his bag.

He paused before jumping down. Ahead of him was an old country house, quite large, red brick, twisted chimneys, tiled roof. The windows looked antique, and there was a slight air of neglect over the place, grass growing from the gutters in some places. To one side were some structures of differing sizes, mainly timber clad, felt roofs. All was set in a large park, a high fence with barbed wire along the top just visible in the distance. There was nobody around; the place looked deserted apart from the officer who opened the van door. He followed him to the big house; the officer called it the Hall. Arriving in the hall, he was invited to wait; a chair was indicated but Berndtt chose to wander, examining the architecture, peeping through open doors, reading notices, and wondering where the toilets were. The Hall was quiet, apart from a low conversation in the room where the officer had gone. After a while, the officer reappeared and called to Berndtt, who requested the toilet. He was shown to a room just off the Hall, unnamed; the window was high up and there were no locks on the two cubicles. Returning to the Hall, he found the officer standing to attention, obviously impatient at the delay. He ushered Berndtt into a large room.

It had been a drawing room; perhaps it was still. The walls were panelled, old dark oak, the ceiling low with carved beams, mullioned lead glazed windows looking out onto a part of the park that was not cluttered with sheds. Mature trees spread their branches over an expanse of lawn and there were benches, here and there. A flock of sparrows passed the window, chattering noisily. At one end of the room was a huge fireplace, complete with irons and fire basket, a darkened beam over, sofas and armchairs. At the other was a desk behind which sat an Army officer, pips on the shoulders, looking relaxed. He watched Berndtt taking in the room, the view, and waited. Berndtt found it refreshing, another man who waited.

After five minutes or so, after he had examined the bookshelves, the pictures, mostly regimental photographs of differing decades, the carpets and the furniture, Berndtt sat at a chair across the desk from the Officer, pulling his chair round so that he sat at ninety degrees to the man, looking out of the window. He relaxed, his right arm resting on the desk, and crossed his legs.

'Bernard Lipmann? How do you do. I'm Colonel Grant, the commanding officer of this establishment. Can I help you?'

Berndtt found it an odd question; he had been conveyed some sixty miles in a closed van to an unknown destination and now was asked whether he could be helped.

'Captain Smith, or whatever he is called; is he your recruiter?'

'Not often.'

'And Corporal "Mike"?'

'Never heard of him.'

'And the Vicar in Bristol?'

'Nice man.'

Berndtt looked at the Colonel; he was younger than he expected, hair not too short by Army standards, a twinkle in his eye. He gazed out of the window again, waiting.

After a while, the Colonel got up from his seat, came

around the desk and sat at another chair, facing Berndtt. He looked at him with interest.

'I had a chat with your Vicar. Nice man. He had an interesting theory, that you have been involved with military at some point, probably not a field regiment, possibly more on the secret side. Does that sound possible to you?'

'I was a mining engineer.'

'And where was that?'

'Europe, mainly.'

'Not this country?'

'No.'

'Not a military man, then?'

'No.'

There was a pause; the Colonel looked amused, a secret amusement that seeped out even though he appeared to be withholding it.

'Well, we may be able to offer you something. If you are no longer descending mines, that is. But I gather that you are retired. Helping the Vicar on the Church, that sort of thing. You would have to sign the Official Secrets Act that was delivered to you, and you would need to go through scrutiny, initiation, and a certain amount of physical examination and exercise. I would not want you to be misled. Alternatively, we can return you to your car, unfortunately by sealed van, but you would be entirely free to go.'

Berndtt looked at him calmly; he was summoning up his life in a few minutes. Escaped from the Conglomerate and losing the only love of his life, he was floating in a life that had no relevance. He could return to his former life, and the idea was repugnant to him, killing for no personal reason except that somebody wanted it done; yes, he had been good at it, no doubt, but it palled on him. He had to admit that he felt no great sense of obligation, of fighting for Great Britain; the thought of serving the Queen was meaningless. And yet the thought of living a life of some risk and using his hard-earned skills did attract. He had no hope of returning to Francine, which would change everything, but she had made it clear that she could not live with him.

'Can you give me some idea of what work I might do, after the initiation?'

'Not really. It's secret, on the other side I might say. We would give you all the training needed, but would still need your dedication. You may have to put your life on the line, make no bones about that.'

Berndtt said nothing.

'Have a glass of something; whisky?' The Colonel poured two stiff measures and offered one to Berndtt. He sipped it; he was not a regular drinker. It would have interfered with his life.

'OK,' he said. 'Let's take it to the next stage.'

'When you have been initiated, you would be unable to leave us for three years. It's a three year service contract; after that, it is possible to leave with a pension. But maybe you are not too concerned about the remuneration.'

Berndtt said nothing. After a few minutes, he took out the form in his pocket, leant on the desk, signed it and passed it to the Colonel. The Colonel stood, shook his hand and told him that if he had any questions or concerns, he could always come and talk to him.

'Welcome to my unit. You'll learn more in due course. And now you will be wanting to settle in. Sergeant!' He called at a parade ground volume.

The sergeant was a powerful man, in his forties, obviously a long-term Army man. His face was expressionless as he examined Berndtt, briefly. He saluted the Colonel smartly, clicking his heels, and gave Berndtt a brief indication to follow him. Berndtt was shown to a hut, his room indicated, told to make himself presentable, and the hour that he should present himself for the evening meal. And not to talk to anyone. New boys are silent, understood? The next day is Scrutiny; he should attend at eight am at Hut H. Lateness is unacceptable.

Berndtt smiled; the sergeant did not like it and told him directly in words of few syllables and that until he was initiated, he was his Sergeant and should remember to address him correctly. Understood? Berndtt sat on the bed, and was informed directly that beds are not for sitting. Stand up!

THREE

'Rise and shine. Two circuits of the Park, a few press-ups and so on. Move!'

Berndtt stretched, and looked at his watch: 5.00 am. He didn't mind waking early. It had been part of his routine but he was not accustomed to being treated like a raw recruit. It had been many decades since he had been a young soldier in the Stasi. He considered felling this ox of a man; the sergeant was not tall but square, a mass of muscle, and he would probably enjoy a tussle with the new recruit, teaching him a few lessons. He would not give him the satisfaction.

He rolled over in bed. 'Got the wrong man. Leave me in peace, please.'

The bedclothes were whipped off the bed and Berndtt's ankle was taken in a steely grip. Berndtt found himself flying through the air to land on the floor. He sat up, rubbing an elbow.

'I said, leave me alone.' He picked up his bedclothes and buried himself under them on the bed.

'I think you may be under some misunderstanding, Mister Lipmann. You have submitted to be a recruit here, I am informed, and it is my job to be your sergeant until you are initiated into the clan, after which I shall salute you, show you the greatest deference, and otherwise kow-tow to you. But, until that time, you are mine; it is my duty to ensure that you go through all due processes to qualify for your work in this unit. And you call me "Sergeant". Is that clear?'

Berndtt was silent. What a bore, he thought. 'How long is this going to go on?'

'That depends upon you. The fastest qualifications have taken no more than three months, some twice that.' The sergeant grinned in an unpleasant way, his thumbs tucked into his belt.

'I didn't sign up for your attention. Leave me; I shall talk to the Colonel.'

'Until then, you will do as I say, or you will be shot as a deserter.' The sergeant grinned again.

'Not possible. I haven't deserted.'

'You would be the first recruit who has chosen to spend his first day in the guardhouse.'

Berndtt rose slowly, washed and dressed. He was wearing his usual slacks, shirt and a leather jacket. He bent to put on his shoes.

'Am I to understand that you have not attended on the department for uniform and dress?'

'I'm not joining the Army. I thought I had made that clear.'

'Well, I am terribly sorry,' rolling the 'r's aggressively, 'but you will need more suitable clothing for these activities.'

Berndtt was taken to another hut; there was nobody present but the sergeant found the necessary clothes, instructed Berndtt what to wear on what occasion, and led him out on a gentle run, twice around the park.

Scrutiny at last. He had submitted to the sergeant's routines and eaten breakfast in silence while surveying the other personnel there. A mixed lot; some were in uniform but many were not and several were even older than him. The conversation was general, muted, and there were many glances in his direction.

Scrutiny was in a room in the Hall; he was directed there by the sergeant, who instructed him to sit upright and answer questions as asked. The sergeant withdrew. He looked around. A pleasant room looking out onto the park, panelled and beamed as the other room, but smaller. No pictures. One desk with three chairs behind, one chair for him; a stiff upright chair. He strolled over to the window. A blackbird was calling. The sun was warm, puffy white clouds.

It was at moments like this that some random memory from the past broke into his consciousness. There was the banker in Italy, so keen to obtain his business, awful wallpaper, slick suit, modern desk uncluttered by paperwork. And the secretary outside. Such a mess, his elimination. Then the hillside with the girl who wished to recruit him. Was she innocent of any crime? He had not thought of innocence or guilt, of the need to eliminate or not. Why were these thoughts creeping into his mind now?

The door opened; two officers came in.

'Blast! Where's Peter? Well, I suppose we can make a start. Do sit down, Mr. Lipmann.' They settled themselves, pushed a few papers around, put them into a folder, laid out a clean pad and a pen. 'Now Mr. Lipmann. Start at the beginning, shall we? Full name, date of birth, place of birth, please.'

'Martin Bernard Lipmann, born 7 June 1935, Walsall.'

'And your father's details?'

That was easy; Berndtt was following the sensible route of using the truth as often as possible. 'Frederick Lipmann, 3 February, 1905, Augsburg, I think.'

'His occupation?'

'Bus driver.'

'Of course, he was too young to be fighting in the First War. Your mother?'

'Frau Mathilde… er… I don't remember her birth name or place of birth.'

'No matter.'

And so it continued; when his parents had left Germany, 1934, primary education, Walsall. Secondary education, Walsall. Tertiary education, apprenticed to a mining firm; he gave a name. They gradually fleshed out his past so that he came to believe it. Much time was taken as they laboriously wrote out his answers, longhand.

Lunchtime. The sergeant was waiting outside the door, took him to lunch, and afterwards to a physical examination.

More questions: general health, any drugs taken, now or in the past, what did his parents die of, bombing in the War, and a can of worms opened in Berndtt's mind. What date had they been killed?

1943, October.

In which case, he hadn't mentioned his adoptive parents to the interrogators. Or even created a history of them. Perhaps this questionnaire would not get back to them.

He had to strip. The nurse's eyes grew large; his physique was that of a professional cyclist, rather than a weight-lifter. He was very fit and was put through a number of exercises with equipment. He had too much knowledge to be given away; he feigned weakness at some point and the doctors gave him a canny look, but said nothing.

An early supper and he was taken back for further examination. This session concentrated on his knowledge of Europe, his attitudes in politics and history. He was not well read and only occasionally read newspapers; he could not satisfy them on many subjects, putting on a blank face. He pretended little knowledge of Europe; though they delved into his mining career, he said he knew nothing of the areas he had visited, whether it was the Ruhr, Czechoslovakia, or North Italy.

He had not expected the degree of questioning; he had assumed that they would be glad of his skills, happy to take him on and put him to work. Why did they question him so? He asked and was told that it was essential that they knew the agents inside out before trusting them with the security of the country. It was the first time that anyone had mentioned agents. It was bizarre; he had carried out many commissions in Europe without anyone checking his past or preferences, as far as he knew.

Secret agent! He had never considered that life, though he supposed that, as a Stasi agent, he had been secret. Did it mean that he was going to be working for the British Secret Service? He had never thought that it would get to that, not part of the Secret Service; he had assumed that he would be an offshoot of Army Intelligence, whatever that meant. He did not question it, waiting to see what would materialise.

The day ended with a short film, showing a variety of jobs that trained agents might be required to carry out. They asked him, very casually, to which of the tasks he had been most attracted. He had given a vague answer, not committing himself. They laughed, said they understood; it was early days, they were sure he would realise his strengths and weaknesses to help him identify a path, a career.

The next day, he was ready for the sergeant; he did not argue or even talk but trotted around the park, carried out his exercises, all without much enthusiasm or drive. Breakfast was the same; a general regard of suspicion. Later, he sat in front of the interrogators, wondering what further questions they had.

Peter had appeared; a young man with sharp features and longish hair, he was dressed in mufti, a casual shirt open at the collar, linen jacket and slacks. He sat very relaxed, leaning back in his seat, often gazing out of the window. None of the interrogators had introduced themselves but regarded Berndtt with the greatest goodwill, as though they were there to help him.

The questions were repeated as the day before; he told them his name, his date of birth, his place of birth, protesting that he had given all this information. They smiled, assured him that it was part of the routine, and continued. When he had completed his record of education and apprentice, there was a pause. The officers muddled through their papers, and whispered to Peter, who laughed.

'So you say that you were born in Walsall,' he said, 'and that your parents were killed in bombing.'

'Yes.' Berndtt sensed a change in atmosphere. Why did it matter where he was born or what happened to his parents?

The leading officer leant forward, a sympathetic look, fixing Berndtt with his eyes. 'That is not quite correct, is it?'

'Oh, have I got the dates wrong?'

'That is not quite what I meant.'

Berndtt was silent, waiting.

'In fact, you were not born in Walsall. I mean, as far as I can make out. That is correct, is it not?'

Berndtt was silent, again.

'I mean, we are quite ready to believe that Bernard Lipmann, or Berndtt – Whatever, was born on that date. But you see, Martin Lipmann was killed in the bombing with his parents, and the secondary school has no record of your attendance. And as for the mining firm, I suspect that it was a fabrication.'

Berndtt looked at them; he was weighing up the pros and cons of telling them more truth, but certainly not the whole truth. There were secrets that he would bury very deep, and he could only protect them by going some way to satisfying the interrogators. He looked them at them directly, almost a challenge.

'So, Mr. Lipmann, or perhaps I should say, Berndtt, who are you?'

Berndtt wondered how much they knew; he was sure that they had the means of finding out, either through their own intelligence or by more brutal means.

'Does it matter?' he said.

Peter burst into loud laughter; the two officers looked embarrassed, though whether at Peter or at Berndtt's comment it was impossible to say.

'Well,' said the leader. 'It may not matter to you, which is an interesting philosophical point of view, but unfortunately it does matter to us. As I have explained.'

Berndtt looked out of the window; a man was mowing.

The puffy white clouds blew over, the distant hills were blue. All looked very pretty and peaceful. Why on earth had he submitted to this torture when he had only been looking to find a bit of interesting action?

'Now,' said the leading officer, quite gently. 'There may be very good reasons why you do not wish to reveal who you are; you may be a criminal seeking a safe harbour. You may be running from the Interpol. You may be running from a wife; oh yes, we have had those! You may be an illegal immigrant. So you see, we need to know where you come from, and whether you are legal, whatever your name, and whether we can use you. Or pass you to the police for processing.'

Give them a little, let them work for the rest, well, some of the rest. 'OK. I was christened Berndtt Grundburg. I was born on the 7 June 1935, in Augsburg. My father was as I told you, my mother also.'

'So, tell us more about your education.'

Berndtt had no difficulty in revealing his primary and secondary education, but faltered at the time that his parents were killed in bombing in Berlin.

'It is the War; you are living in Berlin with your parents. You have siblings?'

'Siblings?' Berndtt's English is good, learnt over decades, but some words escape him. Sibling? It sounds like something unpleasant, or legal. He is sure he has neither.

'Yes; brothers, sisters?'

Ah. 'An older brother, killed on the Eastern Front. My sister disappeared when the Russians came into Berlin.'

'And you were about ten. What did you do?'

'Survived.'

'But only a small boy?'

Berndtt was silent; what could he reveal safely?

'Were you Hitler Youth?'

Aah! What the hell! After all this time. 'We all were; it was a way to survive, food and shelter.'

'And after the War, when occupied by Russians?'

'They took everything. We starved.'

'But you survived.'

'Yes.'

'And?'

Berndtt was silent, gazing out of the window, remembering the worst years of his life. 'There were dormitories for orphans.'

'But not nice dormitories, not like school dorms, I dare say. When did school restart?'

'Not long after; they had to keep us off the streets, out of trouble.'

'You were good at schoolwork.' Not a question.

Berndtt was remembering the years at school and college; how he had survived by a mixture of learning and 'managing' the boys who would descend and beat for any advantage, a coin or food. He learnt to negotiate, and when that failed, to beat them and escape; an important lesson, the evasion or escape after the battle. Stupid boys would stand over the vanquished waiting for punishment from the authorities, grinning with satisfaction. Until they stood before the Teacher.

'So, after school, what college, and what discipline?'

Berndtt named the college, and said how he started on a career in mining technology.

They took him over this stage of his life again and again, until the sergeant appeared to see him fed and put through a gruelling series of exercises, set by a team of three, who stood watching him and making notes on clipboards.

The evening session, after supper, was a repeat of the night before. Berndtt had become withdrawn, a stony expression, answers brief and uncommunicative. The interrogators looked tired; Peter was not there and they stopped the session early. They probed, in particular, the period of Berndtt's life directly after the War, the next ten years; attitudes towards the Russians, the emergence of the East German state, the behaviour of the Germans under an authoritarian state, the role of the police, Army and the Stasi.

Day three.

Berndtt sat in his hard chair, as before, but he was changing. No longer casual about what work they might give him but now defensive, mourning the freedom that he had enjoyed in Bristol. He had one more bargaining piece of information to give them, if they carried on mining his depths, one that carried danger and problems. But deeper, his more recent history festered and he knew that to reveal that would be the end of his life.

They started, as before, by running over his birth date, place of birth, parents' occupations, place of residence, schools and college, his special subjects; most of the interrogation was carried out by the other officer. They talked mainly in an even tone, as though bored or not believing, and Berndtt made the usual brief responses, to confirm and only to elaborate when pushed: the name of his teacher when he was twelve, his best friend at college.

There was a break; coffee was brought in, the

interrogators disappeared and the sergeant and two other men came in, chatting to each other and Berndtt about the weather, girlfriends, anything unimportant and trivial. Berndtt did not relax.

The interrogators returned.

Berndtt was directed to his chair. The other three men were somewhere behind him, seated or standing; he was not going to give them the satisfaction of looking. The leading officer led the interrogation.

'Berndtt, we have determined to give you one opportunity to tell us where you worked, and what unit you were with. We are prepared to believe the story of your young life, even up to college. But we are not convinced of the mining story; do you wish to enlighten us?'

Berndtt looked at them; Peter was now sitting up, looking at him like the other two, as though they were prepared to pounce on him and wondered how much they would need to hear. He became aware of the role of the three men behind him.

'No, I did take interest in mining but there was no work that I could apply for, so I went in to the police.'

'What rank, what station?'

He told them everything about his police career, omitting that it had lasted barely two years. They took him back over it again and again, and pushed for more information. How was it that he had remained at a low rank until he retired? Did he expect them to believe it?

And they produced a photograph.

He had not seen it for many years and he knew that he was in it.

'1957,' said the leading interrogator. 'Your final year at Stasi College. We know you were there; German intelligence has been very useful. Which one are you?'

Berndtt could see it; there he had sat, between two 'friends' third row from the front, four places in from the right.

'That's you, isn't it?' The officer was pointing to third row from the front, four placed from the left. Berndtt nodded; what did it matter which was his mugshot? He was revealed as a Stasi agent, the arch enemy no doubt of the British Secret Service.

'What are you doing in England? We believe that you are a sleeper. I am sure you know what that is; I don't know the German for it. But we don't understand how you could expect to be enrolled here when you must have known that we would find out your background.'

'I retired about five years ago, and was living in France.'

'Place, dates?'

Berndtt provided them. 'They will remember me.'

'And why didn't you reveal yourself to the authorities so that you could become a French citizen?'

'I didn't need to; I had all the papers I needed.'

'And papers for England too, I assume?'

'Yes.'

'And what do you want? Why did you come here?'

Berndtt looked at them, in turn; Peter was grinning, as though he shared the joke, that a Stasi agent should walk into open arms.

'I was bored. The Vicar suggested that there might be something I could do. The Captain recruited me, with his Corporal. Now you seem keener on locking me up; I am not a member of the Stasi. I retired from them; their work in France was boring and pointless and I could not continue to hold their values. I have not been an agent for years.'

There was a pause; the leading officer looked stunned, as though the ceiling had fallen in. He shook his head as though to clear away all of Berndtt's last statement.

'In England, old agents may retire, but they remain on the list. In case they are needed.'

'But I did not return to East Germany; the Stasi have not looked for me, they are afraid that they might just lose an agent eliminating me.'

'They have no records for you for a long time. What were you doing?'

'For a while, I was a sleeper, travelling around France, still carrying out my work. But my instructions came from a different source; I don't know where, but I suspected Russia.'

'We shall look into it.' The Captain stared at Berndtt; what was he thinking? He rallied, summoned the sergeant and told him to lock Berndtt in the guardhouse.

To Berndtt, he said, 'We shall talk further; obviously, we shall expect you to tell us a great deal of information about the Stasi. But at present, for your safety as well as ours, we are going to confine you.'

The sergeant, with a look of great happiness, instructed the two soldiers to take Berndtt in hand and make sure he did not get away; and to watch out! He's dangerous! Berndtt shook them off but walked quietly between them. The cell was small and cold, and the door shut with a loud clang.

FOUR

It appeared to be a trial; that is what it felt like.

He sat in his hard upright chair facing the desk. In the centre sat Colonel Grant, the first time he had seen him since arriving. On either side of him were the interrogation team, the two officers and Peter, who was dressed, surprisingly, in a pinstripe suit, white shirt and regimental tie. There were at least four other persons, three men and a woman, in two groups that sat apart either side of the desk. He had been brought in by the sergeant and the two guards who were somewhere behind him. The air was thick; it was clear that the meeting had been going on for some time before he was brought in. The desk was covered with folders.

After leaving the last interrogation, he had been taken back to the guardroom. The guards' radio had played loudly, day and night, and he had been hauled out for further interrogation at all hours. Sometimes there were all three interrogators, sometimes the two officers only; they had gone over all of his story, from his youth to his retirement, and pursued his knowledge of the Stasi, wanting to know everything from the nature of the organisation to the name of officers and agents, and where they were located and what work he was instructed to carry out. He was not always able to help them; he didn't know anything of the Stasi while he was working for himself, but he could not reveal that secret, his own business as a hitman. So he continued the myth, that he had been a deeply hidden Stasi agent in Western Europe, carrying out commissions as instructed through an office that he never visited. All his equipment and other arrangements he had been expected to source himself, to remove any links to East Germany. He felt little compunction about giving them information about the Stasi; he felt that he had moved on and, in any case, the information was probably out of date. They mentioned assassinations in Europe: the French Baron, an Italian bank manager, a pop singer, and an underwater drowning off Cassis. He was surprised that they had so much information; from where had they received it? Was it Interpol? He declared that he had no knowledge of those deaths; his work had been more political. Sometimes Marxist politicians who were not toeing the line, sometimes financial wizards who had cheated the Russians, even Stasi operatives who had failed the organisation.

For four days the same routine, except that on the fourth day he was given a good meal, a bath, a longer walk round the park, and the radio was turned off. He was allowed a long sleep before being allowed to smarten himself and being led like a condemned man to face the Colonel.

The Colonel looked round the room, eye contact with each person except for his guard, and looked directly at him.

'Well, Berndtt, you have surprised us. We still cannot quite understand why you came to us voluntarily, unless you wished to spy on us, but I find that hard to believe; you would have been found out. You have been found out. These gentlemen and lady have been discussing the situation and really there are three alternative ways to move forward. But before I put those to you, I wondered if there was anything that you wished to say.'

There was a silence. Berndtt looked at the Colonel, out of the window, at the floor. The afternoon sun shone onto the desk, dust motes floating in the sunlight.

'Yes. There is something that I should like to say.'

'Then speak.'

Berndtt felt like a man being allowed his last wish before execution. 'I came to you in good faith, after talking to the Vicar.'

'You all know who he is talking about, I hope. His name is in the report,' said the Colonel. A few people opened their reports, ruffling through the pages.

Berndtt continued. 'I have no allegiance to the East and I have been trained in certain arts that I felt might be useful to the country of my adoption. I would not have come if I had realised that my future would have been put in such a dangerous situation.'

'Thank you,' said the Colonel. He looked around the room. 'Does anyone have any question they wish to address to Berndtt?'

There was a long silence. The lady stirred herself and said, 'We should like to know more of his status in his organisation while he was a sleeper in the West. We know of no other agents in that situation and have doubts that the Stasi would have let him off the leash in such a manner.'

'Thank you,' said the Colonel. 'Berndtt, do you have any comment, further to the evidence that you have already given us?'

'I was always a loner, since boyhood. I—'

'You will recall,' said Peter, 'that he was orphaned in Berlin at the age of nine, or ten, towards the end of the War. It is reported in the folder before you.'

'Thank you,' said the Colonel. 'Shall we let Berndtt continue?' The last with a look directed at Peter.

'I was always a loner since late in the War when I was young. The Stasi found that I was best used operating on my own; indeed, they even used me for taking out inefficient agents. The programme to place me in the West was talked about for some years; I was an agent similar to a sleeper but with executive powers.' He felt he had said enough.

'Everyone happy with that?' said the Colonel.

There was a murmur of approval. Then another man stood up and approached Berndtt.

'How am I to know that you are not infiltrating?'

Berndtt looked at him, a sad look and said nothing.

'You see,' said the man, looking down on Berndtt, 'how do we know that he will feel any allegiance to us?'

There was a stony silence; the Colonel looked uncomfortable, the lady tight-lipped, and Peter grinned.

'I think,' said the Colonel, 'that before we go around the houses again and fly a few kites, I should put the three alternatives, and then you can tell Berndtt what you think.'

There was a murmur of agreement.

'Right. Well, the first option is to wash our hands of him and hand him over to the police as an illegal immigrant. Of course, in the present climate, he would probably be naturalised in three years, and we wouldn't have gained anything.

'The second option is to hand him over to the appropriate department, you lot,' he said indicating the woman and the young man beside her, 'and imprison him after trial as a Stasi spy. I don't know whether they would be interested in a swap; perhaps Berndtt would not wish to be sent back to East Berlin but that would hardly be the issue. Probably he would be executed by them, a waste.

'The third option is to turn him, if you consider that he has not already turned. I suppose that we would regard him as a mercenary, in the first instance. I assume that he could be useful to us; an early mission or two should indicate where his loyalties lie.

'Now, any questions to Berndtt before I banish him.'

Shaking of heads all round. At a sign from the Colonel, the guards came up and ushered Berndtt back to the guardhouse, the sergeant in charge.

''Ow does it feel, then,' he said to Berndtt, ''aving your future in their ands?' He laughed and slammed the door once more.

'He's a sleeper, clear and simple.' The young man with the woman, both representing MI6, spoke out with force, throwing his hands in the air. 'Well, really!' His long hair flew in the air, his tweed jacket was unbuttoned, a shirt with no tie, corduroy trousers.

The woman laid a hand on his arm. 'Slow down, John. Less haste, more speed.'

'Anyone else?' said the Colonel, looking around the room. They had all drawn up to the desk, the MI6 couple staying apart from the Ministry boys. Never the easiest of colleagues, they agreed to disagree; however, everyone present knew that Ministry were the bosses and wielded the big stick.

The Colonel, representing Army Intelligence, said, 'He could be useful to us. We don't need to tell him much; we could send him out on single agent missions to infiltrate or execute, whatever. Don't need to tell him more than what he needs, a need-to-know basis. Let him do all the travel arrangements and so on. Only the Army landscape is rather harder to operate in than a civil one; don't you think?'

'Could he be trusted?' The MI6 man was sceptical, his face twisted in doubt.

'Depends how you use him, I would say. Suppose, for example, you sent him out to eliminate a politician in France? If he were caught, we would deny all knowledge, say that he is obviously a loony, shut him up, whatever.'

The Ministry boys were silent. Then one whispered to the other. The Colonel saw and looked offended. 'Can you share? We are all equal here,' he said, without conviction.

There was a bang on the door, which was opened by a Corporal, standing to attention. A tea trolley was wheeled in and the meeting broke up into three groups, private conversations as they sipped and crunched. The Army, although host, was obviously the weakest party in terms of influence. MI6 looked as though it was all a waste of time; they had experienced agents in the field. The Ministry boys, pinstripe suits, highly polished black shoes, club ties and white shirts, were urbane, an overseeing role without any liability, or so they appeared. They also controlled the finances.

The colonel drew them to the desk again.

'I propose that we look at the liabilities first. Now, he came to us and we have interrogated him and also started the physical evaluation. I have to say that he has remarkable abilities, so much so that the doctors saw him holding back on purpose. He is a loner, by upbringing and pursuit, and probably most effective when he is alone. So what is he useful for? Any views?'

John, the young MI6 man, blurted out, 'He is a liability. We would never be able to control him; how do we know what he would get up to? He has not had a thorough investigation or training. Can you imagine—' His companion, the older woman, dressed in an old-fashioned tweed suit and wearing glasses, a prim person with tightly crossed legs, laid a hand on his arm; he was silent immediately, as though a switch had been thrown.

'All that John has said is true. Of course. But,' she paused, looking down as though assembling her ideas spread out before her, 'he could be useful, on a totally deniable basis.'

'Would you like to say how?' said the Colonel.

'One time insertion for execution, for example. Perhaps one time collection of a safe box. Perhaps even a delivery of a sealed bag.'

The Colonel looked around, in particular at the Ministry men. Apart from a glance at each other, they maintained a relaxed silence, sitting back from the desk, crossed legs, an elegant Oxford extended.

'And his training?' said the Colonel. 'Are you happy for us to continue?'

'Oh yes,' she said with girlish enthusiasm. 'We wouldn't want him anywhere near us, our place. In fact, we wouldn't want him at any of our bases. But you can do all the aspects of training, can't you? You have the facilities.'

'We do, it is true,' said the Colonel. 'There is the matter of who runs him, and the small matter of finance.'

One of the Ministry men sat up and coughed; the Colonel leaned forward, eyebrows raised.

The Ministry man coughed, gave an indistinct gesture as though drawing something in the air, and said, 'Totally deniable, you said. Therefore, by definition, he cannot appear on our budgets; you must appreciate that. Of course, you are going to say that there have been exceptions, but the number of exceptions has been rather high, recently.' He sat back with a satisfied look on his face, as though preparing himself for the off.

The other Ministry man grunted, leaned forward, and said, 'What sort of sum are we talking about? I mean, you gave us the profile of a man who is retired with a satisfactory income and looking for some thing to do. Maybe even something for his country of adoption.'

'Ah yes,' said the Colonel. 'There is the matter of his nationality. I suppose that officially he is East German, even if he has not returned to his country for some years. As he said. If we are to believe it. And do we believe his tale of operating in deep cover in Western Europe for the Stasi? He may have been operating on his own behalf.' He looked round. Everyone seemed to be gazing at the floor, or reading from their folders. There was a long silence.

The MI6 lady broke it. 'It would be a pity not to take advantage of it. We are always short of a certain type of agent, and it seems that we have one here. No, I don't think we should lose him, either to East Germany or to the English law courts. As I said, there is no question of allowing him near our places and little chance of financing him; we are always pushed for finances,' here a side look at the Ministry men, 'but we could use whatever might be gained, one way or another.'

One of the Ministry men sat up abruptly, legs placed square in front of him, hands on knees. 'Now, there is no question of us supplying you with more funds; you already—'

'There is always the mole fund,' she said primly.

'Spent up, last I heard.'

The Colonel interrupted. 'If we can be of service here. With a little nod from the Ministry, a small annual allowance for the information or services obtained, I believe we could manage the training and servicing of him as an agent.'

'Totally deniable, I trust.' John was rudely sharp. The Colonel ignored him; his manners suggested that he would have been happy to have him in the barracks for a week to cut his hair, teach him some manners, and dress him with a little more decorum.

'And the information received? Whose would it be?' said John.

The Colonel looked at the lady; the Ministry men looked on.

'We could certainly use it,' she said.

'Then that clears that up,' said the Colonel with some satisfaction.

One of the Ministry men gave an embarrassed cough. 'There is the small question of sharing.'

'I don't think we have a problem of sharing with our cousins there,' he said, indicating the MI6 couple.

'No, that's not what I was talking about. The standing arrangement of sharing with our allies.'

There was an outburst from John. 'Absolutely not. It would be deeply embarrassing if it were not to work out and we would have the Yanks on our backs yet again. No, really, we—'

'Thank you, John. But he is quite right, if you don't mind. We are going to regard this programme as experimental and therefore not for sharing. Beyond us and our hosts here,' she said with a little bow in the direction of the Colonel.

'And,' said a Ministry man with weight, 'if it is totally deniable, I am not sure that we would want to know anything of this programme at this stage. Call it an experimental Army programme, yes? What shall we call it?'

'Ferret!' said John.

The Colonel ignored him. 'Now, let me see; he comes from abroad offering his service to... er... fight for us. How about Perseus? The slayer of monsters.'

'The man or the programme?' said the Ministry man.

'Oh, the man, I think. Let us avoid a programme, and in terms of your contribution to our finances, we shall invoice you for a unexpected piece of listening technology, of which you would not wish to deprive us.'

The Ministry men looked glum; one wrote a note in his folder. 'His nationality? Perseus' nationality?'

'I think he was Greek, wasn't he?' A rare spark of humour from the Colonel. 'Why don't we leave it as it is, and then we will always have a hold on him.'

MI6 smiled, both the young man, a broad grin, and the lady, a tightening of her lips. Ministry nodded, and started to flap their briefcases, button jackets. The Colonel offered them dinner in the Mess; all refused, said they had to be on their way.

'Well, that's taken care of that,' said Colonel Grant. 'I think we have all their blessings to carry on as we like. Any suggestions at this stage?'

'Training should continue, Sir,' said the Captain.

'Of course. And let's have a look at his marksmanship; we might use him in our area of operation.'

'Do you mean a battlefield, Sir?'

'Well I don't see why not. A totally deniable marksman could be very useful.'

'I didn't think that the Ministry had that in mind—'

'Really? I think you all heard; totally deniable. And MI6 would like the 'information'. Well, if there is no "information" as such, what a pity!' The Colonel looked smug, sitting down behind his desk and stretching out his legs. 'Now, if there is anything else…'

'If I may, Sir,' the Captain stood close to the desk, a deferential bow. 'We could lose him on a battlefield. I mean, he might be killed. Shot by a marksman.'

'Oh dear,' said the Colonel with heavy irony.

'But I thought that MI6 and ourselves regarded him as a valuable commodity. In which case, ought he not to be employed in the civil arena, rather than on a battlefield? Sir.' The Captain sat down.

The Colonel looked irritated, then confused. 'I thought they were leaving him to us to employ him. MI6 didn't bend over backwards to help us, and I don't see why we should always be the arse-licking underdogs. In fact, we might keep him to ourselves for a while; MI6 can whistle for him.'

'No Sir, quite Sir. I only meant that we should take greater care of him than exposing him to a battlefield scenario.'

'Well… I see what you mean. Anyway,' he said with a smile, rubbing his hands together. 'There's no hurry to determine that issue, is there? He has his training to complete. I shall be very interested in his marksmanship and also his grasp of European culture. Carry on.'

'May I have your permission, Sir, to explore arenas in which we might use him?' Peter was unusually earnest, his face lit up with excitement.

'Yes, yes, all right. Carry on.'

The officers saluted, including Peter, and left. The colonel gave a grunt, walked over to the window, gazed out at the setting sun, and returned to his desk where he opened a bottom drawer, took out a bottle and glass and poured himself a stiff Scotch.

In his cell, Berndtt slept.

FIVE

A small car cut in front of him, two young male drivers, chatting, looking at each other, not a care in the world. Berndtt slowed, gave them space and smiled; he knew that he would have reacted rather differently a few years ago. And now? Well, what was the hurry, why get all worked up about two young tykes?

He was driving back to Bristol; a few days leave, they told him. Well done, jolly good work on Initiation, splendid marksmanship; best we've ever seen. It is difficult to say how Berndtt had felt through the three weeks that he had taken to complete the course; in many ways, it was a strange recall of many years before, the necessary bullying by the sergeant, the time to practice and shoot without fear of someone shooting at you, the somewhat dated exercises in traversing an urban scenario without drawing attention. And the details of an agent's life: codebooks, alternative personalities that extended beyond simply changing one's name, secret dropboxes, agent masters, back-up services, emergency procedures including extraction. He was taught all these things, though the Colonel told the teachers not to worry too much about extraction; Berndtt would be able to look after himself. He had found the teachers looking askance at him on many occasions as though they were scared of him, as though they knew that he could fell them without sweating. The Combat training was laughable, really. He had held back for fear of damaging a fellow student or teacher. But he did not mind the refresher; it was many years since he had practised unarmed combat. A long distance from his target and a good snipers rifle was vastly preferable.

The fellow students were an odd lot. They came from all nationalities, including Russian. There was even an East German, a young shy boy who had defected from the Army and wanted to get his girlfriend over the Wall. For the most part, they kept clear of Berndtt; he did not drink with them, did not play games of football, did not play card games in the library. The younger ones treated him with a sense of awe mixed with fear when they saw his skills and false bonhomie when thrown into a group activity. There were a few older ones, one woman among them; they seemed more equal with him, partly due to age but also because they had more history behind them; there were a few defectors and a few teachers of Russian and Chinese.

At the end of the Course, the sergeant had taken him aside, called him Sir, saluted smartly and congratulated him on his skills, particularly marksmanship; he hovered as though he was keen to know Berndtt's past but knew he could not press for it. He also gave him a veiled warning, that Berndtt might be pushed too early into difficult missions and that he should not be embarrassed at calling for help. Berndtt said nothing, as usual. His car had appeared, parked by the gate. The tank was full.

It might be thought that Berndtt was glad to return to his home, his freedom and independence. But Bristol meant the past to him now, a time of drifting and perhaps hiding; the 'friends' in the pub and his neighbours all had concerns that were miles apart from his new life. He did not return to the pub, did not seek out anyone's company, but closed up his house, let his neighbour know that he would be away for a good long time – no, he couldn't say how long, but it could be months – and kindly to keep an eye out – no squatters please and would they hold a key in case of any emergencies. He had already ensured that any materials and possessions that pointed to his past were well concealed, beneath floors, in walls, and not in the roofspace.

On the third day, he called upon the Vicar. He found him in the garden, pruning roses.

'Do you know this breed? Marvellous, a deep red flower and what a scent!'

'No,' said Berndtt. 'I've never had time for gardening. Not at home long enough.'

'Well, how are you? I haven't seen you at the Church for a while.'

'You know why?'

The Vicar looked at him beneath bushy white eyebrows, a little quizzical, a sharp intelligent look. He was wearing an old pair of cords, an old tweed jacket, leather patches on the elbows. Eventually, he spoke. 'Ah. So did you receive an offer that tempts you?'

'You know them, don't you? I mean, the officers at the base.'

'I thought it might be just up your street.'

'They seemed to know you.'

'Let's have some tea.' He busied himself in the kitchen

while Berndtt wandered around his study. There were the rowing photographs, the university groups and an oar hanging over the door. The books were a catholic collection, the religious books that he expected, but also novels, a great deal of history, some geography and politics, biographies. The tea came in on a tray and the Vicar settled himself comfortably in his armchair.

'Help yourself to a biscuit. So... you have completed Initiation?'

Berndtt was silent, sipping this odd drink and eating biscuits.

At last, the Vicar stirred himself. 'Yes, I know them. It goes back a long way. Pupils at Cambridge they were.'

'Just pupils?'

'Well ... I assume you've signed? Yes? Good. Very well.' He sat still for a while, gazing at the floor as though to read the patterns of life in the dusty rug. 'I was at Cambridge early in the century, just after the Great War. There were a number of us who wished never to see a war like that again. You can imagine, I'm sure, the loss of friends and relatives, the awful despoliation of English society.' He was silent for a while, an inward look gazing downwards; at a stroke he looked old, the wrinkles around his eyes growing, his mouth tight and downward turned. He stirred. 'So we turned to the Secret Service; it was founded in 1909, but after the War it needed a bit of a tonic. There were some tutors in the Colleges who pointed us in the right direction, who recruited us.'

'And the Church?'

The Vicar laughed. 'That came later, much later.'

'And so you were an agent?'

'I can't really talk about it, if you don't mind. Another chapter in my life.' He gave Berndtt a look of sadness, still and profound.

'And you taught at Cambridge?'

'One of my favourite chapters. A charmed life; it seemed like a reward for the life that went before. But you know,' he smiled, 'we weren't looking for reward, we did it for our country, because we owed it to the country, surviving the Great War. Then after the Service I taught, and then I was sent out for a retirement job, looking after this parish. I'm not much of a parish priest, I'm afraid.'

Berndtt was silent, absorbing the old man's life.

'There is one area that... er... gives me some concern,' said the Vicar. He chewed a biscuit, gazing out of the window. The late sun warmed his little garden, reds and oranges and warm deep shades. A blackbird started up with a strident call.

'You think I'm a spy?' said Berndtt.

The Vicar laughed, long and roundly, looking at Berndtt with some affection. 'No, no. I don't think that. At least, I hope not. No, no indeed. But, and there is a serious but; where do your affiliations lie, as they say? Where, Bernard or should I call you Berndtt, do you belong? Or to whom do you belong? Why should you, an East German, wish to join the Secret Service unless it is as a sleeper?'

So Berndtt was brought up with a start like a pony at a high hedge; 'East German' belonged back there with the interrogators. The Vicar was up to date with his history, no doubt knew about the Stasi and wondered, as the interrogators had, what had occupied Berndtt during the last fifteen years or so. What could he say? What could he do? He turned to look around the room, at the remnants of a personal history with which he had no cultural connection, a very English life exhibited in English mementoes. And he realised that he could appear to be a sleeper, though he had no intention of acting it, no intention of ever returning to East Germany or serving its masters. And yet, in this room, he felt a foreigner, an outcast, a refugee from another culture.

The Vicar was waiting, looking at Berndtt with a special scrutiny, the old eyes as sharp as they had ever been. His tea had grown cold in the cup, a half-eaten biscuit ignored. Berndtt had had difficulty in explaining himself; it had sounded weak and insufficient at the camp. He did not know what to say to this sharply intelligent old man, so much more intelligent than the interrogators.

The Vicar sensed his difficulty. 'Now Berndtt, I could say that none of this will go outside this room, the rules of a confession. Or I could say that I could summon help within minutes to arrest you. But I am reluctant to take those easy paths. Let us explore your motives.'

It was around this time that Berndtt became aware of a person outside, not far from the window; a watcher, probably the person that the Vicar could summon. But he felt no fear or excitement, rather a wish to explain himself to this nice old man, and to delve a little into his experiences.

'Perhaps we could start at the beginning, like a good story. You were in the police, I take it, and transferred to the Stasi. That is correct, isn't it?'

Berndtt nodded; his mind was full of memories, how the Stasi had been more fulfilling than the police. He began to talk, loose sentences, his history interleaved with impressions and some technical talk, equipment used, the

222

training that he received. He felt the old man open up as perhaps the first man he had spoken to for many years who would understand; he must have some knowledge of the Stasi, he reasoned. The Vicar asked the odd question, being careful not to interrupt the flow. And he felt himself stripping away the layers until he was condemning his past masters, describing his work in Europe, passing all of his private work onto the Stasi so that he believed it himself.

'But didn't you doubt their intentions, to carry out assassinations of bankers and students?'

'You have been in the Army.'

'I? Never. My Service was run by the Foreign Office, I think. It's so long ago that I don't really remember. But are you equating the Stasi with the Army?'

'Absolutely. An order was to be obeyed without question.'

'And you obeyed until… when? What happened?'

Berndtt was silent, transposing his departure from East Germany to his own retirement some five years before, after he had met Francine, after he had assaulted Francine's father. So much history to conceal. It might be doubted that Berndtt could continue to conceal it but his only salvation, his only belief in himself, was to hold to his fabrication. It was more than a simple deception; it was a new life for him, hopefully a cleaner life, even if it carried with it challenges and trials. Otherwise, he had told himself, throw me in a gaol and lose the key.

'I don't know; it was a confusing time. There were the pointless murders and a sense that life could not carry on like that. Is it a matter of age? Did you have the same feelings?'

'I do have some idea of what you speak; yes, indeed. Because the life of an agent is never clean. You are involved in all sorts of deceptions, not only of who you are, but how you treat people, sometimes rather awful people, but sometimes entirely innocent ones. Are you surer that this is the life you want? Now, after what you have told me?'

'I didn't know. I thought that…' There was a silence, broken only by the Vicar taking up his biscuit. A crunch. Silence.

'There remains the question of loyalty.' He looked at Berndtt, a serious stare as though he could read Berndtt's mind. It seemed as if he wanted Berndtt to be true, to be loyal to his adopted country, but needed the confirmation of it. 'Do you believe in our messy democracy?'

'I am not political; I do not understand the need to stand for one's beliefs. It seems a luxury and I am new in the country, new enough to be learning still how things work. Sometimes I am astonished at the freedom to express, but does it always translate into a better life? I don't know. I do believe in the freedom to move and act as one wants and there is more of that here than in any country that I have experienced.' A long speech for Berndtt; he gasped slightly.

'But do you want to embroil yourself again in this messy life that I have described?'

'I had not thought of what might be involved. I was bored, thought I might use some of my skills to help my adopted country. But an agent? I don't know.'

'Where are your loves? Have you not loved a country, or a way of life, or a woman?'

Berndtt was silent; he had not expected this line of questioning and it pushed up against him, constrained his thinking and gave him no option but to respond, to face it.

'The Germany that bred me is no longer; I have spent more time in Western Europe. There is nowhere that I can call home at this moment.'

'No women?'

Again Berndtt stopped, looking down afraid that the Vicar would be able to see into his mind. He coughed, looked out of the window; the sun was setting, shining through a cast iron frame that of an instant reminded him of the style of the Parisian café where he met Francine, ducking below her to his enormous embarrassment. And her coolness, no fear but interest.

'There was someone; no longer.'

'But you are pulled still, pulled to some sort of resolution that has not yet arrived.' The Vicar smiled gently, a perceptive look into Berndtt. He sat quite still, his hands resting in his lap. 'What about fears?'

'Fears?' Berndtt was surprised; fears did not come into his reasoning and if he felt fear, it was only to be conquered, set aside so that it did not interfere with the work.

'Did you not feel fear when a student in the Stasi?'

'There were the times swimming underwater, under ice, and one wondered how long one's breath would hold out. Was that fear?'

'A panic of sorts?'

'Never.'

'Then fear later, when you were surrounded or taken by police, or army, or others… ?' 'There was a fear of being taken, but after that…'

'After that?'

Berndtt looked at him; the Vicar was looking back, a look that was at the same time opaque and at the same time a gentle enquiry. There was a long silence.

The Vicar broke it. 'It is normal to feel fear; it acts to strengthen the body, alert your reactions, and so on. I remember it well, in the field. But perhaps you were not in the field in quite the same way.'

'The same way?'

'Yes, collecting intelligence. That was our main purpose.'

Berndtt looked at him. 'Was it difficult? How did you do it?'

'Ah well, that is a whole branch of agent work. You specialise in it, live the fear every day, and go back for more. Your master directs you but never in the field. The field is your area of work and you learn to survive it.'

'And you liked that work?'

'It wasn't a question of liking it; it was to be done, by someone.'

Berndtt turned and looked out of the window; the sun was low. The shadow of the watcher lay over the grass, with a wreath of tobacco smoke.

'There is something,' he said. 'There are some people in France that I have upset; they were looking for me. They are a threat, but not a great one.' Why did I tell him about the Conglomerate, he wondered. What difference can it make?

The Vicar was interested. 'This arose during your work? For the Stasi?'

Berndtt nodded.

'And what sort of people are they? An organisation, possibly illegal?'

Berndtt nodded.

'Linked to any government?'

'No.'

'And could they find you?'

'Possibly.'

'And when they do?'

'I shall be prepared.'

'And if you are occupied with your task?'

'It won't be a problem.'

'Have a care, Berndtt, have a care.' The Vicar was looking at Berndtt with concern, mulling over this new information. 'It's getting late,' he said. And then he appeared to become a stranger, his face closed and remote, his gestures formal and polite. Berndtt rose, bid him farewell without shaking his hand, and left the house. As he did so, he saw a dark figure disappearing round the corner of the house, leaving a slight aura of Virginia tobacco.

Back at the unit, he was thrown into preparation for a mission, without any indication of what it might be. To a great extent, he was kept apart from the main body of teachers, agents, craftsmen, and technicians. He saw Peter and the Captain, the sergeant a few times, but never Colonel Grant, nor the inside of the Hall or the technical workshops. He was given alternative personalities, though he doubted that he could ever conceal his own. They checked his map reading and his own sense of direction, taking him out to Salisbury Plain and leaving him without food or protection to find his own way out. They taught him about safety, houses to go to in France where he would be safe from everybody. They taught him about the reception and placing of messages and a little about the use of the telephone, an alternative language to be used. They made it clear that his position would be entirely deniable by the English Government and that if he was caught by the authorities abroad it would be the end of his work for the Unit. Berndtt smiled when told; the officers thought he was taking the mick and could not realise that Berndtt had been living that life for years. His training in unarmed and armed combat continued, with instruction as to how he was to find a firearm in France. Again, he chose to ignore the advice.

One morning, he was summoned to a small office in one of the sheds. Peter sat behind the desk, the Captain off to one side; there was nobody else present.

'Sit down, Berndtt,' said Peter. 'I gather that your training has gone well; do you have any questions?' He was sitting dead upright, and looked very young.

Berndtt sat back in his chair, crossed his legs, and addressed the Captain. 'Perhaps you could tell me why I am here.'

'Perhaps,' said Peter, with an exaggerated emphasis. 'I should detail the mission that we are considering for you. You have the option of backing out of it at this stage, if you feel it is beyond your capabilities.'

Impertinent little toad, thought Berndtt, talking to me like that. He thought how satisfying it would be to take the lad in a hold and walk him out of the door. But what would it achieve? He said nothing.

The Captain coughed, gave Peter a fierce look and sat back. Peter seemed untouched by the responses of both and waded pompously into his next speech.

'This is a mission of great importance to both the English Government and the French Government. It is to eliminate a character who has been disrupting French negotiations in Africa and our own relations with France; you could say that he is a random element.'

'Name, location, elimination technique required,' said Berndtt, drawing from his own background.

'Well, that is a little tricky. You see, we don't actually know his name, or indeed, where he can be found.'

'The French have named him Le Boucher, The Butcher,' said the Captain. 'He has an unfortunate habit of killing anybody who comes close, particularly anybody with an official backing. We thought that you might appear to be unofficial, even a trained assassin that he might respect. Of course—'

'Of course,' said Peter. 'He might just try to kill you before you have a chance to negotiate.'

'Negotiate?' Berndtt frowned. He had never negotiated with his targets.

'In addition to his disrupting sensitive negotiations, he has a great deal of information on revolutionary groups that we would very much like to share with the French. Of course, you would have to obtain the information and see it safely deposited before you eliminate him. And it would be good if you could make it appear as if he was killed by one of his revolutionary buddies.'

Berndtt stared at him; whoever had thought up this harebrained scheme? Obtain information from a target of that kind? It would be hard enough taking a long shot. A man like that would be surrounded by bodyguards and sycophantic followers. Break it down; perhaps the information could be obtained from one of the revolutionaries. Before he or she was eliminated, of course. A thought flashed through his mind, that the Conglomerate might be glad to see this Butcher eliminated; he probably disrupted their political ambitions. He said nothing.

Peter was disconcerted by Berndtt's stillness. He started to speak, thought better of it, looked at the Captain and eventually said, 'Any questions? I mean, it is quite a hard mission, particularly the intelligence gathering. Do you think you could tackle it?'

'Do you have any more to give me? Location, newspaper reports, Deuxieme intelligence, photographs?'

'Not much, but there is a possible link: A newspaper reporter. The Butcher has tried to kill her twice but she knows where to find him. Only we are not sure how to find her and she may be one of the revolutionaries.'

SIX

The station was so familiar, the café where he had met the woman, the toilets that had seen the demolition of one of the thugs. He dropped into the café, coffee and a croissant, and sat looking out onto the concourse. A quiet morning, the sun glancing through the glass roof. No suspicious men or girls standing around pretending to be busy, no policemen carrying out a search. And no sign of the Conglomerate.

A passerby might have noted a single man seated at a table at the window, not young, a little grizzled, a tough shaven face, not welcoming. The dress, workers' casual, jeans and a canvas jacket, shirt, no tie. A cap on the table. And no baggage that could be seen. They would have missed the shoulder bag beneath the table, the gun and ammunition, maps and a few clothes. And if they had met his stare, they would have moved on rapidly, chilled by the momentary contact.

Berndtt stood, stretched, tossed a few coins on the table and strode out of the café. Turning towards the town centre, he dropped into the clothing store that he had visited before and bought a leather jacket and a red scarf. He walked through the centre, the same pedestrian street and saw the café where the girl had left him a message, but kept walking and found the cheap hotel where he had stayed before, booked in, and slept for six hours.

Evening and he stirred, assembling his plan. How to find this mysterious journalist. He strolled down the main street; food, that is what he needed. To restore his batteries. He found a small restaurant, sat at the rear, back to wall, his accustomed place in any establishment, and had a large steak with fries. A pint of lager, two cups of black coffee. He felt restored, and strutted down the centre of the street feeling strong, feeling confident.

Until he spied a man, the other side of the street, keeping pace with him. He recognised him; one of the thugs from the boat, probably Serbian, tall, built like a blockhouse, hands like dinner plates. Berndtt dropped into a bar, sat near the window, ordered a lager. Waited.

The man came in, stood in the doorway looking around casually and wandered over to Berndtt. Sat down next to him, smiling. Ordered a lager.

'Nice place, isn't it?'

Berndtt said nothing, looking at the man out of the corner of his eye, waiting for some sudden movement.

'Berndtt, how are you doing? It's been a while.'

Berndtt grunted, still not meeting the man's eye.

'You put me out of a job. You owe me.'

Berndtt turned, looked at him. The man burst into laughter. 'Got you there!'

'How come you're still here then?' said Berndtt.

'Oh, you know, looking for work. You would have thought…' he said, looking at his hands.

'Night clubs?'

'No, no. They all want bouncers who don't frighten the patrons away. Pity.'

'The army?'

'What me? Couldn't stand the hours or discipline. Not again.'

'So what happened to your bankers?'

'And you ask?'

'The organisation. Aren't you still working for them?'

'They've gone underground, ever since your little escapade. Good one, that. Did for them, didn't it? Now I'm out of a job.'

'What work would you do?' said Berndtt. His mind was working on potentials, possibilities, risk factors, weighing need against independence, and looking at his present task. Money was no problem; probably, arms were no problem. Manpower, always a problem. They either gave you away like Marcel or got in the way. Maybe. Perhaps it could be balanced another way, an isolated no-liability sort of way.

'Anything that pays.' The man was not laughing, but playing with his glass, turning it round and round. 'I hope you're paying for the drinks; I'm down on cash just now.'

'Legal or stretching it?'

'Depends what you mean.'

'Your last employment was not legal.'

'And I thought it was.'

'How are you about danger? Life threatening danger?'

The man smiled, raising hands again. 'Well, I was army for a while and we did get up to some operations that weren't exactly Geneva Convention.'

'What rank? What army?' Berndtt knew what the answers would be.

'Serbia. Sergeant.'

Yes, he had guessed right. The man had sergeant written all over him.

'You might have to work independently in an armed context.'

'What's new?' The man gave a big shrug.

'Name?'

'Which one do you want?'

'You tell me,' said Berndtt with half a smile.

'Mack. Mack the Knife. Always fancied that part.'

'Ok, Mack. I don't know you, so how can I trust you?'

'Give me something to do. Unpaid. Then see.'

'OK. If it works out, you'll get paid on a daily basis, cash. If you consider double-crossing me, you might as well leave now because your life expectancy will drop to nil.'

'Fair enough. When do I start?'

'I want you to find the bankers. Tell me where they are. Whether they are a risk to me. How many 'soldiers' they hire, what skills.'

'OK. How do I find you?'

'Here. Two days time. Three pm.'

Mack rose, knocked back his drink, nodded to Berndtt and slipped out of the door. Berndtt watched him go up the street and wondered whether he was going to bring an army of 'soldiers' down on him and deliver him to the Conglomerate. A little care might have to be taken.

It was turning dark, a soft twilight through which the lights of shops and clubs gave a warm glow. Berndtt wandered up the street, examining the bars. Which one would be the home of journalists? Where might he find the mythical reporter who knew Le Boucher?

He had taken his eyes off the street. A stab in the small of his back. He straightened, began to turn. A gruff voice. 'Keep still, or you get it!'

For a moment, he froze and then began to laugh. A rare sound from Berndtt. He wheeled round and smiled. 'Bonsoir, Juliette. How are you?'

She linked her arm in his, saying 'come along,' and led him into a dark bar, a dive that he would not have entered; too dark, too many people, too many unknown risks. But he could not resist Juliette. They sat at a table; there was another couple there, who took a look at Berndtt and left. They slid around to the wall side, Berndtt much easier in mind. It was noisy but the sound disguised their conversation.

'Eh bien, Bernard, what brings you to Lyons again? I thought you had had enough of us after the last time. Poor Marcel; he had a devil of a job looking for you and not finding you and explaining himself to the military.'

'You were good to me,' said Berndtt, a nod to her assistance.

'I didn't give you away. Said you must have discovered something for yourself and escaped. Now he is neurotic, searching for an escape route that you might have found, coming to the conclusion that you jumped out of a window and not believing it. Ah, poor man,' she said, laughing happily.

'And you? What fills your days?'

'This and that. But you haven't answered my question.'

Berndtt looked at her. Would it matter? She might know. It would be foolish to waste time. 'Well, I'm looking for someone.'

'Who? Is she some sort of a glamour woman, should I be jealous?'

'It is a woman.'

'Ah, I should tear your eyes out. And I had such hopes,

finding you again.' She looked away, tugging her face into a grimace.

Berndtt laughed. 'I don't know her, don't know her name.'

'You have seen a picture of her, you are pursuing her across countries, nations, continents, convinced that she is the one!'

'Oh, Juliette. Is this how women think?'

'Eh bien?'

'She has some information that I want.'

'Is this something to do with those men who were hunting you?'

'No. At least, I don't think so.'

'And?' There was a pause. 'My God, Bernard, it is like extracting water from a stone.'

'OK. She is a journalist, or reporter. They are the same thing, aren't they?'

'Not necessarily.'

'Where might I find journalists, or reporters, in this city?'

'What does she have for you?'

'You wouldn't want to know.' Ah Berndtt, you don't know women. A red rag! Juliette looked at Berndtt, gathered her purse and scarf and started to leave.

'Hey, Juliette, what did I say?'

'Ah, you men, you are all the same. You think little women can't handle the big stuff, you think we are no good for more than... than... er... Oh shit, you useless man!' She sat down, tears starting. Berndtt stared in confusion. He went to the bar and bought another round of drinks, a small beer for himself, Pernod for Juliette. When he sat down, she was sitting very upright, cold and stiff; the happy teasing girl had disappeared. Berndtt sat pondering over his problem; should he tell her about his mission? It would be yet another person, Mack and now Juliette. And yet with those two, he might move forward, rather than waste time asking questions until somebody took exception to him and eliminated him.

'It's secret. Do you want to know?'

'If you want to tell me,' she said, tartly.

'Have you heard of a man called Le Boucher?'

'Le Boucher? I guess you don't mean the man who sells us meat.'

'Most unlikely.'

'So. Who is this man called Le Boucher?'

'I don't know but I have to find him. He has something I want.'

'Have you looked in the phone book?'

Berndtt smiled. 'Don't think you'll find him there.'

'Because… ?'

'I gather that he is not a very nice man.'

'You mean… uh oh! Sounds like your bankers all over again.'

'Worse.'

'He kills people for meat.'

'Maybe.'

'You're not serious?'

'I don't know the man.'

'So what are journalists to do with it?'

'I am told that there is a journalist, a revolutionary, who knows where he lives. But I don't know her name.'

'And you want me to find her?'

Berndtt shrugged. 'Do you know where journalists meet? Which bar they use?'

Juliette shrugged at him. 'It won't do any good.'

'What do you mean?'

'How are you going to walk up to a group of journalists and get them to give up their secrets?'

'Secrets?' Berndtt was confused.

'They protect each other; you might be trouble. In fact… '

Berndtt looked glum. 'Go on.'

'Well, you'd probably frighten them.'

'Me?'

'You're not the easiest person to approach.'

'But how—'

'Oh Bernard! Don't you understand? You must become one of them; you must be a radical, maybe a revolutionary, fit in. The clothes, the hair, what you smoke, what you say.'

'Oof!' Berndtt felt lost. There had been times when he had fitted in; an Italian city and a female student came to mind. But that was years ago.

'Eh bien, your leather jacket, OK. Your clothes, not bad. Your manner, terrible.'

'Teach me.'

For an hour or so she lectured him, told him the subjects that might be discussed, brought him up to date on topical affairs and checked that he had acceptable opinions, questioned him about his story, his attitude, his own background that he might reveal, and eventually grudgingly granted him a conditional approval. She led him out into the night.

'It's not far. Are you OK?' She took his arm, smiled, and walked with him up the street. It was full, mostly young people, laughing, joking, shouting to friends. A number greeted Juliette; she introduced them to Berndtt, but many nodded, gave Juliette a questioning look and went on their way. At last, an older man joined them, asked where they were going and went along with them, chatting at first to Juliette and then to Berndtt, quizzing him on his views and his plans. Berndtt answered some questions, avoided others by asking questions himself, tried to relax. If only, he thought, if only I was on a hillside, Le Boucher in my sights, and a powerful sniper rifle in my hands. Then I could go home, job done.

It was like a café; big glass windows to the street, bright lighting inside, a counter at the rear. Tables down either side, packed, overflowing into the central alley. A hubbub of conversation, no music. Juliette waltzed into the centre of the room, gazing around, waving to a few, pushing a young man away with a laugh and a curse, and eventually led Berndtt to a corner table, a group of women, six or eight it was not clear as people kept shifting from table to table. Juliette and Berndtt squeezed into seats apart from each other, either side of the table.

The woman next to him looked him up and down, grunted something he couldn't hear and said, 'Alors, your round, I think.'

Juliette sat up, shouted, 'Eh, he's my guest. What are you doing taking him over like that?' She shook her fist, collapsed into giggles and sat down. Berndtt looked round the table; how the devil do you work out an order based on what everyone was drinking? All different. No waiter. And they were all talking, all at once. Hell!

He turned to his neighbour. 'And what would you like to drink?'

She smiled, a slow smile that never reached her eyes. 'The same as you.'

He squeezed his way to the bar and bought two bottles of cheap red wine. 'Here you are, all I can afford.'

She gave him a doubtful look, gulped wine and asked him where he had come from. He pattered out the profile that he had adopted, an Alsace who had wandered the world a bit, looking into revolutionary groups, looking for a simple cause, a connection. She was interested, pumped him for information, asked him what he did with what he found; he told her that he put it into papers or magazines a little. Many were not interested which was frustrating. She asked him how he met Juliette and he made up a tale about meeting her father once when he had been dossing in a boat alongside the quay. She laughed and said that she was a poet and didn't know anything about the revolutionary lot. Who are they? asked Berndtt. Oh, here and there, she replied vaguely. Berndtt was aware that she didn't know him, suspected that she was protecting friends. He started to spout rubbish that he had read in South American papers about anarchy and grabbing the country's resources. She was interested for a while, then stopped him and said that he should talk to Alice. Is she here? He asked. No, she doesn't come in often. How do I reach her? You don't.

Alice. A name. But no location.

And then he realised that Juliette might have a completely different profile for him and he couldn't remember what he had told her, what her father knew. Except he suspected that it was something about being in the army the other side of the Iron Curtain. Shit. Maybe it wouldn't come out. Maybe Juliette was a dangerous ally.

His neighbour had changed. It was a young man who questioned him acutely about his background and beliefs. He waffled a little, spouted the South American stuff again, told a brief potted history of his life, home, university, research, freelance journalist, travel. The young man nodded, took it all in and vanished. Berndtt began to feel claustrophobic; the noise of talk and the press of people were threatening his sense of autonomy. He wanted to be away. At last, Juliette rose, beckoned and made for the door.

Ahead of them, a girl in army fatigues was flinging a scarf around her neck, blocking the alley as she muttered curses at a man sitting nearby, the young man who had questioned Berndtt. She looked at Juliette and Berndtt, turned on her heel and left.

'Who was that? She was interesting,' said Berndtt.

'Who? Oh, that one. That was Alice; you don't want to get mixed up with her.'

'But wouldn't she know…'

Juliette had walked on through the door. There was no sign of Alice, only the sound and rear lights of a motorcycle way up the street, the smell of exhaust hanging in the air.

Peter stood at ease before the Colonel, who was rummaging through papers on his desk.

'Ah, Peter. Haven't seen Berndtt for a while. Is his training finished?'

'Yes sir.'

'Where is he, then?'

'We thought he should get a bit of experience at underground work, polishing profiles and that sort of thing.'

'Sound sensible. Where is he?'

There was a brief pause. 'France, sir.'

'France?' The Colonel looked up with a start, a hard frown above his moustache. 'Did I sanction a mission abroad?'

'Er... the Captain knew all about it, sir.'

'And what is his mission?'

Peter gulped, looked at the floor, coughed and looked up. 'We thought an exploratory look at Le Boucher would be useful.'

'What?!' The Colonel roared, his colour rising. He was standing now, leaning over his desk, his moustache waving, spittle flying. 'Are you quite mad?'

'Er—'

'You should know... ' the Colonel was struggling to speak. He calmed a little. 'You should know that such an operation would require back-up teams, safe houses, regular agent contact, safe code and telephone emergency numbers?'

His secretary next door heard every word and drew Peter's file, reading it with a slow smile before depositing it in the out tray.

'He wants to be a loner, operate without back-up.'

'I don't care a monkey's arse what he wants. And what was his brief? Exactly, and I shall tell you to bring me the briefing paperwork.'

Peter stared at his ruin, shrugged and said, 'To extract agent information from him and eliminate him.'

The Colonel was staring, perhaps at his own ruin. 'Are you absolutely stupid? And I suppose you haven't informed Deuxieme of this fanciful spree?'

'Er... no, sir.' Peter was standing stiffly at attention.

Silence. The Colonel had sunk back into his seat, with his head in his hands, shaking it from side to side.

'I don't know what to do with you. And you had such promise. A field regiment and square bashing are about all that is good for you now. And there is a hell of a mess to sort out. I suppose that we can contact Berndtt, extract him before we tread any further on Deuxieme's toes?'

'Er... he had a calling routine but he hasn't used it. Sir.'

'You mean... you mean you haven't heard from your agent since his departure?'

'Er... no sir. He said it worked better if he established his own profile and working methods. He seems to have some experience—'

'I don't want to hear any more. You have a rogue agent at work in France and you can't even contact him. I think you had better inform Deuxieme of your idiotic scheme and get over there and find him.'

'Only sir... you see sir... we don't know where he is. Because we don't know where Le Boucher is. Sir.'

'Confined to barracks. You and the Captain on the spot here nine am tomorrow. Get out.'

SEVEN

Juliette was a threat and yet he could not be rid of her; she might take offence, shop him to Marcel, tell the police; there was no knowing what might happen.

He woke with a blinding headache, squinting at the sun that shone full through an uncurtained window. Where the hell was he? He rolled over, exploring the aches in his body, and found a sleeping body in the bed with him. Things were getting worse; what was happening to him? There seemed to be no control, no plan, and he was wandering into trouble.

Did his English background matter? That was some question. What was he doing here if not to pursue his mission? Did it matter? Not when he had a headache like this one. But was he safe? That was a laugh; since when had he lived a 'safe' life? The hilltop village had been the safest haven, but he had been discovered there. And he had felt safe with Francine, in spite of her father's occupation.

He levered himself out of bed, stretching, looking out of the window.

'What a sight!' Juliette's eyes ploughed up and down his naked body. 'Are you going to refuse me now? You weren't up to much last night?'

Berndtt scratched his stomach. 'Time for breakfast?'

'Not until I've—'

'I'm hungry.'

'So am I.'

What should Berndtt do now? You might be saying, don't look a gift horse in the face, or get out of there while you can. But risk annoying Juliette? Ah people! So much better to be free of their influence.

He crawled back into bed; after all, it had been a while…

It was her flat, small, neat and near the centre. They went to a bar for coffee and croissants and after Berndtt made his apologies, said he must be on his way, things to do. And then was pressed into agreeing to meet Juliette for dinner; she would take him to a quiet restaurant and then afterwards…

He did not intend to meet her later but could not progress with the mission without her help. He wandered the town, found the journalists' bar, drank in a corner without seeing Alice though several young reporters came over, chatted to him, cross-examined him on what was happening in South America, what his plans were, where he was going next. Nobody could tell him how to find Alice; indeed they tended to pretend to know little of her, to avoid association with her and always changed the conversation.

The next evening and he was in the restaurant; Juliette greeted him seriously.

'I had wondered whether I might see you again. I'm so happy; I feel it's the start of something.'

Berndtt stared at her. The start of something? They sat, they ate, they drank; Juliette chatted, Berndtt said little but noted a jitteriness that she had never displayed before; she had difficulty maintaining a conversation, dropped her napkin twice, glanced to the door from time to time. What had she done? It must be Marcel. She must have told Marcel and he was going to appear any moment, probably not alone, and he was trapped. Or perhaps they were waiting at her flat.

He rose, bent over the table, kissed her on the cheek. 'Wait here. I am going to get you something,' he said with a smile. The smile took some effort.

'Ah non, mon cherie. Do not leave me now.' She was getting up, but he pushed her back into the seat and laughed.

'A few minutes. Wait for me.' And slipped out of the restaurant.

The night was quite dark, the street not well lit, but he saw two men approaching. There was something about them; were they armed? In their thirties, powerfully built, dark blouson and trousers, silent shoes, short hair cuts. He went the other way.

At once he knew that they had increased speed, put on a spurt as he began to run. He ran for a further hundred metres and slipped sideways into an alley. You can't always run; you have to know what you are running from.

The first man came up fast, missed the alley and ran straight into Berndtt's fist that caught him in the neck, falling onto Berndtt's knee that rose fast into his face. Berndtt stepped over the body and faced the second man.

'What do you want?'

The second man had halted, looking at his comrade and Berndtt, before dropping his hand to his belt. He was not prepared for what happened next. Berndtt charged him at speed, a rugger tackle aimed at his stomach; the man hesitated, no time to draw his weapon at such a difficult target, no time to take evasive action, and crumpled back

246

onto the ground, a piercing pain forcing him to bend double. Berndtt relieved him of the gun, took him by the collar and dragged him over his comrade into the alley, where he sat him against the wall, and pressed the gun into his throat.

'Who sent you?'

A grunt.

'Who sent you. Tell me now.' Berndtt did not raise his voice; the pressure from the gun was a little greater.

'It was... I dunno their names... they—'

'Not good enough. How long do you want to live?'

'I... how long? I... you bugger, they'll catch you anyway!'

Berndtt gave him a hard kick in the groin, watched him keel over and gasp, and knocked him out with a blow to the back of the head. He dragged the man from the street into the alley, leant them next to each other like a pair of drunks and slipped away.

Now Juliette was dangerous; probably told her father and Marcel had contacted... who? Did it make any difference? Police, army or Deuxieme, they must all be after him. And there were always the dear old Brits who had sent him out here; would they support him in such a debacle? Unlikely. Well, he was used to being on his own. Let's go; Italy, Germany, wherever. Free of all obligations, free of police forces; he knew how to melt into a small town, a quiet retired professional man, living an unreproachable life, paying the taxes, visiting the local church, the bar, a smile on his face, a relaxed man. No threat to anyone.

What was the point of that life? No danger and no challenge. It was why he had enrolled with the Brits, wasn't it? The Army Intelligence, though what a terrorist called Le

Boucher in France had to do with English Army Intelligence was beyond him. He groaned, found a small hotel where there were no questions about a man who appears late at night without luggage, and sank into a long and restless night.

After lying low, he was at the bar before time, sitting against the wall, the rear of the room, a beer in front of him. He scanned everyone who came in, assessing them for their degree of threat; the only threat that he observed was a gendarme who wandered in off the street, chatting to the staff, receiving a free coffee, drinking as he stood looking around. Berndtt kept his face down, reading a paper. The gendarme departed, a cheery au-revoir to everyone.

On time, Mack appeared, slipped into the seat beside him, and called for a beer. He smiled, said that he had much to report. Yes, he had caught up with the Conglomerate, in Geneva. They were reassembling their strength, hiring 'soldiers', looking to expand their operations. Were they after me, asked Berndtt. Yes, said Mack. But not in the way that you think. They have an enemy; he's called Le Boucher. Very hard to eliminate, apparently. Has a small army in the Haut Jura; a small place called Arinthod, very quiet and they can see anyone who sneezes within two miles. He is able to slip over the border to Switzerland anytime he wants; keeps his funds in private banks; guess where. Anyway, he is disrupting their operations, a pain in the ass, and they will call the dogs off you, sorry, my expression, if you eliminate him. How do you know? Well, they gave me a serious understanding, and as an indication, they gave me this card and a cheque.

Berndtt examined the card; it was similar to a bankers'

card, some insignia, a pattern that would be hard to forge. The cheque was for twenty-five thousand francs. 'How does this card work?' he said.

'You can present it at any bank in that chain and draw funds. You can show it to any threatening force including the French police they said and you will be given freedom.'

Berndtt doubted it and was unwilling to try it out. 'You have done well, Mack. At present, I can't think of anything you can do, apart from keep an eye on a man called Marcel and his daughter Juliette. I think they are trouble.' And he gave their details and paid him for his time. Mack sat back, a smile of relief.

'Glad to be useful, boss. I hope—'

'Get out now, you don't know me. Chance you were sitting there. Move.'

Mack glanced at Berndtt and slipped away to the bar where he started chatting to the men there. Alice had appeared; she looked around, dropped into the seat next to Berndtt, and said, 'Who was that?'

'I dunno,' said Berndtt. 'Some fool looking for a chat. Seems to have found one now. Can I get you something?'

'You've been asking for me.'

'Yeah. I've been following groups of revolutionaries all over the world, particularly in South America. The other night, someone said you were involved, the person to talk to.' Berndtt hoped he sounded casual.

'What is your history?'

'Oh … army for a while, long ago. Cruising round the world, submitting to journals, research on revolutionary movements. Trying to get them organised. You wouldn't believe…'

'Yes?' Her voice was sharp. 'What wouldn't I believe?'

'Well … you must know, perhaps better than me. But it struck me that it was like a hundred small armies, tight organisation but each limited to a small number, and all pulling in different directions. You would think that … oh, I dunno, I'm not a captain, just a…'

'Just a?' She wasn't looking at him. He shrugged.

'Can you use a gun?'

Berndtt nearly laughed; guns were what he knew, more than people. 'Yes, army you know.'

'Which army?'

He was not prepared for this question; he paused, gave a sideways look at her, and muttered 'East Germany.'

'A communist!' She laughed, a bitter cynical bark.

Berndtt said nothing. After a pause, she said, 'We could use you. If you want.'

'Use?'

'You take a look, we check you out, see how things go. What are you doing now?'

Berndtt shrugged. 'Nothing much.'

'We'll take a ride.'

They rose, and she made for the door while Berndtt paid the bill, a few coins thrown down on the table, and yet, as he reached the door, an old woman was in the opening, struggling to come in, her carer behind her as she swore and rocked, grasping the door frame, no regard for blocking the doorway, an evil eye on Berndtt who had pressed to pass, forced back, a curse in his direction.

Eventually she passed him, waving her sticks about, her carer an ineffective female who wavered in the background carrying shopping bags, coats, and handbags. Berndtt stepped out into the street; no sign of Alice. He breathed slowly, taking in the pedestrians and the weather, slowing his reactions against frustration and anger. Turned to the right, a few steps, turned to the left a little way; swore in French.

A motorcycle engine started up nearby, a harsh coughing becoming a high roar; he turned back, hurrying. The next alley, there she was, the bike roaring, helmet on, shrugging with impatience. He climbed onto the back; miniature footrests, hardly anywhere to hold on, and he wasn't going to put his arms round Alice.

He had little experience of motorbikes. Of course, the Stasi had made sure that he could ride one, had educated him on the different types and engines, two and four stroke, had showed him how to change points, overhaul the electrics, get going in an emergency. But he had never ridden pillion and on the whole decided that he hated bikes; too vulnerable, too noisy and always stood out; he had never ridden one on his own business.

And here he was on the back of a Suzuki 750, a large dangerous machine that accelerated hard, throwing him backwards. They cruised up the pedestrian street, ignoring shoppers, some of whom jumped out of the way at the last moment, swearing and shaking their fists. As they came into roads in the north of the city, still in the speed limit, she opened the throttle and steered a path down the middle, overtaking all before her, weaving around the odd car that dared to pull out, occasionally using her horn, a deep two tone that cleared the way like an ambulance. Berndtt felt the air streaming over his face, plucking at his cheeks, lifting his jacket and pulling him backwards. He clenched his legs over the machine, gripped the brackets under his seat and leant forward into Alice's back.

A siren sounded behind; police of course. For a while, it seemed it approached, but as they pulled out of the city onto open roads and she increased her speed, it fell behind.

Up the road they roared; Berndtt picked out road numbers, A42, town names Meximieux, Pont dAin, others. And now a siren was catching them up, even as they overtook, driving up the middle between lines of hooting trucks; Berndtt saw Alice look back, leaning far out to see the pursuer. The police motorcycle was gaining, four stroke, a deep roar, a tiger on their tail. Alice swore; Berndtt heard it, the words flung into the air, whipped past his head. She overtook a pantechnicon, braked suddenly with a blast of air horn from the truck and dropped into a small side road, accelerating until around a corner, and pulling up in a field entrance, switched off.

Berndtt stepped off, stretching, wiping the water from his eyes, looking away over the fields. Alice sat on the bike in silence; the hot exhaust ticked, a tickle of smoke rose from the cylinders, a smell of hot oil. The police siren continued to the north, fading into the distance.

They returned to the main road. After a time, they turned off the valley road, climbing and twisting, banking hard over on the corners, speed maintained, overtaking vehicles that laboured on the inclines, passing them in a flash to cut the next corner, scaring oncoming traffic. Other places left behind, speed limits ignored, Ceignes, Montréal, and still she rode at the maximum throttle, no lessening, no relaxation. Until. Until a sign indicated Oyonnax ahead, five kilometres, and she slowed, cruising through the suburbs, a model citizen, turning off the main street, back roads, winding around the centre to emerge on the north side of town.

It was an anonymous villa, standing in its own ground. A high metal fence with gates, very traditional, a neat garden reduced to gravel and a few plants, the house two storey, shutters closed. Berndtt opened the gate and watched her ride around the rear of the house. He stood looking up at the house; no sign of anybody, it looked dead to the world. She reappeared, helmet in hand shaking her hair out, beckoning to him. The door was at the side, a small porch, and then inside, a dark hall, the doors to the rooms all closed, a staircase at the end rising into darkness. Berndtt stood still listening; there was a sharp smell of old dust and older women but no sound at all.

Alice said, 'Make yourself comfortable.' And disappeared upstairs.

EIGHT

The Hall: the floor, old chipped tiles, dull colours, stretching away into the depth of the house. Walls papered with some indistinguishable pattern, dark in colour, a muddy brown with cobwebs descending from a high ceiling. Doors and skirtings a dark varnish. The smell of faded face powder. And silence.

A deep impenetrable silence. Berndtt could hear his own breathing; he could not hear traffic. Instinctively he moved to one side, hugging the left-hand wall; the opposite doors would give access to the front rooms, as seen from the road all shuttered.

He opened the first door; a cloakroom, apparently. Coats, hats, some furniture, and, partially hidden behind a hanging Burberry, a 12 bore shotgun. He stayed in the doorway for a while. Nobody hidden. Entered and used the toilet but did not flush, preserving the silence.

The next door. He opened as quietly as he could; the hinges must have been oiled. It swung open fully as he ducked to one side, looking in.

A man sat at the table, drinking coffee. He looked up. 'Ah, Bernard. I have been expecting you. Coffee?'

Must be one of the revolutionaries, Berndtt decided. He sat down opposite the man, back to a wall, watching for anybody else.

'Have no fear, there is noone here. Was your journey comfortable?'

Berndtt thought over his words; noone here, but Alice was upstairs. The journey? Hardly comfortable. He had assumed it was part of a test, a test to see whether he could live the tough life of a mercenary revolutionary. What a joke! He sipped his coffee; it was very good. The man opposite him was in his fifties, he guessed, medium height, a bland forgettable face, dark hair, not long, and smartly dressed, a tweed suit with waistcoat.

'I wonder, Bernard, when you have refreshed yourself, whether we may move upstairs to my study. I have some things to show you and we should discuss your involvement with our group.'

In time, they ascended the stairs together, the man chatting about this and that, a little about the town – it's very quiet, suits our purposes, you know – about Alice – she's very active, a good soldier – and about the house. It belonged to the mother of one of the group; we haven't done anything to it really. It's more of a hostel or temporary resting place; nobody lives here. Upstairs he led Berndtt to a small room at the rear: a low sloping ceiling, a desk against the wall with an upright chair, three easy chairs, a low table. The curtain was drawn against the evening sun, the room lit dimly by a table lamp on the desk.

'Make yourself comfortable,' and he disappeared. Berndtt examined the room; apart from the desk, there was a filing cabinet, locked, and a thin rug on the floor that he guessed had been there for many years. The boards around were bare and worn, an old stain. The walls were papered, peeling in the corner, some vague geometrical pattern dull and dirty; a long dry stain on one wall, drips descending to the floor, a dark brown. No pictures or posters, apart from a small watercolour of a mill in hilly country, dirty glass and frame; Berndtt wondered if it had any significance, whether it was the base of this group. He decided he was over-thinking the issue; it was just an old picture that had hung there for decades. He dropped into one of the chairs; they were very comfortable and he felt himself relaxing after the days of being alert in Lyon, after the strain of the journey.

The man came back into the room. 'I must apologise; I haven't introduced myself. My name is Robert. You'll understand if I don't give my surname; we don't use them. A basic security thing. And you are Bernard.'

He asked about Berndtt's intentions, what he wanted, where he planned to go. Berndtt repeated what he had said before, that he was interested in revolutionary groups, collecting information towards assembling a dossier that might be used by the groups, to concentrate their energies. Robert was interested, asked him questions, probed his background and was not the least concerned to discover that he had been a soldier in East Europe; indeed, he probably had useful skills, didn't he? And would be happy to work on behalf of the group here?

He continued to talk, of nothing in particular, a little history, a little geography, nothing important or relevant, an even tone, gentle, soporific.

Berndtt began to close his eyes, and relax. This man seemed harmless enough; he could not really be much of a revolutionary.

The man was intoning a song now, on one note; Berndtt could not make it out, but it sounded as trivial as a nursery rhyme. He started to drift off to sleep. And then the words changed.

'Open your eyes, Bernard. Open your eyes. Look into my eyes, look into my eyes.' The little insignificant man had become something else entirely; he had moved to the upright chair, placed it before Berndtt and bent down towards him. All his energies focused in his eyes that bored into Berndtt. They had an unusual brightness; Berndtt noticed that they were of different colours, grey and green. 'You are asleep but you can hear me. You will remember all that I say and you will act on my word. My word will be "hammer"; do you hear me. You are my soldier and a hammer; I say "hammer" and you obey me. You will obey me. Now close your eyes and sleep. You are very tired but you will wake refreshed.'

Berndtt resisted the temptation to sit up and walk out of the room. Hypnosis and the resistance to it had been part of his training; he hadn't experienced it for a long time but the lesson came back to him as clear as if it had been the hour before. He slowed his breathing and loosened his muscles; he did not think he was in danger, not yet.

'Now wake.'

He stirred, yawned, shook himself. 'Many apologies,' he said. 'I must have fallen asleep. Sorry.'

The man was smiling, standing looking down at him, an insignificant little man again.

They went downstairs to the kitchen; Alice was preparing a meal. They sat and ate, mostly in silence. His plate cleared, Robert said, 'Hammer.'

Berndtt immediately froze, sitting upright, staring ahead.

Robert said, 'Tomorrow, we are going on a journey. You will come with us. You do not know where you are going. And now you will sleep; Alice will show you to a room.'

Berndtt rose, looking straight ahead, and followed Alice from the room. Upstairs, she showed him to a room at the rear of the house, and he heard the door locked behind him. He shook himself; it was going to be hard work maintaining the image of a drugged servant, obedient to every whim of his master.

The room was very similar to the one in which Robert had interviewed him. A desk and upright chair, one easy chair, a towel rail with a soiled towel and a narrow bed, made up. There were ropes tied to the bed, head and foot. The decorations were similar to the other room but there were no pictures.

He turned to the door and examined the lock. Not difficult, a crude three lever, worn. But he needed a tool, a strong strip of metal. Nothing visible. The desk? Empty, apart from a few scraps of paper and a pencil. He considered stripping the pencil somehow and decided that it would not be strong enough. The curtain was old, hung on rings over a wooden pole; brass rings, a metal tag fixed to the curtain. The bed; a mattress set upon a metal mesh stretched over the frame, an old system. He pulled the mattress off, and went over the mesh, looking for an end. Five minutes and he found one, at the far end. Pulling it loose, he worked it to and fro until it came loose. Replaced the mattress, made the bed, stuffed pillows and his coat under the covers, a suggestion of a sleeping body.

At the door, he listened; there was the same silence that he had experienced when he had arrived. He knelt down and inserted his probe; a couple of minutes later, he was standing on the landing, moving to the staircase. He descended slowly, keeping to the wall, as much in deep shadow as possible; the Hall was unlit but a little evening light came through the fanlight.

The kitchen door stood ajar; he could hear the voices of Robert and Alice.

'I don't know about him. Keep a close eye on him; we shall see how effective my hypnosis is but my guess is that it might need reinforcing at some stage. Anyway, we'll take him out to the mill tomorrow.'

'On my bike?'

'No. The closed van. It will be here in the morning. I don't want to risk him remembering the way. Just yet.'

'What shall I do?'

'You might go back into Lyon. You suspected that he had some contacts there, some girl, was it?'

'He left the bar with a girl; they were just behind me. I didn't get a sight of her or only very brief. Wasn't considering him at that time.'

'Pity. Don't make a mistake like that again.'

Berndtt heard a chair scrape back; he hurried up the stairs, keeping to the wall. He hadn't noticed any creaking treads coming down; it was as well to minimise the risk. He stood on the landing looking down; Robert went into the cloakroom and emerged after a time. Then Alice appeared, making for the stairs. Berndtt slipped back into his room, locked the door, crept into bed and lay silently. He heard steps on the landing pause outside his door, and move on. He put his gun under the pillow; he was mystified that they had not attempted to remove it earlier. He slept.

Lyon was sunny and dry. Peter sat in a café; he had no way of knowing that it was the same one where Berndtt had met Alice and wondered where to start his search. He sipped the coffee, so much better than English coffee; perhaps he should consider moving to France. He was not sure what his prospects were in England anymore.

After university, a Second Class Degree at a Northern University, he had joined the Army. His reasons for doing this were vague though partly a revolt against his family who were churchmen on his father's side going back several generations. His mother was a quiet woman, submissive to his father, and his elder sister, many years older than him, had become a nurse at a hospital in London. The Army did not know what to do with him; while he performed all the tasks required, he did not excel in physical activities. His performance with weapons was good but only when he was given time to consider all the variables, such as wind strength, weight of bullet, size of gun. However, he showed an appetite for military history, keen to cross-examine retired officers at formal dinners and record their experiences. In their wisdom, the Army removed him from Field activities and placed him in the Intelligence Department, under Colonel Grant. He had shown some promise in analysis, though he had not yet progressed beyond Second Lieutenant.

He had stood at attention before the Colonel's desk, his Captain at his side. The Captain was torn off a strip for allowing the Second Lieutenant to have his way, for not informing the Colonel of an overseas mission, for not having contacted Deuxieme of the presence of an English agent, particularly an English Army agent, on French soil.

'You must realise that we just don't do that sort of thing and we certainly wouldn't be happy to hear of French officers making free over here. What were you thinking of? This will be a black mark on your record. Get out while I deal with this miserable young man.'

The Captain saluted stiffly, turned on his heel, and marched to the door, closing it behind him quietly. In the Hall, he removed his cap, took a long breath, and headed for the outside. Coffee, he murmured, not seeing the salute of a Sergeant entering. The Sergeant looked after him, shaking his head. In his office, the Colonel's secretary, a Corporal of long standing, smiled, retrieved the Captain's file and deposited it in Pending.

The Colonel was sitting stiffly upright. 'You realise that I have had to make a very embarrassing call to my equal number in Deuxieme, not that there is an equal number; after all, they are all civilians. But you get my drift.'

'Sir, if I could—'

'Shut up!'

There were several minutes of silence; the Colonel looked Peter up and down, and then stared out of the window. Peter stood to attention, staring over the Colonel's head. He had been thinking for the last twelve hours of what he could say, what he could promise, how he could get out of this mess. The potential reaction of his father had visited his dreams that night and the girl he had been seeing in Oxford would certainly be lost when she learnt that her 'clever' Intelligence officer was becoming something a great deal less, a foot-slogging infantryman. No solution had come to mind; in fact, he realised that he did not really know Berndtt at all. He had assumed that, as a junior in the Intelligence, Berndtt would do as he was instructed. He had forgotten that Berndtt was no Army Officer but an outsider who might be very useful in certain scenarios, if handled with discretion and great care. If he admitted it, he had looked forward to presenting the Colonel with a fait accompli, the elimination of a terrorist with the bonus of useful information about revolutionaries, all without having to endanger himself at all; it would have been worth rapid promotion to First Lieutenant, something to wave in front of his girl, perhaps with an engagement ring. He could kiss goodbye to that.

'I have discussed with Deuxieme what would be the best thing to do. To put it mildly, they were not impressed; murmurs of objections at a political level. They appreciate that we have not done anything to threaten their activities; at least, not yet. They had been planning an operation against Le Boucher, and possibly, just possibly, your foolish ideas may prove useful to them.

'Accordingly, you will cancel any leave that you have planned for the foreseeable future, including weekends, and get over to France by yourself. I need hardly point out that your performance there will have some bearing on your future career in the Army.'

'Sir.'

'Deuxieme revealed that Le Boucher is operating in the Haut Jura, possibly because he can slip over the border to Switzerland when things get a little hot for him. Accordingly, you will make contact with the Deuxieme office in Lyon. There are no photographs of him and they know of no links; or at least, they are not letting us have any further information. You will operate under their orders, make contact with your agent and either extract him to England, or pursue an aggressive operation that Deuxieme have planned. I must point out that you will be on your own; no safe house, numbers, or back-up. Indeed, if you cock it up, you will be totally deniable, acting outside any authority of this Army or Government.'

'Sir.' Peter could hardly take it all in; was this a wonderful opportunity or was he walking into a situation so dangerous that he might never return? No back-up or safe house; he felt himself shaking when he realised how exposed he would be.

'Any questions?'

'Sir... if I... is there any alternative action?'

There was a long silence; the Colonel was staring at Peter as if he had crawled out of a drain.

'Let me get this clear. Are you suggesting that you might not, er, wish to follow my orders? Do you know the punishment for not following an officer's orders?'

'Sir. Sir... but "totally deniabl"... Sir, are these orders legal?'

The Colonel rose like a magma explosion from a volcano, with a similar colour.

'You stupid wretched young man! You have no idea of the trouble you are causing. Do you really wish to spend the next ten years in the glasshouse?'

Peter recoiled; his tongue felt thick, and he had difficulty breathing.

'I said, if you cock up you are deniable. So you have the opportunity of doing well, or at least helping Deuxieme. And I suggest strongly that you bring our agent home.'

'Sir. And if he does not want to—'

'I beg your pardon?' The Colonel was leaning forward over the desk.

'I mean, Sir, I mean ... should he be unwilling to return... well, what should I do?'

'Well, Lieutenant, just consider how it will look on your already appalling record. Now, get out!'

Peter had travelled to Lyon by train; there had been no more than a standard travel allowance. He had had to pay for all his own food out of his own pay and now he was considering how to get by while he was in France. He had called on the Deuxieme office; they had wearily made a note of his presence. When he awaited their commands, they had stared at him and eventually told him to locate his errant agent and get out of their country. Should he be able to eliminate Le Boucher, he may do so but he was not to expect any recognition; it must be seen as a French mission. *Bonne journée.* He was not to visit the office again.

And now he sat in the café; he had hoped that at the very least he would have a French driver and armed guard. But they hadn't even offered him a gun; when he had asked, just before leaving, they had expressed surprise that he was not armed, and gave him an ancient heavy handgun, a Colt 45 with limited ammunition. He felt it weighing down his pocket. But where should he go and to whom should he talk?

A couple of girls came in, talking rapidly to each other. Fortunately, Peter's French was good and he couldn't help hearing their words.

'Hey, Juliette, what are you drinking? You must tell me all about your boyfriend; what was his name?'

'Oh... you mean Bernard. He's disappeared again, *salaud.* I was only starting to have fun; you know what I mean?' She laughed.

Chattering, they settled at a table near the rear. Peter turned the words over in his mind; how many 'Bernard's would there be? In any case, it might be... He lifted himself of his stool, rearranged his jacket so the gun would not stand out and wandered to the back of the café. The two girls were in deep conversation, did not see his approach; he stood, looking around and then interrupted their talk.

'Excuse me...' His normally good French accent deserted him as the girls both scrutinised him from shoes to hair. And then turned to each other with a giggle.

'What have we here? A little Englishman; poor soul, he looks lost. Shall we look after him?'

'Ah Louise, you're wicked.' And to Peter. 'Come, sit with us. We don't meet a young Englishman every day. Say, Louise, did you see his shoes? Not Marks and Spencer, I'll bet.'

'So, young Englishman, what are you doing here? It is not exactly a tourist spot, this café.'

'I am looking for Bernard; he is a friend of mine.'

'Oh really... how many Bernards do I know.' Louise was giggling again.

Juliette was looking at him. 'This Bernard; he is English?'

'Well... no, probably not. He has a German accent, though his English and French are very good.'

'And how would you describe him?'

'Early 40s, tough, very muscular, independent, an action man, you might say. Brown hair, medium height, and... oh yes, those eyes. If you irritate or threaten him, he turns these grey eyes on you and you don't want to be there anymore.'

Juliette sighed. 'I know him.'

'You know him?' said Louise.

Juliette ignored her. 'Where is he? I don't know. He was here a few days ago and then he disappeared.'

Peter groaned, his head sinking.

'But,' said Juliette. 'I might be able to help you. But I don't know you; you might be the police or the Army.'

Peter gave a false laugh. 'Ha, the Army! Me?'

'What is your connection with him?'

'He is a friend and I think he has been having a hard time and needs help.'

'Any help he needs, or I should say, accepts, needs to be armed and as tough as him. You are not. Sorry but it's true.'

'Can I get in touch with him?'

Juliette sat thinking for a time, looking at Peter.

'Look,' she said. 'I don't know where he is. But you might try a café up the road and ask for Alice. I can't promise that she will help you but it's the best that I can do.'

Peter bought them drinks, thanked them again, and set off for the writers' café.

NINE

His first visit to the café had been abortive; there were few people there, it was the wrong time of day, nobody would speak to him but looked at his clothes, his accent, and his Englishness and turned their backs. He wondered how to move forward, feeling both lost and depressed. He could not return to England; there lay complete failure. And probably military prison for a long term. He had no way of finding his agent, Berndtt, whom he was beginning to hate with a fierceness that he had not expected. It was Berndtt's fault, the whole thing. To hell with petty regulations about operating in France. He was sure that MI5 did it all the time. You saw it in James Bond films. No, Berndtt had absconded, not reported back as instructed, a servant of the English Government, an agent of the British Army. It was a court-martial affair, was it not? So why was he, Second Lieutenant Peter, being held to blame for this stupid man's failings?

In the morning, Berndtt came downstairs slowly; he was not sure if he was meant to be hypnotised so he moved slowly, concentrating on the floor in front of him. In the kitchen, Alice was making coffee; she looked up at his entrance and turned away. Robert strode in, brisk and purposeful.

Berndtt looked at him, keeping his face as bland as possible; he did not speak. Robert was wearing casual clothes, utility trousers and jacket, a red handkerchief tied around his neck. The change in clothing could disguise neither the conventional politeness nor the command in his attitude.

They ate breakfast, coffee and rolls, all fresh. Alice left them shortly afterwards without a word; Berndtt heard her motorbike starting and departing along the road, a distinctive low burble. Robert chatted happily, aimlessly, never asking questions, never making demands but maintaining a commanding presence. He moved on to the day.

'Today, we will be going to the Mill. I shall introduce you to the Group and I hope you will find a place among them. There will be plenty of opportunities for you to get to know them, and plenty of opportunities to exercise your undoubted skills. Indeed, I look forward to witnessing them myself.' He asked no questions, gave no directions but led Berndtt out to the yard where they waited in the morning sun.

Half an hour later a van came in; a small, green Citroën, indistinguishable from thousands of traders' vans. Robert was not pleased.

'Half an hour late! What game have you been up to?'

The driver quailed. 'The vegetable merchant was late delivering, sir.'

'Absolute punctuality is the only way forward and absolutely necessary. Remember that.'

'Yes, sir.' He opened the back doors. There were boxes of vegetables and fruit, a side of beef, bottles and caskets.

'You will ride in here,' Robert said to Berndtt.

Berndtt looked at him, saw his expression, decided not to test the system just yet and climbed in, sitting on a sack of potatoes. The doors closed; darkness. He sighed. He would make sure that it would not always be like this, submitting to some petty revolutionary.

The journey was not short, but possibly more comfortable than on the back of the motorbike. At first the roads were quite straight; the driver did not go fast. He could hear no conversation from the front and had little idea of where they were going, though he was sure it was not through town but northwards, away from Oyonnax. After a while, the roads increased in bends and hills, slowing and swinging around tight bends; once the roar of a waterfall, another time the purr of a tractor alongside. At last, they slowed, turned abruptly and climbed at a slow speed, a short toot on the horn before dropping down and coming to a halt on a gravelled surface. Berndtt estimated the time as about one o'clock, distance travelled about eighty kilometres. The doors were opened and he stepped out into bright sunshine, stretching his legs and arms.

Robert stood before him. 'I hope you understand that we could not show you the way here. I trust your journey was not too uncomfortable. Come and meet the Group.'

Berndtt looked about him. They were standing on a large circle of gravel; behind them, the road climbed up between two large rocks, part of a scarp that disappeared in both directions. It would not be difficult to defend the site from attack, particularly by road. In the centre of the circle was a grass patch, two trees growing about five feet apart, a stone mounting block between them.

He turned. Ahead was a stone watermill, three storeys high. There were a number of windows and a large double doorway at first floor level. Walking forward he could see that the mill stood halfway into a small river, a rushing torrent, white water, rocks and steep banks. A channelled divert fed an undershot wheel that turned silently.

At first, he had thought that the mill was in poor condition; the windows were full of cobwebs and paintwork was peeling. But he realised that the doors were fitted with new ironmongery, that the wheel was well maintained and that the roof was sound.

Robert led him away from the mill front and down a track to one side following the river. They came to an encampment, camper vans in variable condition, tents, a large shed with a felt roof and signs of a giant fire in the centre of the clearing. Children were running around, washing hung on lines, and a few women were preparing food on barbecues. There was no sign of the many adults who must have occupied the site.

Robert saw Berndtt looking around. 'They are in the hut, I expect, working.'

Berndtt wondered of what their work consisted but did not ask. Robert took him back to the mill. Going in at the bottom floor he found that the whole of the ground floor was an open area; stocks of food, paper, and boxes stood around; Berndtt thought he recognised ammunition cases. The wheel shaft came in at high level and appeared to be connected to a generator. They walked up a wide staircase to the first floor; in the centre, the grinding stones were still in place but stationary, a centre shaft rising through the floor above. Grain chutes were still in place, descending from above. Tables and chairs filled one side of the open floor, sofas and comfortable seats the other. Up another flight and Robert showed Berndtt a small room, telling him that he would be sleeping there.

They ate, served by two boys from an open kitchen. He noticed that everybody treated Robert with great respect, acquiescing to all his demands and inclinations. He assumed that he must be the mastermind of the revolutionaries. What was his own mission? To get information on the revolutionaries and eliminate Le Boucher. But where was Le Boucher? He thought about moving on, but to where? Meanwhile, he would stay and observe the revolutionaries.

There were two men at the table who he did not think were part of the revolutionaries. Certainly ex-military, they resembled the thugs that he had seen employed by the Conglomerate. They had both given him a long cold stare; he recognised it from his army days, a challenge and a question: who the hell are you, where do you come from, and how tough are you really. He wondered how long it would be before they made a move; he could not imagine that they would not test him at some stage. Robert seemed oblivious to their attitude and maintained the conversation, description of the mill – you might have seen a picture of it at the house – and a brief discussion with the two men about the next few days, places to go to, people to meet, no particulars of which Berndtt could make sense.

The two men made their move directly after lunch. Robert had disappeared, upstairs without a backward glance. Berndtt rose, stretched and made for the stairs down. The men had ignored him, carried on a conversation but when he had reached the staircase, one called out. 'Where the fuck do you think you're going? Bloody rude; you haven't even introduced yourself.'

Berndtt looked them over; they were standing now, both this side of the table; tight army clothes, high boots, shaven heads. He wondered which army had trained them; he did not recognise the clothes or boots. They could be Russian, perhaps Chechen or Ukrainian. Nowhere west of Istanbul. He stared at them and turned to the stairs. In a moment they were both behind him.

He never liked to fight on a staircase, unless it was one of those olden day ones with winding stone steps that gave an advantage to the higher. But on these open tread timber stairs people could get hurt and he did not wish to upset his host just yet. He moved to one side, holding the handrail, stepping down three steps; heard the move after him, not fast as though to measure him up. He sped up and immediately there was a thundering behind him.

It is at moments like these, he thought, that you do get an idea of the intelligence of your opponents. So many armies trained mindless thugs; indeed, they deliberately trained the mind out of them, in exchange for mindless obedience and brute force. Cannon fodder. There was always the odd one who thought before he or she acted; Berndtt enjoyed meeting the ones like that, sought ways to avoid the violence and swap experiences and part in peace without the need for damage to either side.

Clearly, these two were the former type who could endure huge amounts of pain while maintaining a high level of operation. Still, they would have to be taught a lesson. He was looking forward to it; it seemed ages since he had been tested properly.

He turned quickly and head down charged the nearest man. The momentum of a descending body was met by a hard head in the stomach; the reaction was immediate. Unable to use his hands to attack or defend himself, he folded in two and tumbled down the stairs. Berndtt would have liked to follow and ensure that he stayed down; he feared that it might be only a temporary lapse. Jumping down and stamping on his neck would have kept him clear of the second man and eliminated one problem. But he thought Robert might have been unhappy to lose a man so soon after his arrival; he would have to deal with the other man where he was standing. The second man was taking advantage of Berndtt holding his position.

Berndtt was two steps below him and used it to his favour. The man swung an enormous fist, a left-handed blow that would have dislocated Berndtt's jaw and put him out of action for an appreciable period; funny, he hadn't thought that it was Robert's wish to lose him so soon. Anyway, he didn't pause to consider the rightness or wrongness of the issue, but ducked with ease and punched him in the groin, the height being just appropriate, putting all his weight and a driving force behind his fist. The man gasped, looked down in horror, both at Berndtt and his own body, and turned away, hunched in pain.

A lesser man would have taken advantage of a retreating back; a sharp punch in the kidneys or even tripping him on the stairs. Berndtt hoped that both men had a measure of their new colleague and he looked forward to learning more of their tasks. It might take a while but he reckoned that they should see reason. Or more punishment. Only next time, if there was a next time, he might not desist from the stamp on the neck or the punch to the kidneys.

He turned and walked downstairs, past the first man

who was sitting giving him an evil look. Berndtt paused briefly, looming over him, giving him the worst cold stare. The man dropped his eyes. Berndtt continued downstairs.

The next few days were relatively quiet. Robert left him alone. The two men left him alone too, and were occupied from dawn to dusk away from the mill, driving off in the green van. Berndtt took to going down to the encampment and chatting to the group; mostly in their twenties and thirties, they were enthusiastic, naïve and impractical. He guessed that they had all been brought up in the cities, the product of radical schools and cafés where politics were talked. They did not even have the skill to light a fire outside without help. Berndtt was a saviour, a hero; they invited him to share their meals, their table, and, eventually, their meetings in the large shed.

There was no alternative; the only lead he could follow. Peter returned to the café that evening, bought a carafe of red wine and sat near the front, making conversation as he could; there was always the odd kind girl who took pity on him, sat for a while, stroked his hair as though he was a pet, and moved on. Peter felt morose; how was he to develop his mission? He had never been a field officer, in The Army or in the Intelligence. He had no idea how to survive in a hostile environment or even in an easy situation like the present one, because he had no idea of how to develop an alternative persona. He was Peter, a young Army man, passing time in France with the vain hope of tripping over his agent. As though his agent would be sitting there, waiting to be tripped over.

The door swung open with a crash and a leather clad girl came in, taking off a crash helmet and shaking out her long black hair. She was not pretty but quite tall, a firm figure with a manly face, not unattractive. If you liked that sort of thing; Peter didn't. She strode over to his table.

'What the fuck are you doing here? You don't belong.'

Peter reeled at this attack, stared at the table, coughed, and muttered, 'Having a drink.'

'Aren't there nice little cafés in town that cater for the likes of you tourists?' A sneering tone. She did not sound happy or pleased to see a stranger in her drinking-hole.

'I'm looking for some-ne. Called Bernard.' Peter hardly dared to look at her; she loomed over him, the leather creaking quietly. She bent, took Peter's tumbler and knocked back the glassful. He filled it without comment.

There was a pause; the café had gone silent, as though awaiting the outcome of this unusual meeting.

'This Bernard,' she said. 'Describe him.'

'Oh, not tall, no... '

'Forget the "not"s. My God, what an idiot!' she muttered.

'OK. Well, he's of medium height, about 40, tough looking, short hair. Looks as if he was in the army. Very fit. Doesn't talk much. Has a stare that freezes you.'

Alice knocked back the refilled glass, looking Peter over.

'And who the fuck are you?'

'Oh... he's a friend and I got a message that he might be in trouble. So I came looking for him.'

'I said, who the fuck are you?' Alice stamped her foot; Peter backed away, sliding along the bench.

'I... er... work with him.' Peter had not thought that he would be challenged; the Deuxieme office had not been interested and he assumed that he would continue to be himself, but working where? No, he hadn't given it a thought. A bit of mad extemporisation. 'Well, we don't talk about it, but we work for a… er… a bank. Yes, we do active things for the bank. But… but… we're on holiday here, that's all.'

Alice looked at Peter. What was their real connection? Bernard worked for a bank? Pull the other one. Ex-army clearly; still active, probably in an independent unit, perhaps by himself. But with this man? Don't make me laugh. But Robert had said not to leave any loose strings waiting to snag some authority; he would want Peter to disappear. Her expression didn't change as she said, 'Move up! Do you always keep a woman standing?'

There followed a strange conversation, both sides trying to explore the other, neither having much luck. Peter could be intelligent, when he chose, and recognised the situation. It came straight out of training; he almost wished his tutors could watch his performance. Neither side had much luck and became silent, staring at each other.

Eventually, Alice broke the rhythm. 'I'm seeing him tomorrow; shall I take him a message?'

'You know where he is?'

'Not exactly. But I know where he will be tomorrow.'

'Can I be there?'

Alice thought it over. She could take him to the safe house at Oyonnax and contact Robert. She could take him straight to the mill but she thought that might compromise Robert's use of Bernard. Bugger it all! She was fed up with dancing around Robert and his demands; she had her own life to live, away from those crumby revolutionaries lost in their hopeless dreams. It was time to move on, but what to do with this young man? Perhaps she could use him to put a knot in Robert's tail. Yes, that might be rather amusing. What the hell! Life is only lived once.

'I can tell you a little,' she said, pushing an empty tumbler at Peter. Who took the hint, went to the bar and returned with a full bottle and another tumbler.

'He's tied himself up with a terrorist and a group of revolutionaries.' Woops, maybe a bit too far. Peter's eyes had lit up like headlights; she could see his brain turning, faster and faster. She waited.

'Would... would,' he was gasping. 'Would the terrorist be... be called Le Boucher... by any chance?'

Alice frowned. 'Who? I don't recognise that name.' Bugger, perhaps I've gone too far.

Peter stalled; how to get around this obstacle? He became ingenuous, smiling, nodding like a puppet. 'These revolutionaries; what are they after? I mean... sometimes... they are perfectly innocent, looking for a way to change the awful way governments handle things. You know, leaflets and demonstrations.'

Alice stared at him. What an asshole! What could she do with him? 'This... er... what was that name? A butcher? Who is he?'

'Le Boucher. A terrorist: torture, extortion, execution, kidnapping, bank robbery, fraud, that kind of thing. Apparently operates in this area. The French Police have been after him for years.'

'How do you know all this?'

'Oh... came across a bit of intelligence... I mean... some papers at work. Don't know where they came from.'

'Your bank is interested in Le Boucher?'

'I guess it was something to do with the fraud. Nothing to do with my work.'

'And what exactly do you do?'

'Oh… it's confidential, actually. Something to do with large account-holders. Not criminal, of course.'

Of course, Alice thought. And he's not a very good liar. What the hell shall I do with him? Better to use him than leave him floating around like a loose cannon. Perhaps… perhaps if I was to direct him to the mill, by himself, he could kill two problems for me with a single shot.

Alice was not the kind of person who spent much time in planning or looking ahead; she preferred action. Send in Peter, use him as the battering ram, and follow behind to pick up the leavings. Made good sense. She did not consider the two 'soldiers', the revolutionaries in the camp, or, of course, how Peter would be received. She told him to be nearby at eight in the morning, and disappeared.

TEN

What a bore. He had survived the journey on the back of Alice's bike and got off, with relief and a sore backside, in the village of Arinthod. A sleepy little settlement, no shops or cafés; what did people do for entertainment out here, he wondered. Alice had disappeared; he felt some disappointment, and suddenly very alone; how could he tackle a major terrorist by himself? Perhaps he would find Berndtt who might rescue him. And then he thought, rescue him from what? He was still free. He could go down to the Riviera, he could catch a train to Paris and disappear for a while; he could... sod it, none of it answered. He had to find Berndtt.

Berndtt was wondering why Robert had brought him here; he had maintained his myth of locating revolutionary groups and forming an organisation to unify their efforts but the soldiers looked on him with suspicion and would not communicate with him. To his surprise and a small amount of relief, they avoided him, moved away at mealtimes and never took part when Robert initiated conversation. Robert, every now and then, used the 'hammer' word, even in front of the soldiers who smirked; Berndtt dutifully became a machine, carrying out any subservient tasks instructed, thinking how he would take pleasure in revenge, when the time came. In the meantime, Robert and his soldiers were away each day, driving off early, returning before or after the evening meal, no indication of where they had been, or what they had been doing. Berndtt would not ask the soldiers; he did not wish to be seen as over curious.

The camp proved more rewarding. They were friendly from the start, particularly when they learnt of his skills, in fire lighting, in unarmed combat that they were all keen to learn, and in handling firearms. The weapons had been an embarrassment, stowed in a cupboard, not lubricated, boxes of ammunition mixed up, no bandoliers, no training targets. They had told him that they might be called upon, in the distant future, to defend themselves; there was never any question of mounting an armed operation, actually attacking human beings. That was entirely outside their conception of revolution, which was essentially a matter of distributing literature and persuading the general population at meetings that the present system should be overturned. They were very clear that that was the only way forward. But when Berndtt asked them what they would do if the French Army attacked their camp, the women said that they would cook for the soldiers and the men said they would resist them, with force if necessary. And what might that force be, asked Berndtt. There was much muttering, some laughing and then he was shown the munitions cupboard. He asked how they knew when any stranger was approaching, how they could defend themselves; they did not understand him, could not appreciate the concept that a person somewhere might disagree with their work to the extent of attacking them. Even when Berndtt pointed out that they were carrying out illegal activities for

Robert. He suggested that some of the children might be posted on the scarp as lookouts, a portable radio to warn of incomers; they thought about it, wondered whether it would be safe, what hours were necessary, who was reliable enough. Endless democratic discussions.

After that day, he was invited into their big shed; apparently, permission from Robert had been necessary, but they had persuaded him that Berndtt would teach them unarmed combat and to shoot. Robert had been delighted that it was taken out of his hands, they said; his secret operations meant that the two soldiers were too busy to introduce the camp to weapons and, in any case, he knew that his two soldiers had little respect for the camp occupants, the so-called 'revolutionaries'.

When invited, Berndtt strolled into the shed when the women were taking in the morning coffee and sat with the men while they were taking their break. Looking around, the shed appeared to be split into two with a full height partition. Nearby, the room was full of tables, good overhead lighting and piles of paper with some sophisticated printing machines at the far end. He waited to be introduced to their work; it was not long.

One of the men saw him looking. 'You see, Berndtt, we are working to tackle the power of the big banks, the meritocracy and the rich. We will instigate revolution before they realise it. Robert taught us what to do and takes our work away; we only have to produce it.'

Berndtt said that was interesting, and asked what Robert did with it.

'Why,' the young man said with a laugh. 'Make money, of course!'

'You must be making a lot of money,' said Berndtt.

'We don't need it. He pays for our time and we don't care if he makes a profit; that's his business.'

'And, what are you producing?'

'Bearer bonds. You see, they are a very safe way of making money; they can't be traced and the banks have to pay up. Or any organisation that Robert believes he can persuade to pay up. It's ideal!' he said with a laugh.

Forgery and extortion, and perhaps that was not all they were producing. Did he care? Not a great deal. It wasn't his business; they would get caught one day and see the inside of prisons for decades. What was the point in telling them?

'And do you print through those doors?'

The young man became shifty, wriggling in his seat, avoiding Berndtt's stare. 'Well, I don't work there. I don't know what they do in there.'

'Oh yes you do, Michel. Don't be so coy!' One of the women was standing over him, a large coffee pot in hand, barging against his shoulder.

'Well,' said Michel. 'It's very secret but it's our other way of attacking the rich. I mean, as well, and particularly the young.'

Berndtt sat in silence, waiting.

Michel couldn't contain himself. 'You wouldn't believe it but through those doors is a laboratory.'

Berndtt raised his eyebrows. Michel rushed on. 'Drugs. A type of cocaine, I don't know any more than that but it sells like anything and we always make sure that it sells to the young rich. Rot them!' He spat on the floor.

The woman came over. 'Here, you filthy little beast. Now go get a cloth and clear up your mess.' As he slunk off, she gave Berndtt a grin. 'Got to keep these young lads in place. What are you doing here? I can't see you fitting in here.'

Berndtt smiled, said nothing.

She poured him more coffee with a shrug. 'Well, it's no business of mine. But we're very grateful for your help. Will you let the women fire them guns?'

Next morning and Berndtt instructed them in the parts of their weapons; mostly handguns of various types, a few sub-machine guns, Uzis, SiG Sauers and other makes. They had to strip them down, lubricate and reassemble. There was some muttering; 'When are we going to fire them?' and 'Do we need to know how to take it to pieces?' Berndtt pointed out that if they were fighting in the dark and the gun jammed, they would need to strip it down immediately. There was some sceptical muttering about fighting in the dark.

'Won't it just be a case of showing our strength?'

Berndtt asked him what he meant by that.

'Well, you know, like the police. We just appear armed and they will back off.'

'After they have shot you,' was Berndtt's blunt reply.

The revolutionaries looked at each other; it was beginning to seem that things had become more dangerous since Berndtt had arrived. Perhaps it had been a mistake, the learning how to shoot, to fight. They were all right before when the nice Robert helped them in the work and provided money for the essentials and food. Eventually, one of the men said, 'Well, we'll be all right. Robert needs us, he will protect us. He's not called Le Bou—'

'What you saying?' An angry interruption from another man.

The first shrugged. 'I didn't know it was such a secret.' And walked off.

Le Boucher! Robert was Le Boucher! Berndtt made no sign, sipped his coffee, sat in silence. When would he kill Le Boucher?

Hot and frustrated, Peter walked down the lane, over the scarp and paused, looking down at the Mill. A late afternoon sun made all look quiet and peaceful, mellow. He moved his bag onto the other shoulder and wandered down into the gravel circle, to sit down on the stone mounting block in the shade of the trees on either side. What was he meant to do now? Knock on the door? Not a good idea; he had been taught all sorts of techniques for overcoming the enemy, and knocking on their door was not included. And yet he sat there in full view; perhaps he could pretend to be a tourist, coming upon an ancient building, a water mill, not listed in the local guides, his own discovery. But he was getting tired and thirsty.

He looked around. A driveway to one side, running parallel with the river. Worth exploring. He wandered down, as casually as he could as he turned his back on the mill, and came to another clearing, this one more haphazard, camper vans around, a large shed on the left against the river bank, trees around, the remains of a large bonfire in the centre. One car, an ancient Citroën, the grass coming up between its wheels.

And people. Two women and a few children, mostly young, who stopped and stared at him. Old clothes, a bit hippy, he thought. He smiled, put his bag down, and approached one of the women. She stared at him as though he was a fallen from an aeroplane, a being foreign to the area, too smartly dressed, too polite in his approach.

'Excuse me, but—'

'What do you want?' Her suspicions were running high; this smelt of government intrusion, a tax inspector or worse.

'I... er... you wouldn't have a glass of water, would you?'

She sniffed, pointed to a water butt, a tin mug hanging at the side. Peter looked, groaned internally at the thought of a colony of bacteria, and scooped water after wiping the mug with his handkerchief.

'What do you want here?' Her tone was aggressive. She called to one of the children. 'Here, get yer father.'

The child, a boy of about six, darted across the clearing and into the shed. Peter stood still, sure that he could persuade them that he was quite innocent, no threat to them at all. He smiled again. The woman was unmoved, stood with hands on hips looking him up and down. The children edged closer, whispering among themselves. After a short while, a man came out of the shed, followed by the boy. He squinted in the light, shook himself and advanced on Peter.

'What do you want here?'

'I... I'm looking for someone. And I wondered—'

'There's nobody here you could want. Clear off!'

'I thought—'

'I don't care a twopenny kangaroo's fart for your thought. Now, get going before I call out the guns.'

Peter quailed. He hadn't thought that he might meet a resistance of this sort. He had learnt unarmed combat but what was the point when guns came into it? He stood still, gave a slight smile, shuffled his feet.

'Bernard! Bernard!' called the man. 'Give us a hand move this stupid bugger.'

A pause.

Berndtt came out of the shed, saw the situation, and started to turn back to the shed.

'Berndtt! Please, could you tell these good people that I am no threat. And could we have a word or two?'

No point in pretending he didn't know this young idiot. He came over to the woman, shrugged, told her that he had met this idiot on his travels and would see him off the premises. Turning to Peter, he grabbed him, walked up the driveway away from the camp and said, 'What the hell are you doing here? Trying to get me killed? You sent me to find Le Boucher; I'm doing that. You're getting in the way.'

Peter stopped, stared at Berndtt. 'You disappeared. I haven't heard from you. What was I to think? The Colonel sent me to find you and bring you back; you don't have to kill anyone, just return to England, to camp.'

Berndtt shook himself; he could just return to England, could he? And he was so close. But he was not going to tell Peter that, a quick way to get killed. Best to get him away, somehow.

'I'll follow you,' he said. 'You get back to England.'

'I'm not leaving without you. To be honest, my life is worth nothing if I don't return with you.'

Berndtt looked at him. Hopeless; what sort of a soldier was this young man? They went back to the camp and Berndtt went up to the man. 'Can you do something for me, Henri?'

'Of course, Bernard. Just mention it.'

'Keep this young man under wraps, away from Robert

and his goons, and I'll take him away tomorrow. But there must be no gossip.'

'That's hard, Bernard.' He looked to his wife. 'Can we stow him in the camper? Tell the children to keep quiet about him, at least until tomorrow?'

The woman grunted. 'I don't like it. Can't guarantee it won't get around the camp but there's a bit of floor-space he can use. As long as he's clean.' She laughed.

Berndtt turned to Peter. 'Stay hidden. Now. Until I come for you tomorrow.'

He was bustled away into an ancient camper, out of sight. Berndtt went back to the shed where they told the community about Bernard's visitor and asked for privacy.

No sentry had spotted Peter's arrival. The parents had not yet agreed on a rota and felt that it was not necessary, so no sentries were used. The long summer evening passed in peace, Berndtt eating and staying with the community until he returned to the Mill at night. There was no question of how he spent his days; Robert and his soldiers knew and were happy that he was out of their way. That night, they returned from their mission late.

At three a.m., a dozen Deuxieme agents in black outfits, night vision goggles, and armed with sub-machine guns, swarmed over the scarp and surrounded the mill and the camp.

ELEVEN

The Mill showed no signs of life, no lights showing. The Deuxieme agents, wearing black tunics and carrying submachine guns, handguns and tear gas cylinders, assembled in front. The leader of the twelve gave silent hand directions, four to surround the mill, the remainder to follow him to explore the perimeter. He led them down the track into the revolutionaries' camp. All was still. An owl drifted over their heads and bats flitted between the trees; the bonfire glowed red, a thin spiral of smoke rising into the pre-dawn. At a signal from the leader, the eight were posted around the site, including in front of the shed. At a brief flash of a torch, the men knocked on the camper vans and broke into the shed.

It was no accident that they were there. The young officer from England had visited the local office, full of zeal, keen to find Le Boucher. They had pretended a lack of interest, armed him with an old heavy gun, let him think he was on his own. And then followed him. They had seen his meeting with Alice, a person already documented by the office as under suspicion, they had ascertained when he might be leaving Lyon, and it was a relatively simple task to track his progress through the countryside to the mill. They had called up the troops and equipment, prepared a plan of attack and waited for the hour when most people are at their weakest. They would capture Le Boucher, parade him in front of the Judiciaire, and claim the credit due to them. If the young Englishman should be a nuisance, trying to make spurious claims for himself, a quick phone call to Paris would see him recalled to England and told to mind his own business, keep his mouth shut, or worse trouble would descend. Under no conditions would the English be allowed to claim the credit.

The revolutionaries tumbled out of bed, blearily, men, women and children, some crying, and staggered to their doors to be greeted with sharp orders that they must open up, line up outside, silent. They followed the instructions without question or hesitation; some gave a thought to their armament but it was all locked up in the shed to keep it away from the children. Peter was included in their numbers; the agents did not treat him differently but bundled them all into the shed where a guard was mounted while preliminary questioning began. He maintained his story that he was looking for a friend and staying the night; no, he did not know these people, had met them for the first time last night, they were very kind and had put him up. No, he had not been taken to the shed; he had no idea what it contained. He assumed that they were a band of hippies, making a living as best as they could. No, he knew nothing about the mill; there had been nobody there when he arrived. Why did he come here? He believed that his friend was travelling in these parts. What was his occupation? He worked for a bank in England. They left him alone and did not enquire about 'the friend'.

The commander realised that Le Boucher might be in the mill; he had a choice to make. Take control of the camp and its product, or have a gunfight with the mill, by which time the camp and its product might be seriously compromised. He had resolved to deal with the camp first, a softer option, hoping that the mill would remain undisturbed. The camp came first and he waited for word from the four at the mill.

Berndtt woke suddenly; this was no new habit, he had been accustomed to waking at any change in his perimeter, which included the area outside the building. Tip-toeing to the window, he looked out, saw the eight file off to the camp and watched the four spread out around the mill; they had limited access as the mill stood over the river. He had no idea about how they might have been summoned but thought that Peter might have had something to do with it; he wished that Peter had had the common sense to tell him about it.

He dressed silently, checked his weapon, and ripped the flex from the lamp beside the bed. He went to look for Robert. A gentle knock; Robert was asleep; there was no sound from the soldiers.

'Monsieur Robert, we have visitors.'

Robert was awake in a moment, gun in hand. 'Wake the soldiers. Now, hammer.'

Berndtt withdrew, paused about three minutes, and went back in. Robert was dressing with speed. 'Wait outside, you fool.'

Is it now, Berndtt asked himself. Silently, so that the soldiers don't hear. Why wait? What is the advantage?

He stepped back into the room; Robert had his back to him.

'Are they awake?'

Berndtt dropped the flex around Robert's neck, pulling, twisting. Robert dropped to the floor, a dangerous move that might have broken his neck and swung his gun towards Berndtt, gasping 'Hammer! Hammer!'

Berndtt stamped on his wrist, the gun went off, a loud percussive sound exaggerated by the floor. He pulled back on the flex, kicking Robert who was becoming weaker.

There was a pounding on the stairs and Berndtt could hear the men outside the door. 'Are you all right, commander? We heard a shot.'

Berndtt muttered a reply, giving a delay that saw Robert drop to the floor where Berndtt stamped hard on his neck, a crack as a bone broke, the body slumped, dead. Berndtt stood behind the door, muttering again. The men broke into the room, one behind the other; he brought his hand down hard on the neck of the first, pulled him around in front of himself and shot the second, a double tap, head and heart. As the second man fell, he put a bullet into the first man's head.

The trouble with carrying out a commission in a situation where foreign law-enforcing personnel were present was that he was unlikely to be made welcome and would more likely be seen as some kind of assassin who had a grievance against Le Boucher. And he did not wish to give the armed forces outside the benefit of capturing him in addition to claiming, no doubt, the elimination of Le Boucher and his thugs. Records might be examined, his past dragged into question, certain eliminations that involved the Conglomerate.

There was time to spare; the men outside had made no attempt at entry, nor seemed particularly concerned at guarding the mill; two of them were sitting on the mounting block in the centre; they could have been taken out easily, shot by the thugs, no great range. He saw them on their radio, a whoop of joy, a further relaxation of surveillance. Berndtt did not concern himself with Peter; he was sure that the British Army would deal with him in time.

Dropping down to the first floor, he examined the structure of the building around the water wheel shaft. The wheel continued to turn, a loud sloshing sound that drowned out any movement inside the mill. He searched for a few minutes, and found it, a maintenance hatch opening out into the flume. Opening it, he found he was behind the wheel as it rotated, concealed from the opposite bank. A narrow ledge led to either side, covered with green slime. The noise was much greater, the sound of the water in the wheel mixed with the river rushing by, a rocky mountain stream.

He left the hatch, closing it behind him, edging along the ledge. There was little to hold onto, until he noticed a couple of rings let into the wall, presumably to assist in hauling the wheel into place. Swinging from one to the other he reached the furthest extent of the ledge and realised that he was coming into view; there was nobody there. A cow, grazing with two others, looked up, stared at the figure of a man spreadeagled against the mill wall, paused in the chewing briefly, found no more of interest, and returned to grazing. The stream, a fierce current that had prevented the agents from crossing to the other side where they could have extended their perimeter, was before him. He could not be seen, but he could make no progress without being spotted from one side of the mill. He rested.

At the camp, the agents had seen the forgeries, opened the door to the laboratory and even discovered the explosives secured under the benches that Robert had instructed should be blown before any discovery. The revolutionaries, men, women and children, were feeling sorry for themselves, sitting around, hungry, thirsty, and tired. Only Michel put on the façade of a brave resistance, before a quick tap from the butt of a gun reduced him to tears. Peter sat in silence among the others, muttering with them, and wondering how the Deuxieme, who had shown such little interest when he had visited them, had taken the camp. And wondering too what would happen to him.

Berndtt looked around; there seemed to be little choice. There was a small weir at the bottom of the tail race and he stepped across to find himself on the further wall of the flume, the river in front of him. It looked dangerous, the water crashing around large boulders, sliding through the middle at great speed. A dipper hopped from boulder to boulder, lightly. Berndtt sighed, and stepped into the edge of the river.

The current was not so fierce and he found he was able to stand, the water plucking at his legs, cold as ice. He waded to the nearest boulder, two metres but a struggle, and rested on the side of it. Hauling himself up, he sat on it and realised that he was coming into view from the side of the mill and that there was no time to waste.

The top of the rock was dry in a small area, not much larger than his hands. He pulled himself up, sitting and then standing, placing his wet boots on the dry patch. Across the centre of the river was another boulder, about two and a half metres away, the water sliding over the top of it, perhaps ten centimetres deep but fast. A poor landing zone.

Berndtt did not pause; he gathered himself and leapt, trusting to his grip on the boulder he was leaving. Arriving at the further boulder, he spread himself on all fours, clamping over the boulder. But he was sliding inextricably over it towards deep water; he would struggle to survive if he was washed into the current, forced underwater and thrown against rocks, and all in water with a temperature just above freezing. Edging around the rock, he found a ledge about two feet down; finding a grip for his feet, he bounded upwards, diving over the boulder and head first into the water on the far side.

He felt himself whirled around by the current, crashing into a rock, all in a moment before he realised that he could stand, his feet sinking into the gravel bottom as he leant against a boulder, the water chest deep, flowing around him. He waded to the shore and pulled himself out.

Water poured from his clothes, his shoes, his body. He lay back, warming himself in the early sun, resting. The cows, startled at first by the sudden appearance of a river monster, stared in disbelief before returning to grazing.

He rolled over, keeping low between the tussocks of grass; the mill was lit by early sunshine, a few small windows in upper floors. He could see the roofs of the camp below.

A man in black was coming round the upstream side. Berndtt sank into the ground, watching. It would be a long shot if he was seen and he was sure that he would be taken to be one of the terrorists; shoot first, ask questions after. He did not wish them to know that there was a man unaccounted for, even if they came to that conclusion after searching the mill.

The man glanced at the river and turned away; after all, there was no escape there, was there? Even an idiot wouldn't surrender his body to that torrent.

While he lay there, he saw a group of soldiers coming up from the camp to the mill. With the noise of the river, he could hear nothing from the mill and assumed that they broke in and found the bodies. There was a further search at either end, another perusal of the far bank; Berndtt had slid back, concealed by the bank and the grass. Before long, he saw four black buses with bars across the windows appear going down to the camp and depart shortly afterwards.

They were allowed water and to pick up food from their homes. Peter found himself pushed into a black bus, the men separated from the women and children.

There was a great deal of crying, protests and calling out; he sat in silence. The men were beginning to have suspicions and eyed him with hostility; why, he had arrived on the eve of the raid, an unknown, not a revolutionary or even a journalist like Bernard.

In Lyon, he was taken for further questioning alone by agents who had not been on the raid. He told them that there was a man called Robert, who he believed was Le Boucher, who ran the operation; they knew that, they said. He lived in the mill; had they caught him? He was assured that Le Boucher was no longer a threat, taken by French agents, without disclosing that they had found his dead body and the bodies of two others, not known to them but obviously mercenaries. Peter was put onto a plane for England.

At the base, in front of the Colonel, he claimed a great victory; Le Boucher was caught, he had led the Deuxieme agents to his hide-out and discovered his factory. He could not say what it was used for, he had not been allowed to view it, but it was clear that the revolutionaries were working for Le Boucher. When pressed about the location of his agent, he told them that he had seen him, briefly, but Berndtt had taken no part in the action and had disappeared. After a brief discussion, Berndtt's name was removed from the list of Army secret agents and therefore denied any further assistance overseas.

Berndtt felt exhausted and wet. He picked himself up and started trotting upstream. Before long, he came to a plank bridge, green with moss but sound, and crossed back to the familiar side. Circling around the mill and walking just below the scarp, he saw the trucks of the agents pull out and wondered how he was going to get back to Lyon and proceed to Geneva. As he stepped into the road, a motorbike came towards him; he drew back to the rocks. He had been seen; the bike came to a stop, the visor was lifted and Alice said, 'Get on the back. Let's go.'

TWELVE

Midday, and Alice roared through the lanes around Arinthod, Berndtt holding on, wondering why he had entrusted himself to her, why he had not disappeared alone as so often before. But in contrast with so often before, he was stranded in the countryside without car or, more rarely, friendly transport. An unusual situation; how life had changed since his retirement. And all he wanted was to be left alone now. His experiment with the British Army had been amusing but unfulfilling; he had assumed that he would be part of a team, albeit to operate alone, but not sent out with no support to tackle a dangerous terrorist. Not that it had been a great problem but reinforced the belief that he should remain a loner. Forget the British Army, forget Bristol.

Alice was riding fast, clipping the banks, breaking past bicycles at speed to shouts of protest. She came up behind a tractor and trailer. It was trundling along at a slow speed, the driver puffing on a cheroot, a cloud of smoke around his head on which was clamped a filthy cap. He looked back, a shaggy face, low brows, slowed a little, spat to one side, a long stream of spittle, and turned back, the tractor chugging as though breathing its last.

Alice fumed, the high banks prevented her from seeing forward. She revved the engine, throwing the bike around, side to side; the man slowed, turned in his seat, gave her a long look without expression and spat again, before facing forward. Alice tried the horn, a miserable high toot. Again, the man turned, stared and spat, and returned to his slow progress down the road.

A field entrance opened up to one side, and Alice accelerated into it along side the trailer, desperate for a chance to overtake. The man looked down at her, a slight grin as he closed off her escape; she slammed on the brakes, skidded on the wet grass, threw the bike to one side and fell over, sliding to a rest in the hedge. The tractor pulled to a halt; the driver stared, gave a huge shrug and set the tractor in motion once more, a puff of black exhaust, a deliberate chug and disappeared round the corner. Alice swore richly for about five minutes, scraping mud off her leathers.

Berndtt considered his situation. He was stranded in the remote countryside with a woman whose behaviour was random, to put it mildly. He was removing himself from a crime scene with which he did not wish to be associated. It was possible that the French police were still looking for him. It was possible that the Conglomerate had not heard of his success and were still looking to eliminate him. It was possible, remotely, that the British Army were interested in his whereabouts. In Lyons were Juliette and Max who would undoubtedly make life difficult for him. The motorbike might be unusable. Further, his clothes were wet and muddy and he was hungry. The last was the least important. What should he do now?

Investigate the motorbike. Do something about Alice; he did not really want to leave a body near here. The tractor driver had seen too much. Swallow his pride. Even help Alice. Then get rid of her, one way or another.

The bike had little damage; the ground had been too soft. They pulled it upright, scraped some mud off, bent back a foot rest, replaced the oil cooler reservoir, and started it. The electric starter whined; silence. Alice cursed, kicked the bike. Berndtt sat on it, kick-started the bike; at the third kick the fuel ran into the carburettors and the engine caught. Berndtt considered leaving alone, but he ran the engine warm and invited Alice to sit on the back. She looked thunderous, beckoned to him to move, swore at him, called him a *salaud* and a Kraut bastard. He sat impassive, made as if to start; she climbed on, gripping her arms around him. They rode back to Oyonnax without incident. The tractor was long gone.

In the house, Berndtt paused inside the door. 'Is Robert here? Are you expecting him?'

Alice spat, 'He can go to hell! He's a bastard, and I don't want to see him.'

'He's coming here, is he?'

'I don't know. What the hell, am I his keeper, or assistant, or... or something?'

'I'm not waiting for him to find me.' He got up, went to the toilet, and was making for the door when Alice stopped him.

'Hey, hey! Don't go. We've got things to talk about. Won't you stay?'

Berndtt turned and looked at her. She looked contrite; he guessed an apology was not in her vocabulary. He might need her to get to Lyons; buses were not safe. Too many inquisitive people.

They sat; Alice found some food, bread and cheese, a bottle of wine. For a while, they were silent, eating, looking at each other. Berndtt had already determined that Alice was not armed; he had not advertised the weaponry that he was carrying, taken off the two soldiers. He wondered where she had come from, what background, what education. She did not look stupid to him, a keen look from dark eyes, a mass of black hair, sharp face, sharp expression; but the eyes never settled, roaming always from one thing to another. Perhaps she was on drugs.

She sighed. 'I thought we could be good together.'

Berndtt looked at her; what was she thinking now?

She went on. 'Look, there is a great deal of goods and money that we can raid. We could make a killing.'

Berndtt said nothing. Wait, always wait.

'You know where, don't you? At the mill. Robert is minting it, the bastard, and I've only received a pittance. We could raid the mill, when they're away. What do you say?'

'You saw the Deuxieme? You think they will have left anything?'

'They will have seen the shed, the drugs and all that boring paperwork.'

Berndtt sighed to himself. That boring paperwork, the forgery, was the wealth. What did she think she was going to find?

'There's this room in the mill; they won't have found it. He keeps his money in it, valuables from raids, I don't know, whatever.'

Berndtt mentally ran through the mill; the room, if it existed, must be either on the top floor or like a cellar dug into the ground beneath the ground floor. More likely the latter. And then he thought, why should I be interested? The last thing I shall do is return to the mill.

'You don't need me. Keep it all.'

'I need a lookout man, and somebody to help carry the loot.'

'You'll find some petty criminal, somebody on the lookout for a good thing.'

'Can't trust them. And if it comes to a shoot-out, I guess that you must be the guy.'

'So how were you proposing to go about it?' Berndtt was reluctant to make an enemy of Alice; she would shop him to the highest bidder, without doubt. He doubted that she had had a friend for more than a day or two; she would use and misuse.

'We need a truck or a van. Make a daytime raid when they are away. In out, perhaps fifteen minutes.'

'You know where this room is?'

'Can't be difficult. Must be easy to find. And then we split up the proceeds, seventy thirty.'

'Seventy thirty?'

'My masterplan. That's reasonable, isn't it?'

Berndtt felt drawn into a nightmare scenario, a plan devised by somebody who had seen too many thrillers and never had experience of hard crime. Or hard criminals, it seemed, apart from the small leavings that Robert had given her. She had never been on his work trips, he was sure; he had seen Robert and his two soldiers leave most mornings, a single vehicle, quietly at dawn. And they had never discussed the work with him.

'Seventy thirty?' he said, looking her directly in the face, a cold look that could kill. She ducked her head, laughed, a hollow unconvincing laugh, and coughed.

'Sixty forty?' It sounded like a plea.

He let a few minutes pass. 'What things have you been

doing, these last years?'

'Oh, this and that.'

'Money?'

'I was married once. Took him for a bit; I don't have to work, but I could do with a bit extra.'

'What's this and that?'

'I… er, I tried University a bit. Too constricting, didn't have the course that suited me. Bummed around here and there, you know, India and places.'

'What course would suit you?'

She didn't answer, fiddling with a knife. There wasn't a course to suit her, was there. He pitied the husband; perhaps he was a weak man. Got what he deserved.

He let time pass. Eventually, he said, 'I must be on my way. We can talk about this again. I need to get to Lyon.'

'Hey, are you dropping out?'

'Lyon? No. You need Lyon too. The van and guns; guess you can get them in Lyon. Do you know where?'

'Sure, sure. I know things. Yeah, let's get to Lyon.'

Alice was riding, Berndtt perched on the back; not a good bike for a passenger, he thought. She cruised through the town, within the limits, and accelerated hard on the open road, weaving between the traffic, earning hoots and shouts; she seemed oblivious to how others felt, whether she forced them to brake or not.

It could not last. There was a siren behind them, police without doubt. Berndtt tapped on her shoulder; she went faster, taking rash risks between oncoming vehicles, playing Russian roulette with oncoming overtaking cars. The siren fell behind; Berndtt heard her laugh, a hoarse shout caught on the wind. He felt helpless and closer to death than he had been for a long time. It was stupid, a stupid way to go.

When running in their own lane, he bent down, searching. Swore quietly when he touched hot metal. Ah, got it. He turned off the fuel. For some yards the bike ran, then faltered, coughing before cutting out. It slewed to a halt, Alice frantically twisting the throttle, shouting in frustration. Berndtt stepped off as soon as possible and walked away through a hedge into a field and sat down; he found he was shaking, an unaccustomed response to stress. I must be getting old, he thought.

Before long, he heard the siren approaching, braking and halting behind Alice. He knelt, peering through the hedge. The officer, helmet and leathers, gaiters and boots, stood looking at Alice who was still sitting on the bike, checking the controls, searching, searching. He produced a notebook and was taking details when the starter motor whined and the engine coughed. No fuel in the cylinders. With one huge swing, he grasped Alice by the collar and swung her off the bike, depositing her roughly on the ground; she twisted and swore. He cuffed her and left her sitting while he removed the key from the bike and went back to his bike to call for back-up. Returning to Alice, he asked her where she had dropped her passenger.

Berndtt could hear the conversation, tempted to put distance from the police but keen to know whether Alice would give him up; he didn't trust her, and she had no reason to trust him. To his surprise, she said she didn't know, he hadn't been there since she stopped at a junction back there. What junction? I don't know. You'll have to do better than that. He must have leapt off. What junction? I've been following you and I saw no junction. The officer began to look around but was unwilling to leave his prisoner. Who is he, then? Alice coughed, looked around vaguely. I don't know. You mean you carry a passenger and you don't know who they are? He was hitching. Well, I guess he's gone now, said the officer. Let's get you to the station. But my bike? It will be collected, sometime. We don't have staff free to run around the country picking up law-breaking bikes at any time, you know.

Berndtt had heard enough. Here he was, a long way from civilisation, in a field, and possibly under suspicion from the police. Thank you, Alice. He wondered; perhaps she did not know where he was sitting. When the police had departed with Alice, he returned to the road and hitch-hiked; he didn't expect a lift. He was too old, probably didn't look 'safe', but he could think of no other way to arrive at Lyon. A lay-by was ahead. He approached a driver of a cement lorry and, standing well back, asked him politely if he could lift him into Lyon; he would be prepared to pay him. The driver looked him up and down, asked him how much he was going to give, and opened the door for him.

Late afternoon as he wandered down the street in the centre of Lyon. The lorry driver had been taciturn but happy to go out of his way to drop Berndtt near the centre. Berndtt was looking for Mack; he visited the usual bars, hoping not to see Juliette and gave up early, looking for a meal and a hotel.

Next day, he went out again, and almost immediately ran into Alice. There was no chance for escape, without being seen, and there was still a chance that she might shop him to the police; he doubted that they had finished with her.

'Alice, bonjour.'

'Ah there you are, you bastard.'

'The ride, dangerous, asking for trouble.'

'What do you know?' she said, a fierce scowl, sucking on a roll-up. 'Buy me a drink. We'll talk.'

He followed her into the bar. Damn, it was the radicals' bar and Juliette might appear. He bought a bottle of red wine and sat with her near the front of the bar. Towards the rear he could see some girls whom he had met before; he ignored their waves. Alice was a big enough handful.

'So, what did you think of my plan? Pretty good, *n'est ce pas?*'

'How do you know he has a stash?'

'Stands to reason. Anyway, there will be something to rip off. He won't be living like a monk.'

Berndtt bent his head, apparently deep in thought. 'Yes, it's a plan.'

''Course it's a plan, you bastard. Leaving me to face the police!'

'I would only have complicated it for you.'

'I'm out on bail, of sorts. Have to report to the pigs every day until they decide what to do with me.'

'You find a van. I'll look for guns.'

She perked up, made a clenched fist salute, and pulling him to her, gave him a kiss on the cheek. Berndtt considered flooring her, resisted putting an elbow into her ribs, slid off the bench and made for the door.

'Hey, where do we meet next?' She roared out loudly; girls the other end of the room looked up. She flicked them a V-sign, and stood, hands on hips, staring at Berndtt. 'Want to spend the night with me?'

He shrugged. 'Can't. Busy.' And slipped out of the door. There was a roar behind him; he didn't turn but made off down the street fast. Now to get away.

Juliette was walking towards him. Mein Gott, this town was impossible.

She looked up, her face brightening, arms opening. 'Bernard! Mon Dieu, where have you been?'

Without stopping, he caught her arm, whirled her around and continued walking down the street, fast.

'Eh! Not so fast. What is it? The police on your trail?' A short laugh.

'I have to get away. You remember the Conglomerate? The ones who besieged your father's house? How is he, by the way?'

'Papa? He's a darling, always looking for trouble. Where shall we go?'

'Juliette, I must leave Lyon. Now. But I haven't found a friend of mine. Man called Mack. You won't know him.'

'If he comes asking, what shall I tell him?'

'Tell him, I've left for Marseilles.'

'Marseilles? Mon Dieu, Bernard, are you running or something? Anyway, I was hoping to spend a few days with you. You know, the two of us. Somewhere quiet.'

The last time some girl had wanted to spend quiet time with him she had been left strangled on a hillside; he didn't want to leave Juliette like that. She deserved better.

'You want to come to Marseilles? It's a rough town.'

She looked unhappy at the thought.

'Look,' he said. 'I'll be back soon. Have to sort out something. Where can I reach you?'

Her face crumpled; such a child, he thought. Well, all children have to grow up sometime.

He took the train for Geneva that afternoon.

THIRTEEN

Geneva looked the same. He took a room in the same hotel near the station, ate at the same cheap cafés, and walked the same streets.

Until he was recognised.

He had not had a chance to visit his bank, to buy some new clothes, or even to find somewhere better to stay.

A large black Mercedes slid past him, and before he had become aware of any threat, there was a man standing in front of him, another behind, and a third hanging about as though he was window shopping. He wasn't.

Berndtt looked at the car and at the men. The usual East European thugs, poorly fitted dark suits, ties that no man had ever tied. One he recognised from a little trouble at the yacht harbour; the man had fallen in the water. He could get away, but then there would be a fall-out; they would shop him to the police and it would be impossible to travel. Something was not quite right and then he realised what it was; the man window shopping turned round. It was Mack.

'Berndtt, good to see you. The directors asked if you would be so good to spare a few minutes; they would be happy to offer you lunch.'

'What do they want?' Berndtt knew that an invitation often meant a capture, a renewal of danger and trials. But Mack?

'It's OK, really. They don't mean trouble.'

Berndtt looked at the other men; they attempted a smile, more of a crude grimace, backing away. No practice in smiling. 'Do we have to take them?' he said, indicating the 'soldiers'.

'Is it a problem? Oh… all right.' Mack spoke to the men, an Eastern European language that Berndtt did not know. At first, the men looked unhappy, aggressive, looking from Berndtt to Mack; Mack produced some money, gestured down the street and shrugged. They shrugged back, laughed and picked up their heels, taking off down the street at speed. Berndtt raised his eyebrows.

'Oh, it's all right. I told them that there is a bar down the road that does cheap breakfasts until midday, and if they got a move on—'

'That easy?' Berndtt laughed.

Back at the yacht club, Mack ushered Berndtt into a private diningroom. Six men sat around the table, dark suits, polished shoes, urbane expressions. They looked like a committee of bankers and Berndtt realised that is what they were, though possibly not always on the side of the law. They rose as one and bowed, as one, before sitting again, except for one.

'Good to see you, Berndtt. I trust that my men did not appear too aggressive; they don't always know how to behave.'

Berndtt said nothing, standing at the table, Mack behind him.

'Please, will you sit with us? We were about to lunch; you would be very welcome to join us.'

Berndtt looked round; Mack was waiting by the door, waiting to be dismissed, no doubt. 'He stays, of course,' he said.

'Of course,' said the banker, gesturing to Mack to join them.

The table was round; the bankers sat around one side. Berndtt went round the table, apologising in advance for disrupting the silent men, and sat between the two end bankers. Mack sat at the other side; he was clearly unused to sitting with bankers. Noting Berndtt's actions, the spokesperson said, 'Come, let us share the whole table,' and the other bankers spread themselves around. Berndtt found himself between the spokesperson and another man, Mack opposite to him. If there was trouble, he felt safer; there was a door behind him, an escape route at hand.

The food arrived, served by uniformed club staff, a five course meal, ingredients of which Berndtt hardly recognised. The wines were good but he drank little. The conversation was light, comments and stories about Geneva and the Swiss, a few tales of bankers who had been bettered by the Conglomerate. Occasionally, he was asked a question, about his recent whereabouts, his present abode, what car he enjoyed driving, even a delicate question as to his marital state. Or they referred to him for an opinion on a geographical or political matter; he replied vaguely. He read few newspapers and held no political views. Mack sat in silence the whole meal, without showing embarrassment.

At the end of the meal, chairs were pushed back, cigars lit, liqueurs offered, and a silence fell over them all. The chairman, for it was he who had addressed Berndtt before, raised his hand; the other bankers turned to him, except for one, who continued to stare at Berndtt.

'Berndtt, we are very glad to have this opportunity to meet you.'

There was a murmur of agreement from the other men. Berndtt smiled, a rare gesture. The meal had been good, he felt relaxed; the one banker who might have a grudge was in the minority.

'We wished to clear the air between ourselves and yourself.'

Again, a polite subdued murmur.

'We realise that our former way of working with you was not conducive to good relationships.'

Berndtt almost burst out laughing. He recalled how they had captured him at Munich, how they had pursued him in France, disturbing his quiet retirement, kidnapped his girlfriend, and how that had led to her departure, her wish to see no more of him. He remembered the night of the sinking of the Conglomerate yacht clearly, how he had rescued Francine and hoped to kill off some, if not all, of the Conglomerate. He knew nothing of the aftermath of that evening.

'Actually, we had a very fruitful relationship with you. You were the very best operative that we have ever known. Efficient, discreet. And I confess that my former superior, the late chairman, took an aggressive line. Sadly, for some, he did not survive the sinking of the yacht.'

The other bankers bowed their heads; whether it was in respect to their former chairman or to conceal looks of relief was not clear.

'Naturally, following that evening, we had to make a reappraisal of our operating standards and you will be glad to hear that, in spite of the men that we employ, we hold higher standards and do not seek to bring the wrath of official bodies down upon our heads.'

There was a growl from the one odd banker. A swift look from the chairman silenced it.

'However, we are a business concern with interests worldwide and we have to carry out certain operations to maintain our standing. I am sure that you can understand that. It is not as if you have always operated on the side of the law.'

Was this a threat? Were they trying to haul him in with crude blackmail? He glanced at Mack; Mack had withdrawn to a chair on the far side of the room and was gazing out of the window.

'To be frank, we shall always have need of someone of your undoubted skills. Well remunerated, given a free rein in the manner of executing your commissions. A generous pension, in... shall we say... five years?'

The chairman turned to his colleagues and asked if there was anything anyone wished to contribute. One man suggested that if Berndtt was happy to continue working for them, that he should be resident in Geneva, close at hand. Another asked whether Berndtt had difficulty with police forces in Europe that might compromise his operations. And another asked if he was still up to it. It was the dour looking man who stared at Berndtt in a hostile fashion.

Berndtt made no comment to these questions. He was thrown; he was being offered a chance to renew his career as a hitman. His experiences had taught him a great deal and he felt it was possible that he could recreate that persona, move silently around Europe eliminating meaningless bodies, always the long sniper shot, a good gun, prepared in Italy by his armourer with the special armament, a comfortable armoured Audi, the best hotels; perhaps he might learn to appreciate the kind of food he had just eaten and learn a little of good wines. He had no fear of the police forces; he had been out of action as a hitman for a little while and he doubted that there were any open cases, even in Interpol.

He rose, walked over to the window and looked out on the yacht harbour. Mack looked at him but said nothing. It was difficult; in his mind, he had moved on, retired. And then he recalled the recent past, mainly evasions but also the elimination of Robert and his soldiers. He had lost no skills, he thought. They had not mentioned Le Boucher; hadn't Mack said that he would be released if he eliminated him?

He turned to the table; they were all standing.

'Gentlemen, you have been clear and I understand your offer. However, present circumstances prevent me from giving you an answer.' He could not think what circumstances they might be, but he wanted an unlimited time to consider his future. Disrupted from his French home where he had planned to spend the rest of his life and with the loss of his girlfriend, he felt rootless and without purpose. This offer could put him back to work and establish a home. He sighed.

The chairman bowed. 'I can quite understand that you might need time to consider your future, and I would not wish to apply pressure. Too much pressure has been applied in the past. Shall we say lunch here in a week's time?'

He moved residence, to a discreet comfortable hotel in a residential area. He visited his bank and he purchased

312

clothes, shoes, suits, and a car. An Audi, naturally. He did not try to fill his days, but dawdled, walking beside the lake, sitting in coffee shops, even visiting picture galleries. He took a small motorboat out on the lake, motoring to the bay by Chens-sur-Léman where the Conglomerate yacht had sunk and beyond, looking at the shores, anchoring in quiet bays, passing time.

The days passed and he was alone. Always alone. What was the purpose of life? How would he find that stability and happiness that he had enjoyed in France? Before the Conglomerate destroyed it. Could he return to it, the same village, the same arrangement with Francine? Was he interested in eliminating targets, probably mostly innocent? He thought about all these matters, and more; he became morose, as though he needed something or someone to point the way, to advise him about the very best future.

The week was coming to an end; the appointment with the bankers approached. He had come to a decision, how to pursue the future, what to discuss with the Conglomerate.

He was cruising slowly up the lake, feeling stronger. He could see his future now, believed he could make it work. There were few boats out that morning; but in the distance he could make out a fast motorboat, one of the Riva class, coming towards him, a white wash, approaching fast. Someone enjoying an early outing. He wondered what it would be like to live here and own a launch like that.

Too late he realised that the launch had not seen him. Later he realised that the launch had seen him and was determined to sink him. He dived into the water a moment before the launch ploughed into his small boat, cutting it in half, and slowed, circling around the wreckage, engine burbling. Berndtt rose, took a breath and sank beneath the surface. His training with the Stasi came in useful. He could hold his breath for a long time and was as comfortable underwater as he was swimming.

Looking down from the launch was one of the bankers; Berndtt recognised him, the dour one who had stared at him, who had suggested that he might no longer have the skills. As he peered down into the water, he pointed, shouting, and another man, with flippers and goggles, dived into the water from the stern.

Berndtt was dressed, slacks and a shirt, shoes and socks. He kicked off the shoes, surfaced for air close to the hull of the launch and dived, looking for the other man. He was not worried about the man; he never considered being defeated when attacked. It was simply a case of recalling, almost subconsciously, how to succeed underwater. An exercise, of sorts.

The man was coming towards him fast with a knife held forward, his body like an arrow to pierce Berndtt like a fish. Berndtt rolled and kicked at the hand, deflecting the blade that nicked his shin. The momentum of the man carried him past at speed; he started to turn, bringing his weapon round to attack. But Berndtt was too close; he rolled and kicked, this time into the man's stomach. The man folded without control and Berndtt grasped his wrists. For a few moments they were face to face, Berndtt remorseless, the man showing increasing alarm. The dagger dropped away into the depths and the man gave a desperate kick, to escape, to be free. Clamping himself around the man, Berndtt tightened his hold; the man continued to kick vigorously but Berndtt kept clear of the legs that flailed uselessly. They sank, Berndtt wrapped around the man, a fight as to who could hold breath longer. Berndtt knew that he could manage longer than most. The other man had expended a lot of energy coming at Berndtt and was soon fighting for breath; his hands clawed at Berndtt, any advantage that could be gained to escape the hold. For a minute or two, he struggled, then suddenly became weak and stopped fighting, staring into the afterlife. Berndtt released him; he sank slowly, arms outspread. At the last moment, Berndtt pulled the flippers off the man's ankles and holding them, surfaced close to the launch's stern.

The banker was still at the wheel, standing and peering over both sides, searching for signs of his man, for Berndtt, for any signs of success. Berndtt took a few minutes to re-establish his breathing and put the flippers on; he was bleeding a little. He had not seen whether the banker was armed and was unwilling to board into the barrel of a gun. But it was necessary to eliminate him. Now. There could be no future in telling the bankers that one of their number had attempted to kill him; he would not be believed.

He held onto the stern, waiting. Always wait.

The banker sat down, started calling, to either side. He switched off the motor. Called again. Silence.

Berndtt felt him become uneasy; there was a trembling in the hull. He guessed he was moving from side to side, and would come to the stern. He sank down and swam the length of the launch underwater, surfacing by the bow. He waited.

It took about twenty minutes; Berndtt had reckoned on thirty. The motor started again and the launch to move forward slowly. Berndtt slid down the keel to the stern and avoiding the propeller, held onto the corner as the launch started to gain speed. Reaching up, he slipped off his flippers, placing them on the stern, and hauled himself up to look the length of the boat. The banker was back to him; the noise of the engine prevented him from hearing anything.

Berndtt climbed up and moved forward gently until he was standing behind him. Looking around to make sure that there were no other boats nearby, he curled his arms around the man, pulled back on the throttle, and started to lift him over the side.

The banker had been taken by surprise. He started to shout and Berndtt clamped a hand over his mouth. He kicked back at Berndtt, a sharp kick, his dark leather shoe striking the wound on Berndtt's leg.

Berndtt rarely felt anger. Anger was a useless and dangerous mood that often led to a loss of composure and method, and consequently failure. The blow to his leg tested him; he gave the banker's head a sharp twist and released it. He did not want the body to show any signs apart from an accidental drowning.

The banker gave a whimper. 'Please, please. I won't say anything.'

Berndtt paused and recalled the way that the Conglomerate had ruined his rural life. He recalled the behaviour of the man at the yacht club; he could not be trusted. He must belong to the last organisation that had taken him in Munich. The banker had given up resistance, perhaps in the belief that Berndtt would spare him. He was brutally disabused of that a moment later.

Berndtt grasped his body and threw them both over the side; the banker gasped as he fell, drawing water into his lungs as he went into the lake and drowned in a short time. Berndtt released him to sink away. Above him, the launch idled, no hand on the throttle, drifting off a short way. Berndtt recovered the flippers and swam for the beach, about a mile away.

Ashore, he left the flippers by the water. He felt a little conspicuous; wet clothes and a cut on his shin, perhaps where he might have collided with a rock coming in. Obviously a man who had fallen into the lake. He caught a bus back to Geneva, padded into his hotel where the receptionist averted his gaze. Berndtt returned to his room and the shower.

Two days later he sat at table with the bankers. They were one short; the chairman said that the man had made disparaging remarks about Berndtt and been released from his duties. Berndtt said nothing; it had not been the hardest elimination in his career but an unexpected one.

After another excellent meal, this time without Mack, the chairman asked Berndtt if he had come to any thoughts about their proposal.

Berndtt turned in his chair, looked out of the window. He wondered how to start. 'Your offer was generous. I appreciate it. There is a matter of trust; I was retired in France before your thugs disrupted it. I lost my home and my partner.'

The chairman bowed and said, 'I must apologise, deeply. In effect, it was another organisation. Though there are four of us remaining from the former organisation and though our work aims are similar, we do not condone the working practices of the former organisation. Indeed, we will rectify any wrongs, pay compensation where appropriate.'

'There are some things for which compensation cannot be paid.'

'Perhaps you could suggest what we might do in respect of your losses.'

Berndtt had not expected such a move; he was thoughtful. After a pause, he said, 'I thought that I might make you a proposal, that would suit us both.'

The banker inclined his head, and asked Berndtt to speak freely, without prejudice.

'I thought of offering my services in the role of an organiser. That is to say, I would not be undertaking the commissions; I would interview and seek personnel. One of your number asked if I was still able to undertake the commissions and, thinking of it, I proposed a different role. One to supervise the operatives. With retirement in five years. As you proposed.'

The bankers turned to each other; some whispering. The chairman nodded and said, 'You would expect a salary, no doubt.'

Berndtt did not answer.

'It could work,' said the banker. 'We had not considered such an option, but I can see that it would work.' There were smiles among the bankers.

There was a break. The bankers met in a huddle, Berndtt walked down the pier, past the yacht harbour. Happy memories. He went to the end, looking out at the fountain, playing in majesty, and turned, returning to the meeting.

The bankers were sipping coffee. They scrutinised Berndtt as he sat. The chairman rose.

'We have considered your proposal and find it acceptable. However, we require that you live in Geneva so that you are easily available for consultation and we will provide you with an office.'

'And the work that you would like me to undertake?'

'To interview, enlist, and train operatives.'

'And the work for these operatives?'

'The same as you were carrying out before.'

'To carry out eliminations?'

'Yes.'

Berndtt switched off the microphone in his pocket. How to proceed now?

'I was attacked this week, by your organisation. A matter of trust?'

The bankers were stunned; faces fell, there was complete silence in the room, and then an urgent murmuring.

'How did this occur? Where was it?' said the chairman.

'I had understood that the elimination of Le Boucher would relieve me of any threat from yourselves.'

'Yes, yes, that is correct. We do not hold anything against you. We simply thought that you might wish to carry on working. After all, you are very good at it.'

'A matter of trust. It's not working, is it?'

'Who attacked you? In what manner?'

'They sought to eliminate me.'

There were looks of shock around the table. The chairman sank into his seat; a murmur arose, a name. It meant nothing to Berndtt. He stood, gave a brief bow, and left the room.

FOURTEEN

On the street once more. A sharp autumnal day. Two children barged past him, frisking pockets; he tripped one, walked on.

A car backfired down the street.

Should feel safe; after all, what more could he do to guarantee his future, a future without stress and work: Money? No problem. Threats to his person? Unlikely. The police forces of Europe? Nothing recent on their records, hopefully.

And yet, he felt a sense of unfinished business. He sat in a bar and analysed his situation. Well, there was always Francine. Perhaps, in the future, something may be possible; but it seemed all too recent that she had left in a final fashion. Not wanting to see him again. 'Never' had been her word, hadn't it? And what of the Conglomerate? They had seemed shocked by the news of the attack on him, could not conceive that it had been possible. Particularly by one of their number. And yet? He had assumed that they would stick together, thick as the thieves that they were. He wondered whether they had come to the realisation that Berndtt would succeed wherever. And what should he do with the audio tape?

He left the bar and strolled down the road. He must make plans: Paris or the village. And if he were unsettled, either in spirit or by some outside force, he would move on. Drive or train? Definitely drive. He might go to the village first, and see whether his landlady would welcome him.

A car came careering across the pavement and crashed into a lamp standard. There was an old lady at the wheel; she appeared stunned, her head resting on the wheel. Steam rose from the crumpled bonnet. Berndtt looked around; there was no sign of police or help in any direction. Pedestrians paused, shook their heads and passed on; after all, these things did not happen in their city. Berndtt went to the car, opened the door and spoke to the women. No answer.

He was starting to lift her off the wheel, to ascertain her injuries, when there was a whistle, and two uniformed men came across the road, waving and shouting, 'Are you an ambulance man? What do you think you are doing? You come along with us.'

Berndtt stood, faced them and said, quietly, 'Where is the ambulance?'

'Coming soon. None of your business; what, are you a doctor?'

Berndtt shook himself; this was unreal. He started to walk away; again, a whistle. 'Arrest that man. Making off from a crime scene.'

He turned, considered running, and surrendered to the policemen, who placed him between them, cuffed him and started walking at speed.

'Why have you cuffed me?'

No answer.

'Where are you taking me?'

No answer.

He calculated how easy it would be to take them down. And what the fall-out would be; the polite Swiss would be shocked to see a man fighting uniformed officials. He would be a criminal immediately. Even cuffed he reckoned he could bring them to the ground. He stumbled against a kerb, halting and dropping to the ground; the officers picked him up, clasped him between them and frog-marched him up the street. A short distance and they turned into an archway, into a courtyard and into a doorway; there was no sign of a police station, no other police officers. Before he could turn and take action, he felt a violent blow and blackness poured over him.

There was a bright light, a single sharp beam that pierced his consciousness. He closed his eyes tight and started the survey of his body. His arms ached, and were clamped below the elbow. His legs felt sound, a little sore, but he could not move them. He had been kicked in the kidneys, he was sure. He had a sharp headache and a bruise on his back. He felt hungry, and wondered at this; how long had he been lying here? His throat was dry and his eyes itched. He waited.

'So. You want to talk now?' The accent: not Swiss. More guttural, East European, probably.

Water poured over his head; he sucked some into his mouth. Opened his eyes; still the painfully bright light. Closed them again. Licked his lips. Turned his head to one side and opened his eyes.

There was a man sitting in an armchair, a newspaper on his lap. Seeing Berndtt move, he smiled and said, 'Ah, perhaps you would like to talk.'

God, thought Berndtt, this is like a 1970s film, and not a

good one. Where is the laser machine, or the electrical probe to place on sensitive parts? At Stasi college, they all had to endure a spell of torture, essential experience to avoid giving secrets away. As if he had any secrets to give away. The room was quite small, unfurnished apart from the armchair and the table to which he was strapped. It smelt dusty, unused. There was a bare light bulb above him.

He looked at the man. In his forties, an office professional, clean fingernails, hair well groomed, frameless glasses. Some signs of past stress, lines around the eyes, and a restless mood; kept moving. Or rather twitching. Odd. Not tanned. Clothes to suit: a dark suit, white shirt, tie without a strong pattern.

Berndtt sighed; how long would this go on?

The man sighed in response. 'I do apologise for your rude arrest. But we cannot allow unskilled pedestrians to interfere with damaged persons. We felt it necessary to detain you; we feared that you might not have the necessary skills. An unskilled man, we were sure. Are you medically trained?'

Berndtt looked at him and said nothing.

'No, I thought not. In any case, there is a certain matter in which you can help us. Or so we have been brought to believe.'

Ah, so this is what it is all about; they just wanted his attention. Berndtt stared at him, the cold glare; the man looked away.

'Well,' he said, 'the matter I spoke of. How do you feel?'

'Why have you detained me?'

'Absurd, I quite agree. But we could think of no other way of attracting your attention.'

'No other way? Like talking to me in the bar?'

'It is a delicate matter. Not for airing in public bars.'

'So you tie me up, after a beating. And you wish me to help you.'

'That's right.'

'Why should I do that?'

'No reason. Except to be released.'

Berndtt was silent.

After a pause, the man continued. 'You see, we understand that you have recently been involved working for a group of bankers.'

Berndtt was silent.

'Your sphere of operations was in eliminations, I am told. On good authority.'

Berndtt was silent.

'Reply, please.'

'Reply? To what?'

'That attitude will take us nowhere. Or rather,' a brief cynical laugh, 'will take you nowhere.' Another laugh, brief and without substance.

'You know better than me.'

'Do I?' the man said. 'I think not. For the source of our information was one of the bankers.'

'What reply did you expect?'

'Ah, that is better, my dear Bernard; or do you prefer Berndtt? Yes, we know your name; we know a great deal about you.'

Unlikely, thought Berndtt. Standard softening up process, but what did they want of him?

'Yes, a great deal. And this banker told us of your many successes. A hitman, no less. Have you enjoyed your career?'

'I am not comfortable.'

'I am so sorry.'

'Why don't you release me so that we can discuss your matter?'

'Ah, well, that would be civilised, but the people I represent are not civilised, I regret.'

What a surprise! This might take some time, thought Berndtt.

'And it was their men who detained you. In their usual fashion. Not civilised, I admit.'

'Why do you work with them?'

'Let us say, our interests are compatible.'

'And what are they?'

'We are a business concern. We deal in transfers of collateral.'

What did he mean? Clearly an illegal organisation, it was unlikely that they worked with the Conglomerate. There was a difference in language suggesting a difference in country suggesting a difference in working methods.

'What do you know of the bankers?' The man had adopted a gentle wheedling tone. 'You must know something of them.'

'Nothing. Who are you talking of?'

'That attitude wastes time. I do not wish to invite the enforcers in.'

'I have met them. I do not work for them. I retired some time ago. You must have the wrong man.'

'And what was the purpose of your meeting with them? Not to find work?'

'No.'

'And your relationships with them have always been harmonious?'

'What do you want?' Berndtt was loud.

'We wish you to work for them. And us.'

'And how do I do that?'

'We will give you full advice as to how to proceed.'

Who were these people? Another Conglomerate to tussle with? 'They're bastards, that's who they are. I couldn't work for them without attacking them.'

'But that is exactly what we want, my dear Berndtt!'

Berndtt smiled. 'You will help me do them down?'

'Ah now. We have to be a little careful; after all, it is their wealth and power that we want.'

'How will you do that?'

'Not a matter for your concern, Berndtt. But if you are working for them, we shall know all we need to know.'

'Who was your banker, who told you of me? He could be a problem.'

'It seems... it seems that he met his end suddenly. We are not sure how, but the word on the street is that he had a boating accident and drowned. Now we need to replace him.'

In moment, Berndtt saw a way to be released. He smiled. The man looked surprised. 'It's not a joke, I assure you. We need to replace him.'

'It would be good to get back at them.'

'You will help us?'

'What do I get out of it?'

'Well, naturally, we know that the bankers will pay you well. However, as an incentive, I have been instructed to place $50,000 in a bank account that you may access after you are embedded in their organisation and have provided us with information.'

'And what guarantees do I have that I will not be shopped by your boys or involved in any violence between the two organisations?'

'I regret that I can give you no guarantee of that sort. However, we understand that you are very capable of looking after yourself. In most situations,' he said, with a smirk at the bindings.

'I'm ready,' said Berndtt.

The man called the enforcers into the room. Berndtt was released from his bounds; he stretched, rubbed his back and legs, and looked the thugs up and down. Standard army fatigues from East Europe, including the high laced boots. Muscular men with narrow faces, crew cut hair, no sign of humour. Or intelligence. Cannon fodder, he called it. You point and they go. Pain simply a sign of merit. An overpowering smell of Old Spice.

Berndtt was given contact numbers and a safe drop box location. When asked where they could be found, in an emergency, they told him that he didn't need to know that; just stick to the contact numbers. He was assured that he would be left alone, not put under surveillance by the thugs. He was assured also that should he think of absconding, he would be found and dealt with. He assured them that he had no intention of absconding and looked forward to dealing the bankers a deadly blow. And again he was told that it was their money and wealth they were after and for that he needed to be embedded for a time. Could he manage that? He smiled, assured them that he would enjoy living the high life of the bankers and, at the same time, learning their secrets.

And they released him onto the streets. Looking back, the doorway through which he had been dragged appeared one of a dozen, unmarked, no particular decorations or furnishings visible through the front window. Probable that the house had been used for his abduction only and that they had a base elsewhere in Geneva or nearby. Would be useful to know where, but they weren't telling and he was given no clues. Now to find the bankers.

They had not searched for him; he went into a café and ordered a meal and strong coffee. Sat for a while, nursing his bruises. At another table, an old woman spilt her coffee, cursing; the waitress went over and moved her into the street. He wondered why they had found it necessary to give him a beating as though to soften him up, before asking him to work for them. It seemed an odd way to bring someone round to their way of thinking. They must be a rough lot, who did not recognise a civilised way of business, legal or illegal. Well, it was not his problem. He would find the bankers, somehow. Did they live at the yacht club? Unlikely. And they no longer had a fancy yacht on the lake. $50,000 could be useful, but he did not need it. And there was the audiotape.

He strolled into the street. A pigeon swooped low over his head. Visited his bank, made a few transfers, took lunch, and walked down to the yacht club.

He was about to walk down the quay when a black Mercedes drew up beside him. Here we go again, he thought, and considered diving into the harbour, swimming underwater until he could surface safely. He felt the gun in his pocket but was not in a hurry to draw it; it would lead to escalation, police, becoming a fugitive.

The door was opened; the driver invited him to get in. There was only one man in the car and it was Mack. He got in, shook Mack's hand. Mack said nothing but drove into the yacht club car park. There, he turned to Berndtt.

'When are you leaving?'

'Do you like working for them?' asked Berndtt.

'It's good money.'

'Is it?'

'What do you mean?'

'I was hired to be a hitman. Are you a hitman?'

'It's a good life. I have no complaints.'

Berndtt looked out at the yacht club; the sun was low in the west, and all looked mellow and peaceful. 'I've come back,' he said.

'I don't know—' said Mack

'Go tell them. I'll work for them.'

'Really?'

'It's a good life, yes?' And said to contact him at his hotel. 'I'll be there for three days; hope to hear from you.' A smile, shook his hand, and left the car. Walked down the quay, enjoying the quiet evening. There were a few dayboats setting sail; he recognised a couple that had helped him not long ago and accepted a sail with them. A perfect way to finish the day; would they dine with him? A pause, yes, they would be delighted.

Two days later: a note, heavily embossed paper, handwritten over a signature, inviting him to lunch at the yacht club that day. Dress informal. He returned to the coffee shop, two cups of strong black coffee. No old lady spilling her drink. On the street, no thugs, false policemen, or so he assumed.

At the yacht club, he was shown into the private diningroom. Mack was present, avoiding his eye. The chairman was as effusive as usual, invited him to sit, offered drinks, chatted of nothing important. Lunch passed, three courses, no liqueurs, a more business-like air, no stories about skiing experiences or distant foreign holidays.

As they pushed back their chairs, cigars were lit and the chairman turned to Berndtt.

'We have a small problem. The job description that you yourself suggested has been offered to someone else and accepted.' He waved at Mack. 'However, since you have returned, apparently willing to work for us, we are reluctant to let you go.'

Berndtt said nothing. Just waited.

'There is, of course, the role originally offered to you, the duty of eliminating various troublesome persons that we indicate.'

'No.'

'No? I am sorry to hear that; you were always the best.'

'But that was some years ago.'

'A few years only, I believe. I assume that you have lost the skills.'

Assume what you like, thought Berndtt. What will they do with me now?

'There is another role that we have discussed. Our discussions have not yet reached a conclusion, that is to say, we are not agreed on the exact job description; but, to put it in simple terms, we need someone of your skills to… er… to spy for us.'

A spy? Berndtt thought back to Stasi days; that was spying, wasn't it, in addition to the eliminations. He said nothing.

The chairman coughed and looked embarrassed. 'Naturally, our business is built upon trust, not the need to evade the proper standards of our profession. However, in these days, there are other organisations, those who do not work within the confines of appropriate and legal standards, and we need to know more of these organisations. To protect ourselves, of course.'

Berndtt frowned, looked down at the table. 'Do you know of the existence, practice and locality of these organisations?'

The chairman looked around the table. Eventually, he nodded to another banker, who spoke up. 'Well, there was the organisation run by Le Boucher. I understand that you had something to do with the eradication of that organisation.' He paused, looking to Berndtt for confirmation. A fly buzzed noisily across the table, alighting on Berndtt's cup. 'And then, there is another organisation operating here in Geneva. We know little of them, except that they seem to have come out of the East. East Europe, I meant,' he added hastily.

There was a pall of cigar smoke hanging over the table. The chairman glanced at it, an irritated expression; coughed. Two bankers put their cigars out.

The other banker continued. 'We are not aware of other organisations nearby, though there is the Mafia in Italy, and an Algerian outfit in Paris. I imagine that the Deuxieme know all about them.'

The chairman thanked the other banker for his contribution, and said, 'Do you think you would be interested in this more widely roving appointment?'

Berndtt thought about his own plans, to escape Switzerland for good. He thought of the other organisation, the Group as he called them. How could he engineer this operation? 'I would need to know more of your own organisation, so that I can recognise ways in which they are a danger to you.'

There were frowns around the table. The chairman had a whispered conference; Berndtt heard the words 'not much' and 'have to give him something' and a few grunts.

The chairman said, 'There is not a great deal that we can tell you, but you may be inducted into the framework so that you understand how we work, where the outside threats lie.'

'Inducted into the framework'? What did that mean? Oh well, it was a step forward.

'The terms will be as before? A five year contract?'

'Yes, of course. It may be that your work will be so efficient that the contract might be shorter, in which case you would be suitably rewarded.'

'Accepted,' said Berndtt, looking to Mack, who smiled, a relieved smile.

Outside the club, as he walked back to the city, a car slowed. Berndtt recognised one of the thugs of the Group; he ignored him.

FIFTEEN

6.50 am. A light drizzle, low cloud, south-westerly force 3.

The traffic on the D884 was busy for that time of day: cars, vans, lorries, pick-ups, articulated trucks and motorcycles. Even the odd bold cyclist.

A white panel van, driven by a young man, was speeding in the fast lane; the driver was dreaming of how far he could go with the girl he took out the night before, and who had spent the night deflecting his advances. He did not notice the traffic congestion ahead, caused by a line of lorries pulling out to overtake a tractor pulling a harvester. He hit the back of a pick-up truck, breaking an oil line, though he did not realise the problem until later, when his engine began to seize up. The two drivers did not stop, limited their communication to physical gestures. A motorcyclist, following at a cautious distance, hit the hot oil, skidded, fell over and slid on his side for approximately 100 metres. The car-carrier behind him, carrying a full load of new Mercedes, braked hard and jack-knifed, the trailer skidding through the central reservation into the oncoming lane, towards a minibus of nuns. Sister Angelica acted with commendable speed; she turned the wheel, missed the trailer, crossed both lanes across the nose of a police car in the nearside lane, and embedded the minibus in the soft ground beyond the hard shoulder. The nuns overcame their shock with prayer, ignoring the appeals of the police and ambulance crew.

Three kilometres down the road into Geneva, the traffic built up, the outgoing lane blocked and preventing the incoming traffic from proceeding into the city. Even in this civilised city of considerate citizens, tempers were raised.

Berndtt found himself stationary at a junction; the traffic lights changed from Go to Stop to Go while not a vehicle moved. Next to him, a young man in a white van was eyeing up a girl in a new convertible; she ignored him, in spite of his use of the horn and significant hand gestures. And meanwhile, the time moved on, past the hour that he had agreed to meet the Group.

A few weeks had passed since he had been employed by the Conglomerate. He had been assiduous in pursuing any clues about rogue groups that might threaten the Conglomerate's business, and he had been equally assiduous in passing on secret information concerning the Conglomerate's method of working to the Group, as he now called the East Europeans. He had been unable, until now, to learn codes and passwords to the accounts and correspondence of either group, but he had kept his fund of recorded information as an insurance against police action.

One might wonder at Berndtt's behaviour, in betraying both sides to the other. But his past had been simple; he was loyal only to himself. Since escaping the Stasi, no organisation, country or person had claimed his loyalty. It was true that Francine had broken that insularity, and that he had been prepared to die for her. But that was not the same as loyalty in terms of obedience or respect to some person or organisation who paid him. Though he was obliged to take an oath of secrecy when he worked for the British Army, he was never fully inducted and felt no ties or concerns at leaving them behind. When the Conglomerate captured him in Munich and revealed how they had been issuing his commissions, at the same time reminding him with some force that he was to react with more speed and less objection to any of their instructions, he had fought to release himself and hoped that he had eliminated them in the sinking of the yacht. The new Conglomerate was civilised, considerate and not demanding as the old organisation had been. But they were still the group that had ruined his French village life and broken the relationship with Francine, which had become more important to him than anything else. As for the East European Group, he would destroy them in time. He was building the framework for it.

An hour later, he was still extricating himself from the city. Diversions had been organised and he found that he was being directed away from his destination, a farmhouse near a small village south of the city. He arrived two hours late, told them of the road blocks and diversions and sat down for their meeting.

A rope was thrown around him, binding him to the chair. A sack was pulled over his head. He sat still, waiting.

A voice, that he did not recognise. 'We understand that you are providing us with information. However, you are our man and you're late. We expect obedience. You are here when we say.'

Berndtt was silent.

'Do you understand?'

Berndtt was listening; how many people were in the room? There was the man in front of him, the speaker, and certainly one man behind him, but more likely two; unlikely to be more. Yes, there was a sniff, behind him to the left; and then a foot moved, behind him to the right. Moved again. Restless, perhaps a little drug problem. The man in front was the other side of the table; there were chairs either side of Berndtt, light metal frame, canvas seats. The table was wide, a farmhouse kitchen table. His hands were unbound, the cord placed above his elbows. His feet were unbound. Did he need to see?

He bent, as though in humility, grasped the chair on his right and rose, swinging the chair fast to the right behind him. It hit the man behind him; he heard a bone crack, a hiss of pain, before he turned to the other man. He was too late. He felt a gun pressed in to his neck. Bending, he pulled the sack off his head, turned to the table, sitting again on the chair tied to him. 'You want information?'

The man sitting the other side of the table was huge. His face was faceted, scarred from burns, the eyes little pits of darkness. Possibly Serbian; Berndtt had met a few during his time in East Germany. He gazed at Berndtt without expression, but gestured to his men to stand back.

'Always good to see that our men are still up to it,' he said, with a coarse laugh. Berndtt wondered whether he was talking of the two behind him, or of himself. The wounded man burst into a torrent of words, all unknown to Berndtt, angry, spitting. The boss gave him a glare and ignored him. 'Now,' he said, 'when do we get to it?'

Berndtt was silent; what was 'it'?

'All this pussyfooting like little Swiss cow maidens.'

Berndtt looked at him; the man was grinning. And then he wasn't. 'I want them, and I want them soon.'

'The bankers?'

'Who else?'

'When?'

'When what?'

'When do you want them?'

'Now, you dunderhead. All this dawdling; I want their organisation, their money, their business. I want to string them up by their bollocks until they squeal and give me... give me everything!'

'All right.'

'Ah, at last. A man of action. What will you do?'

'Organise a little meeting.' Berndtt had been planning it for some time, the logistics of bringing the two groups together. He thought that they might have mutual interests.

It was chance that he met Mack in the street; there was a visit, some congress or other, a slow procession of cars that brought pedestrians to a stop, lining the route as though they could see the occupants, hidden behind darkened glass. And they met, standing within a metre of each other. They shook hands and went to a bar, a private conversation.

'Are you content with your role, Berndtt?'

'And what about you, Mack? Can you train your operatives?'

Mack sighed. 'It's difficult, and recruitment is a problem. You get these men who have been chucked out of armed forces, all brute force and no brains – not their fault, I guess – and they have no idea of a delicate operation.'

Mack had changed; the worn fatigues were replaced

with a dark suit, not Armani but more hard-wearing. He was even wearing a tie; Berndtt suspected a clip-on.

'You have some soldiers?'

'Soldiers! That's exactly what they are.'

'Might be needed.'

'Really?'

'Where are you based?'

'Tiny office in one of the banks. Most unsuitable.'

'Why do we always meet in the yacht club?'

'They don't have a headquarters as such. Couldn't meet in one of their banks; the security systems would go mad. So they meet at the club where they're all members; most of them sail.'

'Boys' club.'

'The club has good service, as you know. It works well.'

'Can you summon a meeting?'

'You got something in mind?'

'A quiet little meeting. Just you and the chairman.'

'We can go to his bank.'

Berndtt thought about it. No reason why not. 'When?'

'Today? I'll get in touch.' Mack went to a phone. A brief conversation. 'He'll see us now.'

Down the street, onto a parade of grand commercial establishments, some old stone buildings, some vast modernist creations in glass and steel. Went into a new building. Marble floor, full height windows, a ceiling six metres above them, a professional hush; no vulgar bank counter, no signs of hard cash. A uniformed guard lounged by a small desk; took his cap off and wiped his forehead. Replaced the cap. Gave Mack and Berndtt a careful check; nodded at Mack. No frisking. The receptionist looked up, nodded at Mack and indicated the lift. They rose, a quiet Otis hum, surrounded by dark suits and glossy secretaries. Top floor. Greeted by a secretary who greeted Mack as an old friend. Sat in a waiting area. More hush, a background of murmured conversations and electric typewriters. Offered coffee; both refused.

The chairman sat behind a large mahogany desk, two telephones, a few family photographs in guilt frames, no files or papers. His room looked out onto the lake, the fountain performing for him, sunlight glinting in the spray. The carpet was deep, the chairs deeper and comfortable. He beckoned them to sit around a small table with him, and sat in silence.

'Sir, Berndtt has asked for this meeting.'

'I have infiltrated an organisation operating in this area. I believe that their aims are similar to yours.'

'Are they a problem?' The chairman looked as if there was an unpleasant aroma in the room.

'Yes.'

'In what way?'

'They want your business.'

'Can you eliminate them?'

'Not my business.' A pause. 'There are many, and I don't have their headquarters.'

'What will they do to take our business?'

'Use force.'

The chairman rose from his chair, went to the window, looking out onto the lake, hands twisting together. Turned back to Berndtt.

'I was afraid that something like this might occur.'

Berndtt stood. 'Might a meeting with their boss be a way to alleviate violence?' Unlikely, he thought, but he was interested to see the chairman's response.

The chairman shuddered. 'No... no. I don't think that's the way. Berndtt, thank you for your intelligence, very useful. Could you brief Mack on what needs doing? Mack, you'll let me know how it goes, won't you? You know when the next lunchtime meeting is programmed. And now, gentlemen, please excuse me; I have a meeting.'

On the way down in the lift, Berndtt told Mack of the first meeting with the 'civilised' man, and of the farm and the aggressive boss who threatened violence. He did not reveal the information that he had passed on between the meetings.

A few days later, Mack called for a meeting; a quiet bar, as usual, a slow drink and an excitable Mack.

'We went there. This morning.'

Berndtt asked, 'Where?'

'The farm, of course. Planned a take-out, old-fashioned gang warfare pattern. Perhaps more CIA. Automatics, flak vests, helmets, masks, the lot.'

'You're well armed.'

'The budget is generous. We expect it; their protection is what counts.'

'They have protection all the time?'

'Hadn't you spotted it?'

'At the Yacht Club as well?'

'Particularly at the Yacht Club: The car park attendant, the doorman, and a few waiters. The Club is only too happy to have the organisation provide paid staff. We provide others when the bankers are there.'

'I was always freelance,' said Berndtt.

A pause, fresh drinks. Two young women, cruising the

room, passed by them slowly; a single look from Berndtt sent them on their way. Mack watched them as they went; was it a look of regret, Berndtt wondered. How easily could he be distracted?

'Anyway, the farm,' said Mack.

'Did you succeed?'

'Yes and no. The boss wasn't there. Or at least, we couldn't find him. Killed three of his operatives. They weren't the brightest. You know the type.'

Berndtt thought about his visit to the farm, the 'soldiers' who handled him, and the huge boss the other side of the table. Whose man was he at this moment?

'How did you plan it?'

'Surrounded at dawn. The dozy buggers had no sentries, no warning alarms. Chucked in tear gas, you know the ones. One of them was a bit more aware than the others; hid up in the kitchen, armed, and we had to weasel him out. Poor bugger; his arm was all bandaged up.'

'I hope you had the right place.'

'Where you said. It was as if they had no fears of being surprised at all. Didn't seem right; we were afraid of a trap, or booby bombs. Man in the kitchen; we gave him the chance to give us some information, about traps or where the boss was, or how many they were. But he didn't feel like talking; he isn't now.'

'Pity,' said Berndtt. 'Could have done with the intelligence.'

They talked some more. It had been Mack's first operation, and he was open about the performance of his men.

'Not a bad bunch, clearly at home with an operation like that. Not sure about the bodyguarding. We'll see.'

Berndtt learnt when the next lunchtime meeting was at the Club, and the monthly programme. Asked if he should be present.

It was no more than twenty-four hours after their meeting that Berndtt received a call.

'You got any more for me?'

He recognised the voice of the boss, a harsh bark.

'Yes.'

'Spill it, before I... the bastards are onto us. Raided the farm; you know anything about it''

'When?'

'When? Yesterday, the bastards. Killed three of my men. I'll have their guts for bowstrings, their eyeballs for slings, their—'

'They meet at the Yacht Club. Lunchtimes, they have—'

'Right. They've got it coming, and they won't enjoy it.' The line went dead.

Berndtt shrugged. Might be interesting to see whether anything was going to happen today, he thought.

Two hours later, he was on the quay, looking over the harbour while keeping a discreet eye on the Club car park. A quiet sunny day. A few yachts were out on the lake, and others were being rigged; there was a little breeze. A day for motoring, he thought. A packed lunch and a cool bottle of wine over the side, to enjoy in a quiet cove up the lake. Roll on retirement.

A loud screeching of tyres. Berndtt retired to the seclusion of a tree, and watched three Toyota four-wheel drives pull into the car park, slamming to a halt in the alley near the door; a crowd of black dressed soldiers spilled out, shouting. They were heavily armed: sub-machine guns, knives, helmets, the long boots. The parking attendant and the doorman had disappeared, and the crowd of soldiers charged up the steps and through the doors, pushing aside a couple who were coming out.

A pause. Then the sound of automatic fire, prolonged bursts. A few people on the quay stared, frozen in incomprehension, the abrupt interruption to their peaceful sunny afternoon. Berndtt could imagine the destruction, the club being obliged to close for extensive renovations; what would the Conglomerate do for a meeting place? A maid came out of the door, screaming, followed by a huddle of well-dressed people, all shocked, some still clutching napkins. Inside, there was more screaming than gunfire.

After a few minutes, silence fell. In the car park, the four-wheel drives had not moved and were still blocking the parking; when a customer had the courage to ask them to move, a driver waved a gun and the customers retreated to the quay in shock. Some women were sobbing, some of the men were conferring, tight huddles against the women. But nobody was challenging the drivers.

Sirens could now be heard, a chorus growing in volume. Five police cars screamed to a halt around the entrances to the car park, disgorging armed police who spread out rapidly around the club and down the quay, and set up a line around the four-wheel cars; the drivers within closed their windows, locked their doors and waited. The customers who had fled down the quay were escorted away up to the road, behind the police cars; many of the women were still weeping, the men in shock. Berndtt had moved further down the quay, beyond the club; the police did not bother to come so far, but beckoned that he was to stay there. Armed policemen had now moved into the club in a tight column, weapons to the fore.

A quiet fell, full of promise of exciting things to come.

.

SIXTEEN

There was a period of quiet. Berndtt could imagine the police inside, a hard phalanx of men, bullet-proof vests, helmets, radios and automatics, advancing slowly through the club, clearing rooms one by one. He couldn't imagine that the Group would wish to take them on, a pitched battle that they could never escape from, however many police they took down; but where were the Conglomerate? Had Mack succeeded in protecting them with his green guards?

Cooks emerged from the front door, followed by reception staff, waiters and a few more customers. It was just a question of time now; the police would have the Group in their hands. Berndtt started to walk up the quay.

There was a fresh burst of gunfire from inside the club. A side door, a fire door facing onto the quay, burst open. A tight cluster of the Group emerged, guns pointing in all directions; at the centre of them was the boss. Berndtt slipped behind a tree; he was wondering how they thought they could escape.

A tight line of police, holding their fire, started to advance down the quay towards the Group. They called out, 'Three of your men have been shot, a further two captured. There's no escape. Give up while you can!' They sent a few warning shots over the heads of the Group.

There was a scream. From inside the cluster of the Group. Berndtt could make out a woman, a dark green silk dress, high heels, hair coiffured, twisting in the grasp of the boss. She screamed again. The police stopped shooting and stopped. There was nowhere for the Group to go, trapped on the quay, water on three sides, the police blocking their way out. And Berndtt concealed on the other side of them behind a tree, but he was unarmed.

One of the thugs pointed to one side of the quay, shouted to the boss. Berndtt followed his gesture; a launch, a beautiful Riva, glistening varnish, white leather seats, had started its engines; a rich burble, twin exhausts. The two men on board were hurrying to untie, to escape the mayhem on the quay.

They were too slow.

Two of the thugs were on the pontoon beside the launch in a moment, waving their guns; the men on board gazed in horror, and dived overboard. The thugs untied the ropes, calling to the others who jostled off the quay on to the pontoon, and crowded aboard the launch. The police pursued them, and started to fire, but were limited in their scope; there were a number of sailors nearby in the harbour, preparing their boats, or tying up, unaware of the danger. They managed to hit one or two of the Group in the legs, but not enough to stop them, and fire was returned; an officer wheeled round, hit in the shoulder.

At the last moment, the boss threw his hostage into the water and squeezed into the front seat, eight bodies in a boat designed for four. The launch roared, accelerating fast out of the yacht harbour, carving up a small sailing dinghy that capsized, the two girls shouting and swearing, now rapidly disappearing in a cloud of wash. The smartly dressed woman had landed in shallow water; she stood up and started to scream, her hair bedraggled, her dress dripping, and was joined by the two men who had escaped the launch; they were a sad sight, waiting for help.

Berndtt emerged from behind his tree. The police were coming down the quay, wary of him appearing. They held guns on him, until one officer confirmed that he had been on the quay before the gang arrived and had remained at the far end.

'Who were they?' Berndtt said.

'Some gang. We'll catch them. Soon. Don't worry about that, sir.'

'They were heavily armed, weren't they?'

'Yes sir. All too common these days, unfortunately. But they never succeed. Have a good day, sir.'

Berndtt walked up the quay. Overhead, a police helicopter headed up the lake. In the car park, there was a lot of noise; the Toyotas were trying to ram their way out of the car park, in spite of being surrounded by the police. He watched one accelerate into a Ferrari, back into a Bentley, and charge a police car before the driver was killed, an easy shot through the driver's window. The vehicle subsided with a crunch on the front of a police car; the policeman looked on, shaking his fist at the dead driver. One of the drivers had surrendered immediately; the other one was shot after causing a lot of expensive damage.

The police were manning the doors and allowing no one to enter. Berndtt knew that there were three dead gangsters and learned that there was one dead waiter, who had unfortunately been holding a gun. One of Mack's men.

A phone call at Berndtt's hotel.

'They weren't there. What the fuck are you playing at?'

There was no mistaking that voice.

'Two of my men killed, no five, and one in police cells. If he talks, his life won't be worth living, but he knows that. Is your life worth living, eh?'

'You cut me off.'

'What do you mean, I cut you off? Who do you think you are? You give me information, or... or your life isn't worth a cent.'

'They meet at the club on a monthly basis.'

'You didn't say that.'

'You cut me off.'

'You say that one more time, and I'll come down and cut you off.'

Berndtt gave him the dates. And refused an invitation to be there. Not his job; would give him away. Wouldn't want to let him down after all. Rang off. Changed hotel.

He went to Mack's office.

Mack was irritable, jumping from one thing to another. He couldn't sit still. The chairman had been onto him; could he provide enough protection? Should they change their meeting place? Berndtt flourished a newspaper report, a glamorised version of the raid.

'Sounds like the gang you busted at the farm.'

'Or didn't bust. What do I do? Can't find them, can't promise they won't attack again.'

'Where would you like them to attack?'

'What? What do you mean? I don't want them to attack.'

'But they will.'

'When?'

'The next meeting. That's my guess. And I'll bet that a club employee gave them the dates. At the point of a gun. You would too, wouldn't you.'

Mack subsided into a chair.

'So,' said Berndtt. 'Where would you like them to attack?'

'That's a new way of looking at it.'

'A restaurant is a nightmare. They would be in a private room, a cul-de-sac. No way out, difficult to guard, and a busy street outside. A lot of peripheral damage potential.'

'A private house?'

'Too many escape routes for the attackers, if they are overcome. Quite apart from damage and intrusion into a private home; the occupiers would have to move out for good.'

'An office?'

'Same problems as a restaurant.'

'What do you reckon?'

Berndtt paused, thinking around the problem.

'It has to be the Yacht Club,' he said. 'You know it well. The best place to mount a defence, and after the gang has arrived, easy for the police to surround.'

'Escape routes?'

'Yes, there's always the water. But escape is risky; it was chance that they took the launch. The police would have captured them, if it hadn't been for the launch.'

'Did the paper say where they went?'

Berndtt flung down the paper. 'Now you know what to do.'

'Will you be there?'

'Not my job.'

'Will you help?'

'Aren't I?'

Mack shrugged, then smiled, shook his hand. 'Thank you. I'll prepare, warn the bankers. Might move them to another room, with an escape. I'll see.'

A crack of thunder.

Berndtt was walking along the harbour wall. A splint of lightning descended into the lake; silence for a moment, before a rumble of thunder as dark clouds rolled out of the north towards the city. Up the lake, all was lost in a grey curtain of rain that advanced, drowning the fountain, drowning the quay, drowning Berndtt who swore and ran for the Yacht Club.

He had not intended to go to the Club; it was the day of the bankers' luncheon, and he did not want to get drawn into the maelstrom that might follow. Why, oh why, he asked himself, had he been tempted to come on the chance, a very good one, that the Group would attack. Simple curiosity.

The car park was a flurry of people hurrying from car to door, bumping into each other, speedy apologies, women covering their heads with bags, scarves, newspapers. Berndtt saw the doorman extending an umbrella over one of the bankers who was getting out of a parked car. Berndtt kept out of sight, slipping into the Club and making for the bar. He chose a stool with a sight of the entrance, watching the car park filling. The rain was falling hard, vertically, an instant flood that sluiced through the car park, over the quay and into the water. He watched a lady arrive with a small dog; it lost its feet immediately, swept towards the edge of the quay. She pulled it in on the lead and scooped it up, water running from its coat, her clothes, her hat. The doorman bowed; someone of rank, thought Berndtt.

The club had come alive. The diningroom buzzed with conversation, the bar was full, and the lobby was busy with damp clothes, dripping umbrellas, and complaining ladies. Outside the rain kept up a dense curtain, visibility no more than 50 metres.

Through the gloom appeared a black Toyota LandCruiser, wading into the car park off the road, up to the door, spraying late arrivals; they took one look and returned to their cars. Three more Landcruisers followed, a line down the central lane of the car park, blocking it to all newcomers. And those attempting to drive away. A huddle of soldiers dressed in black fatigues, helmets, masks, and long boots, carrying carbines and handguns, emerged. Was this Mack's defence, hired in for the day?

In the bar, nobody seemed to have noticed the arrival of the soldiers; Berndtt looked around, a friendly face that he could call to raise the alarm. The two barmen were busy. At the other end of the bar he spotted Mack, deep in conversation with two pretty girls; he waved, an urgent signal. Ignored. He started to make his way towards him but at that moment, two soldiers appeared in the doorway from the lobby. Berndtt ducked down, to avoid being seen.

There was a burst of automatic fire from the lobby.

Alarm and shock took hold of the crowd in the bar; screaming, they huddled away from the two soldiers, crouching on the floor, hands up, pushing their handbags towards them as though it was a hold-up. Berndtt couldn't see Mack. Slipping around the end of the bar, he crawled through the open service door into a store, and went to the door at the back. It was locked. Hunted around. There must be a key nearby. Yes, hanging on a hook to one side. Unlocking it, he slipped through the door and found himself on a service alley at the rear of the building. Beyond the low wall in front of him, the lake had become a storm of breaking waves, the wash adding to the rain falling. Berndtt was soon soaked.

In spite of the noise of the waves and the rain, he could hear gunfire from inside the club. He wondered how Mack's soldiers were standing up to the Group; had Mack rejoined them? And what could he, Berndtt, do now? He remembered his original aim, to see both the Group and the bankers eliminated, but he could not be sure that both sides would eliminate each other. The Group had the advantage of surprise, but Mack's men had had good warning.

To his right was to go to the front of the Club and run into the gangsters. To his left, the alley terminated a few metres away. Beyond, the wall of the club appeared at first to descend into the water. He went to the end of the alley, stepped onto the low wall, and saw that there was a ledge, about fifteen centimetres wide, running around the wall of the club, where the concrete retaining wall was covered with an alloy flashing and surmounted by the metal cladding of the club.

He stepped onto it. The ledge was running with water. He wondered about dropping into the lake and swimming around, but looking at the breaking waves, decided to pursue the ledge further. It was slippery with wash from the lake and hard rain running off the wall. And a little algal growth, no doubt. The cladding of the wall was a dark anodised aluminium, vertical sheeting with standing seams.

He found that he could just grasp the seams with his fingers, pulling himself along the ledge a seam at a time, face to the wall. The wash pounded his legs and rain poured off him. His fingers ached. He wondered why he had come to be there, why he had not simply walked up the service lane to the car park. And remembered.

After a while, he came to a window. Crouching down as he grasped the cill, easier hold than the seams, he peered through a corner.

Directly inside the window were three of Mack's operatives, crouching behind an upturned table, aiming their guns at the double doors the other side. To the far side, he could see the heads of some bankers, also protected by an upturned table.

As he watched, the doors burst open and two gangsters charged in, firing wildly. A number of shots pierced the window, which cracked but held. Thank goodness for laminated glass, Berndtt thought. One of the gangsters fell back, a bullet between the eyes; the other went down, blood spurting from his leg, still firing until a bullet hit him in the face. One of Mack's men had swung round, clutching his left shoulder.

There was a pause. Berndtt heard a banker whimpering, calling for help. Three armed police appeared in the doorway, checked the gangsters, and stood with their backs to the room, ignoring the occupants.

Berndtt crossed the window, not bothering to conceal himself, and continued his slow journey around the building. The wind was lessening, the wash dying down and the rain had ceased, to be followed by a cold wind. He shivered in his wet clothing, unable to move fast enough to warm himself.

At last, he reached the quay and sank down in a squat beneath the wall, rubbing his hands to get feeling back into them. He did not have long to wait.

The fire door burst open. Here we go again, thought Berndtt as he pulled out his gun.

The police had focussed on the interior of the club and the car park. And forgotten the fire door. There was nobody on the quay; the weather was too foul for sailors and tourists had been driven indoors by the rain.

Again, the boss came out with a hostage, again another well-dressed woman, surrounded closely by six or eight 'soldiers'. Berndtt was surprised. He thought that they would have held the club longer against Mack's men and the police. Perhaps they preferred a quick guerrilla raid, guns firing in all directions, and left before greater losses. And he had thought that they wished to hang up the bankers by their balls.

The Group stopped. It was quiet on the quay, quiet behind them in the club. One even pushed the door to behind him. They looked around; there was no obvious means of escape, no launch ready with motor running.

The boss spotted Berndtt. 'So, there you are.'

'Did you get them?' said Berndtt.

'You didn't tell me they had their own army, you useless bugger.'

'What do you think? They have no protection?'

'Yeah. It's a lunch club, isn't it?'

'Bankers always have protection. But didn't you get them?'

'I never saw them. Where were they?'

'Aren't they there? It's the right day.'

'Lot of good now. How the fuck do we get out of here?'

'Up the quay. Or swim.'

'Into the arms of the police? Yeah, bright boy. You've run your time, no more use to us.'

There was a pause; his soldiers were looking around, each thinking for himself, not interested in the boss's conversation. The boss pushed his hostage aside, pulled a gun from his belt, released the safety catch, raised it. Berndtt found it comical; so slow. He drew his gun, shot him between the eyes. And dived backwards into the lake. The water did not feel cold, after the chilling he had had.

He could see a couple of the gangsters looking over the wall for a short time, before disappearing. He surfaced. Climbing a ladder, he peered over the wall. The Group had disappeared; there was no sign of them, apart from the body of the boss and a whimpering lady, who looked at him with horror. He could hear gunfire from the car park. They would have met the police.

He waited, doing exercises to warm up, waiting for the police to clear the club. The lady watched him with an air somewhere between fear and wonder. Could he regard the Group as no longer a danger to him? It seemed probable. But the Conglomerate? Still alive and kicking.

SEVENTEEN

She hammered on the door. 'Sir, sir, please open up. I haven't done your room for three days. Please sir, open the door.'

A groan and a hoarse shout, followed by silence. She hammered again, and went off down the corridor.

Berndt rolled over on the floor. It's safer, he thought. I can get under the bed and maybe he won't see me. Where the hell is he? He keeps finding me wherever I am, bed, bathroom, dressed or undressed. What do I do? And he's got that hole between his eyes. Like a third eye, winking at me. Where can I go?

He stood, and the man was before him, leering, waving a bloody arm.

'Won't you leave me alone? Aren't you dead, what am I to do? Leave me alone!' Berndt swung at him, shattering the cheval mirror, glass exploding over the carpet. He danced in it, his feet soon oozing blood, and suddenly, a lady was there, screaming at him. Screaming and screaming. He put his hand over his ears and the screaming was just as loud. And then he could see the two people, fading into and out of each other, the man and the lady. Then it was the man.

'What do I have to do? How long? Taste this.' And he drew his gun and shot the man in the mouth. The man appeared to enjoy it; the bullet embedded in the wall after passing through a chair.

Reeling, he collapsed onto the bed, clutching his head. The screaming went on, and he knew, he had to get out. It must be time to go, but where did I leave my car, my Audi? I can see it now... if only I could stand... who is this? What's that?

A siren. It's stopped outside. They're coming to catch me; they have caught up with me. Who will it be? What... No! Francine's father; is he outside the door? Is he coming to get me, after all this time? I must get out of Paris. Oh, Francine! Must escape, can't shoot my way out of this one, which way is the back staircase, the rear extension? How many of them are there? Oh, leave me alone, you bastard! Where shall I go? It's so dark, I can't see the way...

And then his head went into a fog and he was struggling to follow, follow a little man who said to come with him, through this passage. This is the way, sir, out of here, come quickly... quickly... it became narrower and narrower...

The hotel manager opened the door. The Geneva city police came in, took one look, and called for an ambulance. With a quick survey of the room, they handcuffed him as he lay unconscious.

It was days before he woke. After being brought into the ward, he had reared up and started running; it had taken three orderlies to control him, after he had knocked out one. He had even been put in a strait jacket for a while, until the Consultant had seen it, barked at the ward sister, had it removed, and ensured that he was bound to the bed, a more humane restraint. And asked to be called when the fever had abated.

He lay in silence.

His mind was in retreat, and he could not tackle the recent past; it remained a tangle of experiences and pressures. His body had rebelled, and even his bowels were strangers. Lifting an arm, when allowed, was exhausting. He looked upon the male nursing assistant who checked his medications, filled the drip feed and fed him, as an unavoidable embarrassment. As he gained control of his thoughts, he felt demolished, worthless; he had never lost so much control in all his life.

He lay in silence.

It took days for Berndt to realise that he was the object of scrutiny on ward rounds: a circle of white-coated physicians, students and nurses. The Consultant had introduced himself, and came to see him more often; he checked the physical signs, his eyes and responses. He would ask questions, gently; who was he, how did he get ill, what could he do for him.

One day, when he was showing signs of comprehension during a ward round, the Consultant sat down and explained what he believed was the problem.

'At first,' he said, 'we thought that you were suffering a psychological breakdown; certainly, the symptoms indicated a breakdown: hallucinations, erratic behaviour verging on the dangerously aggressive, self-harming, and the inability to communicate with us. However, we have moved on from that situation, though there are definite signs of a mental breakdown. It seems that you are suffering from a virus, a strain not known to us until we had the opportunity to compare your specimens with other institutions. One of the side effects of the virus is an attack on the brain, causing hallucinations and uncontrolled behaviour. The origin of this virus is hard to locate, but there are examples in Africa and Eastern Europe. We have sought expert advice in the treatment of the virus; can you tell us, do you think you might have had contact with someone who might have been affected? From those areas? It was certainly exacerbated by your condition when admitted; you had a chill and your body temperature had dropped excessively.'

Berndt ran his mind back over past time; much of it was muddled, a fog through which odd things stood out, like the sheeting on the Yacht Club, the temperature of the water of the lake, the colour of his sister's hair, the smell of another woman; but who was she?

He spoke. The Consultant made no comment on the fact that it was the first time that he had spoken since admittance.

'I… I was here, wasn't I?'

The Consultant smiled. 'Of course. Yes, you have been here. We wondered why, where you came from. Is there anybody we can contact?'

Berndtt felt a jar in his thoughts, a vague spectre of peace. 'My sister.'

'Can you tell us where she is?'

'She disappeared, when the Russians came. Are they still here?'

The Consultant smiled. 'They didn't get this far. Is there anybody else?'

Berndt turned his head away; tears ran down his cheeks. The doctors left him, quietly.

He lay there for some weeks. The virus flared up again and they feared that they would lose him. At such times, he knew neither where he was nor who he was. The treatment was, to a degree, experimental; the hospital was tackling a virus that showed no similarities to well-known viruses, such as flu. He had been moved into an isolation ward, the silence broken only by the wails and cries of the patients.

Eventually, he showed signs of recovery. He was very weak, but was encouraged to walk a little each day. From the fourth floor, he looked out over Geneva, the fountain, the harbour, the Yacht Club. They sang a brilliant tune to him, as though he had spent much time there, time that was not easy. But he still did not dare to look into his memories and feelings.

He waited. Until he felt stronger.

And then he started to write. He could not rely on retaining memories, but he found that resurrecting a memory brought other memories alive. He asked where he had been found, and was able to organise the collection of his belongings; the hotel was reluctant at first. A large bill for repairs awaited his return; on hearing of the virus, they had been advised to burn all the soft materials, replace the bed, redecorate, and carry out a careful anti-bacterial cleaning. It was not in their experience and raised the cost of his stay substantially. The bill was settled, without his knowledge.

His writing, at first a few notes on scraps left by the nurses, became a diary; the Consultant purchased one for him. He filled the pages with all his memories, both recent and also of his past life. And learnt what he had been. And wondered who he was now.

The diary was a cause of concern, of stress. It was full of information that the police forces of a number of countries would be delighted to obtain; he had to keep it secret, and carried it with him wherever he went. The staff teased him; were these about his old lovers, his assignations? Can we have a look?

Berndt would not reply; sometimes it was the cold look, still sufficiently chilling, sometimes a slight smile.

One day, a police officer came to see him. Berndt froze, and avoided his eye. He took to an armchair, thought of his gun, apparently lost, and waited.

'Sir, you have been identified as the man who released a lady from the boss of the gang who attacked the Yacht Club, some weeks ago. Please could you tell us how you came to be there, and who you are. We have no name for you.'

Berndt had not yet uncovered what had happened on that day; his memories had blacked out, from the time that he had approached the Club. There was someone called Mack, and something about a gang called the Group. But he could not connect the gang with the Yacht Club, nor could he remember why he had been there. There was something in his mind, a clash, a confusion concerning the Group and some other group called... yes... the Conglomerate. He grabbed his diary, wrote down the name. And woven throughout his memories was the scintilla of a person, a French woman, name lost but a close relationship, someone to find. The policeman watched, saw the confusion, but did not interrupt. The doctors had been firm; do not push, do not probe. He needs time.

Berndt was silent.

'Is there anything that you can tell us, sir? We would be very grateful. We are still trying to complete our investigations; it seems that you shot the head of the gang, and we captured or shot the rest. The lady is very grateful for your assistance and would like to meet you in person.'

Berndt shuddered. Was the lady the spectre in his dreams? He had no idea when he had met her.

'You should know that she is the Mayor's wife, a lady of some importance. I am sure that the Mayor would also like to express his gratitude.'

Berndt felt only the need for flight.

'There is one other thing. When the officers came to the hotel, to arrest you, they had no idea of your illness; they apologise if they treated you inappropriately. They recovered your weapon; we are holding it at the police station and you may come and collect it whenever you please.'

Berndt felt his stomach clenching automatically; he did not think that he had ever been so close to a police officer since… yes, dining in Paris. Why did that come back with such force? A window in his memories opened, as though he was hovering outside a window looking in at a dinner party, two men, two women… he was one of the men, and one of the women… the French woman. It was her, somehow so familiar now. Who were the others? An older couple, something about policemen. And it took the visit of a policeman to bring it back. And there had been a siren.

He turned away; needed to write it down before it was lost. But what was this about a gun? The thought of visiting a police station seemed all wrong. Actually life threatening. Did he have a gun at the Yacht Club? Well, he must have done, but he had no memory of it.

He spoke. 'I'm sorry, I have no memory of being at a Yacht Club.'

'Well sir, if you should recall—'

A nurse came into the room, looked at Berndt, and ushered the police officer away. Berndt started writing; a memory brought a small smile that flickered briefly.

The memories gradually came back. There was a village, a place where he had felt great contentment, and was linked to the woman as well. There was a flat in Paris. There was a trip to England, more vague; he couldn't think why he had been there, something to do with the woman. There was Lyon, a mass of things happening that overlapped and tripped upon each other, a house like a fort, a café, and then there was Le Boucher. Who was he? Geneva had a number of overlaid images; perhaps he had been here more than once. At least he could remember his bank, from old.

One night, the Consultant came to see him.

'I hear that you are improving. Your physical condition is much better; I have the impression that you were in peak physical condition before your illness. How are you getting on with your memories?' He nodded at the diary.

Who was this man? Friend or foe? Would he report anything to the police? It was unlikely; he was a doctor was he not, bound by laws of confidentiality?

The Consultant watched Berndt; he could guess what he was thinking. It was common with patients of a certain sort. 'You should know that anything you tell me goes no further; all I do is to record the general level of your recovery.'

'There are some memories that I cannot recall.'

'What distinguishes them?'

'I don't know. But there is one that crops up often, a woman. She was important to me, I think, but I know no name or location.'

His wife, thought the Consultant. 'It is not uncommon that memories that have a strong effect are the hardest to recall; you know, people who have been important in your life and are associated with different times and places. If you asked me what my wife looks like, I would have great difficulty describing her exactly, whereas if you have met someone one or two times only, you could describe them exactly. Do you have addresses?'

'No.' Berndt remembered a Paris flat, but it did not relate to the woman in his memories. He felt that he might find the village, almost certainly French. Was the woman there?

'I can only suggest that you keep writing. It is the best way of recovering memories. And you should see a psychologist; I can arrange it.'

'Thank you. I'll keep writing, no psychologist.' My God, what a psychologist or psychiatrist might discover! He couldn't go there; it would be better to be dead.

The consultant noticed Berndt's expression; he has things to hide, he thought. Well, don't we all? I wonder what they are. All the same, I wouldn't want to push him to regression or suicide.

'How soon can I leave?'

'Where will you go?'

'France. I have somewhere to go. I'll be safe there.' Safe! He had meant to say that he would be looked after there.

'But the woman won't be there?'

Berndt looked at him, and said nothing.

'Well, I would give it a few days, and then you will be ready to leave. I want to improve your diet, more protein. Give you some strength.'

'Would it be possible... could I borrow a tape recorder?'

'Yes. No problem. I'll ask the sister to bring you one.'

The consultant left feeling a little disappointed; he did not usually feel such an interest in a patient, and he would have liked to learn more of this man.

He had found the tapes in his things brought over from the hotel. Perhaps they would help him recover some memories. He played them through; at first, he could make no sense of them. The voices seemed familiar, but he could put no names to them. The threats and instructions were clearly illegal, and rang true with his past life. Why did he have the tapes?

It was only on the third or fourth time of playing them that images began to fall into place. He could remember where he had recorded them, but not why. He began to make a laborious record of the tapes in his diary. The tapes he tucked away in his bag.

On the street again. He felt like a foreigner, seeing it for the first time. Except that, after a time, flashes of recognition brought buildings to life, or an alley or café. He felt tired soon, and sat on a bench, content to watch pedestrians and traffic go by, without any feeling of fear. He had feared fear itself, knowing that his lack of particular memories and his current physical state made him vulnerable. He could be taken or overcome. And yet he sat without any fear, more a sense of relief, perhaps gratitude, that he was alive. Though alive to do what he had no idea.

A man sat down on the other end of the bench. Berndt glanced at him, saw only a youngish man, dressed in a polite manner, shoes polished, and looked away. He had an arm in a sling.

'Berndt, where have you been?'

Berndt turned and looked at him again. Yes, he knew him, from Lyon and... and here. Why? What was his name? He seemed friendly.

'They came, you know.'

What was he talking about?

'You were right, they came, and we were prepared. Lost one man, sadly, and I picked up this.' He held up his bandaged arm. 'You don't look well.'

Berndt was silent. He was waiting; perhaps he would learn something of the recent past.

'Do you wish to meet the chairman?'

The chairman. Faint bells rang; a smart office, overlooking water and boats. The yacht harbour that he had seen from the hospital.

'I can take you to see him, if you wish. I believe they were very grateful for your intelligence. The hotel bill has been settled.'

My intelligence? What was I doing? This is enough, I have to move.

He stood. 'Excuse me, I must take some exercise.'

Mack stared after him; what had happened? He hurried after him, took his arm, and was thrown off immediately. 'Let me buy you a cup of chocolate. Here, we can go in here.' And he directed Berndt into a smart café, ordered two hot chocolates, and sat in silence until the drinks arrived.

'Berndt, I don't know where you are. Let me help you, as you have helped me. I am Mack, you met me in Lyon.' He watched Berndt closely.

Berndt stared at Mack. 'Yes, in a café. Yes, and here. You were working here. What were you doing?'

'I was working for the bankers. So were you.'

Berndt was silent; this was news. Mack saw Berndt's confusion.

'You were providing intelligence; you warned me of the attack on the Yacht Club. Indeed, you said that was the best place to have the battle. You were right. Were you there?'

'I don't know.'

Mack was silent. They sipped and stared at the table.

'I was in the hospital. Some illness.'

'I'm sorry.'

More silence.

'You shot the boss of the gangsters. The police told us about a man who came from the water; we guessed it was you. There was a hostage that you released. The Mayor's wife.'

Berndt remembered the policeman. 'What happened in the Club?'

'They came in from the rain, took everybody by surprise. Lots of shooting. The police were there in ten minutes, but my men were guarding the bankers.'

'Who are they?'

'The people we were working for, here in Geneva.'

'Did the bankers escape?'

'Yes.'

'Where did they go?'

Mack looked confused. 'They belong here, they live and work here.'

Berndt nodded. 'And the gangsters? Where did they go?'

Mack looked at the table; this was going to take time. 'They were all captured.'

Silence.

'Mack, I must leave. I don't want to meet a… chairman.'

'Yes.'

Silence.

'Where will you go?'

'France.'

Mack wondered where in France, but did not dare to ask. Perhaps Berndt would find somewhere safe.

'Mack, I have something. Can you take them? I don't know why I have them; they are tapes of people talking. Talking about eliminating certain persons. I must have recorded them here. You can have them.'

Mack took him to his office, said he might leave anything there. Berndt told him about the gun, said he might recover it; he had no use for it. They shook hands, Mack promising to tell the bankers and ensure that full payment had been made.

Berndt returned to the hospital, thanked the Consultant, and left with his things.

That day, he caught a train to Paris.

EIGHTEEN

'Pardon, mais… is it Bernard?'

He stopped chewing, dropped his knife and fork, his hands fell to his sides. The voice was so familiar, so dear, and yet he feared that it was yet another mirage. He stared out into the restaurant, not daring to look, afraid of being deceived.

He had travelled to Paris by train, a shy man wearing the same bland supermarket clothes, no hat, dark glasses and carrying a small suitcase. He carried no armament, no special equipment of any sort; the police could have frisked him, searched his belongings and found nothing worse than a chewed toothbrush. He carried papers, of course, the papers as a Frenchman that he had used for years.

The train was busy: the occasional inquisitive child who retreated when Berndt gave him a brief stare; businessmen, some travelling with secretaries, or so it appeared; a small party of nuns, sitting in silence; an army sergeant, not young; and families, who created the most noise. He could not sleep; such relaxation had not come to him yet, but he looked forward to a time when he might be completely accepting of any situation.

He had left Geneva with no regrets. Mack had reported

that the bankers understood his state of health and accepted his resignation with regret; they sent condolences and a cheque as a sign of their gratitude. Mack had ensured that they learnt of the elimination of the gang's boss. Berndt had not been able to remember who the bankers were, why they should wish to reward him; he accepted the situation, thanked Mack, bid him adieu and wished him well. That had not been too difficult.

He had been obliged to change trains at Lyon. It was a city that rang with half-remembered images, mostly uncomfortable. He had no wish to relive them, and kept to the station, waiting for the Paris train in the café. The woman behind the counter said good day, it was nice to see him again, it was good of him looking after that lady, how was she? How was he? He stared at her, could remember nothing of a lady, or even of an earlier visit; she turned away, embarrassed. He sat with his back to her.

At one point, he had seen a young woman walking briskly across the concourse. A sharp tag in his mind, not unpleasant. No name accompanied the memory.

In Paris, he had walked from the station. He could not have taken a taxi in any case; he could not remember the address. But he had a feeling that if he walked, and walked, a pattern would reassert itself and lead him to his home. In an hour or so, he found himself in Le Marais, and thirty minutes later at the building where his apartement was. The concierge gave him a suspicious look, in the manner of all French concierges. But she did not stop him as he climbed to the top floor.

And then he stopped. A key. Where was the key? He descended to the concierge. 'Madam, I have mislaid my key.'

'And what should I do? Walk up five storeys? With my legs?'

'I have been away for some time. I apologise.'

'Here, use my master key, but please return it immediately. Immediately, do you hear?'

The apartement was strange, at first, as though he had broken into a hotel suite. There was nothing personal and even the toothbrush in the basin was new. After returning the key, and been assured that a replacement would be available in two days, at cost, he sat in the livingroom.

He had waited. The *apartement* was quiet, and there were no sounds from the other floors. A distant rumble reminded him of the city but otherwise all was quiet.

An hour passed, and past thoughts and actions began to emerge, like animals at night. He knew now that he had not worked in this city. He had worked away; his work was... no, he couldn't face it. It was a dark cloud that threatened his hold on life. But here, in Paris, there was a lightness, a warmth that took him back to his childhood, the warmth of a familiar relationship, and it had a name... a name...

It was no good. You don't go through a wall by walking into it, he told himself. Better to let time pass. To wait.

He was hungry and took to the streets; in time, some street, some restaurant or café, would mean something. After an hour, having passed numerous restaurants and cafés, he saw a front, Art Deco like the Metro stations, that was at once familiar and at the same time was loud with warning bells. It was busy with young people. He turned away, shrinking from the aura of familiar associations, but it would not do; he had to face it, whatever it was. He entered and automatically made for a table on the left, back to the wall, a view of the front and the street, and a quick access to the kitchen and the rear.

It was as natural an impulse as avoiding a car when crossing a road. He could not question it, not now. It would come, perhaps with some pain.

And now someone knew his name.

'Ah Bernard... you want to play strangers? Are you going to crawl at my feet again?'

He turned. A woman, good clothes, long dark hair that was swept back... it was the hair, rather than the slightly severe look, that gave him a shock.

'It's you... I had hoped...'

'*Mais naturellement*, it's me. Who did you think it was?'

He sat, bemused at his luck, shocked at the sudden meeting. There was no doubt, the woman next to him was the source of the lightness, the person for whom he had returned to Paris, the one of whom he had the greatest hopes. He had expected that it would take time, perhaps a distant sighting, and then... 'It is good to see you.'

'Is it?'

'I have hoped... it was wrong... I didn't...'

She examined him, without embarrassment. She took in the thinness, his face drawn, the eyes that flickered and dropped, the hands that had difficulty in keeping still. But this was the man with whom she had shared her life, her bed, her hopes.

'You don't look well, Bernard. Very pale.'

'How are you? We parted... I was so sorry... I was lost.'

'Have you been in hospital?'

'And then I rescued you, didn't I?'

'You don't remember?'

'I was in hospital in Geneva. Some illness; it's over now.'

'But you don't remember rescuing me?'

Bernard looked at her as times spent with her began to appear, some more vividly. But before that? Before that? Some violence, concerning her. Where was it? But he did rescue her, he knew that; he couldn't remember how or where.

'I... I... it was this illness. It took my memories and I am just discovering them now.'

'Are you still working? The mining engineer?' she said with a sad look.

He stared. 'Was I a mining engineer? I don't think so.'

'Nor do I.'

'No, I don't work. I want a quiet life. There was a village...'

'Yes, there was a village, a good place. I loved the man who I stayed with there.'

Berndt was shocked; he hadn't expected that.

'But the man in Geneva,' she said, 'was not the man I loved. Who are you now, Bernard?'

He wondered; how do you answer a question like that? You can say what you do, what you like, what you eat – steak and frites – whether you are religious or not, what size shoes you wear, but how do you say who you are? A hard question to answer when you cannot remember how you arrived at this point.

'I am Bernard, who wants only to live a quiet life, no work.'

'Ah! So simple. If only life was like that!' She spat her words, looking away.

Berndt suspected tears. 'Please, tell me, how have you been?'

'It is so easy for you ... well, perhaps not. But I invested a lot in you, Bernard, and I, Francine, am not so young to be played with like a doll.'

The name rang like a warning siren, at once so familiar and at once with some recall of what had befallen her, the capture by the Conglomerate, the violence involved in her release. And he was aware of how he had deceived her, unable to describe his work, talking of a mining engineer it seemed.

'I am sorry, for all that I mislead you, and what I led you into. I never wanted it, I never wanted to leave the village, but they came for me. And left me with no choice; either that or be killed.'

'What sort of people did you associate with? Awful!' She shuddered.

'Yes, awful, but I did not seek to associate with them. They... they captured me, made me work for them.' As he talked, memories revealed themselves, sliding into view, one unfolding to another. At last he knew why he could not speak of his work.

'I have been working, of course,' she said. 'It is what I do, though my work does not involve violence.'

'Your teaching?'

'Yes? My teaching... what is it you want to know?'

'Does it go well? How long will you continue to teach? Do you have other work?'

'Ah, who knows how long. The University... you know, they have their fashions... perhaps, I may be there until I die, perhaps I may be walking the streets tomorrow.'

'No, you will never walk the streets.'

A pause. 'Pardon?'

'I apologise, I meant no impertinence. But I could not live if I thought you were walking the streets.'

The food had been forgotten, congealing upon the plates. She sipped her wine. Berndt did not dare say anything. The buzz of the restaurant was a distant clamour.

At last, she spoke. 'And you, Bernard, what exactly do you propose to do, now, when you leave this restaurant?'

'I shall return to my *apartement*—'

'That I have never seen!'

'And I shall wait for the next opportunity to sit here next to you.'

'And then?'

'I shall invite you to my *apartement*.'

'And you never enquired whether I have met someone.'

Berndt reeled; he had not imagined it. Was it so many weeks since he had last seen her? It would not be surprising, perhaps; she was worth so much more than him, and he had failed. Miserably. He started to gather himself to leave.

She put a hand on his arm. 'Well, aren't you going to ask me?'

'Francine, if you want never to see me again, please tell me now, and I shall leave. Now.'

There was a long silence. Francine beckoned to the waitress, who removed the plates, and ordered another glass of wine for herself. She ignored Berndt, who sat still, looking out on the restaurant, the activity and noise another world.

She stirred. 'It is difficult. I don't know you as once I thought I knew you. And I have to find some means, some way of understanding you.'

'Would you like to go somewhere, a day trip to somewhere? Or spend an afternoon at …' – he rummaged in his mind, what did city people do for recreation? – 'a museum?'

She broke into laughter. Peals and peals of laughter. People turned, smiled at her. Tears ran from her eyes, and she turned to him. 'Oh Bernard. You don't know how to pass time, do you, doing nothing?'

He said nothing.

'Well,' she said. 'We could try… something.'

She reached out, laid her hand on his. He stared down at it, the warmth spreading from it into his soul. 'I had hoped—'

'Enough for now. I'm hungry; have you ordered?'

He looked at her; hadn't they ordered and talked, and were they now starting again? Oh, how he hoped they would start again.

They met the following day, and the day after that. Francine visited the *apartement*; she disarmed the concierge's look of thunder and lightning with charm, declared that the place looked no better than a hotel suite, and teased Berndt on his taste in clothes.

Berndt allowed himself to be re-educated, in clothing, in culture, in conversation, though he hated being taken into smart clothing outfitters, hated the use of money on something that he felt had no value. But he would not challenge Francine on these matters and came to accept that it was part of Francine's life. He even came to accompany her into women's shops and paid for her clothes. He was changed; he was no longer the man whom she had loved in the village but he was not the man she had known in

Geneva. She would occasionally ask him who he was, why she was going around with a stranger; he learnt to smile, gain confidence and trust her.

There was a man, who appeared from time to time, a slow perusing look as though memorising Berndt's face, who had disappeared when Berndt thought to see who he was. Each time, a slow alarm spread through him, though he could not recall why there should be a threat; had not Mack reassured him... And each time, Francine recalled him to the present, with a word or a touch, and he turned away from the past.

Of his background, his working life, he sometimes would go quiet, with regret and a little shock, when he remembered particular eliminations. He never spoke of them, and learnt to pass a policeman without crossing the road. One day, she said that she would like to visit her parents. They had moved, not to the South of France but to a small town in Normandy, where her mother complained constantly of the weather, and her father pursued his interest in the English Civil War, taking annual journeys across Le Manche.

They arrived by train on a Friday night; Francine had been working that day, and was tired, not prepared for a confrontation with her mother. Berndt had no more than vague memories of the supper with her parents, so long ago.

The evening started quietly; a good meal, wine, time to relax. Céline had recovered some energy since leaving Paris, and enjoyed bargaining with the local farmers at the markets. François was quiet; Francine worried that he was not happy with the reappearance of Bernard. She had never understood

377

why her father had become reticent about Bernard, though he had never made any accusation. She knew that he knew that she visited him in the village. Something seemed to have happened after Berndt had been to supper with her parents, and she had never learnt of it.

Berndt, after Francine had told him that he had met her parents, felt some anticipation at meeting them again, like placing his head in the lion's mouth, but he did not know why. He could not clearly remember meeting them or what had occurred, and did not wish to raise it; something told him that it would destroy his relationship with Francine.

After supper, they sat around a dead fire. François offered Calvados and they sipped in silence. Eventually, Céline rose, beckoned to Francine, and retired with her to the kitchen. Sounds of a fraught conversation emerged until François got up and closed two doors.

'Céline has been missing her,' he said. 'She has a number of things she wants from Paris; I guess Francine is not so keen to be messenger boy.'

Berndt nodded and did not believe a word.

'But you, Bernard, tell me about yourself.'

Berndt sat up, leaned towards the fire, and wondered what tale to tell. What could he tell anyway? His memories were vague, historic images mixed with those of yesterday. Had Francine warned them that he had been ill?

'I live in Paris. I am retired, a quiet life.'

'And what work did you retire from?'

'I'm not clear on that. My memory... I was ill, a virus. I lost my memory, my mind was wiped clean.'

'I'm sorry to hear that; was it recent?'

'Only a month ago was I able to return to Paris.'

'Oh. You were not ill in Paris?'

'Geneva. I had been travelling, a holiday... I could not tell you where I was before Switzerland. I believe it was France, but I remember no detail.'

'Do you remember your youth?'

'Yes.' He smiled. How strange. When reminded, ancient memories flooded back, his parents, his sister, their move to Berlin, the war.

'And?'

'I was born in Germany. But I have lived in France for a long time.'

'Where about in Germany? I like that country, it has a good police force.'

'Police force?'

'*Mais oui*. I was a police officer, you know.'

'What sort of work did you do?'

'Oh, over my career, all sorts. But mostly detective work.'

'Interesting.' Berndt was not sure that he wanted to hear any more.

'Very interesting. Particularly my last posting.'

Berndt was silent, waiting.

'I was posted to Interpol for my last months,' said François. 'I pursued old cases, ones that police forces of various European countries had set aside, unsolved. But surely I told you that, when you came to supper.'

Berndt reeled; they had met before and he had been a police officer? A black shadow covered his mind, with a threat, though he could remember almost nothing of his past, that this would be the end of Francine, of his retirement, of all that he now knew. He had met this police officer before? He couldn't bring things together, gather the memories into a recognisable pattern.

'I'm sorry. I don't remember. We have met before?'

François shrugged. '*Alors* Bernard, what do you propose to do with your retirement? You are still a young man.'

Berndt coughed, spoke in a whisper. 'I should like to live in a small village, like this one, with Francine. A quiet life.'

'Francine will wish to continue working; have you discussed it with her?'

'A little.'

'And do you wish to marry?'

'François!' They had not heard Céline come into the room. 'That is very direct; is this the way to speak to Bernard?'

François' face closed; he sat in silence. Céline sat down, addressed herself to Berndt. 'Now Bernard, Francine has gone to bed, very tired. But I wish to hear something of you; it has been a while since you came to supper at our *apartement* in Paris.'

What could he say? He now had vague memories of meeting her, of a crowded *apartement*, a siren in the street, but not of a supper.

'I know that my poor husband does not remember well; he had an accident on his last day at work. He had no business being there. A railway station where they were pursuing drug runners. I can't think why he thought to involve himself. And then he had a serious accident, hit by a train or something; they never told me the full story. He shouldn't have been there.

'Fortunately, he has his English battlefields to visit. I had wished to move to somewhere warmer, the South… but there we are. I had to give him something that meant a lot to him, and here we are. But you Bernard, where are you now?'

'Paris. I have been very ill and I must take it easy.' Did he just say that? What had happened to him? He used to be a hard man, didn't he? A mirage of his working life passed in front of him, contracts to be carried out, equipment and safe processes, though he could remember no details, only obligations, constraints, negative shades. All as though it had been someone quite separate from him, someone whom he observed and now rejected.

'What will you do?'

'Travel a little, read, perhaps learn to cook. It's about time.'

'Francine says that you need to take care of yourself. She says that you have an *apartement* in Le Marais; very nice, I must say. What happened to your mining job? You said you were a mining engineer.'

Berndt gulped; is that what he said? He was sure that he had not been an engineer. He felt François' eyes on him. 'I can't work at all; I don't remember anything.'

'Yes,' said François. 'A mining engineer. I remember now. That's what you said.'

'Oh François, leave him be. You can see he has been ill.'

François looked down, sipped his drink. Gazed into the dead fire.

'Do you plan to marry?' Celine was demanding.

François caught Berndt's eye, and smiled. Raised his eyebrows. They waited for Berndt to say something.

'If Francine will have me,' he said. There, that should do it.

'And where,' said Céline. 'Where will you live?'

Berndt was silent; he had not discussed it with Francine, he had no idea where they might go, if indeed there were the two of them. He shrugged, a Gallic shrug.

The weekend passed. There were no more confrontations, and they ate well, walked, slept, and chatted to neighbours. Back in Paris, life continued as before, Francine visiting Berndt's *apartement*, Berndt visiting Francine's *apartement*. By day, Berndt walked, further every day, exploring Paris, while Francine worked.

One day, Francine said, 'It's about time, wouldn't you say?'

Berndt frowned. 'About time?'

'To... to decide where we live, and... perhaps...'

Berndt stared, nodded. 'Would you like to move to my *apartement*?'

'No. Berndt. That's not what I meant at all.'

'Then, shall we find our village?'

'Well, that would be a start.'

'A start?'

'Well, Berndt, what do you want to do with your life?'

There was a long pause. Berndt was staring at the wall; was he so stupid?

'Francine, will you marry me?'

'Of course. I mean, yes. Yes.'

They found their village and a small house, not far from Paris. They were married by the *curé*, her parents the only persons present, apart from half the village.

One day, they were shopping in the local town. Berndt was learning to recognise a good vegetable, and to bargain for it. Francine was spending more time at home; she had reduced her hours at the Sorbonne. They visited her parents, on occasion, and lived a sociable village life.

They passed a game shop, rifles and shotguns in the window. Berndt stared and entered; Francine was surprised, but watched him. He moved slowly, looking at the guns in the cases, handguns, rifles with scopes, boxes of ammunition.

The proprietor came forward. 'Is monsieur interested? What can I show you? Is it a shotgun you are after, the hunting? Or perhaps something smaller?'

He offered Berndt a handgun, a SIG Sauer; without a pause, Berndt stripped it down, ejected the magazine, weighing it in his hands, put it together, looked through the sights... and froze. The proprietor stared. 'Monsieur was an army man,' he said with admiration.

Berndt was staring at his hands; they were shaking. His face had become rigid; he began to crumple, standing there on the shop floor. Francine apologised to the man, handed the gun back to the man, took him by the arm, and led him out into the street.

There was a man across the street; Francine never saw him, but Berndt looked him in the eyes and at that moment the man raised a gun and fired. Berndt spun round, met Francine's look of astonishment with a look of regret, of sadness, and fell. Before long, the street erupted with the blare of sirens.